Anvil

V Plague Book Ten

Dirk
Patton

Dirk Patton

Published by Voodoo Dog Publishing, LLC
2824 N Power Road
Suite #113-256
Mesa, AZ 85215

Printed in the United States of America
First Printing, 2015
ISBN-13: 978-1518704611
ISBN-10: 1518704611

This is a work of fiction. Names, characters, businesses, brands, places, events and incidents are either the products of the author's imagination or used in a fictitious manner. Any resemblance to actual persons, living or dead, or actual events is purely coincidental.

Table of Contents

Dirk Patton

Anvil

Also by Dirk Patton

Unleashed: V Plague Book 1

Crucifixion: V Plague Book 2

Rolling Thunder: V Plague Book 3

Red Hammer: V Plague Book 4

Transmission: V Plague Book 5

Days Of Perdition: V Plague Book 6

Indestructible: V Plague Book 7

Recovery: V Plague Book 8

Precipice: V Plague Book 9

Anvil: V Plague Book 10

Merciless: V Plague Book 11

Fulcrum: V Plague Book 12

Rules Of Engagement: A John Chase Short
Story

Other titles by Dirk Patton

36: A Novel

Author's Note

Thank you for purchasing Anvil, Book 10 in the V Plague series. If you haven't read the first nine books, you need to stop reading now and pick them up. Otherwise, you will be utterly lost as this book is intended to continue the story in a serialized format. I intentionally did nothing to explain comments and events that reference books 1 through 9. Regardless, you have my heartfelt thanks for reading my work, and I hope you're enjoying the adventure as much as I am. As always, a good review on Amazon is greatly appreciated.

You can always correspond with me via email at dirk@dirkpatton.com and find me on the internet at www.dirkpatton.com and follow me on Twitter @DirkPatton and if you're on Facebook, please like my page at www.facebook.com/FearThePlague .

Thanks again for reading!

Dirk Patton

November 2015

Anvil

       I look inside myself and see my heart is
black
       I see my red door I must have it painted
black
       Maybe then I'll fade away and not have to
face the facts
       It's not easy facing up when your whole
world is black

       No more will my green sea go turn a deeper
blue
       I could not foresee this thing happening to
you
       If I look hard enough into the setting sun
       My love will laugh with me before the
morning comes

       The Rolling Stones – *Paint It Black*

Dirk Patton

Anvil

Anvil

1

I couldn't move. I was in shock, staring at my wife. She screamed one more time before going still and watching me. I desperately searched the blood red eyes for any sign that even a small part of her was still in there. I didn't find what I was looking for.

I glanced at Rachel, and she was frozen in place, staring at Katie. Turning back, I was surprised to see that Katie had moved next to Martinez' corpse and was nudging it with her shoulder. When she saw me watching, Katie stopped and stared at me. I stared back, tears running down my face. I couldn't breathe.

"We have to go," Irina grabbed my arm to get my attention before moving to Rachel.

"I can't," I mumbled, unable to take my eyes off the terrifying sight my wife had become.

"Bring her," Rachel said as Irina removed the grenade strapped to her throat and began working on her cuffs. "Maybe there's help in Seattle."

My heart leapt with faint hope. Swallowing hard, I took a deep breath before stepping closer and doing something I'd never done before. I hit my wife. Hard. With my rifle's stock, right on the temple. Her horrible eyes rolled up in her head, and she slumped into unconsciousness.

I stood there looking at her, vision blurry from the tears in my eyes. Absently, I noted the metallic jingling sound as Irina freed Rachel's hands. Finally turning away from Katie, I looked at Martinez. Another woman I realized I loved. Not romantically, but the kind of love you have for a kindred spirit who has become family. I started to reach for her, to hold her lifeless body in my arms, but Rachel wrapped me in an iron-hard hug.

"There's Russians all around us," she said in my ear. "If we're going to have a chance to save Katie you need to get your shit together. Now, goddamn it!"

I turned and met Rachel's eyes as Irina snatched up the dead medic's rifle and began removing spare magazines from his corpse.

"We have maybe thirty seconds before someone decides to come see what is happening," Irina said, swapping mags so a full one was in the AKMS and it was ready to go. "How are we getting out of here?"

"You got four of them fuckers headin' your way."

Anvil

I had forgotten about Titus, but his voice in the radio earpiece reminded me I still had a slight edge.

"What about the sniper on the far edge of the park?" I asked, stepping out of Rachel's arms.

"Who are you talking to?" Rachel silently mouthed the question, but I ignored her as I reached up to press the device deeper into my ear.

"They're still there," Titus said. "Don't look like they noticed nothin'. Yet."

My mind slowly began to spin back up to speed, and I looked around the area.

"What direction are the ones approaching from?" I asked.

"From the west. Same direction you came in," Titus answered immediately. "Just crossing that small parking lot."

I took a moment to warn Rachel and Irina about the sniper and told them to stay close to the helicopter, so he didn't have a shot at them. Pulling out the remote trigger, I changed it to the final setting, lifted the protective cover and pressed the button.

All around the perimeter of the park, the small C-4 charges I'd planted on the underside of every manhole cover detonated. The noise was furious as the plastic explosive blasted dozens of cast iron plates free of their resting places and into the air.

"Whooooeeeee!" Titus shouted over the radio. "That got them fucker's attention! You probably just killed about thirty of 'em. The ones in the parking lot are headin' the other way. But you still got a whole lot of 'em running all around like you kicked an ant hill."

"What about the sniper?" I asked.

No matter how many of the Russian soldiers on the perimeter went down, I wasn't going anywhere until he was out of commission. He was definitely the first priority.

"He's still there and looks all pissed off. Sit tight and be ready to run when I tell you. Got something up my sleeve."

"Titus, what the hell are you doing?" I shouted into the radio, but he didn't answer me.

"Goddamn it!" I said, dropping my pack and digging out the six Claymore mines I'd brought with me.

Quickly, I set them up to form a small, defensive perimeter around where we were sheltering. Stringing the wires back to a trigger, I pressed it into Irina's hand.

Anvil

"Only fire when I tell you," I said, looking into her eyes as I kept my hands wrapped around her's.

She nodded and squatted down with her back against the hull of the Hind.

"Titus," I called into the radio. I needed to know what was about to come my way.

"Hold your fuckin' horses," he panted back, obviously running as he spoke.

"What the hell are you doing?"

I pointed in the direction I wanted Rachel to watch for anyone trying to flank us. I was scanning in the opposite quadrant. She took the AKMS from Irina and brought it up to her shoulder.

"Tryin' to save your narrow ass," he panted back. "Got my deer rifle and headin' for the bell tower in a church. Should get me higher than this fucker. Now shut the hell up and let me be for a bit."

Grumbling, I reversed the direction of my scan, pausing when I saw five soldiers walking towards the helo. One of them appeared to have a leg injury as he was being helped by two others while the remaining two guarded them. They looked jumpy as hell, rifles in constant motion as they kept checking all around.

They were probably bringing their comrade to the medic and hadn't seen me. I wanted to shoot but hesitated because they were in full view of the sniper's position. If they suddenly started dropping it would alert him to the fact that something wasn't right. He might not be able to shoot me, but he could sure as hell make a call on the radio and send a whole bunch of his buddies running to ruin my night.

The five soldiers were about a hundred yards away when Rachel called out that she had three more approaching from her side. Fuck me, this was going to get ugly in a hurry.

"Titus, whatever you're doing, you'd better do it quick," I said.

"Shhhh," was all he said, then there was the loud crack of a rifle from the far side of the park. A moment later there was a second, then a third shot.

"You're good, son. Get the fuck out of there," he said, satisfaction clear in his voice.

"Sniper's down?" I asked in surprise.

"Yep, and his buddy, too. Get going. If you can make the tunnels, I'll see you in the shelter."

What the fuck? How had he just pulled that off? But then I learned a long time ago not to count out an old dog just because he was old.

Anvil

"Rachel, hold your fire," I said as I pulled the trigger on the Russian walking point.

He crumpled to the ground, dead, and I quickly shifted aim and dropped the second man. That left the two helping their wounded friend, and they had reacted when the first one fell. One of them threw himself to the side, prone on the wet grass, looking for where the shot had come from. The second one pulled the injured man down with him, a second later both of them bringing their rifles up.

The turf in the park was billiard table flat, and there was no cover. Sure, going prone had reduced their profile and presented me with much smaller targets, but they were inside eighty yards by now. I shot one of them, his head snapping back before it flopped onto the ground. That was the shot that let the other two zero in on me and open up with their unsuppressed rifles.

Bullets pinged off the armored hide of the helicopter I was pressed tightly against. Rolling to the side, I scrambled behind the cover provided by the Hind's landing gear. Popping up, I braced my rifle on a tire and drilled a round into one of them. His rifle went quiet. The last remaining guy decided it was time to retreat, leaping to his feet and running a zig-zag pattern away from me.

"Got a lot more coming. Fast!" Rachel shouted.

She started firing the AKMS. I knew they must be close for her to have decided it was more important to start shooting than it was to obey my instruction to hold her fire. Trusting her decision, I took a couple of seconds to track my guy before pulling the trigger. My aim was true, and his corpse tumbled to the wet grass.

A quick scan showed more coming, responding to the gunfire, and it sounded like Rachel had more than she could handle. To her credit, she was firing single shots. But she was also firing as fast as she could pull the trigger.

There was heavy return fire, and I suddenly realized that Katie was still out in the open, hanging unconscious from the winch cable. One stray round was all it would take to permanently eliminate any chance she might have, no matter how fantastical it might be.

Scrambling along the side of the Hind, I moved to where Rachel was firing steadily and peeked around her head. Nearly twenty Russians were charging, firing as they ran, and they were no more than forty yards away.

"Irina, fire!" I shouted.

A moment later all of the Claymores detonated with enough force to rattle my teeth.

Anvil

Mud and grass were thrown into the air, the water on the surface of the ground atomized and turned into a fine mist by the force of the explosion. It hung there, obscuring my view, but the incoming fire stopped.

Grabbing Irina's wrist, I pulled her along as I dashed to Katie. I didn't need to tell her what I wanted. As I wrapped my wife up and took her weight off the cuffs, Irina quickly unlocked them with a key she'd taken off the medic's body. Scooping Katie into my arms, I shouted for Rachel to follow me.

2

I ran with Katie's body cradled against my chest, bouncing with each step I took. Irina and Rachel were right behind me and slightly to either side. Rachel was still firing the Russian rifle. Irina grabbed mine where it hung from its sling and released it so she could join the fight.

Within ten yards we ran out of the concealing mist that had been created by the detonation of the Claymores, and even though it was night the remaining Russians spotted us and opened up. Rachel had abandoned single shots in favor of short bursts, and I could also hear my rifle being fired in the same manner. I angled for the corner of the building I'd been behind when I'd shot the Russian Major, rounding the bend and running directly into two soldiers who were charging towards us.

I stumbled from the impact, somehow managing to maintain my footing as both of them were sent sprawling. One of them fired as he landed on his back, but the bullet went wide. Rachel put a round through his head and pushed me. I kept running.

Directly ahead was the small parking lot, and though I couldn't see the manhole I had a pretty good idea of its general location. There were two bodies near the center of the asphalt area and I headed for them, glad to hear both rifles still firing behind me. I nearly tripped over the cast iron cover, not seeing it in the dark and rain, lying on the pavement where it had been blasted by the charge of C-4.

Boots skidding on the ground, I came to a stop at the open hole and looked down. There was the sound of water rushing through the tunnel beneath my feet and I cursed, somehow having forgotten the torrent that had nearly washed me away earlier. If we went down there, we'd be swept up and carried who knows where, but my hesitation was resolved when a bullet blasted a chunk out of the asphalt at my feet.

"Down the hole," I shouted at the two women. "Storm tunnels and they're full of water, but we don't have a choice."

I put Katie down and yanked the rifle sling over my head. Extending it to its full length, I put a loop around Katie's wrist and snugged it tight before attaching the other end to my belt. Irina and Rachel were keeping up a steady rate of fire, but I didn't have time to look and see how close the Russians had pushed in on us.

Reaching up, I grabbed Irina and took my rifle back, pushing her towards the hole. She balked at the edge. I lifted her off the ground and dropped her through, a short squeal cutting off when she went into the water.

"Get in the hole!" I yelled at Rachel, dropping to a knee and targeting several soldiers who were heading our way.

Without a word, Rachel stepped to the opening. She sat and swung her legs into the void, then with the rifle tucked tight to her chest scooted her ass forward and dropped out of sight. I fired a long burst at the approaching Russians, dropped the rifle and shoved Katie's unconscious body through the opening. Her weight hit the end of the sling and nearly pinned me across the manhole, but I was able to swing my legs around and drop through with her.

The water I plunged into was cold, taking my breath away as I went under. I was immediately in the pull of the current and was turned upside down and slammed into the wall as the sling attached to my belt jerked hard. Fighting the force of the flood and the weight of Katie's body, I flailed for the surface. After what felt like hours, my face broke into the air, and I was able to take a partial breath before being dragged beneath again.

I was worried about Katie; afraid she would drown or be slammed into a wall. It took every ounce of energy and concentration I possessed to even manage an occasional breath. The rest of the time I was completely submerged, tumbling in the current and completely disoriented.

22

Anvil

This went on for a long time as I was carried along in the pitch dark of the tunnel system. I was battered at intersections with other tunnels, getting spun about like a top when the flows merged, then the main current would take over again and pull me under. I had no sense of time or direction; my entire world compressed into a battle for air.

Breaking the surface for a rare breath, I had a second to hear what sounded like the roar of a massive waterfall. Before I could confirm the sound, I was savagely tugged back under by the sling that secured Katie to my body. Fear for her coursed through me, worry that she was unconscious and couldn't fight to get a breath. There was absolutely nothing I could do to help her. I was barely keeping myself alive.

Lungs burning, I kept struggling, breaking into the air again and taking a ragged breath that felt like there was a fair amount of water in it. The roar was louder now, deafening, and the turbulence that had kept me pulled under was subsiding. That was the good news. The bad news was it felt like I was accelerating as the water sped towards whatever was making the din.

Then I remembered Titus telling me all of the storm drains fed into a single giant tunnel that disappeared underground, supposedly filling a reservoir for the air base. Was that the roar? Were we about to be swept into an underground storage tank where we'd be trapped and die?

Fear surged anew, and I fought harder, trying to reach anything to grasp onto, hoping to stop our progress. But the tunnel walls were smooth, and there was nothing for my flailing hands to grip. Just blank concrete.

The water was smoother now, flowing very fast as we approached the bone-shaking roar. I looked for Katie, but there was no light. Only perfect darkness. Kicking to keep my head above the surface, I grasped the sling and started pulling. At first, I didn't understand why it was jerking, then an elbow slammed into my face.

Reaching out, I grabbed Katie's arm, intending to pull her to me. I was caught completely unprepared when she yanked it away and grabbed my arm with both of her hands. She was alive!

But she was infected and immediately began pulling herself to me. A hand brushed my neck, and I realized she was attacking. Or trying to attack. Using both hands I shoved her away from my body, feeling a hard tug on my belt when she reached the end of the sling.

I don't know if she tried to continue the attack. Perhaps it wasn't an attack at all, rather an attempt at survival. I never found out. Without warning, the world dropped out from beneath us, and we were falling.

We were still in the water, and it took me a moment to realize we were in a waterfall. Would there be a deep pool beneath us or would we crash onto rocks or perhaps more concrete? Were we about to be sucked into an underground storage reservoir that was full to the ceiling? There was time for those thoughts to run through my head, then I was plunging deep into more cold.

Struggling against the force of the water falling on top of me, then a tug on my belt as Katie struggled, I thought I was done. My lungs were on fire, spasming from all the water I'd inhaled. My body wanted nothing more than to cough, expel the bad air and take a deep breath. With a supreme effort of will, I controlled the urge as I was pushed deeper.

My ears popped from the pressure before the downward momentum ceased, finally allowing me to move farther away from the tons of water falling into the pool. Fighting a current, and now what felt like Katie's dead weight pulling on my belt, I stroked for the surface as hard as I could.

Another current caught me and dragged me along as I ascended. After an eternity I broke

Dirk Patton

through, sputtering and coughing. There was a hard tug from the sling that pulled me back under as I was drawing in a breath. What felt like several gallons of water came with it, causing my lungs to seize up and rebel. Madly fighting, I reached air again, racking coughs expelling partially inhaled water through both my nose and mouth.

There was another tug on my belt, not as hard, and I realized that Katie was unconscious again. Or drowned. Panic set in, and I frantically pulled on the sling until I could grip her arm and pull her to me. She was limp, head flopping lifelessly to the side when it cleared the surface.

The surface of the water was smoother than it had been in the tunnels, growing calmer by the moment as the strong current swept us along. It took me a second to realize I was able to faintly see Katie's head, wet hair obscuring her face. Glancing up as I kicked to keep us on the surface, I was surprised to see a night sky. Not stars and the moon, and I noticed there was a soft rain falling, but even with the cloud cover, there was enough light for me to faintly see in a few shades of grey. We were above ground in a river!

There wasn't enough illumination for me to be able to see far enough to spot either bank. I assumed the current was close to the middle, so I made it simple and struck out in the direction I was already facing. I had my left arm around Katie's chest and snaked under both of her arms. I held her on her back, tight against me with her face out of the water as I swam.

My body was battered, cold and numb. I couldn't feel much, and everything I could feel was hurting. I didn't think I was moving faster than a slow crawl, but I refused to let my limbs stop moving. If I stopped, we'd be pulled under, and it would be over.

I have no idea how long I kept at it, fighting the current and the dead weight of my wife's body. It could have only been five minutes or five hours. I was operating in the mode I remembered from Special Forces selection and training. The body has gone farther than it wants to, farther than it thinks it can, but the mind refuses to allow it to stop.

Until you're dead, there's always that one more ounce of fight in your limbs. As long as you *believe* you can go on, you can. Give up and fail, or be determined and succeed. In selection and training, giving up just means you don't pass. In the field, it will usually mean you're going to die.

With awareness of nothing other than focusing on continuing to swim, I was surprised when my feet struck bottom. I had made it out of the current and reached the shore, finally looking up and seeing a narrow strip of rock studded sand only a few feet in front of me. Trying to stand, my legs wouldn't obey the command from my brain and I wound up on my knees.

Crawling forward, I dragged Katie through the water and finally succeeded in pulling both of us onto the bank. I was panting, shivering and nearly delirious as I turned and began performing rescue breathing on her. The first couple of breaths were almost more than my tortured lungs could take, eliciting deep coughs that didn't do her any good and just made me light headed.

Calming myself, I put my hand under her neck to tilt her head back, bent over and pressed my mouth tightly against hers. I breathed for her, growing dizzier with each exhale. I kept at it, the world around me shrinking with each breath into her body until it completely closed in and everything went dark.

Anvil

3

Rachel dragged herself out of the water. She was shaking from the cold, teeth chattering as she got on her hands and knees and tried to make her way up the sandy bank. The wind was blowing from the north, instantly leaching away, even more, body heat than the dunking. She raised a shaking hand and shoved dripping hair out of her face, trying to see her surroundings.

She was on a steep embankment, the roiling surface of the river only a few inches from her boots. Shivering hard, she wanted to curl into a ball and rest but knew that if she didn't find a way to warm herself she would die of hypothermia. Maybe there was some shelter from the wind if she could make it over the top of the bank.

Pushing on, she caught her breath when a figure silhouetted against the dark sky suddenly appeared over her. She had no weapons, having lost the rifle when she jumped through the manhole. Her mind screamed at her to fight as hands reached out to grasp her arms, but her body refused to respond. She just stayed where she was, not really feeling the strong grip on each of her upper arms.

"You have to stand," Irina said to her.

At first, Rachel thought she was hallucinating. Irina? How was she here and able to be up and moving around? It must be an infected that had grabbed her! She tried to resist, tried to pull away, but the hands were too strong.

"Rachel! It is me, Irina! We have to get out of the wind!"

Irina pulled hard, finally lifting Rachel's upper body until she was resting on her knees. She stared back with vacant eyes, a flicker of recognition passing through when the Russian woman put her face close.

Pulling hard, Irina got Rachel to her feet, wrapping her arms around her body to keep her from tumbling back to the ground. Guiding the taller woman, Irina helped her reach the top of the bank. The wind was stronger here. Rachel began shivering uncontrollably and would have fallen if not for Irina's support.

"You have to walk, or we are going to die," Irina gasped, taking a step and pulling Rachel with her.

It took them several minutes to cross forty yards. Both stumbled several times, somehow managing to stay on their feet. Irina was heading for the leeward side of a small bluff, the wind steadily decreasing as they approached.

Anvil

They finally made it into the shelter of the terrain, both women collapsing to the sandy ground.

Rachel immediately curled into the fetal position, her entire body racked with violent shivers. Irina was cold, her extremities numb, but she was also proudly Russian. From early childhood, she'd delighted in participating in annual polar bear plunges. Competitive to a fault, she would stay in the ice-choked water until all the rest of the participants had returned to shore and donned warming cloaks. This water was cold, but it was far from what she'd done for fun when she was growing up.

Despite her ability to endure the cold, Irina knew that Rachel was already in trouble and she, too, would be soon if she didn't do something quickly. Looking around, she moved to check a darker shadow at the base of the bluff, but it wasn't what she hoped for. Continuing her stumbling walk she paused at a small hole, getting on her knees to peer inside.

The hole opened into a cramped cave. She couldn't see into the darkness, but pushed herself through the opening anyway. She had to make sure it was large enough for both her and Rachel, or it would be a waste of time to go get the other woman. Finally satisfied there was room, she crawled back out and made her way to where Rachel still lay shivering. Irina could hear her teeth chattering before she could see her on the sand.

"You have to get up. I have found us shelter," Irina said, pulling hard on Rachel's arms.

It took a lot of effort to get Rachel on her feet. She was taller, and weighed twenty pounds more, but Irina was persistent. Twice they crashed back to the sand when Rachel's frozen legs wouldn't respond, but eventually, Irina's determination paid off. With her support, Rachel was able to begin walking.

Reaching the cave, the next challenge was to get Rachel inside. As soon as they stopped, she sank to the ground and tried to curl back into a ball. Irina had to settle for grabbing her wrists and slowly dragging her inside. Once she had Rachel lying against the rear wall, she went back out and gathered brush to conceal the entrance, piling it up as she backed into the cave. She had no idea how well the camouflage would work, but it was the best she could do.

Rachel was shivering so hard her muscles were beginning to stay clenched. Working as quickly as her numb fingers would allow, Irina removed the other woman's soaked clothing. If the wet garments remained against her skin, they would continue to draw out her body heat.

Anvil

With Rachel stripped bare except for a pair of cotton panties, Irina quickly took off her own wet clothing. She pressed her body against Rachel's bare back, the skin so cold she momentarily shrank away. Steeling herself for the discomfort, Irina wrapped her arms around Rachel and adjusted her hips, so her pelvis and legs were tightly spooned against Rachel. Together they shivered, Irina concerned that their bodies wouldn't warm up.

Irina squeezed tight as she began shivering. This told her that the small amount of heat that had remained in her body was being sucked out by Rachel's frigid skin. Together they shook, Rachel drifting in and out of consciousness and Irina struggling to remain awake.

She was frightened that she would fall asleep. If that happened, she would relax, and her body would shift away, allowing cold air to circulate and rob both of them of the precious warmth. As she lay there, her mind went to thoughts of the past few hours.

The deaths of Scott and Martinez, both defiant to the end. She grieved for Scott, who she had grown to like, but thoughts of Martinez brought a profound sense of loss. Tears flowed as she thought about what might have been.

Dirk Patton

The two women hadn't particularly cared for each other at first, but over the past few days, they'd had an opportunity to talk and come to know each other. Irina sobbed as she replayed the last moments of Martinez' life in her head. She couldn't say that she had fallen in love with her, but it was closer than she'd been in many years.

"Are you OK?" Rachel's voice startled her.

Irina was surprised that Rachel was awake, then she realized that she had lost all track of time and had been in a state of near delirium as she reminisced about Martinez. Both of them had stopped shivering. While she was definitely not cozy, she recognized that they had warmed enough to be out of immediate danger.

"I am fine."

Irina raised her face from the tangle of Rachel's long hair, realizing she had been crying into it.

"I think you saved me," Rachel said, gently lifting Irina's arm off her body but not scooting away from the warmth of the other woman.

"No more than you would have done for me," Irina replied.

"How did you find me?" Rachel asked a moment later, sensing Irina's mood.

Anvil

"I was already out of the water and saw your head bobbing. I ran along the bank after you until you made it to shore."

"Thank you, again," Rachel said. "I haven't exactly been kind to you. I'm sorry for that."

"Emotions have been running high," Irina said, finally releasing her hold on Rachel and sitting up. She scooted a foot away and crossed her legs.

"Did you see John and Katie?" Rachel asked, sitting and turning to face Irina, who crossed her arms to conceal her bare breasts.

"No. I do not even know if they made it into the tunnel. It is fortunate that I saw you," Irina answered.

"We need to look for them." Rachel reached for her wet clothes.

"If you put those on they will draw out your body heat," Irina warned. "We must wait until they are dry."

"We don't have that much time," Rachel said. "They could be in real trouble; just like I was."

Despite Irina's warning, Rachel dug through the pile until she found her pants. Rolling back on her ass, she stuck her feet into the legs and pulled them over her knees. That was as far as she got before peeling them back off.

"Oh shit! They're freezing," she breathed. "Can we start a fire to dry them?"

"With what?" Irina shrugged her shoulders without removing her arms from over her breasts.

"There's ways to start a fire without matches. Aren't there?" Rachel asked in a plaintive voice.

"Yes, there are. But those ways only work if you have dry wood, tinder and a source of heat. We have none of that."

Rachel stared back at her, finally shaking her head.

"Then we should put them out in the wind. They'll dry faster."

"It is still raining," Irina said.

"You're not helping," Rachel grumbled even though she realized the Russian woman was right. "But we can't wait."

"Wet clothes in the wind will drain body heat very fast," Irina said, reaching out and placing a restraining hand on Rachel's arm when she reached for her discarded pants. "We cannot help them if we are incapacitated by the weather."

Rachel cursed, knowing Irina was correct, but still reluctant to give up. She racked her brain, trying to come up with a way to dry the clothes faster.

4

I came awake feeling like I was frozen to my core. My hands were so numb, I had no feeling, and I was shivering violently. At least I didn't feel warm, which would have meant my body had shut down, and I was about to die.

It may have been seconds or minutes, but the current situation finally dawned on me, and I tried to sit up. Tried. The mind told the body to do it, but the body told the mind to go pound sand.

The side of my face resting on the wet ground seemed to have some feeling, but the other side was fully exposed to the rain and wind and all it registered was... numbness. I couldn't even tell it was still raining by feel other than when an occasional drop splashed into my eye.

Finally, I forced my battered body to start moving. Slowly, with every tiny motion causing a cry of agony from a muscle or joint, I managed to lever myself up onto my hands and knees. Behind me, the water was still rushing. I was lucky it hadn't risen and washed me away while I was unconscious.

I turned my head to check on Katie, momentarily confused when I didn't see her. Confusion turned to panic, and I frantically checked the sling that was attached to my belt. It was still there, the loop that had been secured around Katie's wrist pulled open and lying on the sand. She had freed herself?

Standing up as fast as I could, I looked around, failing to see her. Forcing my feet to move, I clambered to the top of the embankment. Spinning through a slow circle, I shielded my eyes from the wind and rain with my hand. The landscape was bleak, nothing more than sand, rock and scrub in every direction. And there was no movement.

Turning back to the water I tried to look for Katie, but it was still dark. All I could tell was that the river was very straight. Too straight to be natural. It must have been a flood control channel for the water coming out of Mountain Home.

Perhaps the underground reservoir was full, and it was being diverted? Or maybe there wasn't a reservoir, and Titus had repeated a rumor. Regardless, the water was running fast. If Katie had gone back in, she'd be miles away by now. But I doubted she had.

There was still enough intelligence in there for her to loosen the sling loop and slip her hand out. That meant it was very doubtful that she'd make a decision as bad as going back into the water. And I was still alive!

Dirk Patton

I'd been out cold, but she hadn't attacked or killed me. Why not? Were there still some memories in there? Enough to override what seemed to be an uncontrollable urge to kill?

I'm generally a pretty logical guy. I don't normally fall prey to unfounded theories or suppositions, but the faint hope that Katie wasn't completely gone pushed all logic aside. Right then and there I accepted the idea that she was still capable of love and reason, otherwise, why was I not a rotting corpse. Now I just had to find her so I could help her.

Shivering in the biting wind, water dripping from my clothing, I tried to think about how I was going to go about locating my wife. Where would she have gone and why had she run off? It didn't make sense, but not much made sense at the moment. But how the hell was I going to track her?

Tracks! That's it! Stumbling back down the embankment, momentum overcame my exhausted body, and I wound up falling and splashing into the water. Freshly soaked and shivering harder, I crawled to the point where I had dragged her earlier. The sand was wet and had taken prints that were easy to see, even in the near darkness.

It was a jumble in the area where both of us had lain, but as I cast around, I found a clear set of prints heading up and over the embankment. Slowly getting to my feet, I followed them as best I could. I stumbled and tripped over a rock as I reached the crest. Getting back up, I finally thought to check for weapons.

I wasn't surprised that only the Kukri, sheathed at the small of my back, was still attached to my body. No rifle. No pistol. No Ka-Bar knife. Several full magazines were still secure in my vest, but without a rifle, they were about as useful as a rock. Almost dumping them to shed weight, I thought better of it at the last moment and began stumbling along the path my wife had taken.

Moving slow, I followed her weaving trek. The wind was getting stronger, working in concert with my drenched clothing to sap my body heat. I could feel myself growing weaker with each step, but I stayed focused on the trail and kept putting one foot in front of the other.

I rounded a low hill and had gone another fifty yards before realizing the path had suddenly straightened. Had she decided where to go or seen something? Standing there, I stared at the prints in the sand. I was so cold I couldn't feel any part of my body, but it seemed as if the shivering had stopped. That was good. Right?

Dirk Patton

Walking again, I trudged along following Katie's trail. My head was bent to look at the ground, all of my energy focused on not losing my way. One foot at a time, I kept going, failing to notice that the rain that had been falling had turned to snow. Wind drove it against the side of my face. Where it began to stick, I actually felt warmer.

Pushing on, fighting the wind, I wanted to sit down and rest. Just for a few minutes. But I wouldn't let myself stop. There was a part of me that still had enough awareness to recognize the danger of stopping. A part that knew if I sat down I'd never get up again. Wherever I sat would be my final resting place.

Then the hallucinations began. Katie suddenly appeared right in front of me. She didn't speak, just stood in the steadily falling snow and looked at me. I reached for her, but she stepped away before turning and walking off in a new direction. I called out to her, but she didn't respond.

Forcing my frozen legs to move, I followed. I called her name and reached for her, but she was too far in front and ignored me. Just kept walking, her long, red hair whipping in the wind. A couple of times she looked over her shoulder to make sure I was still there, and my heart leapt when I didn't see red eyes. She was OK! But why wasn't she talking to me?

Anvil

I tried to put on enough speed to catch her, but she easily outpaced me. Stumbling, I fell face first into the snow, unable to look up when she screamed. I heard her race away into the storm when I called her name. With a supreme effort of will, I pushed myself up and tried to follow my wife. I was taking a step to pursue when Rachel suddenly appeared in front of me, wrapped her arms around my shoulders and pulled me down towards the ground.

5

"There, sir."

Petty Officer Jessica Simmons pointed at a spot on the large display. Admiral Packard, his aide and Jessica's CO, Lieutenant Hunt, stood behind her and looked where she indicated. The giant, flat panel monitor showed a pallet of greys with two red blobs. They were watching a thermal image of Idaho, having tracked Major Chase and his companions after the havoc he had unleashed on the Russians.

One of the red blobs was following the other. The one in the lead was bright red and easily followed. The one behind enough cooler for the difference to be detectable by satellite. They came to a stop, and Jessica zoomed the image.

After a moment, the hotter of the two bodies raced away to the northwest, leaving the other where it was. Then a third person appeared, glowing bright red. The new arrival merged with the one that had been left behind.

"Where the hell did that one come from?" Packard asked, riveted to the image.

"Must have been under or in some sort of shelter, sir," Jessica replied as the two blobs began to move, then disappeared from the display.

"They're screened from the bird, sir."

Jessica zoomed back out. The person who had led the way was still moving fast and Jessica used her mouse to draw a box around the blob. She marked it as target Bravo.

The system's software would continue to track the target as long as it was visible. A new window opened in the display and began scrolling data related to the target. The location, direction of travel and speed on the ground were continually updated.

"I think that must be an infected female, sir," Jessica said, peering at the data scrolling through the smaller window.

"Explain," Lieutenant Hunt said.

"The speed, sir. She's moving at a steady twenty miles an hour. That's damn fast. Too fast for an infected male and too fast for an uninfected person unless they're a professional athlete. I've seen some of the females hit twenty-five miles an hour for short distances, and that's... uh oh."

The red blob suddenly slowed to three miles an hour before also disappearing from the view of the orbiting thermal imager. Jessica's fingers flew across the keyboard, the displayed image rotating through several colors as she tried to reacquire the target with different light and heat spectrums, but she was unsuccessful.

"We've lost her for the moment, sir, but the system will keep watching the point where she disappeared and lock on again when she's visible."

"Did you target Major Chase as well?" The Admiral asked.

"Yes, sir."

"Commander," the Admiral spoke to his aide without taking his eyes off the monitor. "I want an update on the extraction plan for those people on my desk in fifteen minutes."

"Sir, the Russians have complete control of the airspace and there are still ground troops arriving as we speak. We have no assets remaining in North America other than the SEAL team at the lab in Seattle. If we go in too soon, we'll tip our hand."

"Commander," Packard's voice grew hard as he turned his steely gaze on the junior officer. "I didn't ask you to tell me why it was going to be hard. We are not leaving one of our own behind. You now have fourteen minutes. I suggest you get busy."

"Yes, sir."

The younger man snapped to attention before turning and rushing out of the room.

"Petty Officer, are you able to keep track of all of the targets?" Packard asked in a calmer voice.

"Yes, sir. The system will do that, and I'll personally monitor it. The only thing is, if they've gone into some sort of cave system and come out at a different location I may lose them. Or if the weather worsens it will blank out the thermal, and we won't have any eyes on them. Sir."

"Young lady, you've done a great job, and I have faith in you. Lieutenant, update me immediately if there's any change."

"Yes, sir," they chorused as the Admiral turned on his heel and strode out of the room.

"Good work, Jessica," Lieutenant Hunt said once the Admiral was gone. "You're making both of us look good."

"Just doing my job, sir."

Jessica smiled at the praise. Hunt smiled back then returned to his workstation to continue monitoring Russian troop movements in the western US. Jessica double checked the system to make sure it was properly set to maintain surveillance of the targets, closed out two files she'd been working on and locked her terminal.

"Sir, if it's OK I'm going to step out for some air," she said, rolling her chair back and looking at her CO.

"The system will alert me if there's any activity?" He asked, looking up over the rim of his glasses.

"Yes, sir. It will beep and transfer to your station."

Jessica stood and stretched, trying to remember the last time she had eaten or slept. He nodded and returned his attention to his screen.

"OK. Try and keep it short in case the Admiral comes back."

"Ten minutes, sir. Thank you."

Jessica grabbed her small purse that held nothing other than a lighter, a pack of cigarettes and two condoms, and headed for the exit. She checked out through the layers of security, finally emerging into fresh air. Taking a deep breath, she ignored the million-dollar view of Pearl Harbor and headed for the bench she liked to sit on while on break.

Anvil

Rounding a thick planting of Birds of Paradise bushes, she smiled when she spotted the figure seated on the bench. Chief Petty Officer Mark Hiram heard her approach, standing to greet her with open arms. Jessica ran the last few steps, falling into his embrace and lifting her face to accept his kiss.

"Do you have time?" He asked, squeezing her ass with both hands when they finally came up for air.

"I wish," Jessica breathed, shuddering with pleasure as he pulled her pelvis tight against his. She could feel his manhood pressing hard against her abdomen. "That Army Major I told you about is still alive, and there's going to be an attempt to extract him. They're going to be needing data from me very soon."

"We don't need long," he purred in her ear, making her knees go weak.

"Maybe you don't, but I do."

Jessica smiled and placed her hands on his chest, opening some space between them before she lost all control and took him right there on the bench. Taking a deep breath, she sat, digging out a cigarette and lighting it. Hiram set next to her, circling his arm around her narrow waist and pulled her close.

"How is he still alive? I thought the Russians were closing in on him," he said, gently rubbing her thigh with his other hand.

"They were. They did. He had some surprises for them and escaped through a storm tunnel. I'm watching him on thermal right now, about ten miles south of town. It's snowing there, and I hope we can get to him in time. At least he made a clean escape from the goddamn Russians," Jessica said, leaning her head onto his shoulder.

The two lovers talked for a few more minutes as Jessica finished her smoke. They embraced and kissed deeply after checking to make sure no one was around, then she broke away and dashed back to the building where she worked.

When Jessica was out of sight, Hiram turned and strode across the neatly mown grass to the parking lot where he had left his personal vehicle. He had been waiting for two hours for her to take a break and was relieved to be moving again. Getting behind the wheel, he drove across the sprawling base, careful to stay below the posted speed limit.

Reaching the cargo area of the harbor, he parked and stepped out, looking around and seeing no one else. Keeping a close watch, he moved deep into a maze of stacked shipping containers. Stopping close to the middle of the massive storage area, he checked for observers again before removing a key from his pocket and approaching a container at ground level.

He had carefully selected this one, reviewing its history and satisfying himself that it hadn't moved in over a year. Due to its unique size and shape, it would likely sit for another year or more before being loaded on a ship. Well, that would be if the world hadn't ended. Now, it would probably never move again. It would just sit there until the salt air rusted it into oblivion.

Stepping to the door, he pulled on a pair of thin, latex gloves so he wouldn't leave fingerprints. He inserted the key into an old lock scrounged from the motor pool where he worked. It was tarnished with age on the outside, but well lubricated and the key turned easily, the hasp popping open. Removing it, he raised the locking lever and tugged the door open, taking another look around before stepping into the container.

Clicking on a small flashlight, he ignored the debris scattered across the floor and stepped quickly to a battered shoe box lying amidst a pile of loose packing material. Raising the lid on the box, he retrieved a small satellite phone and pressed the power button to turn it on as he walked back into the open air to get a signal.

A minute later the phone finished its boot sequence and had locked onto a signal. Hiram pressed a speed dial button and listened as a phone deep within GRU headquarters in Moscow began ringing.

6

I stumbled and fell to my knees when Rachel pulled on me. She was dragging me towards a small hole in the side of a bluff, but I didn't want to go. I wanted to keep following Katie. To catch up with her and protect her. I tried to push Rachel away, but she was stronger than I was.

A moment later Irina's face appeared in front of me as Rachel worked my body through the hole. Together, they pulled me into the darkness and rolled me onto my back. Immediately, fingers began unhooking, unfastening and unbuttoning my clothing.

"W-w-w-w-w-hat the hell?" I stammered through a shiver.

"You're hypothermic," Rachel's voice said from the darkness as my vest was pulled over my head. "If we don't get these wet clothes off and warm you up you're going to die."

"K-k-k-k-k-atie," I mumbled.

"We heard her," Irina said in my ear as she raised my upper body to work the shirt off my arms. "We thought we were being attacked, but I think she brought you to us. She saved you."

Dirk Patton

I understood the words Irina was speaking, but the concept wasn't registering. All I could think about was that Katie was getting farther away, and I was wasting time. I raised an arm and tried to push them away, but I was too weak. Irina worked my final shirt over my head and began rubbing my arms with her hands as she pressed her body against mine.

Rachel had my boots and socks off, now struggling with my pants. I tried to push Irina away, but she held me in a tight embrace. Her face was close to mine, and she whispered into my ear as Rachel tugged on my pants.

"Katie is infected. She brought you to us so we could save you. If you go back out there, you will die. She is obviously thinking. She will seek shelter."

I finally understood what Irina was saying. Emotion overwhelmed me, and a sob escaped my lips. Tears began flowing, and there was nothing I could do to stop them. Laying in Irina's embrace, I cried like a child.

I felt my pants come off and heard Rachel tell Irina to move me on my side. No longer fighting, I cooperated when she gently pushed me into position. A moment later one of them spooned against my back as the other pressed in against the front of my body. I couldn't tell

which was which. Whoever was behind me was
vigorously rubbing my exposed arm.

We lay that way for some time as their
combined body heat slowly warmed me. Neither
of them spoke as I cried, not battling the
emotions that had taken over. I drifted,
somewhere below the level of consciousness yet
still awake and aware of what had happened.
Then I slept, but not for long.

Feeling began returning. My skin tingled
as it warmed, feeling like ants were crawling
over every inch of me. Then the pain set in. Soon
it was all I could do to not cry out as every fiber
in my body felt like it was on fire.

The pain finally subsided, and I was
itching all over like I'd been dragged through a
patch of poison ivy. As feeling returned, so did
greater awareness of the situation and a measure
of control over my emotions.

"I need to go after Katie," I mumbled.

I felt the body in front of me shift as she
turned over. Then it was pressed tightly against
me as arms went around my neck, pulling me
into an embrace.

"The wind is howling, and your clothes
are still soaked," Rachel said in my ear. So now I
knew which one was where.

"Fire," I said, wondering why they hadn't already lit one.

"No way to start one. Wood is wet," Rachel answered without loosening her hold.

"My vest," I said. "Ammunition. Open a round and use the powder to start the wood burning. Lighter in my pants pocket."

I was still warming, and with the warmth came exhaustion. It was comfortable between the two women, and my eyes were growing heavy. I just wanted to sleep, unable to force my body to start moving to go search for Katie.

My back was suddenly cold as Irina moved away from me and I shivered. Rachel began rubbing her hand across the exposed skin and threw her leg over mine in an attempt to make up for the loss of Irina's heat.

I could hear Irina going through my clothing as she searched for the items I'd mentioned. A gust of frigid air blew across my bare skin when she moved the jacket covered bush that was mostly sealing the entrance. A few minutes later there was another blast of cold air when she returned.

There was the sound of ammo being ejected from a magazine, then a scrape as she worked bullets out of their brass cases. Branches rustled as she broke and arranged them, then the

Anvil

scrape of the wheel on flint from a disposable lighter. Over and over.

"Flint's wet," I said, recognizing the problem without having to see it.

For several minutes, I could hear Irina blowing air, presumably across the lighter's flint. Rachel continued to stay tightly wrapped around me. When Irina tried the lighter again, it must have lit as it only scraped once then there was enough light in the small cave for me to see Rachel's face inches from mine.

The gun powder ignited with a whoosh, the air immediately filling with the odor of burnt sulfur. Irina said something in Russian I didn't recognize, then lit another round's worth of powder. This time, after the initial flare of light and acrid odor, there was the crackle of wood starting to burn.

Soon it was brightly lit inside the cave, and Rachel slowly peeled herself away from me. For the first time, I realized she was nude other than a pair of panties. Painfully sitting up and turning to face the fire, I saw that Irina was in the same state of dress. Looking down, I noted that I hadn't been given the same courtesy as I was completely nude.

"Really? Couldn't leave my underwear on?" I asked Rachel.

Dirk Patton

She didn't say anything, just dug through a pile of clothing I recognized as mine. Finding my underwear, she held it up so I could see and gently wrung the thin fabric. Water poured out and soaked into the sandy floor of the cave.

"Point taken," I mumbled, looking around for something I could use to cover myself.

Irina was busily spreading clothing across sticks she had stuck into the sand. She had built the fire at the entrance so the smoke would vent and not suffocate us, and was now positioning our garments to dry.

"Thank you," I said, looking first at Irina then Rachel.

They both nodded, Rachel reaching out and gently touching my arm.

"Katie brought you to us," she said softly. "Stood right outside the opening and screamed, then took off as soon as she saw me."

"She must still be able to think. She's not all the way gone," I said, hearing the optimism in my own voice. Irina and Rachel exchanged a glance.

"What?" I asked, not liking how they'd looked at each other.

Anvil

"Maybe she isn't, but she's still infected," Rachel said, looking into my eyes.

"What the hell is wrong with you?" I asked, starting to get mad.

"Nothing. I'm sorry. I just don't want you to think she's still the same woman and let your guard down. Yes, she brought you here. Saved you. Some part of her is still in there. But just because it's there now doesn't mean the infection doesn't progress, and…" Rachel's voice trailed off and she lowered her gaze.

I had been getting mad, and what Rachel said didn't help. Anger threatening to boil over, I was starting to open my mouth when Irina spoke.

"You are both right," she said in a stern voice. "There is some of Katie still inside. Otherwise, she would have killed you rather than bringing you to us. But you cannot count on that the next time you see her. This is not her fault. It is the virus to blame. Rachel is giving you sound advice; the same advice I am giving you. I know it hurts to hear, but you need to hear it. And listen to it."

I stared back at her for a few moments, anger coursing through my veins. But not anger at Irina or Rachel, just a blind rage at the situation in general. I had thought our biggest threat was from the Russians or the infected. It had been a while since I'd worried about the virus. Now…

"How the fuck did this happen?" I asked, turning to Rachel.

"I have no idea," she said after a moment of making sure I wasn't about to explode. "You're sure she had the vaccine?"

"She said she received it when they were vaccinating everyone on base at Tinker," I said, blowing a deep breath out.

"Then it makes no sense," Irina said. "The vaccine was tested for over two years and was found to be one hundred percent effective."

"Unless the virus has mutated," Rachel whispered, a haunted look crossing her face.

7

We spent the next hour or so constantly turning our clothing as close to the flames as possible. It dried slowly, and I selfishly made sure the first item to be ready to wear was my underwear. Not that there's anything wrong with sitting around naked with two beautiful women, but I was feeling self-conscious. Odd for me as I've never been one to give a crap if someone gets an eyeful.

Perhaps it was the stress and emotion of our situation, but I sat near the fire with my legs tightly pressed together until I could pull them back on. There were warm spots and spots that were still damp and cold. Naturally, the dampest and coldest spot wound up tight against my balls. But it wasn't wet enough to be a concern, and I felt about a thousand percent better with just that little bit of modesty restored. Genitals covered, I scooted away to make room for the girls to finish drying their shirts.

"What do we do now?" Rachel asked, turning her shirt and fluffing it to get warm air inside.

"I don't know yet," I said, staring into the flames. "I've been trying to figure that out. I want to go after Katie, but I don't know what the hell to do if and when I find her. She's going to be fast and strong. Hard as hell to catch. And if I do catch her, I don't even know how I'll control her. There's no option other than knocking her out again, and I'm not sure continuing to pound on her head is such a great idea."

Irina opened her mouth to say something but caught her breath and turned to look at the opening to our tiny cave. I knew better than to speak when someone is trying to identify a sound, but Rachel asked her what she heard.

"Shhhh," Irina hissed, moving as close to the fire as she dared and cocking her head for a better angle to hear.

Rachel looked at me, and I shook my head, telling her I didn't hear anything. After a few long moments, Irina spoke softly without changing the direction she was facing.

"Rotors," she whispered. "They're looking for us."

"The fire," I said, worried about the smoke leading the Russians directly to us.

Irina already had the same thought and quickly scooped up handfuls of sand from the floor of the cave and smothered the flames. The temperature in our refuge quickly began dropping.

Anvil

"Get dressed," I said, reaching for my pants. "This is as dry as we're going to get."

The two women nodded and after a few seconds of sorting through the clothing they began covering themselves with the less than dry garments. Damp fabric against your skin isn't comfortable, but it was the best we could do. At least we'd had time to remove the majority of the moisture and weren't sitting in soaked clothing.

I changed places with Irina, leaning my head through the opening to scan the area. It was a grey morning, snow still falling slowly. The sound of two separate rotors was clear on the cold air, but neither seemed to be particularly close. As I listened it sounded like one of them was slowly moving along the flood control channel, heading south, as the other was in a large orbit over an area on the opposite side of the water.

At least for the moment they weren't searching the specific area where we were hiding. Shifting my attention, I looked at the ground outside the cave. From my angle, I could make out the jumble of prints that had been left when Katie led me to safety. They had been mostly filled in by fresh snow. I knew where to look and what I was looking at. It was doubtful the tracks could be spotted from the air.

"We're OK for the moment," I said, moving fully back into the darkness.

My eyes had adjusted to the light outside, and I couldn't see either of the women.

"Will they send ground troops to search?" Rachel asked from the gloom.

"I don't think so," I said, looking in the direction her voice had come from. "Too much country to cover on foot when you have air assets available. They've probably got them waiting to load onto trucks and head to any area..."

"What?" Irina asked when my voice trailed off to silence.

"I was thinking about regular ground troops. There were quite a few Spetsnaz, and they may very well send out a bunch of small squads to sweep the area. Either of you have any idea how far from town we are?"

My eyes were adjusting to the lack of light, and I could make out both of them shaking their heads.

"We must have traveled several miles," Irina finally said. "We were in the water for a long time, and it was moving swiftly."

That thought comforted me to a degree. The farther away we had been swept by the flood, the less likely it would be for the Russians to be able to find us. I relaxed a notch but reminded myself to remain vigilant.

"So what do we do? Where do we go?" Rachel asked.

"For now, we stay put. We have shelter and a pretty good hiding place. The Russians aren't searching in the immediate area, but if we start moving while it's light we'll be pretty easy to spot."

We lapsed into silence for a few minutes, each of us lost in our own thoughts. Occasionally the sound of a rotor reached my ears, but I wasn't hearing anything to indicate they were approaching. But it was only a matter of time. I had no doubt they were performing a grid search and eventually one of them would pass directly over us.

"Tell me what happened after I got out of the Jeep," I said to Rachel.

She nodded, pausing as she collected her thoughts. Her story wasn't surprising, now that I knew I hadn't killed everyone with the grenade launcher. Pain and anger swept over me when she told me Scott had been killed by the tall Russian I'd shot while rescuing them. She didn't know what had become of Colonel Crawford, Igor or Dog.

"You didn't see them?" I asked.

"The Colonel was running with Katie and me when we were attacked. Dog was with us, too. Scott was hit in the leg, and Dog was heading for him when the helicopter Martinez was in went down. That's the last I saw of him or the Colonel, and I never saw Igor after the firefight started."

"Could they have survived?" I asked, not ready to contemplate the loss of so many more.

Katie turning. Martinez dead. Scott dead. Sure, I've lost friends and fellow soldiers in combat before, but that doesn't make it any less of an emotional impact when it happens.

"I just don't know," Rachel said. "Oh, and they did kill the prisoner. The one we thought was immune."

"Who?" I asked.

"Johnnie something. They found him in a jail, I think."

"Not surprised at that one," I mumbled, remembering finding the man.

"Who were you talking to that was helping?" Irina asked.

Anvil

"A survivor I ran into when I got to town," I said.

I'd already forgotten about Titus and a wave of worry passed over me. The man had saved my life and hopefully hadn't given his in the process.

"Survivor? Was he vaccinated?" Rachel asked, excitement causing her to raise her voice. Irina and I shushed her simultaneously.

"No vaccine. He was in a bomb shelter with his family. They turned. He didn't."

"Immune!" Rachel whispered.

"Probably," I said. "What's the big deal?"

"The same reason the Colonel was taking the prisoner to Seattle!" Rachel was growing more excited and reached out and grasped my arm.

"Katie and I left to find you before Crawford decided what to do with him."

"With an immune subject there's a possibility a cure can be created," Rachel said. "Where is the man in Mountain Home?"

"If he survived, he's probably back in his bunker," I said, hope lifting my spirits and making me antsy to go find Titus.

"Then that's what we should do," Rachel said. "Find him and Katie and get both of them to Seattle."

"Can it really work?" I asked, trying to control the growing optimism I was feeling.

"It's possible, but by no means certain. There's a lot of factors I don't understand related to virology. It might not work, but it's the best chance we have."

"Quiet," Irina mumbled barely loud enough to be heard.

I looked at her. She was staring intently out of the opening. I turned my head and saw four Russian soldiers slowly working their way across the open ground.

8

We huddled in the cave watching the Russian troops carefully make their way through the area. My only remaining weapon, the Kukri, was gripped tightly in my right hand. I didn't have much optimism that if we were discovered, I'd have an opportunity to use it. But, it was better than bare hands against rifles.

As I watched, I noted they were being very cautious as they moved. The bombs and smaller charges on the manhole covers, then the Claymore mines I'd set off in town had made them nervous. And I didn't blame them one bit. I'd be tiptoeing too, worrying that at any moment there was going to be the sudden flash of high explosives that would be the last thing I'd ever see.

The downside to having put the fear of God in them is they were moving so slowly and were so alert to their surroundings. They were in a modified diamond formation, one in front or on point, the two in the middle close together and the rear guard holding back a good ten yards. Too spread out for me to have any hope of successfully attacking with only a blade.

The Russian on point was hyper-focused on the ground in front of them, most certainly concerned about encountering one of my IEDs.

The two in the middle had their heads on swivels, constantly scanning the full one hundred and eighty degrees on their individual sides. The rear guard spent as much time walking backwards as he did forwards. Yes, they were spooked.

But why the hell were there already ground troops in the area? We were miles from town, or I was pretty sure we were. And I was confident we hadn't been spotted by any of the helicopters. Miles from town meant there was a LOT of open country which translated into a LOT of square miles to search. They didn't have enough men to cover all of that territory on foot. No one does. So how was it I was huddled in a cave looking at Russians?

Something was wrong. Either the enemy had regained access to our satellite imaging feed, or someone was able to track me and supply information to the Russians. My mind once again went to Jessica. There was no one else I was aware of that could possibly know where I had wound up. But suspicion of her was once again tempered by realization that she would have me pinpointed. If it was her giving intel to the enemy, I'd already be dead.

No, this was something or someone else. Could they have broken the encryption and regained access to Echelon? Doubtful. If that was the case, they would have me pinpointed as well, and I wouldn't be watching them search the area. That left someone with peripheral knowledge or information about my movements.

I had no idea how many people might be working with or close to Jessica. As soon as I could get my hands on a sat phone, I was going to have a conversation with Admiral Packard. He needed to know there was a bad apple in the barrel.

As all of this went through my head, the Spetsnaz had only covered maybe twenty-five careful yards. Shutting down that line of thought, I focused on the emergency at hand. I had already thoroughly checked the tiny cave, and there was no other way out. The entrance was well hidden in the shadows at the base of the bluff, but we were trapped.

I caught my breath and tensed my arm when the small squad came to a stop. The point man was frozen in place, his left hand held up and clenched into a fist. He was focused on the ground where I had followed Katie. I stared hard at the snow, grimacing when I was able to faintly make out our trail.

All around, the light snow that was falling had covered the ground in a perfectly smooth blanket of white. It was only a couple of inches deep but had settled evenly. Except for where

71

Dirk Patton

the passage of mine and Katie's feet had compressed a layer.

More snow had fallen, filling in the tracks. But not enough to completely erase them. The point man understood what he was looking at, even if it was only variations in the surface of what should be smooth, virgin snow.

His head turned as he followed the path with his eyes. At first, I had hope they would move away and follow the trail to the flood channel. Those hopes were dashed when the lead soldier pointed at the ground and moved his arm up to highlight the bluff we were hiding in. He stepped off, moving parallel to the trail, the others spreading out slightly as they followed.

"When they get close enough I'm going to go," I mumbled. "You two make a run for it while I've got them distracted."

"Are you crazy?" Rachel hissed, reaching out and grabbing my upper arm. "They're armed and too spread out. You might get the first one, but they'll kill you."

"No, they won't," I said, gently removing her hand. "They want me alive. Their orders are to take me alive. They'll be focused on me, and you just might be able to get away."

"No," Irina interjected. "You have killed too many. They are angry, and no matter what

72

their orders may be, they will kill you if you attack."

"No choice," I said, waving for them to be quiet as the Russians drew closer to our hiding place.

There was a rustling behind me that I ignored as I repositioned my feet under my hips to help me get a good lunge through the opening.

"There is always another way," Irina said from behind me.

She reached out and grabbed the Kukri, yanking it from my hand. I spun to see her lift it as she held her hair back. With a quick slice, she split open her scalp, then handed the blade back to me. I was stunned into immobility, thinking she must have lost her mind. It was only a moment before blood began pouring from her self-inflicted wound, running down across her forehead.

The rustling I had heard was Irina removing some of her clothing. She was nude from the waist up and quickly reached to her forehead and rubbed her hands in the fresh blood. Smearing it across her face, she pressed directly on the cut to cover her hands again, rubbing a slick coating across her chest and bare breasts.

Dirk Patton

Grabbing my hand, she slapped it onto the freely bleeding slice in her scalp. She held it there for a moment to soak my skin with her blood, then holding my wrist with both hands put my hand on her throat. When I removed my hand, there was a bright, bloody handprint left on her neck as if I had been choking her.

"Stay here unless you see an opportunity," she hissed.

Scrambling forward, Irina passed through the narrow door. As she emerged from the cave, she began screaming in Russian. She was a frightful sight, blood smeared on her pale skin, staining her blonde hair and running down her face. Moving forward on hands and knees, she kept screaming, shouting to the soldiers in her native tongue.

They had frozen, rifles snapping up when she had first appeared. As she struggled towards them in the snow, she slipped and fell, leaving a bright red stain on the pure white. Still screaming, her tone was somewhere between panic and begging for help, she finally collapsed onto the ground no more than three yards from where Rachel and I remained concealed in the bluff. She rolled onto her back, making sure the blood covering her bare skin was starkly visible.

Looking around nervously, the soldiers glanced at each other. As Irina continued to scream and plead, the point man finally walked forward. He stood over her for a moment before sinking to a knee and reaching out to touch her shoulder. She was sobbing now, and even though I didn't know what she was saying I could tell she was putting on a masterful performance.

Irina reached up and grasped the man's arm, pulling him closer. She was speaking fast, in between sobs, and finally began pointing in the direction Katie had gone. The soldier looked where she pointed, then glanced back at the rest of his squad. Slowly, the two from the middle of the formation began walking forward.

"Good girl," I mumbled, amazed at what Irina was doing.

But there was still the fourth Spetsnaz. The rear guard. He wasn't a fool, and he wasn't moving. He had stopped about thirty yards away from where Irina lay crying in the snow. Just like he should, he was scanning the surrounding terrain. He wasn't watching the distraction of a half-naked, blood-covered woman. The other two had reached the commotion now and stood watching their comrade try to calm the hysterical stranger.

They stood close together, one of them with his back to me, watching as she wailed and grasped onto the man on the ground with her. Irina had given me an opportunity. I could be out the door and on the Spetsnaz in one step. And she appeared to have a death grip on the point man's arm. She intended to hold him back from the fight. I was confident I could take the other two with the Kukri, but the fucker on rear guard wasn't budging.

And he was too far away. Sure, I could charge out of the cave and quickly dispatch two of them while Irina occupied the third, but then what. The guy on rear guard would just shoot me before his buddies even hit the ground. I needed him closer.

Irina recognized this and amped up her wails and screams, writhing on the ground in a good imitation of pain. The man wasn't budging, and she somehow kicked it up another notch, arching her back and screaming at the top of her lungs. One of the other soldiers knelt on the far side of her, trying to comfort her.

Finally, the fourth man, who's attention was now drawn to Irina's wails, took a step closer. He paused, scanned through a full three hundred and sixty degrees, then moved a few more steps. He was either very nervous or a combat vet. And if the woman that had so suddenly appeared hadn't been speaking in Russian I don't think he would have been drawn in.

Anvil

Slowly, he kept moving closer. Only a few steps before he'd stop and scan all around, but the distance was closing. Once he was inside five yards, Irina twisted onto her side and began emphatically pointing in a direction away from the bluff.

As she shook her arm she screamed a few Russian curses I did recognize, then I thought I heard my name. Four heads turned to look in the direction she was pointing.

9

I had been waiting for this moment, legs coiled beneath me, Kukri tightly gripped in my right hand. As their attention turned away from the bluff, I launched myself through into the open air. On all fours to squeeze through the low door, I pumped with my legs to keep forward momentum. Pushing off with my hands, I came into a crouch as I charged forward.

Irina saw my movement and screamed louder to cover the sound of my approach. As she screamed, she gripped the upper arm of each kneeling man and pulled them towards her. The rear guard soldier looked down at her and saw me from the corner of his eye.

Everything slowed as I took my first full step. Suddenly I went from a normal world to a super high definition, slow motion world. Colors were vivid; details were incredibly sharp, and only the sounds I was focused on could be heard.

The soldier who saw me snapped his head around, and as I stretched to cover the last of the open ground between us I clearly saw the stubble on his chin, the dirt ground into his brow and even the color of his eyes. The Kukri was up, held high for a killing slash as I came even with the Spetsnaz, who had stood over Irina with his back to me.

Anvil

With all of the power in my shoulder and arm, I swung the heavy blade. There was a moment of resistance when it met the side of his neck, then it was free. Continuing the swing, I noted several drops of blood fly off the tip and strike the rear guard soldier on the face. Irina was still screaming, now struggling with the two soldiers who were trying to respond to my attack.

In front of me, the man was swinging his rifle up, not to shoot me, but to block the strike of my weapon. He raised it just in time, the steel of the Kukri ringing loudly on the barrel, then we collided and tumbled to the ground. Behind, I could hear the struggle Irina was engaged in, but I had my hands full.

We rolled, each of us gripping the other in an attempt to get the upper hand. The thing about hand to hand combat is that it is brutal. There's no other word for it. Between two trained fighters, it is fast, violent and almost always fatal for one. More often than you'd think, it's fatal for both as there is typically a lot of damage inflicted by both parties.

I still had the blade, and he was trying to control my arm as I threw punches and searched for leverage. He was strong as hell, equaling the power I was able to summon, and the Kukri wasn't moving one-inch closer to his flesh. Knees pounded into my back as I shifted my weight and crashed my forehead into his face.

Two fingers on my left hand snapped as he found a momentary purchase and twisted them savagely to the side. Yanking my hand away, I twisted as he reached to get a grip on the back of my neck. He moved with me, and I wound up on my back as he rolled his full body weight onto my chest. I tried to roll him off, but he countered the move and slipped a hand past my defenses and locked it on my throat, pressing with everything he had.

I pounded on the side of his head and clapped his ear with an open palm, trying to rupture his eardrum. He seemed impervious to pain. Unable to breathe, I began bucking, trying to throw him off or even loosen the pressure on my windpipe long enough to gasp for air. He wasn't budging, his legs now in a hold around my hips, pinning me. My hand with the Kukri was still in an iron grip and blows with my damaged hand were ineffective. He looked into my eyes and grinned with bloody teeth as he continued to lean pressure into my throat.

Blood pounded in my ears, and my vision was starting to tunnel as the big Russian kept squeezing my throat. I hit him in the face twice, feeling his nose break with the second blow, but the pressure didn't lessen by even an ounce.

Anvil

Grasping, I tried to work my fingers beneath his, failing to overcome the strength in his hand.

Feeling myself losing consciousness, I flailed out with my hand, hoping to feel a stick or rock or anything I could use for a weapon. There was nothing within reach other than snow on top of smooth sand. Still struggling, but losing strength as I felt consciousness waning, the vicious pressure on my throat was suddenly gone.

Taking a ragged breath, I turned my head in the direction the Russian had gone, levering up on my elbows. He lay on his back trying to fend off slashing blows as Katie tore at his neck and head. Frozen in shock for a moment, I shook off the surprise and rolled, plunging the Kukri into the side of his exposed neck.

Katie leapt away from him, coming into a crouch and watching me. I wanted to keep looking at her, but the sounds of fighting from behind reminded me there were still two more Spetsnaz that I hadn't dealt with. Tearing my attention off of my wife, I stood and dashed to where Irina and Rachel were struggling with the last soldier.

One of the two lay on the ground, his head deformed from a savage blow. The last guy was trying to shake Rachel off his back. She had leapt on, wrapping her arms around his neck and long legs around his waist. Irina was pounding on him with her fists to little effect. As I rushed to help he delivered a solid punch to the side of her head that sent her sprawling.

Reaching over his head, he grabbed Rachel's hair in both fists before falling backwards and crushing her against the ground with his full body weight. I heard the air whistle out of her lungs as I arrived. The Russian's eyes went big when he saw me, knowing he was done.

I hit him twice in the face, hard, not wanting to stab or slash with the Kukri and risk injuring Rachel. His eyes lost focus after the second blow, and I grabbed the front of his vest and hauled him up and off of her. He reached for me, trying to wrap me up. My blade was already turned in the right direction, and I buried it in his body, sliced to make sure he was done, then pushed his corpse away.

Pausing, I looked down at Rachel as she gulped air like a fish out of water, trying to get her lungs working again. Irina was unconscious, having been knocked out by the blow she'd received. With no urgent injuries or threats, I turned to face Katie.

She still watched me, standing several yards beyond the body of the Russian she'd saved me from. Saved me! Again! She was still in there! But I couldn't see any sign of the

Anvil

woman I loved in the horrid red eyes that stared back at me. There was only cold aggression and anger.

"What the hell?" Rachel mumbled as she regained her feet and came to stand beside me. She placed her hand on my shoulder in an unconscious gesture of fear.

When she touched me, Katie took two steps forward and snarled. After a moment she leapt over the corpse and dropped into a crouch, still snarling as she prepared to leap at Rachel. I moved between the two women without even thinking.

"No!" I said to Katie, dropping the Kukri into the snow and holding both hands up, palms towards her.

She paused, the snarl dying out. Slowly she relaxed her posture and returned to a standing position.

"Can you understand me?" I asked in a gentle voice, afraid of provoking her or scaring her off.

She remained motionless, only her eyes giving away her anger at Rachel. They continually flicked back and forth between the two of us. Perhaps I was reading too much into the moment, but for me, this confirmed that there was still some part of my wife buried under the infection induced rage. The jealous part. That in combination with her having attacked the Russian to save me strengthened my hope that I hadn't completely lost her.

"Please come with me," I said. "I'll take you someplace safe where there's help. Please. Trust me. I'll get you help."

I had slowly moved forward as I spoke, maintaining eye contact with her. As I drew closer, I thought I could see a war of emotions taking place, but maybe that was only what I wanted to see. When I came to a stop, we were separated by no more than five feet. Katie's posture was guarded, but she didn't look like she was about to attack.

"It will be alright," I whispered to her. "Just trust me and everything will be ok."

As I pleaded with Katie, there were tears running down my face. I didn't know if I really believed what I was saying. All I knew was there was nothing I wouldn't do to get her back. Carefully, I took another half a step and very slowly raised my arm, extending my hand towards her.

"Take my hand," I said. "Please, honey. Take my hand. Let me help."

We stood like that for close to a minute; my hand extended to within easy reach for her as

Anvil

my tears flowed. She stared back at me, some of the anger in her eyes dissipating. She tilted her head to the side and lowered her gaze to my offered hand and for a moment I thought she was going to reach out and take it. Thought I was getting through to her.

But suddenly her head snapped up to look at the horizon. Time froze for several heartbeats, then she looked me in the eye and screamed before turning and racing away. I was rooted to the spot, watching her disappear over a low hill, not processing what Rachel was shouting. She finally grabbed my arm and tugged hard enough to get my attention.

"Rotors!" She yelled in my face. "Helicopters coming!"

10

Rachel's warning snapped me back to the moment and got me moving. I took half a second to listen, identifying the rotor noise as a Russian Hind. It was approaching from the north, probably one of the helicopters assigned to a search orbit, but it was possible one of the dead Spetsnaz had managed to get an emergency call out over the radio, and it was responding.

Either way, we were pretty much fucked if it flew within visual range. Four dead Russians lay on the ground, three of them having been slashed open with my Kukri. Their bright red blood formed large, neon red stains on the white blanket of snow. There was no way I had time to conceal the bodies and evidence of the fight.

Dashing to Irina's still unconscious form, I bent, grabbed her wrists and cursed at the stab of pain from my broken fingers. Ignoring it, I yanked and pulled her limp form up and over my shoulder. As I was doing this, the thrum of the approaching rotor steadily grew in volume. I was out of time.

Straightening with the burden, I turned as a Havoc attack helicopter popped up over a low hill. The pilot was apparently surprised to see us as it took him a moment to react and swing the aircraft around into a hover. He held in the air, three hundred yards away and maybe five hundred feet above the ground.

"Do we run?" Rachel asked from beside me.

"We can't outrun him," I said, anger and frustration churning in my gut.

We were caught. Completely. It was daylight. We were in unforgiving terrain with few places to hide and certainly none that could protect us from the Havoc's weapons. We stood out like a beacon against the snow on the ground. I was out of rabbits.

"What do we do?" Rachel asked, grabbing my arm. "There has to be something."

"Wait for the right moment..." I started to say, pausing when the sound of another aircraft reached my ears.

It was a jet, coming fast from the southeast. Turning my head, I spotted it and didn't understand what I was seeing. So far the Russians had only flown aircraft of their own design and manufacture. Despite hundreds, if not thousands, of American military aircraft available to them, I had yet to see them put one into operation.

But here was an A-10 Warthog barreling down on the scene, only a few hundred feet in the air. The Warthog is the red-headed stepchild of the Air Force because it's not a sleek, sexy fighter or bomber with more gadgets than James Bond would know what to do with. The Air Force brass has hated it for decades, repeatedly trying to kill or replace it. But other than his own rifle, there's nothing a ground combat soldier loves more than seeing a Warthog overhead. His chances of survival just went way up.

Designed to be a close support weapons platform for ground troops, and a tank buster to counter Soviet armor during the Cold War, it flies low and slow. And it can effectively obliterate anything on the ground with its 30 mm Gatling Gun firing depleted uranium slugs. When it fires it sounds like the very fabric of the Earth is being ripped apart, and at 4,200 rounds per minute, it is absolutely devastating.

But why the hell were the Russians flying one of these? They weren't designed for, nor very effective at air to air combat. They were a ground attack weapon, and there wasn't anything of the American military left on the ground. Maybe I should be flattered that it had been brought out just for me.

The A-10 bobbed up and down as the pilot maintained a constant altitude above the rolling terrain. It was definitely coming in at attack velocity and when I realized it was staying in the Havoc's blind spot a light bulb finally came on.

"Down!" I shouted to Rachel as I dumped Irina and fell across her inert form.

A heartbeat later the ripping sound of the Warthog's gun sounded for perhaps a second. My head was turned towards the Russian helicopter, watching, and almost instantly it was torn in half by the heavy slugs from the A-10's gun. The main rotor was sheared off to spin away, the crippled aircraft falling in several large pieces.

Before it struck the ground, it erupted in a massive explosion as the ruptured fuel tanks ignited. A wave of searing heat blasted across us as the pressure wave pummeled us with snow, sand, small rocks and other debris. A moment later the Warthog screamed overhead at no more than three hundred feet, banking sharply and gaining altitude.

It flew out of sight for several seconds, then the sound of more weapons being fired came to us. There was another explosion in the distance, a thick column of black smoke soon staining the grey sky to mark whatever else the pilot had just destroyed.

Slowly I climbed to my feet, tracking the plane by sound until it came back into sight due south. It was approaching but at a much slower pace this time. Passing a few hundred yards to the side so the pilot would have a good view of us, it waggled its wings before gaining altitude and going into a broad orbit of the area.

"What the hell just happened?" Rachel asked, climbing to her feet and brushing herself off.

"I think the good guys just showed up," I said, tearing my eyes away from the orbiting aircraft and kneeling beside Irina.

Her pulse was strong when I pressed my fingers to her neck, and she was breathing. She had just been knocked out and would hopefully regain consciousness soon. The self-inflicted scalp wound was still oozing blood, and her naked upper body was completely covered in the stuff.

"Grab her clothes out of the cave," I said to Rachel.

A few minutes later, Rachel and I had finished dressing Irina. No matter how Russian or how tough she was, bare skin in this weather wasn't a good idea. As we had worked, I kept a sharp ear out, noting our guardian angel was still orbiting. I didn't want to say anything and get Rachel's hopes up, but I suspected he was keeping watch over us until a rescue helo could arrive.

But who the hell were these guys and where had they come from?

11

"Son of a bitch!" I exclaimed when Rachel pulled the first of my two broken fingers back into place.

"Don't be a pussy," she said, holding my hand tightly to prevent me from yanking it away. "Now quit whining and hold still. One more to go."

"You can be a real bitch. Did I ever tell you that?"

"No, I don't think you have. Are you sure you want to be calling me names right now?" She smiled and snapped the second finger back straight.

"Goddamn it," I mumbled, my hand throbbing all the way to my elbow.

"Alright, hold still and stop being such a big baby. I've seen you take worse without nearly as much complaining. Getting soft?"

As she spoke, Rachel probed the two broken fingers. Both were swollen and hurt like hell, but I had to admit that after being set the level of pain had dropped a couple of notches.

"As soon as I can find some splints and tape, these need immobilized. I don't think

Anvil

there's any permanent damage, but if we don't take care of them, there're all kinds of bad things that can happen. Including losing them or your hand."

Rachel met my eyes, and she wasn't smiling. I nodded, no longer worried about the pain of having them set. A moan from behind drew my attention, and I turned to see Irina slowly moving her head back and forth. I knelt down next to her, pulled my jacket off and gently slipped it under her head after folding it over a couple of times.

"You saved our asses," I said when her eyes fluttered open and focused on my face.

"My head hurts," she groaned.

"I'm sure," I smiled. "Between slashing your own scalp open and getting clobbered in a fight, you're having a rough day."

Irina started to sit up. Rachel, kneeling on the other side of her reached down and restrained her.

"Give it a minute," she said. "You likely have a concussion, and you don't want to sit up too fast."

"Did you get all of them?" Irina asked, happy to lay her head back on the pillow I'd made from my jacket. I was shivering without it

93

but figured she'd earned a little discomfort on my part.

"They're all dead. What the hell were you screaming to distract them like that?"

"I told them you had kidnapped and raped me," Irina said with a small smile. "You must already be a monster to them, so it was not hard for them to believe."

"Hell of a risk, Irina. What if they had been suspicious of a Russian woman out here in the middle of nowhere?"

"I thought of that. There are women in the Russian military, and I am sure there are civilians that have been brought in by now. So it is possible you could have captured one. Enough screaming and tears and emotion and they were more concerned about helping the bloody, half-naked woman than asking questions about what she was doing here."

"Well, thank you," I said, impressed with her quick thinking and acting skills.

"What happened?" Irina asked, noticing the burning wreckage of the Havoc for the first time.

I spent a few minutes filling her in, including the part about Katie saving me. She stared in shock, turning to look at Rachel to make sure I wasn't completely off my rocker. Rachel nodded her head in confirmation.

"She saved you?" Irina asked, her blue eyes wide with surprise.

I nodded. She started to say something else, stopping when I held my hand up. I'd just picked up the sound of rotors, faint on the wind, but definitely there. Looking up, I spotted the Warthog, relaxing slightly to see the plane still in its orbit. Must be friendly helicopters coming. Otherwise, he wouldn't still be calmly circling.

I stood, facing the direction of the approaching sound. Nearly a minute later I was able to make out several black dots on the horizon. They quickly resolved into a pair of Black Hawks escorted by four Apaches. As always, it was a relief to see the cavalry arriving.

The Apaches split apart, heading to the four points of the compass to set up a picket line as the two Black Hawks came directly in for a landing between us and the burning Havoc. Their rotor wash caught the smoke from the wreck, swirling it in fantastical patterns before slowing. The side doors on both opened, disgorging several Rangers who quickly formed a perimeter around the area. Right behind them a man I recognized jumped down, escorted by a heavily armed Army Captain.

Striding forward, I accepted the outstretched hand of Colonel Blanchard, reminding myself that he had been promoted several ranks since the last time I saw him.

"Damn good to see you, sir," I said.

"Likewise, Major. I'm sorry we couldn't get here faster, but it's been a bit of an adventure. Let's load up and get you out of here. I'm on my way to the front."

He turned and nodded to Rachel and Irina as they walked up behind me.

"The front?"

"We've engaged the Russians," he said with a stern look on his face. "It's been in the works for a while, just took some time to put all the pieces together. Right now we need to get moving."

"No, sir," I said. "My wife is still out there somewhere, and I'm not leaving without her. There's also an immune in Mountain Home that needs to get to Seattle."

"Why is your wife out there?" Blanchard asked, not quite comfortable enough with his new rank to get in my face for refusing to do as he said.

"She's infected, sir."

This caught him by surprise. His attention snapped into focus on me, his head tilting slightly to the side as he looked closely to make sure I wasn't playing a sick joke or had another head injury. Finally satisfied, he took my arm and walked me a few yards away.

"Tell me," he said.

12

"How do you plan to find her?" Blanchard asked when I finished filling him in.

"I'm working on an idea but don't really have a good answer to that, yet," I said, shaking my head. "But getting in a Black Hawk and going the other direction isn't going to help."

He nodded, acknowledging the validity of my statement.

"OK, we don't have time to go into details, but here's what you need to know. We're hitting the Russians hard. The plans have been held very close over concerns about moles. I don't know even half of what's in the works, but we only left a skeleton crew in the Bahamas to protect the civilians.

"We've been leapfrogging our way across the continent, stopping at Air Force bases and Army posts along the way to gather equipment and munitions. The Navy has moved into the north Pacific and is engaging the Russian Navy. Colonel Pointere and his MEU have finished clearing out Mountain Home Air Force Base. They moved and engaged with a large enemy force about thirty klicks northwest of Boise.

Anvil

"Except for support personnel and the handful of Rangers with me, everyone is in the fight. That's where I was headed when I got the call from the A-10 pilot. That's why we need to get moving. We're outnumbered three to one, but holding our own for the moment."

"Leave me a rifle and take the women," I said. "If the front moves this way Katie could easily get caught up in the fighting and killed."

I was torn. As badly as I wanted to find my wife and bring her to safety, it was killing me to know that Soldiers and Marines were fighting and dying, and I wasn't joining the battle. Not that one more rifle would make much difference, but it's not in my nature to let someone else do the fighting for me.

Blanchard stared at me for a long moment, turning when a young Lieutenant ran up, radio handset extended. The Colonel snatched it from his hand and pressed it to his ear. He listened for a few seconds, both of us looking up as a flight of eight F-16s screamed overhead heading west.

"I'm on my way," he said before returning the handset.

"Lieutenant, get a rifle, pistol, and ammo for the Major. Also a radio. Load the women. We're leaving. Now."

"Yes, sir!" The man left at a dead run, shouting to the Rangers who had formed the perimeter to mount up.

"I'm sorry, Major. You're on your own. The Russians have broken through our lines, and we're in danger of losing a whole company of men. I've got to get to the front. Good luck, and if I can help, I will."

He extended his hand, and I shook it, feeling selfish that I wasn't headed into battle with him. Wondering what the hell I was doing. I didn't know where to start looking for Katie. Didn't know what I'd do once I found her. I had no illusions that there was any way I could catch her if she didn't want to be caught.

And even if I could, what then? Hog tie her and carry her on my back to Seattle? And what about Titus? Even supposing I could somehow capture and control Katie and make the journey, without an immune for the scientists wouldn't it be a futile effort? I needed Blanchard's resources. There were no two ways about it.

"Thank you, Colonel, but hold on. I'm coming with you. As long as I can get some help when we finish with the Russians."

Blanchard smiled and clapped me on the shoulder.

Anvil

"I'll do everything I can," he said, turning and setting off at a jog to the waiting Black Hawks.

"Let's go," I shouted to Rachel and Irina, falling in behind him.

Another flight of F-16s roared over, a moment later a large formation of Apaches following at a lower altitude. Looking to the northwest, I could see a smudge of black smoke against the swollen, grey clouds.

"Where are we going?" Rachel asked as she and Irina ran on either side of me.

"War," I said. "You two stick close to Blanchard. It's going to be chaos."

"What about Katie?" Irina asked.

"I'll come back for her," I said, then we arrived at the Black Hawk.

The Lieutenant was just climbing down, arms loaded with the equipment the Colonel had told him to give me. Blanchard waved him back inside the aircraft, leaping up after him. I came to a stop, helping Rachel and Irina board, then jumped in and slid my legs out of the way as one of the Rangers slammed the door closed.

We were in the air immediately, the pilot transitioning to forward flight only yards above the ground before quickly gaining altitude. Reaching towards the Lieutenant, I collected the weapons and quickly checked them over. He held out a field radio for me, Blanchard telling him to put it away. Instead, I was outfitted with a small unit that slipped into a pouch on my vest and had a tough, thin wire leading to a throat mic and earpiece.

Getting myself outfitted, I looked around, meeting the eyes of the other men. Each of them had the look I expected. The look of a blooded warrior who is heading back into battle. Irina and Rachel huddled against the rear bulkhead, looking out of sorts from the sudden turn of events.

"How do we have enough forces to engage the Russians?" I shouted to Blanchard over the roar of the engines.

"The USS Reagan Carrier Strike Group put into Nassau after we arrived. They had been hanging around in the Gulf but were in the Persian Gulf when this all started and had a full MEU on board. There was nearly a full Infantry Division they pulled out of Iraq. Over 10,000 Soldiers. They were stuffed on those ships like sardines."

"How did they bring armor?" I had to lean close to the Colonel and shout in his ear.

"They didn't," he shouted back, shaking his head. "That was one of several stops we had to make on the way."

I nodded, wanting to ask more questions but it was too hard to communicate without a headset.

"What the hell are we doing?" Rachel shouted in my ear.

She was squeezed in next to me, shoulder and hip pressed tight against mine.

"We're in a battle with the Russians a little way northwest of Boise," I said, my mouth pressed close to her ear.

"What about Katie? You're coming back?"

"With help," I said. "I can't handle her by myself without hurting her. And it's still a very long way to Seattle. If I've got help, just maybe there's some hope."

"How are you going to find her?" Rachel asked, placing her hand on top of mine.

"I have a couple of ideas," I said, turning to look at Blanchard when I remembered something that had been bugging me.

He was busy on the radio; a rugged laptop open on the vibrating deck next to him. Not wanting to interrupt, I waved the Lieutenant over. I explained what I needed, and he set to work on a communications set that was connected to the helicopter's satellite radio. A couple of minutes later he passed me a headset.

When I put it on the built-in noise canceling silenced most of the roar of the Black Hawk in flight, and I could hear sounds of someone breathing over the clarity of a digital circuit. I identified myself, happy to hear Petty Officer Simmons respond.

"It's great to hear your voice, sir!"

"You too, Jessica," I responded, intentionally using her given name instead of her rank. "I don't have much time, and I need to ask you something."

"Anything, sir," she replied, curiosity clear in her tone.

"How do you think the Russians found me in Twin Falls? How did they know where to start looking? And again, just today, they were able to start searching the exact area where I wound up south of Mountain Home."

I didn't say anything else, and there was complete silence for several heartbeats before she spoke.

"You think..."

"Yes, I do," I said when she didn't finish her thought. "One coincidence, no matter how unlikely, can be passed off as exactly that. Twice? No fucking way, Petty Officer. They're either in the feed again, or someone is passing them information."

"You don't think it was me?" Her voice rose a couple of octaves, and I could hear that she was both hurt and indignant.

"No, Jessica. I don't. If it was you, they would have had me pinpointed each time and not had to search. This is someone that has enough information to point them in my direction, but can't give them my exact location. Who would that be?"

It was quiet for a long time, and I let her stew and think. I had originally intended to contact Admiral Packard directly with my suspicions, but for some reason, I knew I could trust Jessica to do the right thing. I've been around the military much of my adult life and had no doubt that if I had called the Admiral, he would immediately lock down all personnel with any access to or knowledge of my whereabouts.

Naval counter-intelligence would start an investigation. Depending on who was running things, that investigation could easily become a witch hunt. With the current state of affairs, I wouldn't be surprised if everyone who was even remotely involved got thrown into a jail cell and left to rot. I didn't want to lose Jessica while the bureaucrats got things sorted out. She'd saved my ass more than a few times. It would be better for her to come forward with the suspicions.

Not that she wouldn't be looked at closely. It's not uncommon for moles and traitors to accuse others of their crimes in an attempt to deflect suspicion. But if I was correct about her, and I was betting my life on it right about now, she would come out of the other end of this and be just fine.

"Still there?" I finally asked.

"Yes, sir. Just running over a list of possibilities in my head. And getting really pissed off." I could hear the tightness in her voice.

"Just be sure you've got your ducks in a row before you talk to anyone," I advised. "And, be prepared to be put under the microscope. Also, I need one more thing."

"Sir, you just talked to me directly about this instead of throwing me to the wolves in intel. Anything you want, you get."

"Get into what's left of the CIA's network. Find out if it's still possible to activate personal locators. If it is, I'd like you to ping my wife's locator and start tracking her."

Anvil

"Your wife's? She's CIA? I thought she was with you, sir."

Shit. Jessica didn't know. But then, how could she?

"She turned, Jessica. Infected. I lost her somewhere south of Mountain Home. I'm in a Black Hawk on my way to the front, and I'm going to need to find her when this is over."

Jessica was quiet for a few moments, and I could imagine the thoughts going through her head.

"OK, sir. I'll do everything I can, but I'm not optimistic this is going to work. If that system is even still up and running, the very nature of what it is means it will have one hell of security layer in front of it."

"Do the best you can," I said, hope that I'd be able to find Katie again flickering and threatening to go out.

"Already working on it, sir," she said, the sound of rapid keyboarding coming over the circuit.

"Thank you, Jessica. And be careful who you talk to about the other matter. You don't know who you can trust."

"Yes, sir," she said.

Dirk Patton

I could hear an undercurrent of fear creep in when she spoke. Breaking the connection, I pulled the headset off and handed it back to the Lieutenant.

13

It was only a few more minutes before the pilot made a sharp turn and descended quickly. One of the Rangers opened the side door as we touched down, jumping to the ground. The rest followed, and I leapt out right behind them. Blanchard, his aide, then Rachel and Irina brought up the rear.

We were at a temporary command post. Five Hummers were parked in a reasonable facsimile of a circle and two Bradley fighting vehicles bracketed the camp. The sounds of the battle were loud, and we couldn't have been more than half a klick from the front.

Blanchard ran to where a Major and two Captains were leaned over a large, plastic-covered paper map. All three of them had radios pressed to their faces, listening to reports and shouting orders as they made marks on the map with grease pencils. A little old school, but then so am I.

I stepped behind the shortest man and looked over his head at the map. To the uninitiated it looked like uncontrolled mayhem, the symbols they were drawing appearing to mean nothing. But they did mean something, and if you knew how to read them, they told a story.

And it wasn't a good story. The Russians were spread across a five-mile front and had both light and heavy armor supporting them. The Infantry Division was spread thin but appeared to be holding the higher ground. The Marines had broken through enemy lines to the north, flanking a company of Russian armor, but they were now pinned down.

Two companies of Rangers were holding fast, using the terrain to their advantage, but another was in serious trouble. They were flanked on two sides by Russian infantry and were in danger of being encircled as a spearhead of light armor and ground troops pushed ahead.

Another company of Rangers was trying to reach them but had made contact with the largest concentration of enemy armor. They were stalled, unable to make progress. I turned my radio on, the shouts and screams of men in contact with the enemy immediately filling my ear. I listened for a few moments, sorting out who was who as I kept studying the map.

Rachel stepped up next to me and grabbed my injured hand. She'd apparently found a medic kit, probably in one of the Hummers. While I studied the map, she splinted and taped my broken fingers.

Anvil

"Going to be a bitch handling a rifle with that," I mumbled to her without taking my attention off the map.

"I'm sure you'll figure it out," she said, applying a final piece of tape and stepping away.

"Pull them back!" Blanchard said to one of the Captains, stabbing a point on the map where there was still a chance for the company in dire straits to escape before being completely surrounded and decimated.

"No comms," the man replied. "We can't reach them."

"Send a runner," Blanchard shouted.

"We've sent two. Neither made it. Third's on the way, but we've lost contact with him."

Everyone ducked as a pair of A-10s roared overhead, seemingly low enough to count the rivets in their skin. The sounds of rifle fire, light automatic weapons, and high explosives seemed to be coming closer. From farther away there were several explosions as American and Russian jets joined in aerial combat. Two hundred yards to our front, a pair of Apaches were hovering only feet above the ground.

They were screened from the battle by a low hill, using the sensor suite mounted above their rotors to see over the terrain and select their targets. As I watched, they popped up in unison. Clear of their cover, each fired two hellfire missiles at targets I couldn't see.

Before they could drop back into protection, one of them exploded as a Russian missile found it. The other jerked sideways, away from the blast, making it to safety. The shockwave ripped over us a second later, nearly knocking everyone to the ground. The smell of burning aviation fuel came with the wave of heat that arrived moments after.

"Goddamn it, get a squad out of Charlie Company in there to pull these men out. What do we have available for air support?" Blanchard shouted to be heard.

"All ground attack air assets are fully engaged with their armor, and we will lose the MEU if we re-task," the Captain I was standing behind answered.

"A-10s?" The Colonel turned to the other Captain who I realized was wearing an Air Force uniform.

"Working on it, sir. The enemy has multiple rotor-wing assets and anti-air that are keeping them back. We've lost four birds already and are trying to get fighter support to clear a path."

Anvil

I'd seen enough. Turning, I reminded Rachel and Irina to stay close to Blanchard before running to where ten Rangers had set up a security line between the front and the command post. I ignored the cries from both Rachel and Blanchard.

"You five with me," I shouted, pointing at them as I ran past.

None of them hesitated to leap to their feet and follow. It didn't really surprise me. Rangers prefer being on the offensive to the defensive.

We ran a wide circle to avoid the heat from the burning Apache. As soon as we were far enough past to turn west towards the front, without roasting ourselves, we headed for the base of the low line of hills the helicopters had been hiding behind. To my left was a cut in the terrain and I angled towards it, the five Rangers on my heels.

Slowing as I entered the break, I cautiously approached the high spot. Motioning them down, I dropped to my stomach to crawl the final few yards. There was a battle raging on the other side of the crest, and it's generally not a good idea to silhouette yourself against the sky when entering a fight. If the enemy doesn't see you and blow your ass off, there's a good chance of friendly fire taking you out. Suddenly popping up isn't a good way to stay healthy.

Taking advantage of the cover afforded by a small rock resting on the lip, I peered around and grimaced. There weren't just a lot of Russians, there were a LOT of Russians. And the battlefield was massive, spread across the horizon as far as I could see in either direction. Dozens of light and heavy armor vehicles belonging to both sides sat burning, black smoke billowing into the sky and creating a hellish pall.

Farther out were multiple locations where aircraft had been shot down and crashed to the ground, adding to the haze. The sound of small arms fire was constant and larger vehicle-mounted guns were firing, adding to the din. Helicopters buzzed over the fight, engaging each other as well as ground targets, while higher up I could see the trails of missiles as the fighter jocks tangled.

Mortars were firing, both sides using them to keep troops from advancing. The only thing missing was heavy artillery, which I didn't understand as I'd seen a fire battery notated on the map.

The screams of men fighting and dying. The smell of munitions and spilled blood. The choking smoke from burning machines and expended ordnance. This was truly hell on Earth,

Anvil
and with a wave to the Rangers behind me, I
stood and ran directly into it.

14

Admiral Packard stood in Pearl Harbor's shore based Combat Information Center, staring at multiple monitors. The four largest displays were satellite images of two Carrier Strike Groups (CSGs) operating in the north Pacific Ocean. The remaining two were zoomed on Russian naval facilities located near Vladivostok and on the Kamchatka Peninsula. CSG Nine with the USS George Washington supercarrier at the center was positioned three hundred miles due west of Portland, Oregon. CSG Eleven, with the USS Nimitz, was one hundred miles north of the Washington.

All but one of the remaining displays monitored Russian naval and land based activity within the striking range of the two fleets. Finally, he checked the last screen, unhappy with the heavy losses the Marines and Rangers were taking in the land battle with enemy forces in southern Idaho. He didn't understand why the Kremlin had committed so many ground troops to a tactically valueless chunk of the country, but in doing so, they had divided their forces on the ground in North America.

Shifting his attention back to the looming naval engagement, he nodded in satisfaction when he noted the ships of the CSGs were in the proper positions. He wanted to be on board the Washington, leading the fight at sea, but knew the Captains well and had full confidence in their abilities.

Still, to stand on the catwalk outside the bridge and watch his warplanes. To feel his bones vibrate, from the sheer power of the jet engines as they went to full throttle a moment before being hurled into the sky by the catapult. That was what he missed.

Chastising himself for losing focus, he issued the order for the commencement of Operation Anvil. The images drew back slightly, allowing for a wider view of the operational area, and in moments, both carriers began launching aircraft. The first planes in the air were tankers that would top off each fighter once it reached altitude, then tag along behind so they could refuel before returning home.

As the two CSGs launched aircraft, the views of the Russian naval bases panned a hundred miles off shore to seemingly empty stretches of ocean. On each monitor, which provided a view of over one hundred square miles, multiple cruise missiles erupted from the surface and gained altitude before tipping over and stabilizing into horizontal flight.

These were Tomahawk missiles, launched by eight American, Ohio class submarines. Each weapon was fitted with a one-thousand-pound conventional warhead as the Navy had so far been unsuccessful in enabling its inventory of nuclear warheads in the absence of National Command Authority (NCA) codes. The Russians had seen to that quite effectively by eliminating all political and senior military leadership through strikes on Mt. Weather and Cheyenne Mountain.

Each sub carried 154 Tomahawks and would send two-thirds of their missiles. Packard divided his attention between the launches in the eastern Pacific and the activity of the CSGs off the west coast of the United States, which were busily sending waves of cruise missiles to Russian targets within the US.

That wave launched from four Ticonderoga Class, Aegis guided missile cruisers. Each of the ships disappeared in clouds of billowing white smoke. Soon, eight hundred missiles were on their way to a variety of targets in Russia and four hundred were streaking east to the US mainland, low over the blue waters of the Pacific.

Cruising at five hundred and fifty miles an hour with a range of fifteen hundred miles, Tomahawks aren't fast. But they approach enemy targets so low to the ground that they are all but undetectable until it is too late to do anything. They are also deadly accurate, and nearly half of the airborne weapons were set to seek and destroy electronic emissions. Russian radar and radio communications.

Next came Electronic Warfare (EW) aircraft from the CSGs. Their job would be to monitor enemy communications and disrupt them, gaining an advantage for the attacking Americans. Finally came waves of F-18s, looking like needle-nosed darts on the displays as they took to the air and queued up to take a drink of fuel.

Full, each flight group formed up and began heading for the west coast of the United States. They were flying slow, staying below the sound barrier to conserve fuel as well as to not arrive on target ahead of the initial attack wave. Throttling back, the F-18s held their speed slightly below that of the Tomahawk missiles.

"Turn that up!" The Admiral snapped when a snatch of conversation coming over a console speaker caught his attention.

The Senior Chief Petty Officer operating the station spun the volume control and hit a button to send the audio to overhead speakers. Packard listened for a moment to the fleet communications as first one, then all of the ships in CSG Eleven reported detecting torpedoes in the water with their sonar.

On the screen he watched as each ship responded exactly to US Navy doctrine, accelerating to flank speed and maneuvering based on the bearing and distance to the inbound weapons. Several of the ships launched countermeasures into the water, large canisters that would create noise intended to fool the torpedoes into locking onto them instead of the sound of a ship racing to safety.

Anti-Submarine Warfare (ASW) helicopters were already in the air, and as he watched, two of them dropped torpedoes into the sea. Before the weapons had time to destroy the enemy submarine, there was a brilliant flash from the stern of one of the destroyers that had dashed to place itself between the incoming torpedoes and the Nimitz. A moment later a second explosion bloomed from amid ship on the destroyer, and it went dead in the water. Flames and thick smoke poured from its damaged hull.

The CSG continued to maneuver, and more torpedoes were dropped by the helicopters searching for the Russian vessel. Packard cursed as new warnings were sounded when an attack from the opposite side of the formation was detected. More torpedoes were dropped, and additional helicopters launched as a destroyer and a frigate dashed to the probable location of the new submarine.

Anvil

The battle raged on, one of the Guided Missile Cruisers taking hits from three torpedoes. The Cruiser's back was broken, the hull splitting in half and the ship disappearing under the waves in minutes. One more leaked through the defenses and countermeasures, striking the Nimitz and damaging its massive propellers and rudder. The giant ship, without propulsion or steering, came to a stop in the water and began rolling in the large swells.

When it was over, both Russian subs had been destroyed. But the Americans had lost a destroyer and a cruiser. And even though it was still floating, the Nimitz couldn't launch or recover aircraft without the ability to maneuver.

One of the console operators was busily marking every sailor in the water he and the system could identify, sharing the data with the CSG as rescue operations got underway.

"What's the water temperature?" Packard asked without taking his eyes off the hundreds of men and women bobbing on the surface.

"Forty-five degrees, sir," a voice he didn't bother to identify answered.

"Goddamn it," he mumbled to himself.

He well knew that in water that cold a human would lapse into unconsciousness in less than thirty minutes. It would only be the lucky individual who survived an hour before succumbing to hypothermia. As frantically as sailors were being pulled out of the ocean, there just wasn't enough time before many of them died.

"Status of CSG Nine?" He barked out, compartmenting his anger over the loss of so many.

"ASW has detected and engaged three targets, sir. One destroyed. They are still pursuing the other two. No damage or casualties to any CSG assets at this time." The Senior Chief, who was monitoring communications, answered.

"Time to first targets for the Tomahawks?" He asked the Surface Warfare Officer seated at a station directly beside him.

"Eleven minutes, sir," the woman answered immediately.

"Launch the second wave," he ordered, watching as more sailors were pulled out of the water into RIBs and winched up into hovering helicopters.

"Launch second wave, aye, sir," she replied.

Fifteen seconds later, the remaining three Guided Missile Cruisers began sending the last of their missiles to target. Half were programmed to seek any enemy radar signal that hadn't been destroyed by the first wave, the remainder flying slow and loitering. The launching ships were in communication with them and would be able to designate targets of opportunity that had survived the initial attack.

The displays showing the eastern Pacific changed to two more stretches of open ocean, moments later the surface boiling as more Tomahawks took flight. The location was the North Sea, fifty miles off the western coast of Denmark. Six more subs launched another eight hundred cruise missiles between them, half heading for military targets deep inside Russia. The remaining four hundred spread out as they raced to political and command and control locations within Moscow itself.

"Admiral, CSG Nine reports detection of multiple inbound bogies. They are maneuvering to engage."

"Show me," Packard barked. "Where the hell did they come from?"

The view on one of the screens changed as did a monitor that mirrored what was displayed in the Washington's CIC. Multiple tracks were racing across the surface of the ocean, heading directly for the super carrier.

"Submarine launched anti-ship missiles, sir," the Surface Warfare Officer said. "Most likely Shipwreck missiles."

"How many?" The Admiral asked, dreading the answer before he heard it.

"Nineteen, sir," she answered.

As he watched on the satellite image, all of the ships in CSG Nine maneuvered to place themselves between the approaching threats and the Nimitz. Every man in the fleet, from the Captains to the cooks, knew that in a situation like this his ship was expendable if it would save the carrier.

"Any way to tell if they're specials or conventional?" By 'special', Packard was referring to nuclear warheads in the missiles. He knew there was no way to know until the first one detonated, but couldn't stop himself from asking.

"No, sir," she answered in a quiet voice.

Anvil

15

The Russian Shipwreck anti-ship missiles rushed towards their targets, constantly confirming their current position and speed as they maintained a running calculation of time to impact. All nineteen weapons were equipped with 500 Kiloton thermonuclear warheads. Ten were targeting the Washington. Two each for the two Aegis Guided Missile Cruisers and the remainder for the Arleigh Burke-class guided missile destroyers.

Shipwrecks are big and fast, streaking towards the CSG at nearly twice the speed of sound. Every ship so equipped fired defensive missiles as they raced to set up a screen to protect the carrier. Three of the Russian missiles were destroyed in the initial salvo, additional anti-missile missiles roaring off their rails and heading downrange.

Five more Shipwrecks were knocked out of the air by the second and third wave of defensive fire. Eleven remained, tracked and engaged by a final launch. Three more were destroyed.

By now the Shipwrecks were close enough to heavily damage the fleet simply by detonating their warheads. But they kept coming. The Phalanx, Close In Weapons Systems

(CIWS – *pronounced see-whiz*), spread across the fleet locked on and began firing when the Russian missiles came within two miles.

Four inbound missiles were destroyed by the hail of fire from the CIWS, a fifth shredded by the depleted uranium slugs of the Phalanx. Three missiles remained, and it was the Washington's bad luck that all three were targeted on it. The carrier's CIWS managed to knock two of them down, leaving only one to leak through the defenses.

When the Shipwreck's electronics determined that it was within one hundred meters of its target, a command was sent to the warhead. The nuclear trigger was initiated, and milliseconds later, a thermonuclear explosion equivalent to five hundred thousand tons of TNT bloomed.

Millions of gallons of seawater instantly flashed to steam as the fireball expanded, engulfing the Washington and the majority of the CSG in a ball of radioactive fire. While the fireball was still expanding, ten more Shipwrecks were launched, targeting the Washington's CSG. Fifteen more took flight from a Russian submarine that had remained quiet and deep, hiding within fifty miles of the crippled Nimitz.

Again, the US Navy successfully stopped all but one of the inbound threats with a flurry of launches. But the single missile screamed over the tops of the waves, slightly gaining altitude seconds before arriving. The CSG's defenses had been overwhelmed, none of them targeting the Russian nuclear weapon which detonated one hundred meters above the Nimitz' flight deck.

The Tomahawks launched by the two American Carrier Strike Groups spread out as they approached the coastline of the western United States. Some were adjusting course to reach designated targets, others seeking and locking on to electronic emissions. When communication with the CSG was lost due to the nuclear attack, the missiles without assigned targets defaulted to searching for sources of electromagnetic energy.

For reasons unknown to the Americans, the Russians had only moved into Seattle, Portland, and San Francisco. The remainder of the west coast remained unoccupied. Theories abounded for why this was so, but that was all they were.

The first eight missiles to arrive on target had been selected to attack a Russian destroyer guarding the mouth of the Columbia River. The Admiral Panteleyev, an older Russian destroyer, detected the inbound cruise missiles less than three minutes before they arrived. But three minutes was more than enough time for the Captain to bring the ship to general quarters and

Dirk Patton

turn the bow to face the approaching threats. As the Tomahawks drew closer, they lost altitude until they were barely skimming the surface of the ocean.

Equipped with two Kashtan CIWS systems, the Captain and crew stood nervously watching as the computers took control of the ship's defenses. The Kashtan system boasts two 30 mm cannons as well as eight radar guided surface to air missiles. Each cannon can fire 4,500 rounds per minute and the entire turret is self-contained and fully automated when activated.

Sirens blared as the two systems swung into operation, tracking the inbound targets on radar. Quickly, missiles streaked into the air, rapidly covering the distance to the Tomahawks. Of the eight targets, two were intercepted and destroyed in the opening salvo. More defensive missiles launched, splashing another Tomahawk before all four of the auto-cannons began firing.

Three more Tomahawks went down, both turrets attacking the remaining threat and destroying it when it was within half a mile of the ship. Sirens continued to sound, and the Kashtans were swiveling to engage newly detected threats when three Tomahawks slammed into the ship in quick succession.

Anvil

These were radar seeking missiles that had homed in on the Kashtans' electronic emissions, changing course and coming in at a sharp angle to the bow of the ship. Three, 1,000 pound high explosive warheads detonated, blowing massive holes in the deck of the destroyer and instantly killing all aboard except for a select few who were deep in the bowels of the ship in sealed compartments. Burning, the ship quickly began listing to port as cold seawater poured in through multiple breaches in the hull.

Up and down the coast, from Northern California to Seattle, the Tomahawks began arriving on target. The Russian Navy had a large presence in the area, many of the ships launching anti-missile missiles and engaging with their Kashtan systems. But the Americans had successfully attacked with enough cruise missiles to overwhelm the Russian's ability to effectively defend their positions.

Over two-thirds of Russian Navy ships on and near the west coast of the United States were either sunk or damaged so severely they had to be abandoned. No ship that did not have defensive systems survived the barrage. But the Americans had targeted much more than just enemy ships.

Shore based operations centers set up by the occupying military were devastated in Seattle

and San Francisco. Infrastructure critical to the
new tenants of the cities was also targeted. In
San Francisco, the Golden Gate and Bay Bridge
were the recipients of multiple strikes, both
collapsing into the water. In Portland, bridges
across the Columbia were taken down. In the
mountains above Seattle, hydroelectric dams
were destroyed, denying power to the Russians
and sending billions of gallons of water flooding
downstream.

Follow-up waves of Tomahawks seeking
radar and radio emissions arrived, killing more
Russian civilians than military. US military bases
all along the coast were attacked and heavily
damaged, denying their use to the invaders.
Finally, port facilities were targeted. Dozens of
Russian cargo and passenger ships were caught
tied up at the docks. Many were damaged
beyond repair, burning and adding thick, black
smoke to the choking miasma that hung over
each city.

The Russian naval bases near Vladivostok
and on the Kamchatka Peninsula were
significantly damaged. Heavily defended, they
were able to stop nearly six hundred of the
inbound missiles, but again the sheer numbers
overwhelmed them, and over two hundred
Tomahawks reached their targets.

The final wave of the American attack was
the eight hundred Tomahawks launched from

the North Sea. Several Russian air bases in Eastern Europe sustained damage as they were not expecting or prepared for an assault. That left four hundred missiles streaking across the Russian steppes for Moscow and multiple military installations surrounding it.

Moscow is the most heavily defended city on Earth. Ringed by multiple, redundant anti-aircraft and anti-missile batteries, it was prepared to fend off just the type of attack that had been launched against it. Only because part of the system was down for maintenance did any of the Tomahawks slip through and reach their targets.

But none of the over one hundred missiles designated to destroy the Kremlin came within ten miles of the seat of the Russian government. A total of eleven explosions rattled the windows in the city as the weapons succeeded in damaging some hangars and two runways at Kubinka Air Base, several miles west of Moscow.

Before the fires on the flight line had been extinguished, four long-range nuclear missiles were launched from a Russian submarine patrolling above the arctic circle. NORAD would have normally been the US Military organization to identify, track and attempt intercept of the missiles, but it no longer existed.

Dirk Patton

In Pearl Harbor, console operators stared at their screens in disbelief for a few moments before warnings began being shouted across the CIC. Admiral Packard stepped quickly to a terminal, clenching his jaw when he saw the four tracks plotted on the screen. The man working the station was typing furiously, unaware of the Admiral peering over his shoulder.

"Fuck me," he breathed when the tracks updated and the computer drew the projected flight paths of each missile.

The dotted tracks formed neat parabolas that terminated in Hawaii. They were undoubtedly ICBMs.

16

I dashed through the break in the terrain, the five Rangers following in single file and keeping good spacing. There were lots of small hillocks as well as depressions in the terrain, and I used them to my full advantage as we moved down the slope. I would run for a few seconds before throwing myself to the ground, not wanting to give anyone an opportunity to zero in and drill a bullet through my hide.

Half way to the valley below, where the main battle was being fought, I paused behind a car-sized boulder. The Rangers spread out on either side, prone with their bodies shielded by the earth. Only their heads and rifles were visible from downslope. A quarter of a mile away the fighting raged as Russian troops tried to advance and complete the encirclement of several hundred Soldiers.

Bullets were flying, mortars were thumping, men were screaming as they fought and died. The air was foul with the acrid stench of burned gunpowder and explosives. On the left flank, the enemy was making progress, using light armored vehicles, RPGs and grenade launchers to supplement the heavy fire they were laying down. If they succeeded in moving behind the American forces, it would be a slaughter.

I didn't understand why the officers in command hadn't already pulled back or why their comms with the Command Post weren't working. Bravery in battle is one thing, but holding ground against a superior force when there's no value in the terrain you're fighting for is foolish. Retreating and regrouping is a valuable tool that every infantry officer in the world is taught.

"Why the fuck aren't they falling back?"

One of the Rangers, a First Sergeant, had moved to lay next to me as I surveyed the battle.

"Beats the hell out of me, Top. But if we don't get them out fast, there won't be any idiots left to ask," I said. "Ready to get your hands dirty?"

"Thought you'd never ask, sir," he grinned.

He followed me as I ran around the rock and headed for a shallow depression in the side of the hill. Halfway to my destination, bullets began cracking all around. Some of them screamed by close enough for me to hear their passage, others slammed into the wet ground and kicked up gouts of mud and snow. They were too heavy, and too many were coming in, for it to be anything other than a machine gun firing at us.

Adjusting my run for the final twenty yards, I zigged, twisted and threw myself into the hole. The First Sergeant was right on my ass and crashed against me a heartbeat later.

"You see the fucker?"

I had to shout over the noise of the battle, hoping he'd gotten a bead on where the gunner was set up. I hadn't been able to spot the source of the incoming fire that was currently chewing up the lip of the hole where we huddled. The son of a bitch had certainly seen us and was making sure we kept our heads down.

"No luck," he said, shifting around and stabbing his radio's earpiece back in his ear.

I looked up the slope as he made a call, not seeing the four other Rangers. That was usually a good sign. If they'd been hit, most likely their bodies would be out in the open and visible. Maybe.

While he shouted into his radio, the withering machine gun fire stopped. I gave it a moment before popping my head up and pulling it right back down. The movement was too quick for me to see anything, but if the gunner was just waiting for one of us to show ourselves, I hoped

I'd entice him to show his hand and send some more rounds my way.

He was either occupied with a more immediate threat or was a wily little shit who realized what I was doing and was waiting for a better target. Either way, I didn't have much choice other than to take a risk. Moving laterally, so my head would appear in a different spot, I carefully raised up and exposed only enough of myself to get my eyes above the edge.

No bullets came my way, but I didn't relax. First priority was to find the gunner so he could be dealt with. I didn't even bother checking on the progress of the Russian troops. With that machine gun in play, we weren't going to be advancing. Getting caught on open ground would be tantamount to suicide. He'd chew us up and go on about his day without a second thought.

"There," the First Sergeant tapped my arm and pointed. He'd finished on the radio and moved next to me.

I looked where he indicated and saw the muzzle flashes of the machine gun being fired. He had dismissed us for the moment, using his position to keep a group of Soldiers pinned down so the Russians coming around the flank could advance.

Anvil

"Dug in like a fucking tick," I said, noting the nice, deep depression the gunner had found to set up his weapon.

He was well protected from return fire in addition to having a commanding view in almost every direction. Almost. Behind and to his side there appeared to be a narrow slice of terrain that would hide someone sneaking up on him. Maybe.

"Anyone got anything other than a rifle?" I asked.

"No, sir, but I'd surely give my right nut for a two-oh-four right about now."

He was referring to an M-204 grenade launcher, and I agreed with him.

"Give me covering fire," I said, making my decision and pushing up and out of the hole at a run.

Charging a machine gun emplacement is not the brightest of ideas on the best of days. But we were stuck, and if we just sat there and kept our heads down, the Russians were going to overwhelm and wipe out a whole bunch of Soldiers. There wasn't any other option. Besides, no one ever promised that being in the Army was a safe occupation.

Dirk Patton

I covered about a third of the distance, with two stops behind rocks, before the gunner looked up the slope and spotted me. Swiveling his weapon, he opened up, blasting chips of stone off the small boulder I was sheltering behind. I glanced behind me, gratified to see the First Sergeant and two other Rangers with their heads up as they poured full auto fire at the machine gun's position.

They didn't hit him, but they sure as hell got his attention. I watched closely, and when the muzzle of his gun traversed to engage them, I leapt to my feet and ran. My destination was a shallow ravine that had been carved by water and ran down the hill. It passed only a short distance behind the gunner's position, and I planned to follow it, pop up and ruin his day.

Running flat out, I dove the final few yards as bullets began tearing up the ground all around me. A tracer round passed inches in front of my eyes as I stretched for the safety of the ground. Crashing down, I bounced off a couple of exposed rocks and came to rest on my back, a soft bed of sand beneath the cushion of snow. Fuck that hurt!

My body wanted to just stay there until the pain of pin-balling off the rocks eased, but staying in one spot too long in combat is a good way to die young. Ignoring the protests of what I hoped were only bruises, I rolled over and began making my way down the ravine. The din of battle was growing louder as I advanced, scrambling on my knees and elbows.

Twenty yards to my front, something of the high explosive variety detonated on the very edge of the ditch I was using for cover. Dirt, rocks, and filthy snow fountained into the air and rained down on me. I was stunned from being too close to the blast, hearing as if I was underwater and my vision blurry and tunneled to narrow pinpoints of light. My body refused to respond to my brain's commands to keep moving.

Well, I thought it refused, then realized I was still crawling forward. I was operating on auto-pilot and it took a few more yards of movement to regain control. Stopping, I looked around, unsure where I was in relation to the gunner. My hearing was slowly coming back, and I was pretty certain I could hear the machine gun hammering from behind me. I'd crawled past him?

Shaking my head, trying to clear it, I turned and poked my eyes over the edge of the ravine. Sure enough, I'd kept on going and overshot my target. Reversing course, I scrambled to the point I'd identified as a blind spot for the gunner and crawled over the lip onto open ground.

Dirk Patton

There were two more explosions, close, but not close enough to affect me like the last one. Now I was able to identify them as mortar bombs dropping in and it dawned on me that someone was trying to lob one on top of the gunner's head. They seemed to have him bracketed, but as more fell the accuracy wasn't improving. I needed to shut this fucker down and get out of the area before one of them found me, which was probably all too likely since they were beginning to rain down at a much faster pace.

Flattening myself on the ground, I wormed my way forward, rifle held in both hands. Another mortar fell close enough to rattle my teeth and leave me with a fresh coating of dirt. Spitting mud and blood, I kept moving, eyes focused on the very small hump in the ground that was all that screened my approach from the gunner. Slithering up to it, I pressed my face to the ground as more mortars fell, one on either side of me.

By now I was mostly deaf and questioning whether I really needed to engage the gunner. All that was really needed was some accurate mortar fire. But then maybe they were firing blind. They were probably pinned down and doing the best they could to send some shells in the direction of the machine gun and hoping for a lucky drop.

Anvil

Mentally yelling at myself, I gripped the rifle tighter and rolled around the hump into the open, aiming into the depression. Two Russian soldiers were there. The gunner who was currently working a stream of lead onto American positions, and another man operating as the gun crew. He was facing my direction, opening the lid on an ammo can.

He detected my movement, whipping his head up and staring in surprise. He was just a fucking kid. Eighteen, maybe nineteen. He just stood there staring at me with his mouth open. I shot him in the chest, three rounds shredding his uniform blouse and sending him staggering backwards to fall against the gunner.

The man jerked away from the body of his comrade, starting to turn in my direction. He never completed the movement. Three rounds shattered his skull, and he fell across the other body. Dropping into the depression, I dashed forward and dragged the two corpses out of my way. Raising up enough to see upslope I waved at the First Sergeant.

He saw me and began racing down the slope as I traversed the machine gun and opened up on the front ranks of the advancing Russians. As I walked the heavy slugs across them, I grinned an evil grin as bodies were torn apart and fell to stain the snow a brilliant crimson. Continuing to mow down enemy troops, I

Dirk Patton

couldn't help the good feeling you get from turning the enemy's weapon on him.

17

"Still no comms," the First Sergeant shouted a few seconds later when he leapt into the hole next to me.

He was referring to continued attempts to contact the command element of the Soldiers that were about to be cut off. I was still firing the captured machine gun, heavy on the trigger. This was definitely one of those times that you didn't worry about overheating and damaging a weapon. All that mattered was sending as much lead downrange as quickly as you could.

"Need ammo," I shouted, noting the belt was about to run out.

He grabbed the same can the first Russian I'd shot had been opening, snatched up the end of a fresh belt of ammunition and moved next to me. When the last round fired I yanked the breech cover open, and he slapped the new belt into place. A second later, I was back in action. But the damn Russians weren't cooperating.

Instead of standing out in the open for me to shoot, they had taken cover and were firing back. Bullets were screaming overhead and slamming into the dirt I was sheltered behind. Fortunately, only the barrel of the machine gun was exposed through one of several slots the gunner had cut in the surrounding berm.

To add to the fun, mortars were still falling all around. No more or less accurate, but I was getting an itch on my back, worried the troops firing that particular weapon were about due for a lucky drop.

With the Russians eating dirt, their advance stalled. They didn't pull back and give even an inch of the ground they'd taken, but at least they weren't still progressing. The remaining four Rangers arrived and set up to guard our rear. We were within Russian lines, and it was only a matter of time before someone behind us realized that it was American hands firing the machine gun.

"Now that just ain't fair," the First Sergeant drawled when two Russian BTRs appeared over a rise to our front.

The BTR was first developed by the Soviets during the Cold War, having been continually updated and upgraded. Not to simplify it too much, it's their version of a Bradley. Only with eight wheels instead of tracks, so it looks less like a tank. But it's no less deadly, sporting a 30 mm auto-cannon.

I didn't even bother targeting either of the vehicles. They have an armored hide that the best I could hope for would be to chip the paint. But what wasn't armored were the tires. BTRs have been around for a long time, with that one glaring vulnerability, and the Russian answer has been to install winches on each vehicle so it can be more easily recovered if disabled by multiple flats.

Using the tracers to direct my aim, I began shredding the left side tires on the vehicle closest to me. Soon it was bogged down, unable to do more than move in a circle as all four tires on one side were destroyed and the heavy vehicle crushed its steel wheels into the dirt. It was a good thing that it couldn't move, but a few flat tires didn't have any impact on its weapons.

"Down," I screamed as the BTR's turret turned and lined up its cannon on our position.

Diving into the bottom of the hole, I cursed when someone's boot struck the side of my face. Then I didn't care as the first of the 30 mm rounds slammed into the edge of the berm surrounding the hole. The Russian fired for several seconds, thoroughly saturating the area with high explosive shells. If we hadn't been below the grade of the surrounding terrain, well, let's just say it wouldn't have been pretty.

The First Sergeant's face was inches from mine as we both pressed as tight to the bottom of the hole as we could.

"I saw an Arty unit on the map at the CP," I shouted. "Time to bring some smoke."

He nodded and began squirming, reaching into a pocket and pulling out a small map book. Mortars continued to drop all around us as the second BTR joined the party. We were in the eye of the storm as both the Russians and our own troops tried to turn us into jelly stains.

The First Sergeant, Dutch I finally had time to read the name tape on his uniform, started screaming into his radio. He referred to the map book, calling in the fire mission. He listened for two seconds and confirmed the read back before stuffing it back into his pocket.

It couldn't have been more than twenty seconds, but it felt like a lifetime before the first artillery shell arrived. Dutch poked his head up when he heard it coming in, verified where it struck and got back on the radio and screamed, "Fire for effect!"

The artillery battery must have been close because it wasn't long before even over the nearly deafening roar of battle I could hear the freight train rumble of approaching shells.

"Gotta be 155s," Dutch shouted, referring to 155 mm shells.

I didn't argue or do much of anything else other than hold my mouth open to equalize the pressure in my head and hopefully preserve my eardrums from the pounding that was about to begin. Then the shells arrived, the earth shaking hard enough to bounce me an inch or two into the air. By the time the third shell struck, all fire from the BTRs had stopped. Then the Red Leg Soldiers manning the battery went to town.

The barrage continued for nearly three minutes. Three minutes of explosion upon explosion, drowning out all sounds and shrinking my world to a near constant roar. I couldn't tell if the mortars were still dropping in my immediate area and couldn't have done a damn thing if they were. When it was finally over, an eerie quiet descended over this part of the battlefield.

Weapons of all descriptions were still being fired just a few hundred yards away, but within reach of the artillery barrage, nothing was happening. Anyone that was still alive was face down, trying to dig their way to China. Opening my eyes, I saw Dutch speaking on his radio and I couldn't figure out how the hell he could hear to carry on a conversation. Raising up slightly, I looked around at the total devastation.

The ground in the area of the BTRs and the leading edge of the Russian advance had been churned up and cratered, looking very much like a desolate moonscape. One of the BTRs was burning furiously, the other unrecognizable. It must have taken a direct hit as not much more than the steel frame was left. As I watched, a few Russian heads began poking up from locations that had somehow survived the attack. I looked down when Dutch banged on my arm.

"What?" I shouted when I could see his lips moving but wasn't hearing anything other than a high pitched tone in both ears.

"Second fire mission?" He shouted back.

I looked back out at the Russian lines, seeing more heads still emerging from cover. Farther back I could see movement and wished for a pair of binoculars. At the limit of my vision, I could see several large trucks maneuvering into a line. I stared for a moment to make sure of what was mounted on the back.

"Tell the Red Legs to bug the fuck out," I shouted, grabbing Dutch's arm and pulling him up onto his knees.

He looked where I was pointing, cursed and relayed the message. The Russian trucks were carrying the Tornado, multiple rocket launching system. They'd probably had time to track the inbound artillery on radar, determine the location of the battery and were about to send a few dozen high explosive warheads in return for the pounding we'd just delivered.

Anvil

Dutch continued shouting into his radio, and as my hearing slowly returned, I was able to make out what he was saying. I was also hearing another voice in my ear, and it took me a moment to remember I also had a radio with an earpiece. I had apparently landed on the frequency being used by the Air Force and was hearing targeting missions being relayed to pilots. Sometimes even I get lucky!

One of the flyboys had already spotted the Tornados and called it in. I listened as an A-10 pilot acknowledged the new target. Standing and watching the destruction of the Russian rocket launchers would have been fun, but more troops were pushing into the area that had been devastated by the artillery attack. We were running out of time.

"On me," I shouted, leaping out of the hole and running across the hill.

The Russians regrouped quickly, and before we had covered fifty yards, there were bullets coming our way. Fortunately, we were running away from them, and there weren't any additional BTRs to light us up with cannon fire. Still, we sought cover as we moved, none of us particularly enamored with the thought of getting shot in the ass.

There was a bloom of white smoke from the direction of the Tornados and moments later multiple rockets streaked overhead. Almost before I even registered that the Russians had fired, a pair of A-10s screamed by on my right, seemingly only feet above the ground. I had lost elevation and could no longer see the truck-mounted launchers, but I heard the buzz of the Warthogs' guns a heartbeat before a massive explosion erupted on the horizon.

Still running, I glanced back and was happy to see all of the Rangers were still with me. Turning back to the front, I rounded a low hill and damn near got my head blown off by friendly fire. Three soldiers, a Corporal, and two Privates were huddled behind the hill.

I wasn't in uniform, still wearing the all black tactical clothing Titus had given me. If not for Dutch shouting that we were Americans, my day would have ended right then. We were in a low area that for the moment was screened from the battle raging all around. I didn't know why these three were here and didn't give a shit.

"Where's your CO, Corporal?" I asked, skidding on the snow as I pulled to a stop.

"Who the hell are you?" He asked, not lowering his rifle.

"Major Chase. Now where is he?" I stepped forward and pushed on the muzzle of his weapon until it was pointing at the ground.

"Dead, sir," he said. "So's our Top."

"Who's in command?" Dutch asked, looming over the frightened man.

"Lieutenant Willis," he said, sparing a glance at the two Privates with him.

"Take me to him," I said.

The Corporal looked at me for a few long moments, swallowing nervously. I saw the fear in his eyes and realized what he and the other men were doing. They were running. Well, I'd deal with that later. If there was a later. It sounded like the fighting was growing closer.

"Now, Corporal," I said, staring hard.

"Yes, sir," he mumbled, dropping his gaze and turning back towards the sounds of the heaviest fighting.

I pushed him to a run, the Rangers corralling the other two and keeping them in front. We rounded a couple of hills, small arms fire steadily growing louder. Incoming RPGs and grenades punctuated the sounds, and we had to slow and start using the terrain as protection from Russian fire.

Soon we were moving past fighting positions that had been hastily dug in the hard soil. Bullets were passing overhead, and the occasional enemy mortar dropped in to keep things interesting. I was dismayed to see a large number of bodies on the ground. For every two men still fighting there was probably one of their brothers lying dead. This was insane. These men should have been pulled back.

To my left, beyond a low line of short, rolling hills, the bulk of the Soldiers were spread across the terrain facing an advancing wall of Russian troops supported by BTRs. They had maybe five minutes before every single one of them was dead. There're overwhelming odds, then there was what I was seeing. Maybe two hundred men faced off against five thousand.

"Dutch, get those men pulled back behind these hills," I shouted.

He peeled off, taking two of the Rangers with him. The other two stayed with me, following the Corporal around another hill. I pulled to a stop when I looked up and saw a tall, thin man standing on the top. He was completely exposed to enemy fire and held a large pair of binoculars to his eyes, watching the approaching Russians.

"There," the Corporal pointed and tried to slip away before being body-checked to a stop by one of the Rangers.

Anvil

Before I could speak, the man turned slightly, looking at something closer. I saw his back stiffen as he spun and leapt down the side of the hill.

"Who ordered those men to withdraw, goddamn it?" He screamed. His eyes were wild, face florid and spittle flew from his lips.

"I did," I said, stepping so I was directly in front of him when he reached the bottom of the hill.

"Who the fuck are you?" He shouted, eyes searching my clothing and not finding any indication of name or rank.

"Major Chase. You're relieved, Lieutenant."

"Like hell I am," he yelled, stepping forward until the toes of his boots bumped into mine. "We're holding this ground! No one's going anywhere until the Russians are stopped!"

Before I could take his head off, mortars began dropping much too close. The Russians were responding to seeing the troops repositioning behind the hills. We all turned as a Havoc attack helicopter popped up from behind a larger fold in the terrain. He was no more than a quarter of a mile away, directly facing us.

"Oh fuck," went through my head the instant I saw the helo.

18

"Hey, LT. You're wanted on the sat phone."

Navy SEAL Lieutenant Sam looked over from the observation window he was standing in front of to see Master Chief Petty Officer Gonzales holding out a small handset. It was connected via an encrypted wireless signal to the satellite phone system they had placed on the roof of the building. Taking the offered device, he raised it to his ear and turned back to watching the three infected males that were in secure isolation. They were test subjects for Dr. Kanger's efforts at creating a Terminator virus.

"Go for Sam," he spoke into the handset.

"Do you show secure on your end?" A voice asked.

Sam lowered the handset and checked the display, verifying that the call was properly encrypted and secure.

"Confirmed," he replied.

"This is Lieutenant Hunt at Pearl Harbor. I'm in charge of the Cyber Warfare unit, and we wound up in control of the remaining surveillance satellites. We have been monitoring your area since the sinking of the Russian battlecruiser, Peter the Great. The reactor core was breached, and radiation levels are continuing to rise."

"How bad?" Sam asked, turning his attention away from the infected.

"We're unable to determine that from orbital based analysis. The system was a former black budget NSA project, and we're still learning how to use it. What we can tell is that there has been an increase, but we're unable to measure the values. That's why I'm calling."

"I don't understand," Sam said, hiding his irritation and wishing the man would get to the point. "If you can't measure it, how do you know it's rising?"

"We are receiving a radiation alert from the satellite, and are also observing wildlife and infected in the area of the docks that are dead or dying."

"I'm sure it's bad right next to the reactor, but the docks are several miles away, and there's terrain between here and there," Sam said.

"Correct, but there's also a steady wind blowing directly over you from across the site. I've checked with several nuclear power engineers here in Hawaii, and they all agree that there's a high possibility you are at risk. But there's also another problem."

"Of course, there is. What else?"

"We engaged the Russians a few hundred miles off the coast. The Russians used nuclear Shipwrecks to take out two of our carriers. Weather patterns are bringing the radiation your way. Much of it's falling into the sea, but combined with the reactor breach on your doorstep…"

"So what do we do? Pack up and move? There's nowhere else for the scientists to do their work."

"Moving has not been advised yet. The recommendation is you need to isolate the building's environment from contaminated air, make preparations in the event you do have to relocate and monitor the fallout levels where you are," Hunt said.

"The building is already sealed. It's a bio-research lab. Any ideas where I can get my hands on a Geiger Counter and radiation suits?" Sam asked sarcastically.

Few things scared him, but here was one of the two at the top of his list. Radiation. The irony wasn't lost on him that he was most afraid of the things that could stealthily kill him before he even realized he was being attacked.

"The experts' best suggestion is the University of Washington. It's close to your location, and you can get there by boat. We've identified the nuclear physics lab, which is the most likely place to have the equipment you need. There should be exposure suits in the lab in the event you have to move, as well as potassium iodide pills to protect your thyroid glands against radioactive fallout. I'll text the specifics to you momentarily."

Sam took a deep breath and let it out quietly. Another damn trip outside. Another risk of detection by the Russians. And if that happened, they'd come in here and wipe out the work the virologists had done. His orders were to keep the facility buttoned up and off the enemy's radar, but if he had to keep taking trips outside...

"What's the status of the Russians? Still evacuating?"

"They've evacuated all civilian and military from a ten-mile radius around the docks. The University is not within the evacuation zone, but you are at the moment. We threw a lot of conventional Tomahawks at them. Took out a lot of infrastructure they were using, but they're still coming in."

"Do we really need to be concerned inside this facility?" Sam asked, doing a masterful job of disguising his frustration.

Anvil

"According to the experts, yes, you do. You are most likely safe, but after briefing the Admiral he wants to make sure. There are other labs where the work could be conducted if we need to move you."

"Other labs? Where?"

"Two, actually," Hunt said. "One here in Hawaii, but it's not well equipped. The other is in Australia."

Sam was quiet for a few moments, digesting everything he'd been told. He was by no means knowledgeable about what Kanger and Revard were doing to create a virus that would kill the infected, but he doubted it would be a simple thing to just pick up and move. And the risk of losing one or both of the scientists during an extraction from occupied territory was higher than acceptable.

"Understood. Text me the location of the University's lab and I'll put a plan together."

Sam broke the connection without waiting to see if Hunt had anything else to say.

"What's up, LT?" Gonzales had stayed within earshot during the call.

"That's just fucking great," he said when Sam filled him in on the conversation. "What if the levels are too high when we go on our little boat trip to the University? We get exposed to find out we'll be dead if we go outside?"

"We're not paid to like it, Master Chief. We're just paid to do it," Sam said, handing him the handset and leading the way down a long hall.

"Yes, sir," Gonzales grinned. "Maybe I should have listened to my mother and joined the Peace Corps."

"Travel the world and meet strange new people? But the Peace Corps doesn't let you shoot them and blow shit up."

Sam grinned back as they turned into a new corridor.

"Yes, sir. There's that little drawback, for sure."

By this time, they had reached a common area of the large facility. A radio call gathered all the SEALs that weren't on sentry duty. Within ten minutes they were all in a large cafeteria, occupying a small corner. Sam briefed the men, a couple of them voicing the same concerns Gonzales had in the hallway. This time, the Master Chief shut down their objections with a few terse words.

Anvil

"We're going tonight," Sam said, wrapping up the briefing. "Master Chief, I want a run through ready for review in an hour."

"Aye, sir," Gonzales answered as the young Lieutenant strode out of the room to give Kanger and Revard a heads up.

The SEALs settled in around several laptops that were connected to the satellite signal and allowed them to access maps and sat imagery from the servers in Hawaii. Getting to the University was easy. The hard part was going to be getting to the Nuclear Physics Lab building once they disembarked their boat. While the sprawling campus wasn't thronged with infected, there were still enough to overwhelm the men if they were caught in the open and couldn't concentrate their firepower.

Then they had the problem of breaching the lab itself. Any facility dealing with nuclear physics had always been well secured, but after 9/11, the US Government had conducted a review of all such locations within America and installed dramatically stronger defenses. Any glass in the building would be thick and ballistic rated. Very tough stuff that could only be breached with explosives. Doors would be tough, heavy and just as difficult to penetrate.

While the SEALs were more than capable of penetrating the building, it was the noise involved that concerned them. No one could estimate the amount of time it would take to find the equipment they needed once they made entry. If they made a lot of noise going in, the infected would be attracted in large numbers, and there was a very real possibility that they would become trapped. Outnumbered beyond their ability to fight through to return to their boat.

The only positive was they did have some C-4 explosive which they would need to breach doors or windows. When Sam and Gonzales had stopped at the National Guard Armory with the crazy Army Colonel, the Master Chief had stuffed a few extra bricks and some detonators into his pack. He had more than enough and as the team discussed the plan, part of his mind was already working on the design for a small, shaped breaching charge that would get them inside with minimal noise.

Precisely an hour after he had left, Sam returned to be briefed on the plan his men had developed. It was simple and straightforward, as most plans made by the men who actually have to execute them are. After several questions, he approved it without changes.

"Sunset is at seventeen-fifty-three," he said, glancing at his watch. "We launch at twenty-hundred. Questions?"

Anvil

A SEAL who looked more like a movie star/California surfer than a warrior spoke up from the back of the room.

"LT, think there'll be any hot co-eds on campus?" He grinned with perfectly straight and white teeth.

"There's plenty of them," Master Chief Gonzales answered. "And the best part is they'll all be running right to you."

19

"Is GMD online?" Admiral Packard snapped, rushing to stand behind a Master Chief Petty Officer manning a console at the far side of the large CIC.

GMD stands for Ground-based Midcourse Defense and is comprised of anti-ballistic missiles. The missile shield that had become so prominent in the news when the United States proposed installing the system in Poland. Russia had flipped out, threatening all sorts of horrible things until the US President abandoned the idea.

"Green across the board, sir," the man answered, fingers flying across his keyboard.

"Set the system to automatic and execute," Packard ordered.

The console operator quickly entered the appropriate commands, the Admiral providing his authorization code when requested by the software that controlled the missiles. Within seconds, several Navy ships were networked into the targeting system as the GMD utilized their Aegis AN/SPY radar to augment its own.

"I want every ship that can move exiting the area at flank speed!"

Anvil

Packard looked around the CIC as he shouted, satisfied to see several operators immediately begin issuing emergency orders. While the GMD's targeting software identified, tracked and calculated the intercept, four missile silos buried deep in the earth at Fort Greely, Alaska came to life.

There was no one left on the post, even the infected having succumbed to the bitter cold, but the GMD system was more than capable of operating independently. Millions of dollars had been spent to ensure that nothing short of a direct hit from a ground penetrating thermonuclear weapon could prevent it from functioning.

Blast doors at ground level opened in preparation for launch. Restraining arms fell away from the sides of the missiles and inside each, a computer woke up. Readiness for launch was verified, and the authorization codes accepted. Seconds later, the missiles received their flight trajectory data. This was only a preliminary track which would get them into the general vicinity of the Russian ICBMs. Once in flight, they would maintain communication with the command system, constantly updating their individual target's location.

With a ground shaking roar, four anti-missiles streaked skyward. Cameras positioned around the massive field where the silos were located gave a view of the launch to the CIC in Pearl Harbor. The Master Chief had taken over one of the large displays at the front of the room, putting up a computer-generated plot of the incoming ICBMs as well as the intercepting GMD missiles.

"How long to intercept?" Packard asked quietly, eyes glued to the display.

"Five minutes, sir."

The Master Chief used his mouse cursor to point out a small set of numbers in the lower right corner of the screen that were counting backwards. The tracks went nearly straight up from the launch platform, a Russian sub. The lines drawn on the display were solid to show where the weapons had already traveled, changing to dashed to indicate the predicted path.

The ICBMs had completed their five-minute boost phase. The engines had burned out and dropped away when they were two hundred miles above the Earth's surface. Still gaining altitude from the tremendous velocity of the launch, the missiles were headed for an apogee of eight hundred miles. Once there, gravity would overcome their momentum, and they would tip over and begin to fall back towards the atmosphere.

Anvil

This is the midcourse phase and can last from fifteen to twenty-five minutes, depending on the distance from the launch site to target. It is during this phase, before re-entry, when there is an opportunity to intercept and destroy the warhead.

"Sir, I recommend launching a second wave of interceptors. We have intelligence that Russian missiles deploy decoy warheads when they reach apogee. There is still time to get additional missiles on target."

Packard turned and met the eyes of a Captain from Naval Intelligence. Without hesitating, he issued the order to the Master Chief operating the system. In short order, the tracks of four more anti-missiles appeared on the display. They raced to intercept the small objects traveling at greater than 15,000 miles per hour, eight hundred miles above the surface of the planet.

The GMD system had never been used to intercept a real ICBM. There had been multiple tests for nearly two decades, but the track record of the system was anything but confidence inspiring. The success rate had never been greater than fifty percent. The Admiral knew this but also recognized there was no other option.

Dirk Patton

Once the ICBMs re-entered the atmosphere, they would be traveling at speeds exceeding four miles per second. There was nothing that could be done at that point. No defensive weapon ever devised by man was capable of tracking and hitting something moving that fast.

It was deathly quiet in the CIC as all eyes watched the display. The view zoomed as the first wave of interceptors closed the distance to the Russian missiles. The ICBMs were almost at their apogee; speed reduced as their flight path flattened out.

"Missiles are at apogee."

The Master Chief confirmed what everyone could see on the screen. There were gasps and curses from around the room when the four dots on the screen representing the inbound missiles suddenly separated and became sixteen.

"MIRVs?" Packard asked the Master Chief.

A MIRV is a Multiple Independent Re-entry Vehicle, or in simpler terms, several nuclear warheads packed onto one missile that separate and strike different targets.

"Decoys, I believe, sir. But unable to confirm," the Master Chief answered after a moment of carefully analyzing the data that was streaming into his system.

Packard and the Captain exchanged worried glances as silence fell across the room. The clock kept counting down the time to intercept of the first wave, ticking to under fifteen seconds. Everyone held their breath as the tracks of the Russian weapons and the American interceptors converged.

For a few moments, nothing could be seen on the display other than a large flare that marked the point in space where all of the tracks had converged. The Master Chief was closely watching different data sets on his console, ignoring the monitor at the front of the room.

"Two successful intercepts, sir," he reported. "The other two were misses."

"Can you tell if we hit warheads or decoys?" The Admiral asked.

"No, sir. I cannot."

The man answered in a professional monotone that belied the seriousness of the situation. Packard looked back up at the master display, noting the second wave was less than two minutes from intercept.

"Time to re-entry?" He asked.

"Twelve minutes, sir."

The Master Chief highlighted a different location where another countdown clock was running.

"Send another wave, Master Chief. As many as you can."

"Aye, sir."

The man banged out commands on his keyboard, quickly overriding the GMD system and ordering twelve more interceptors to launch. Their tracks quickly appeared at the bottom of the display as the second wave converged on the inbound targets. Once again, the tracking of individual objects on the screen merged into a large blob of light. The Master Chief was watching one of his displays as he typed furiously. Soon, the remaining interceptors left their silos in Alaska.

"Three targets destroyed and one miss, sir," he reported. "All silos at Fort Greely are now empty. Without personnel on site to reload, we cannot launch any additional."

"What about Vandenberg?" The Admiral asked, referring to the other location in the California desert where the GMD system was located.

Anvil

"Unable to communicate with the system at Vandenberg, sir. It's been offline since the attacks in the LA area."

Packard cursed to himself, maintaining a calm outer appearance. There was nothing else they could do. If the Russians threw short range, or theatre, ballistic missiles at them, the Navy had more than enough ships remaining that were capable of knocking them down. But defense against ICBMs? He was out of rabbits.

"Time to impact on target?" He asked, the Master Chief understanding he meant how long before any warheads that made it through would detonate in Hawaii.

"Ten minutes, twenty-three seconds. Sir."

"Do we sound an alarm for the civilians, sir?" The Captain asked in a quiet voice.

"If even one of those leaks through, it won't matter," the Admiral shook his head as he spoke. "There's not enough time and besides, where would they go? It's a small island, Captain."

"Yes, sir," the man answered, nervously fingering the Naval Academy ring on his right hand.

The third wave arrived, the room waiting anxiously for a report.

"We have nine kills and three misses, sir," the Master Chief said. "One target remains inbound."

"Odds are in our favor. Ten interceptors for one target," Packard said quietly.

"Respectfully, sir, the odds are getting worse. The remaining target is accelerating as it falls back towards the atmosphere. That makes it more difficult to knock down."

The Master Chief had turned and spoken so softly that the Admiral had to lean in to hear him. He appreciated the man's discretion. Nodding, he turned his attention back to the display, willing one of the anti-missiles to find its target.

It wasn't long before all of the tracks converged. Everyone in the CIC knew the drill by now, turning to look at the console where the Master Chief worked, waiting for his report. This one took slightly longer, the man double checking before turning to face Admiral Packard.

"All interceptors missed, sir. One target remains inbound."

This time, he spoke loud enough for the whole room to hear. There was stunned silence as the enormity of the report weighed on each man and woman.

"Can you tell exactly where it's targeted?" Packard asked after several moments of silence.

The man turned back to his console and opened a new window on one of his screens. Several clicks of the mouse fed data into the software which quickly provided a set of coordinates in a textual display before drawing them on a map. The Master Chief looked up as he sent the results to be displayed on another of the large screens.

A satellite image of Oahu slowly zoomed, a pulsing red dot appearing directly over the USS Arizona memorial in Pearl Harbor. Packard looked at the image for a couple of heartbeats before turning to the Captain at his side.

"Get all essential personnel into shelter," he ordered.

20

As quickly as the Russian helo appeared, it exploded into a massive ball of flame. I flattened myself on the ground as shrapnel from the destroyed Havoc whistled past my ear. A heartbeat later an Apache roared overhead, banking away from several lines of tracers that reached out from the advancing enemy.

The pilot dropped until he was nearly scraping the ground, juking side to side in a desperate attempt to evade the enemy anti-aircraft fire. Body pressed to the ground; I looked up as he fired off a pair of hellfire missiles. Then the stream of tracers found the aircraft.

Most of the tail section was shredded, the Apache beginning a sideways twist before belly flopping into the snow. It slid several yards before striking a rock and flipping onto its side. The main rotor contacted the ground and shattered, sending chunks slashing through the air.

"You two," I leapt to my feet and pointed at the two Rangers who had accompanied me. "Grab some men and go get those pilots!"

The Apache had come down inside the shrinking perimeter, and I didn't want the men flying it to fall into Russian hands. The Rangers grabbed the Corporal and two Privates who we'd caught trying to run and dashed in the direction of the crash. The Lieutenant was still on the ground, and I bumped him with my boot, none too gently, telling him to get on his feet.

He didn't respond. I could tell by feel the moment my foot touched him that he was either unconscious or dead. Kneeling, I grasped his shoulder and rolled him over. Vacant, dead eyes stared up at the grey clouds as his limp corpse flopped onto its back. A neat, almost bloodless, wound was in the middle of his forehead. Shrapnel from the Havoc.

Standing, I looked around, glad to see the Soldiers I'd sent Dutch to retrieve. They were streaming through gaps between the hills, running as Russian mortar fire tore up the ground behind them. As happy as I was to see them, I was dismayed at how few were still alive. And healthy. Nearly a third of the men running towards me were supporting a buddy who had been injured, too many more paired up and carrying a body between them.

Voices screamed for medics as they approached, but there wasn't much help available. The two men wearing armbands with muted red crosses on them dashed about, trying to triage the overwhelming amount of injuries. Many of the Soldiers were mortally wounded and wouldn't make it through the day without immediate evac. But there were no hospitals anymore, at least not within reach of the battlefield. Maybe the Navy still had a hospital ship in operation, but...

As the remaining men of the company approached, I shouted for them to get formed up and prepare to fall back. I ran around the edges, meeting many of them as they arrived, pointing and yelling orders. Keeping my eyes moving, I was looking for any NCOs amongst the survivors but wasn't finding any.

All too soon, men stopped appearing. Dutch and the two Rangers brought up the rear. He saw what I was doing and immediately added his voice to the commands, helping get the Soldiers rallied and ready to move as a group.

"Any NCOs survive?" I asked him when he passed close to where I was standing.

"Not that I could find. This is one big cluster fuck, and the Russians are close enough I can smell the goddamn borscht," he answered.

"I sent two of your men to pull the pilots out of that downed Apache, and they aren't back yet. Can you get them on the radio?"

We both ducked as mortar shells began falling closer, heralding the continued approach of the Russians. Dutch transmitted several times, pausing to listen in between each broadcast, but he wasn't getting a response.

"What freq are you on?" I pulled out my radio and adjusted the channel when he told me, making a note of his call sign.

"Take point and get these men out of here," I said, tucking the radio back into its Velcro pouch. "I'll go get our Rangers."

I turned to run for the column of smoke that clearly marked the site of the crash, pausing when Dutch touched my arm.

"My job, sir," he said, trying to move past me.

"Negative, Top. I sent them; I'll go get them."

I didn't give him a chance to argue the point, though I understood what he was doing. In the military, officers are considered more valuable than NCOs. That's probably true as there are only a fraction as many officers as there are NCOs. The principle is drilled into every Soldier from early on in their military career, and for NCOs, it is second nature.

But I wasn't a tactician. I wasn't a highly skilled technician or engineer. I wasn't a General that could draw up battle plans and change them on the fly as the fighting unfolded. I was a dog-faced grunt that was nothing more than an NCO until the world fell apart and a well-intentioned Colonel promoted me to Major. Sitting back and letting someone else do the fighting just didn't mesh with my mindset.

The incoming fire intensified as I ran towards the downed Apache. Mortars were getting closer and a couple of times machine gun fire came my way. I ran in a crouch, changing direction often and slowing then sprinting to the cover offered by different terrain features. It's an exhausting way to cover ground, but running a steady pace in a nice straight line is a great way to let an enemy lock on and shoot you.

I was able to get an occasional glimpse of the advancing Russians, and I didn't have much time. Dashing to the base of a small hill, I threw myself flat and skidded to a stop as more machine gun fire whipped over my head. Worming forward, I looked around the shoulder of what was really no more than just a small mound of earth. I could see the crash site fifty yards in front of me.

The Apache was on its side, smoke pouring from the engine compartment. No flames were visible, but it was only a matter of time. Taking shelter behind the hull were the five men I'd sent and the pilot and gunner from the helicopter. They were still alive, for the moment, pinned down by a couple of squads of Russians.

I needed to get them out of there. Fast. If the enemy didn't get them, there was the very real concern of the fire reaching the Apache's fuel tanks. Sure, they're made tough, are ballistic resistant and self-sealing, but fire has a way of finding fuel. When that happened, the seven men would be engulfed in the fireball of an explosion.

The rifle in my hands was new to me, and I had no idea how well, if at all, the battle scope had been sighted. The Russians pushed forward, leapfrogging towards my men while maintaining a blistering suppressive fire. I decided it didn't matter if the sight was zeroed or not. I also needed some help.

Settling into the rifle's stock, I called Dutch on the radio. He answered as I pulled the trigger for the first time and saw a puff of dust a foot to the left of my intended target. The Russian soldier, who was throwing down much of the cover fire, either didn't notice or wasn't fazed. I adjusted my aiming point and pulled the trigger, drilling a round through his neck.

When I called Dutch, I had asked for the radio frequency for the artillery unit. He gave it to me, and even though I didn't have a map book to provide grid coordinates I placed the call anyway. It took some shouting and longer than it should have, but I finally convinced them to check with Colonel Blanchard to verify I was legit. While this was going on, I took out three more Russians.

That was good, as it slowed their advance on the men pinned behind the crashed Apache, but it was also bad as they finally noticed me. A large volume of fire started coming my way, and I had to roll behind the protection of the hill. Clicking over to the channel the Rangers were using I reached the men below my position and told them to sit tight for another few minutes. The reply was sarcastic, and profanity laced and, despite the circumstances, made me smile.

Clicking back to the artillery channel, I was glad to hear that they were satisfied I wasn't the enemy trying to call a fire mission in on American troops. I didn't have a map book, had no idea what my location was, but they had terrain maps, and I had a set of eyes. It took some doing, but I was able to spot and describe enough unique topographical features for them to find the general area.

Knowing it was a best guess, and not wanting to drop a shell on the men I was trying to save, I requested a ranging shell or one that would only produce smoke. The Red Legs were on the ball, and it wasn't long before I heard the rumble of incoming arty. A moment later there was a huge blossom of white smoke, a couple of hundred yards behind and far to the right of the Russians.

I called in adjustments for direction and drop, doing some rough math in my head and hoping like hell I remembered how to do this. Calling in a fire mission isn't complicated, but it wasn't something I'd ever done in real life before. It's rare that an SF operator finds himself in a situation where artillery is available. It had never happened for me, and I had only ever done this in training.

The second round arrived quickly, closer, but not close enough. Still too far and slightly right. The Russians had noticed the ranging rounds and were pushing hard to move forward, knowing the best protection would be to get as close as possible to the Americans. They didn't give me a lot of choices even though I would have liked another round to fine tune the bombardment.

Crossing my fingers, I called in another adjustment and ordered the battery to "fire for effect". If I had fucked up, I'd either just brought the shells down on the heads of my men, or was sending them into empty terrain where they'd do nothing other than make a lot of noise. Hoping I was due for some luck, I started sending as many rounds at the Russians as I could, trying to slow them.

I heard the roar of the shells in flight over the report of my rifle. Ceasing fire, I watched and waited. It didn't take much more than a second for the shells to start dropping and they were on target. Well, not perfectly. They were still coming in long, detonating fifty yards behind the rear of the Russian squads, but half the enemy soldiers were killed by the first three rounds, and the rest were too busy looking for cover to keep firing.

Back on the radio, I shouted a new adjustment and watched as the fire was walked closer to the Apache. The Russians were devastated, and I lost sight of all of them in the clouds of dirt, dust, and smoke that were thrown up by the 155 mm shells.

"Fall back now!" I screamed into the radio after switching channels.

A moment later one of the Rangers leapt to his feet, four others jumping up when he shouted. They scooped the Apache crew off the ground and ran. I stayed prone, rifle up and ready if a Russian popped up behind them. I didn't think that was going to happen as the artillery was pounding the ever loving shit out of that part of Idaho.

When they reached my position, I waved them on, getting to my feet and following as the last one passed. Mortars started up again when the other advancing enemy units spotted our movement. Machine gun fire was sprinkled in and ahead I saw one of the Privates flop lifelessly to the ground after half his head disintegrated.

The Ranger in the lead pulled to a stop behind the cover of a slightly larger hill, the rest of the men bunching tightly around him. I started to ask what the hell he thought he was doing, then dove for cover when I saw a Russian BTR nosing its way towards us.

21

"Sir!"

Admiral Packard turned when a communications specialist called out from the far side of the CIC. He had been watching as each console operator worked to shut down and secure their station before heading to a bunker located deep underground. He glanced at the countdown clock tracking the inbound thermonuclear warhead as the woman who had called out to him stood up.

"Phone call for you, sir. It is Fleet Admiral Chirkov. I've confirmed the call as originating in Moscow."

Packard was normally not a man who could be surprised, but the news that the head of the Russian Navy was on the phone and wanted to speak with him caught him completely unprepared. He knew Chirkov, having met him twice at diplomatic functions throughout the span of his career, and had always thought the man an arrogant simpleton. But, regardless of the man's intelligence, he had shown himself to be an incredibly astute politician.

"Here," he pointed at the phone on the console closest to him.

Anvil

While the comm specialist worked to reroute the call, Packard ordered the Captain to continue clearing the room and move personnel to the bunker. Waiting a moment to collect his thoughts, letting the phone buzz on its cradle, he took a deep breath and lifted the handset.

"Admiral Packard speaking," he barked.

"Admiral, so good to hear your voice. How long has it been? Eight years, no?"

"If you'll excuse me Viktor, one of your warheads is about to drop into my lap. I'm a little busy. What do you want?" Packard snarled, struggling to contain his anger.

"My old friend, I am calling to deliver a present to you. I assume you are watching the track of the inbound device?"

Packard glanced at the screen, wincing when he saw the ICBM still tracking along a dotted line ending in Hawaii.

"Again, what do you want, Viktor?"

"Admiral, please," the Russian purred into the phone. "Can't two old warriors have a civil conversation?"

"If you want civil, you shouldn't have attacked my country," Packard responded, finally getting his emotions under control and speaking calmly.

"Ahh... well, perhaps it is time for all of this to end. That is why I'm calling."

Packard was quiet for a moment, wondering what game the Russian was playing. He looked at the countdown clock. Five minutes and twelve seconds remained.

"I'm listening," he said. "But you'd better talk fast."

"First, allow me to demonstrate my goodwill," the Russian said. "Keep watching the incoming nuclear warhead."

There was silence on the phone as Packard glared at the screen. The clock kept running, counting down the time to detonation. He was aware of the continuing evacuation of the room and decided he was hanging up and heading for the bunker when the time reached three minutes remaining.

"I'm going to hang up, Viktor," he said when the clock reached four minutes, and radar still tracked the missile.

"Keep watching," the Russian said with a note of supreme confidence in his Oxford accented English.

Anvil

Three seconds later the screen blinked and the icon representing the ICBM disappeared. At the same time, the clock stopped, displaying 03:56:59. Packard stared at it for a moment before stabbing the mute button on the phone console.

"Confirm that, Master Chief," he shouted at the console operator.

"Already on it, sir," the man answered, typing furiously.

After what seemed an eternity, but was actually less than thirty seconds, the Master Chief heaved a deep sigh and turned to face Packard.

"Confirmed, sir. The missile was destroyed in flight, above the atmosphere."

The man couldn't contain the smile that spread across his face. Cheers broke out around the room, Packard barking them to silence as he turned back to the phone and took it off mute.

"Am I supposed to thank you, Viktor?" He asked.

"To be honest, Admiral, you should thank President Barinov. It is on his orders that the missile was aborted. He is ready to end hostilities with the United States if certain conditions are met."

"What are the conditions?" Packard growled.

"See, I knew you were a reasonable man. There is no need for further bloodshed. If you agree to these conditions, Russia will leave all surviving Americans unmolested. If you do not, the next missiles will not be aborted. And there will be more of them. Many more. Shall I read the President's conditions to you now?"

Packard gripped the handset so tight his hand throbbed. Anger boiled in his gut, but as he looked around the room, he realized he had no option other than to listen to the Russian. Muting the phone again, he turned to the comm specialist.

"Is this being recorded?"

"Yes, sir," she replied after confirming the conversation was being saved to disc.

"Proceed, Viktor," he said in a tight voice after un-muting the call.

"Very well. I assume you are recording and do not need to take notes.

"First, the full and immediate cessation of all military actions by the United States against any Russian military or civilians. Anywhere on the globe.

Anvil

"The complete decommissioning of all American military forces and assets. Immediately, all American submarines must come to the surface and remain there until we direct them to a port of our choosing. All operational naval surface vessels shall be handed over to Russia within one week. All aircraft other than un-armed commercial craft shall also be handed over, and inspections shall be performed in Hawaii to inventory and remove all military munitions.

"The complete evacuation of North America, including Alaska, by all surviving Americans. Russia now claims the entire continent as sovereign territory.

"Americans are limited to the Hawaiian Islands and their immediate waters. The survivors in the Bahamas shall be evacuated to Hawaii within one week. Travel to, and trade with, Australia shall be permitted if approved in advance.

"Finally, we want Major John Chase. Deliver him to any Russian commander, but he must be in our custody within twenty-four hours.

"None of these conditions are negotiable. If you do not agree, or if you violate any of the terms, all remaining Americans shall be destroyed by Russian nuclear rocket forces. Do you understand, Admiral?"

Packard stood very still, only the bunched muscles in his jaw betraying his mood. His mind was racing, but as he considered his options it became painfully aware that without America's nuclear deterrent, it was suicide to stand against the Russians.

"I don't know where Major Chase is," he finally spoke, trying to buy time. "I don't even know if he's still alive."

"I think you are being less than honest with me, Admiral," Chirkov chuckled into the phone. "You are as aware as I am that he is in Idaho. Perhaps you do not know his precise location at this moment, but he is with your forces. President Barinov has a personal score to settle with this man and delays or obfuscation on your part will be considered a violation of the terms I've laid out. I need your answer. Now. Do you agree?"

"Agreed," Packard growled through his teeth as he seethed internally.

"You are a wise man," Chirkov laughed again. "I'm sure you can imagine how many warheads are targeted on Hawaii at the moment, awaiting the President's order. My aides will contact you to arrange the details of the turnover of your fleet. And, I will be coming to Hawaii to personally accept your surrender. Isn't it a shame that the USS Missouri has been decommissioned? What a marvelous setting that would be for a surrender signing."

The Russian was laughing when he broke the connection, leaving Packard listening to a dead circuit. The Admiral stood perfectly still for several moments, the CIC completely silent as every remaining person watched him. Finally, with a shout of anger, he snatched the phone off the console and threw it against the wall, shattering the device into dozens of pieces.

"Get me Colonel Blanchard in Idaho," he snapped at the comm specialist. "I'll take it in my office."

Packard turned and stormed out of the room, motioning the intel Captain to follow.

Petty Officer Simmons had been even quieter than normal after speaking with the Army Major. She thought about what he'd told her, brooding as she pulled archives and confirmed his suspicions. The Russians were always right behind him. Just like he said. Just like someone was feeding them information. But who?

Jessica looked around the room at the five other occupants. There was Lieutenant Hunt, her CO. She eliminated him from the mental list of suspects she was compiling. He had the same access she did and would have been able to pinpoint the Major's location. No, this was someone who had a good idea of where he was but wasn't in the system.

Pulling up a security system window, she spent several minutes going through the logs. She was looking for any record of one of her co-workers having accessed the data stream specific to Major Chase. None of them had, but there was something else she needed to check.

Closing the security logs, Jessica initiated an admin login directly to the orbiting satellite. Once in, she ran through three different logs. Still no access by anyone other than her. Sighing in frustration, she began to log out but paused, deciding to perform a keyword search in case she had missed something in her review of the records.

One by one she searched for the login IDs of everyone who worked in her unit. The IDs were comprised of the first three letters of the user's first name, followed by a middle initial and the first three letters of the last name. Glancing at each console, she noted middle initials which were not something she had committed to memory.

ROBWROB – No results found.

CHAHZEM – No results found.

MELKSTE – No results found.

THORSYS – THOR SYSTEM LOGIN.

Jessica blinked, surprised by the results. She had been searching for Chief Petty Officer Thomas R. Sysko. He hadn't logged in to the satellite, but what the hell was Thor System? Curiosity got the best of her, and she selected the response.

There was a slight delay before a new screen appeared. It gave no indication of what it was for, containing only a password prompt. Opening an additional window, Jessica began digging into the satellite's operating system. It took some doing, but she finally determined that the password prompt was coming from another satellite which was communicating through the NSA bird.

"Sir, you need to see this," she called to Lieutenant Hunt.

A moment later he was leaning over her shoulder, peering at her console.

"What's up?"

"There's another bird up there, sir. One of ours apparently. I'm communicating through the NSA satellite and got to a login prompt."

"What is it?" He asked.

"No idea," Jessica said, staring at the blinking cursor in the password field. "I was poking around and found it. It's called Thor System. Ever heard of it?"

"No," he replied, shaking his head. "Can you get in?"

"Haven't tried yet. Didn't want to try without checking with you first. Just in case it's something I shouldn't be messing around with." She looked over her shoulder and met his eyes.

"Probably a good idea," he said, straightening up. "Let me make some calls, see if anyone knows what it is before you start breaking in."

"Yes, sir," Jessica said as Hunt headed for his console and snatched up a phone.

Dismissing the new discovery from her mind for the moment, she returned to working on her list of suspects. She was confident the people in the room with her were clear. Besides, the very nature of their jobs had required an incredibly extensive and intrusive background check before each of them received a security clearance. And the clearances were updated every six months. The odds of someone being a Russian agent or sympathizer were so small; they were microscopic.

That left people that didn't work directly in her unit. Who had been in the room or had access to the information about Major Chase?

Admiral Packard. Jessica briefly considered the possibility before dismissing it outright. Besides, if the Admiral was in the Russian's pocket, they had much bigger problems than who was feeding intel about one Army Major.

The Captain from Naval Intelligence. More possible than the Admiral, but unlikely. Still, he had been present in the room and had seen and heard enough information to put the Russians on the Major's trail without being able to give them precise coordinates. Jessica mentally labeled him as a possibility.

Dirk Patton

Who else? She had no knowledge of who the Admiral or Captain may have told. Staffers, fellow officers, lovers...

Jessica caught her breath when the last word went through her head. Mark? No, it wasn't possible. With an internal groan, she forced herself to acknowledge that it was possible. And if it was Mark, that meant she was the leak. But what had she told him if anything?

Their relationship was relatively young and still in the phase that was ruled by physical passion. She went to sleep each night thinking about the things he did to her, let her do to him, and woke up with a smile on her face. But what had she told him? It was hard to remember, difficult to separate the things she had said when the majority of their encounters were limited to heart pounding sex.

Setting aside their trysts and focusing, she felt a hot flush of guilt when she remembered having made off the cuff comments to Mark about her work. She had told him the general area that Major Chase was in, south of Mountain Home, and a short time later the Russians had been searching for him in precisely that area.

Thinking back, she remembered several other little bits of information she'd shared. None of them had been specific but certainly were enough to compromise Major Chase's escape. Guilt turned to anger, burning until there was a ball of white hot fury in her chest. Her suspicions weren't proof, but the seed of doubt had been planted in her head.

"Start working on getting in."

Jessica was so wrapped up in her thoughts about Mark that she was startled when Lieutenant Hunt spoke directly behind her. She jumped in her seat and let out with an involuntary squeak of fright, drawing the attention of everyone in the room.

"Are you alright, Petty Officer?" Hunt asked, taken aback by her reaction.

"Yes, sir. I'm fine. Was just lost in thought and didn't hear you walk up. Sorry, sir. I'll get on it right away," she said, lowering her head and concentrating on not meeting any of the eyes that were looking at her.

Working quickly, she began looking for a back door around the password prompt. She knew it would be there, was confident she'd find it. Once she did, she would be able to start working on defeating the layers of security that were almost certainly in place to protect the new satellite.

Jessica worked for several minutes but was distracted. Thoughts of Mark tumbled through her head, and the pain of her suspicions gnawed at her like a cancer. Finally, she sighed, acknowledging she was too distracted at the moment to be trying to hack into a heavily secured system. Knowing there was only one thing she could do, she secured her terminal and walked over to where Lieutenant Hunt was wrapping up a phone call.

"Sir, can we speak in private?" Jessica asked when he replaced the handset.

He looked momentarily surprised, then nodded. Standing, he led the way to a small, secure conference room and closed the door behind them. He took a seat at the head of the table, but Jessica remained standing, staring at a large map of the western hemisphere that was attached to the far wall.

"Petty Officer?" Hunt prompted after several moments of uncomfortable silence.

Jessica turned, and he could see the moisture in her eyes. Moving slowly, she took a seat at the opposite end of the table and began telling him about the call from Major Chase and what she'd done since receiving the information. He listened attentively, letting her speak without interruption.

"This isn't good," he breathed when she was done. "Is there anything else you need to tell me?"

"No, sir. That's all of it."

"Stay put. Don't move," he said, standing and walking out of the conference room.

He closed the door behind him, and since there were no windows looking into the working area of the unit, a security feature, Jessica was left feeling as if she were already in prison. It was close to five minutes before Hunt returned, a legal pad and pen in hand.

"Here," he said, placing the items on the table in front of her. "I want you to write down everything you just told me. Don't leave anything out. There's someone from NIS on the way to talk to you."

He was referring to the Naval Intelligence Service. Jessica nodded, picking up the pen after wiping tears from her eyes. Hunt looked like he wanted to say something else, but after a long pause left the room, pulling the door softly shut.

23

The BTR slowly wheeled around the base of a large hill, bouncing over mounds that weren't much smaller than the one we were using for cover. I didn't think the driver or gunner had spotted us yet as there wasn't any fire coming our way, but it was probably only a matter of time. I took a couple of seconds to glance over the men around me, hoping someone had something capable of penetrating the Russian vehicle's armor. I didn't really expect to get that lucky, and I didn't.

Scrambling through the dirt, shoving legs and feet out of my way, I moved to where I could get a look at the BTR's supporting ground troops as well as the main body of advancing enemy. The news wasn't good. We were cut off. The only good news here was that it looked as if Dutch had gotten the main body of the company out of the area just in time.

Mortars were still falling around us. Fortunately, they didn't have us zeroed. They were close enough to make us duck and press our bodies against the ground, but they weren't close enough for us to be taking shrapnel. Yet. It was only a matter of time before the Russians began making adjustments and dropped one right in the middle of us.

Anvil

The two Rangers had spread apart and were set up to start sending defensive fire. They were holding off as long as possible, not wanting the BTR to spot us and open up with its 30 mm cannon. The Corporal and surviving Private were sheltering with one of the Rangers while the Apache pilot worked to stop the blood flowing from his gunner's leg wound.

More Russians were approaching than I could count. We needed artillery and air support, or we weren't going to last more than five minutes. Keeping my head down, I dialed in the channel for the artillery battery. The fire mission I'd called in a few minutes ago had stopped, and I needed these guys back in the battle.

After several unanswered calls, I cursed and switched to the frequency I'd heard the Air Force using. The channel was flooded with orders being issued and pilots shouting over screaming engines. I broke in, transmitting a distress call. It took several attempts before a calm voice with a heavy Georgia accent answered, asking me to identify myself.

Turning to the Corporal, I grabbed his arm and shouted to be heard over the blast of a detonating mortar bomb that was way too close for comfort.

"What Company are you with?"

"Alpha Company, third platoon," he shouted back.

I relayed this info over the radio and requested immediate air support to our east and south. I was told to "stand by" and screamed that we didn't have time to wait. A mortar dropped on the top of the hill screening us from the Russians, the blast deafening and stunning us. Dirt and rocks rained down, covering everyone in a thick layer of dirt.

Ears ringing, I looked around and saw the Apache pilot sitting up. He had thrown his body across the gunner's face to protect it from the dirt cascading down. He paused when he saw the man's eyes, reaching out to find the pulse in his neck. He didn't find one, looking up and shaking his head when he saw me watching.

The Private chose that moment to break, leaping to his feet and running into the open. He was heading west, running hard, panic lending wings to his feet. A hundred yards away was a short bluff overlooking a narrow channel that had been carved by water during rainstorms. I had already seen it and dismissed it as crossing that much open ground was suicide.

He had covered a third of the distance before the Russians saw him and swung a machine gun in his direction. The gunner tracked him for several steps, the bullets striking the ground all around him. But none of them hit, and he kept running. He was two-thirds of the way to safety, and I was starting to think he might actually make it.

There were three loud, rapid reports from the BTR, smoke swirling around the muzzle of its cannon before the wind whipped it away. The three shells arrived on target in fast succession. An area the size of a small house disappeared in the blasts, and I lost sight of the fleeing man.

The wind was freshening and quickly cleared the dust and smoke. I looked for the Private but couldn't find him in the churned soil. There were a couple of things that could have been body parts, or maybe they were just rocks, but he was gone. I didn't feel sorry for him because his panic induced sprint had given our precise location to the Russians. A moment later there was more firing by the BTR and shells began tearing up the ground all around our hill.

The blasts were brutal, the mortar drawing in tighter until we were completely bracketed. There was a scream to my left an instant after a particularly close strike from one of the BTR's shells, but I wasn't about to raise my head off the ground to see who had been hit.

The ringing in my ears was subsiding, and I thought I could hear a voice in my earpiece over the near constant crump of exploding munitions.

Dirk Patton

Pressing it tighter, I listened, relief flooding over me when the radio call was from a pilot that had been redirected to my location.

"... pop smoke and call it." I heard.

The pilot wanted me to mark my position with a smoke grenade, so he knew where to avoid as he came in. But that was a problem as I didn't have one. I turned and shouted, coughing from the thick, acrid smoke produced by the exploding shells that had us pinned down. No one had one.

"No smoke," I shouted into the radio, lifting my head for half a second to get a look at the BTR. "We're pinned down three hundred meters due north of the BTR."

The pilot told me to hold on and a few seconds later a pair of A-10s roared directly over our position. The lead one was already firing and as they banked away there was a large explosion from the direction of the Russian vehicle. Poking my head around I breathed a sigh when I saw it burning furiously.

"Good shooting," I shouted. "Now, to my east, half a klick. Get that fucking mortar and I owe you a beer."

This time, I didn't see the Warthogs until the sound of their guns firing helped me spot them. Their grey paint scheme blended well with

204

the heavy clouds, hiding them from sight. The ground along the advancing Russians erupted, captured Hummers as well as infantry being shredded by the heavy slugs.

The pair of jets banked away, dropping lower to stay close to the safety of the ground. They were turning, aligning for another strafing run when the trail of an air-to-air missile streaked in from the west. It was traveling almost impossibly fast, the lead pilot standing his aircraft on its wing and turning, trying to evade. But the missile was locked on and homed in, destroying the A-10 and sending flaming wreckage scattering across the terrain.

The second jet changed course, turning away from the fireball that marked the grave of the first one. He jinked hard when a shoulder fired anti-aircraft missile screamed skyward from the rear of the Russian lines. The pilot dropped so low I was losing sight of the plane as hills and bluffs blocked my view, finally disappearing completely from sight. I didn't see an explosion, so hoped he'd been successful in evading the missile.

The Mortar had stopped firing and for the moment, all we had to worry about was rifle and light machine gun fire. The shout I'd heard was the Ranger on the left, and when I checked on him, he was dead. A piece of shrapnel had pierced his chest. The Corporal was huddled behind the corpse, but at least he had his weapon up to cover that flank.

Ahead, the BTR still burned, and I could make out several bodies on the ground, but there were still nearly fifty Russians on foot that were pushing in on us. They had set up a couple of machine guns on the tops of hills and were using them to hose down our hiding spot while the rest of them dashed forward.

The one surviving Ranger was firing, picking his targets, and dropping a running enemy with almost every pull of the trigger. I slapped the Corporal on his helmet and told him to start shooting. As he began firing, I pulled the rifle and spare magazines off the dead Ranger and tossed them to the Apache pilot. His right arm was broken, the hand dangling uselessly, but he pulled the rifle up to his left shoulder and joined the fight.

The Russians kept advancing. Slowing, as they drew inside a hundred and fifty yards and our fire became more accurate, but we didn't stop them. To the west, Apaches had shown up and were harassing the larger force. But the Russians called in their own helicopters to counter and soon our air support was driven off, outnumbered three to one.

They brought the machine gunners closer, first one then both opening up and putting out much more accurate fire due to the reduced range. The Corporal was killed when he raised up to change magazines, several slugs ripping his throat and chest open. That left one of the Rangers, an injured helicopter pilot and me.

Behind us, the battle was picking up. The rate of fire and the sounds of large caliber cannons was drawing closer. I tried several times to use the radio, hoping for some artillery support, but it wasn't working. The Ranger was also equipped with a comm unit that wasn't working. The Russians were jamming the airwaves, disrupting our communications.

On the horizon to the west, an aerial dogfight was taking place between two large flights of helicopters. They were too far away for me to see much more than a basic outline and I couldn't tell who was getting the worst of it. Not having time to watch, I focused on the approaching Russians, carefully picking targets.

The surviving Ranger and I were finding an enemy soldier with almost every shot, but we weren't firing very often. Machine gun fire was forcing us to stay behind cover, each getting to spot a target only when there was a lull in the incoming suppressive fire. The Apache pilot had settled for holding the rifle at the ready for when the Russians overran our position.

Dirk Patton

Mortar fire resumed from the main body of the advance, and they damn near had us zeroed. The second shell that dropped rang my bell. The only good news was that its shrapnel missed all three of us. I felt like I was wrapped in heavy gauze, my senses dulled from the concussion of the blast and felt more than heard the beat of a rotor as a helicopter suddenly appeared behind me.

Spinning, I began firing at the aircraft when I recognized a Russian Havoc attack helo. But, it's well armored, and my rifle bullets did nothing. The Apache pilot was screaming something at me that I couldn't understand as he held the trigger down and emptied his rifle at the new arrival. His first couple of rounds were deflected off the ballistic windscreen, then the recoil from full auto lifted his rifle's muzzle up and to the side, sending the remaining fire flying harmlessly off target.

The Havoc just hung there, weapons staring back at us. It was no more than fifty yards away, and we'd be dead before our brains even registered that it had fired a rocket or cannon. With nowhere to run and nothing to effectively fight back, I let my rifle drop as thoughts of Katie ran through my head.

Not the infected Katie, but the girl I'd married. I guess this was my life passing before my eyes. Not all of it, just the best part. The part I'd spent with her.

24

Jessica Simmons was angry. And frightened. But mostly she was pissed off. Waiting in the conference room as ordered by Lieutenant Hunt, she was apprehensive about what was coming. In less than ten minutes a Commander from Naval Intelligence had arrived with four large Marines in tow. He had walked into the room as the Marines took up positions to prevent anyone from entering or leaving.

Jessica leapt to her feet and came to attention when he walked in. He looked at her with hooded eyes and tossed the legal pad she had used to write out her confession onto the polished table top.

"I'm Commander Tillman," he said in a somber tone. "Take a seat, Petty Officer."

He sat at the head of the table and began reading from the pad. Jessica lowered herself into a chair at the opposite end, back perfectly straight and hands folded in her lap. Tillman quickly read through the four, hand-written pages, then re-read them at a slower pace.

"We have a problem, Petty Officer," he said, pushing the legal pad to the side and leaning forward with his arms resting on the conference table.

Anvil

"Yes, sir. We do," she replied, meeting his accusing gaze.

"You realize I have enough here already to refer you to NCIS for charges of espionage and treason."

Jessica was stunned into silence. This wasn't what she'd expected. Sure, she'd spoken out of turn, revealing sensitive information. But treason? Espionage? She wasn't the spy!

"I'm not a spy, sir!" She said through clenched teeth. "I acknowledge I've made a mistake, but I'm not the one talking to the enemy."

"Semantics, Petty Officer. Revealing classified information to anyone not authorized to receive that information is a serious offense. And this is not a grey area. It's very black and white, and with your clearance level, you are very well aware of that."

"Sir, I'm more concerned with the information that has and is being relayed to the Russians. That's why I came forward."

"You mean the information that you provided?"

Tillman looked at her with raised eyebrows, and a lump began to form in her stomach.

"Yes, sir," she answered, breaking eye contact and looking down at her hands for the first time.

"What else have you told the Russians about?"

"What else?" Jessica's head snapped back up, her mouth open in surprise. "I haven't told the Russians about anything! I made a mistake in talking about something I shouldn't have, and that's all it was. A mistake!"

"A mistake. Is that how you'd categorize your relationship with Chief Petty Officer Hiram? A relationship that is clearly inappropriate and prohibited by Navy regulations?"

Jessica sat staring at the man, stunned by the direction this was going. She alerts her CO to a breach in security, and the possible dissemination of information to the enemy and this guy is sitting here talking about an inappropriate sexual relationship?

"Sir, if you want to charge me with something, call me a lawyer and get on with it. I thought the bigger issue here would be the fact that it appears we have someone feeding intel to the enemy."

Jessica's eyes flashed as she spoke, fear and anger fueling her frustration. She wasn't sure what she expected when she decided to confess all to Lieutenant Hunt, but it wasn't this. Who she was or wasn't having sex with didn't seem to be nearly as important as a traitor in their midst.

"Oh, it is an issue, Petty Officer," Tillman said with a condescending tone. "But I'm trying to understand why it happened in the first place. Who initiated the relationship? What else has he asked you to tell him? What else have you told him?"

It was starting to make sense. They didn't believe her. Didn't trust that she was telling the full truth and wasn't just trying to deflect suspicion so she could continue passing secrets.

"I want a lawyer, sir," Jessica said, realizing the warnings from Major Chase were nearly prophetic.

"A lawyer? But you haven't been charged with anything, and I'm not a criminal investigator," Tillman smiled.

Jessica didn't know what to say. She had been around long enough to understand that until NCIS got involved this wasn't a criminal matter. Mind racing, she looked up when the door opened and shot to her feet. Commander Tillman turned, annoyance clear on his face until he saw Admiral Packard standing in the doorway. He too leapt to his feet and came to attention.

"Petty Officer, please excuse us," the Admiral said, stepping aside so she could leave the room.

"At ease, Commander," he said, closing the door behind Jessica. "Can she be trusted?"

"Sir, I've only begun speaking with her. I can't answer that at this point."

"Commander, we're at war. The Russians are about to start dropping nukes on our heads and according to her CO, that young lady is the only person that has the ability to give us an edge. So, I'll ask you again. Your gut feel. Can she be trusted?"

Tillman met the Admiral's eyes for a few moments as the gravity of the statement hit him.

"Sir, my gut feel after speaking with her CO and ten minutes of conversation with her is that she is genuine. She made a mistake, and when she realized it, she came forward. But there could be many more layers to this. She may well be a Russian agent. There are many aspects of this that bother me."

"Thank you, Commander. If we survive the next twenty-four hours, there will be time for a thorough investigation. Leave one of the

Marines to keep watch on her activities and pursue other avenues at this time. I have a job for her."

"But, sir..."

"Dismissed, Commander," Packard barked.

"Yes, sir!" Tillman snapped to attention, held the position for a few heartbeats then left the room.

Packard stepped to the open door and called for Jessica and Lieutenant Hunt to join him. Moments later they stepped in, one of the Marines looking inside the room before closing the door behind them.

"Sir, I..." Jessica began, falling silent when the Admiral raised a hand.

"Petty Officer, we don't have time for that now. You made a mistake, and you are going to have to live with the consequences of your actions. However, we have an emergency and a higher priority at the moment."

Packard waved them into chairs, remaining on his feet.

"You found something called the Thor System, and the Lieutenant contacted NIS," the Admiral began. "I was just briefed on what it is, and candidly it is our last and only hope. Lieutenant Hunt assures me that you are the best person to break into the system and take operational control. Perhaps the only person."

Jessica's head was spinning. Two minutes ago she was being interrogated by an officer from Naval Intelligence. Being accused of spying for the Russians and committing treason. Being threatened with criminal charges for everything from sexual misconduct to operating as a foreign agent. Now she was being put back to work?

"Sir, I'll do whatever is asked of me," she finally said. "I'm not a spy!"

Packard stood motionless, staring down into her eyes. He wanted to believe her, in fact, did believe her. But he had dealt with traitors before and knew from experience that their most valuable skill was the ability to lie to your face and convince you they were telling the truth.

"I sincerely hope not," he said after a long pause. "And if I had any other option, you wouldn't go near a terminal or any classified data until NIS is satisfied that you're who and what you say you are. But I don't have a choice. You need to break into that system, and you have twenty-three hours. After that, it won't matter. We're on a deadline, and if you can't get us in with enough time remaining to deploy it, I don't have a choice but to surrender to the Russians."

Anvil

"I understand, sir," Jessica said. "What is the Thor System?"

"That's classified, Petty Officer. Get us in. That's your job. Knowing what it is isn't necessary for you to do your job," the Admiral said, his voice stern.

"Understood, sir," Jessica said. "I'll get you in."

25

The Havoc suddenly gained altitude, banked and flew away. What the fuck? Thinking I was about to die, I was so surprised that I just lay there for a few moments watching it disappear over the horizon. Then I realized the incoming mortar and machine gun fire had stopped. I exchanged glances with the Ranger and Apache pilot, then carefully poked my head out to check on the Russian advance.

They were withdrawing! Again, what the fuck? They had us. The ground forces had us pinned, and an attack helicopter was close enough to chew us up into hamburger. What the hell was going on?

I involuntarily jumped when my earpiece came to life. Orders were being shouted. And questioned, which is very unusual. But the overall command was to cease fire and fall back to designated rally points.

"What the fuck?" The Ranger called from where he was watching the Russians pull back.

"That's what I want to know," I answered, slowly climbing to my feet.

A few moments later the two other men stood up next to me, and together we watched the enemy retreat. Only it wasn't a real retreat. We hadn't won the engagement, forcing them back. Someone had negotiated a cease fire. And as far as I was concerned, they had done it just in time.

"Let's go," I said, helping the Ranger lift his fallen brother onto his shoulder.

There were more bodies than we could carry so other than the dead Ranger I decided to leave them where they were for the moment. Details would be sent out to retrieve the dead, but I couldn't imagine what would be done with the remains. We didn't have a morgue. That only left the option of hand dug graves for those killed in battle.

It was a long hike back, farther than it had seemed when I'd run into the battle. The ground was littered with bodies, both American and Russian. It was dotted with armored vehicles that were burning or burned out. There were more crash sites within visual range than I could count, and perhaps an aviation expert could have recognized the difference between our planes and the enemy's. I couldn't. I just hoped that most of them had been built by Ivan.

After most of half an hour, we reached the temporary command post. When I appeared around the base of a low hill, Rachel spotted me and broke into a run. She slammed into me, throwing her arms around my neck and nearly taking me off my feet. Holding me in a tight embrace, she whispered in my ear.

"I thought you were dead."

I squeezed her back, then released her when she stepped away.

"What the hell is wrong with you?" She shouted in my face as tears ran down hers.

I was touched by the show of raw emotion but wasn't in the frame of mind to deal with it. Standing there looking at Rachel's tears I was relieved when Irina walked up and leaned in to kiss me on each cheek. Ignoring the looks, I was getting from Soldiers and Marines that were trudging past where we stood, I took Rachel's hand in mine and headed for where Colonel Blanchard stood with a sat phone pressed to his ear.

"What the fuck, sir?" I asked when he lowered the handset and pressed the red button to end the call.

"Temporary cease-fire," he said, blowing out a deep breath. "The Russians launched ICBMs at Hawaii. We shot down most of them before running out of missiles. They destroyed the last one before it re-entered the atmosphere, then called Admiral Packard with terms for our surrender."

"What? What terms?" I asked.

"We stop fighting and hand over all of our assets. And evacuate North America and the Bahamas. We're restricted to Hawaii. The Admiral agreed, and that bought us a twenty-four-hour cease-fire until the final condition is met."

"What's the final condition?" I asked.

"You," he said, holding my eyes with his. "We have twenty-three hours left to deliver you to any Russian commander. If we don't, they nuke Hawaii."

I stood there staring at him, half expecting him to smile and say he was just fucking with me. But I knew he wasn't. Knew my time was almost up.

"You can't be serious," Rachel cried. "We don't hand people over to the enemy. That's not what we do!"

"How many people left alive in Hawaii?" I asked Blanchard.

"One point four million civilians," he said. "And another thirty thousand military."

"No you don't," Rachel released my hand and grabbed my upper arm, trying to pull me around to face her. "They haven't used nukes so far; there's no reason to think they will now!"

"There's every reason to believe they will," I said, turning to look at her. "And I'm not worth all those lives."

"Tell him," Rachel looked to Irina, pleading for her to help convince me that I didn't need to turn myself over to the Russians.

"I am sorry, but he is correct," she said in a soft voice. "President Barinov is quite capable of using nuclear weapons. He has not done so up until now because he was intent upon maintaining the fallacy with the Russian people that this plague was the doing of the Chinese. Something has changed, giving him an excuse to wipe the few remaining Americans from the face of the planet."

"Rachel..." I said gently, stopping her from continuing to protest. At least for the moment.

"Do you think he'll actually honor the terms if I surrender?" I asked Irina. "Or is he just doing this to get his hands on me and he'll launch anyway once they have me?"

Irina stood quietly for a moment, considering the question. Blanchard, Rachel and I remained silent, watching her.

"I do not know, but I have a difficult time trusting him. He has shown in the past that commitments and treaties he has entered into are only respected for as long as is convenient."

"So you're saying we shouldn't trust him?" Blanchard asked.

"I am saying that his past actions have shown him to be untrustworthy," Irina said. "I was trained as an intelligence officer, and in the absence of current information about a subject's intentions, the only way to predict their potential course of action is to analyze how they have behaved in similar situations in the past."

"She should speak with the Admiral," I said to Blanchard.

He nodded and called over an aide, instructing him to arrange a secure call with Packard. The man immediately set to work.

"I have twenty-three hours?" I asked Blanchard.

"Slightly less," he said, checking his watch.

I was unprepared for the turn of events, but can't say that I was terribly surprised. Barinov wanted revenge and had shown that he wasn't going to rest until I was either dead on the battlefield or rotting in a damp cell at the

Lubyanka Prison, waiting for my very public execution.

Sighing, struggling to accept the inevitable, I turned and looked at the horizon to the southeast. The sun was setting, and it was already dark in that direction. Katie was somewhere out there. Infected. If I turned myself over to the Russians...

"If I do this, I want your word that you will find my wife and take her to the researchers," I said, turning back to face Colonel Blanchard.

"You have my word," he said without hesitation. "But I'm not sure how we're going to track her down. You said earlier that you had an idea."

"She was CIA," I said. "Not long before she left the Agency they began putting tracker beacons in selected officers. Just a small chip that was surgically implanted in her upper thigh. It's dormant until activated by a coded signal, then is supposed to transmit her location for forty-eight hours."

"You're sure it's still there?" He asked.

"Positive. I felt it a few days ago," I said, not bothering to explain what my hand had been doing on my wife's upper thigh.

Anvil

"Any clue how to activate it?"

"Speak to a Petty Officer Simmons at Pearl Harbor. I've already mentioned it to her, and she can help."

By this time the call to Admiral Packard had gone through and Blanchard and Irina stepped aside to speak with him. Rachel stood next to me, distress clear on her face.

"I don't have a choice," I said softly, leading her away from the command post.

"Yes, you do. Don't stop fighting. It's going to be dark soon. Let's slip away. We can find Katie and get her to Seattle," Rachel pleaded.

"And more than a million people in Hawaii die? And all of these Soldiers and Marines? They'll be wiped out. No, that's not something I'm willing to do. Not something I could live with," I said, shaking my head.

Rachel stood in front of me, staring into my eyes. Fresh tears began flowing as she accepted I wasn't going to change my mind. With a sob, she stepped in and wrapped her arms around me, burying her face against my chest. I held her as she cried.

26

It had been dark for close to two hours, but I had no idea what time it was. I sat with Rachel near a small campfire a few dozen yards away from the command post. The Russians had withdrawn a few miles, and there was the constant thrum of rotors in the dark sky as both sides patrolled the neutral zone that had formed between us.

Irina had spoken with the Admiral for close to an hour, joining us by the fire as Colonel Blanchard made several more phone calls. She didn't have any idea if the conversation she'd had with Packard had changed his mind about agreeing to the terms offered by the Russian president. Now we sat in silence, eating some MREs I had scrounged.

"Twenty-one hours," Rachel said, breaking the silence.

I didn't have a response to that and didn't want to spend my last few hours of freedom thinking about what was in store for me. Well, thinking about it anymore than I already had. Though I had never been a guest of the Russians, I'd read de-briefs of people who had and knew I wasn't in for a good time. Most likely I'd welcome death with open arms once Barinov grew tired of my presence.

Anvil

"We need to talk."

I looked up, surprised to see Blanchard standing on the other side of the fire. I had been so lost in thought I had failed to notice his approach. Handing the rest of my meal to Rachel, I stood and followed him out into the darkness.

"What's going on?" I asked.

"It's been a busy couple of hours. I spoke with the Petty Officer's CO. She's on a priority project, and he had another of his staff get in to a part of the CIA system that's still operating on the Echelon network. They can't get into the area where individual codes are stored."

"Can't they just activate them all?" I asked, a feeling of defeat coming over me.

"The system doesn't work that way. One at a time, and without the code specific to her beacon, there's no way to trigger it. The database where they are stored is very heavily encrypted and pretty much impenetrable without the proper CIA credentials."

"They can't break in? Come on; they got into the NSA satellites and a few other things," I complained.

"They tried, but the system has safeguards because of concerns over an enemy being able to do just this and locate an agent. Three

227

consecutive failed attempts, and it will erase all the data."

Fuck me, if it wasn't one thing, it was another. I was a little short tempered at the moment but managed to stop myself from snapping at Blanchard. He was just the messenger, not the problem. Then an idea struck me.

"Can I borrow your phone?" I asked.

Blanchard gave me an odd look but handed it over without asking why I wanted it. I had one phone number memorized, and it was the direct line to Jessica's desk. Punching it in, I raised the phone to my ear as it began ringing.

"Lieutenant Hunt," a voice answered, surprising me as I was expecting to hear Jessica's voice.

"Lieutenant, Major Chase. I need to speak with Petty Officer Simmons."

"I'm sorry, sir. She is unavailable. May I be of assistance?"

What the hell did they have her working on? Whatever it was must be a pretty big deal.

"I hope so," I said, suppressing my frustration. "A few days ago she connected me to a phone in Australia. I need to be put through to that number again. Can you do that?"

"I should be able to pull it out of the logs," he said. "But I need to ask who you're calling and why."

I paused for a moment, surprised by the response. Something was up. Had Jessica talked to them about my suspicions of a Russian agent? Or was something else in play? Either way, the man was just doing his job and following protocol, so I told him. Blanchard's eyebrows went up as he listened to my end of the conversation.

"Sir, I'm connecting the call now," Hunt said a few minutes later.

"John?" Lucas Martin's voice came over the phone after a series of clicks.

"Lucas, I need your help again," I said.

"Didn't think you were calling to talk about the weather, mate. What can I do?"

"The CIA officer you pulled out of the listening post for me a few days ago. He still amongst the living?"

"Aye, he is. Stuck him in a deep, dark cell while the bloody politicians figure out what to do with him."

"Can you get to him?" I asked.

"Maybe. Probably. Why? Knocking off the tosser while he's in custody isn't a wise career move," Lucas said with a chuckle.

"Career move? You back with the Regiment?"

"I am, much to my missus displeasure. But you didn't call to hear about my domestic woes. What do you need from him?"

I explained in as brief a version as possible what was going on and what I needed from Steve. There was silence from the other end for a few moments when I finished speaking.

"Bloody hell, mate. This is a tall order. If he figures out there's something we want from him, and he's a smart little fuck so he'll pick up on that right off, it's going to be tough to get it out of him."

"I know you better than that, Lucas," I said, remembering some of the things I'd seen him do in the past.

"Sorry, mate. This isn't the middle of Africa. He's in official custody, and it's going to be hard enough just to get to him. There's no way I can persuade him to cooperate without having something to offer in return. Not unless I want to wind up in the cell next to his," Lucas said, sounding genuinely sorry.

"What if it was your wife, Lucas?"

I sincerely hated playing that card. It wasn't fair. Not even by a long shot. But this was the only chance I had to make sure Katie was found. The odds were stacked against her ever being anything other than a raging infected, but if I could at least make sure she had a shot at treatment...

"There's more you're not telling me," Lucas said, after a long silence.

He was right. I hadn't told him anything about the Russian threat to nuke the last surviving Americans if I didn't hand myself over. If I had the opportunity to search for Katie myself, I wouldn't put him in the position I just had.

"I'm sorry Lucas," I said. "They've delivered some non-negotiable terms, and I'm trying like hell to keep Hawaii from being nuked off the face of the Earth."

"What do you need from him?" He asked after a very long pause.

I told him exactly what was needed and what to do with the information when he had it. He still had the direct line to Jessica saved in his phone, and I made sure he also had Colonel Blanchard's number.

"I'll start working on it right away," Lucas said after an uncomfortable silence.

"Thank you for doing this," I said.

There was a long pause; then Lucas settled for just saying goodbye.

"Goodbye, Lucas," I said and broke the connection.

I handed the phone back to Colonel Blanchard, who had heard my end of the conversation.

"Can he pull it off?" He asked.

"If anyone can, he can," I said.

Turning away, I walked back to where Rachel and Irina were seated on the ground next to the fire. It was snowing again, and they had both scooted closer to the heat. I sat down between them and filled them in on what was going on.

"Both of you should go to Australia. Soon," I said. "I've got some leverage at the moment, and I'm going to call Admiral Packard and make sure you've got transportation. A friend of mine named Lucas Martin will take you

232

in. He's on a big spread in South Australia and has plenty of room."

"I'm not leaving..." Rachel started to say, but I cut her off with a raised hand.

"There's nothing left here for you," I said, looking at her first before turning my head to gauge Irina's reaction. "The country is lost. If you evacuate to Hawaii, you'll always be living under the threat of a Russian nuke. For some reason, Australia has been spared. That could change tomorrow, but for now, it's the last safe place on Earth."

We argued for several minutes, Rachel raising several different objections. None of them swayed my position. Sure, she could go to Hawaii, but how long before Barinov decided to eliminate the last vestiges of America? I was aware of some of the things he'd done as President and didn't disagree one bit with Irina's assessment.

Leaving the warmth of the fire, walking away and ignoring Rachel's renewed argument, I found Blanchard and asked for him to put me in touch with Admiral Packard. He didn't ask why just turned to an aide and nodded. Several minutes later the man handed a sat phone to me, and I spoke to Packard, explaining what I wanted.

He immediately agreed to put the two women on a flight. I thanked him, grateful that he hadn't thanked me for voluntarily surrendering to the Russians. I didn't want his thanks. I just wanted it to be over with.

27

"All clear?" Lieutenant Sam asked over the radio.

He was speaking to the most junior of the SEALs, who was sitting in the buildings security office, monitoring multiple screens which were receiving security camera feeds from the exterior. The man double checked everything in view, switching to several other cameras to perform a final survey of the area.

"Clear. Good to go," he said, continuing to click through the system.

A moment later four figures stepped through a steel security door. They immediately spread into a diamond formation, rifles up and ready as they ran across a broad, sloping lawn. It was dark, and a cold, steady rain made it even darker and masked the sounds of their footfalls on the soggy grass.

At the bottom of the slope was a long dock with two boats tied to it. One was the creaky cruiser that had been taken from the marina near the locks when the SEALs RIB had been damaged while bringing Dr. Kanger to the facility. The other was a sleek, thirty-foot, luxury runabout with inboard engines. It had lots of teak and

shiny details. There was a bet amongst the
SEALs that it had belonged to Paul Allen.

They had performed an exhaustive search
of the research institute, failing to find the keys
for it, but hotwiring a boat was all in a day's work
for them. Reaching the dock, three of the men
remained on it, spread out and keeping watch.
While they scanned the area with their rifles,
Master Chief Gonzales jumped aboard and set to
work. Two minutes later a starter whined, and
the motors rumbled to life.

The three SEALs on the dock collapsed
their formation and stepped onto the boat. The
last one to board, Lieutenant Sam, released the
ropes that held the craft tight to the shore. With
one foot he reached out and gave a small shove,
pushing the boat a few feet out into the lake.

The first two took up station at either
corner of the stern, rifles pointing out. Sam
stretched out on the bow, rifle facing forward.
The Master Chief notched the throttle forward
and steered for open water.

They were moving north on Lake Union, a
small lake surrounded by the urban sprawl of
Seattle. The area had been lit after the Russians
moved in and restored the power grid. One of
the targets of the Tomahawks fired by the Navy
had been the dams in the mountains that
provided hydroelectric power to the city. The

attacks had been successful, denying the occupying enemy access to electricity and plunging the city back into darkness.

The SEALs were equipped with night vision and weren't hampered by the lack of light. They watched as the shoreline slipped by. Marina after marina, some almost empty of boats, others with every slip occupied. A large community of floating houses appeared on their right.

The SEAL responsible for watching that area reported that he could see multiple infected moving on the docks the houses were moored to. They were reacting to the muted sound of the boat's motors but were unable to spot the small craft which was running without lights.

It didn't take long to reach the northern end of the lake, which forked like the top of a Y. The left would take them back to the locks and Puget Sound. The right arm was the one they wanted, the water narrowing into a broad canal as they turned to the east. Ahead, Sam could make out the massive double decked bridge of Interstate 5 that soared nearly two hundred feet above the surface of the canal.

Approaching slowly, he called a halt when an object flashed in his night vision goggles, impacting the water with a loud splash. Whatever it was, had come down only a few yards to their front. Boat bobbing in place, he looked up at the massive steel structure but didn't see anything or anyone. He checked with the two SEALs watching their flanks, both reporting all clear.

Making another scan of the bridge and shoreline to either side, he still didn't spot anything concerning. Motioning to Gonzales, he adjusted the position of his rifle against his shoulder as the boat began moving forward again. They slowly approached the bridge and Sam frequently looked up to check the steel trusses far above his head.

They made it under the bridge without anything else falling into the water. Another older and much smaller bridge appeared in Sam's night vision as they made a bend to the right. This was a drawbridge and appeared to have been built to carry local, neighborhood traffic.

The canal narrowed even more. Dikes had been placed in the channel to direct boat traffic through a small space directly beneath the portion of the bridge that would raise to allow tall-masted sail boats and larger ships to pass.

It was only wide enough for a lane in each direction with low rails on each side. Along the rail facing the approaching SEALs, nearly twenty infected males bumped around trying to locate

Anvil

the source of the sound their motors were making. The Master Chief backed off on the throttle without being told, speaking softly so his radio would let him communicate with the Lieutenant.

"Wanna bet that's what that big ass splash was? One of them fuckers coming off the bridge?"

"No bet," Sam answered.

He was concerned. Even though this new bridge was less than fifty feet above the water, if one or more of the males came over the rail and landed on them it could seriously damage their boat or even sink it. He looked over his shoulder when there was another loud splash from behind.

Night vision let him see the disturbed water where what he now believed was an infected body had fallen. Turning back to the front, he noted that the males were growing more agitated. They pushed up against the railing, which was no more than waist high for most of them.

Looking around and assessing the situation, he wasn't happy. They were going to have to motor under the bridge and hope a two-hundred-pound body didn't slam into them or their boat. They were more than capable of swimming to shore and completing the mission on foot if the boat sank. But the more time they spent on the ground, the greater the chances of running into a large group of infected. Or maybe even worse, a Russian patrol.

"Sit tight," Sam said quietly, sighting in on a shaggy haired male that was leaning over the rail and waving his arms.

Even though his rifle was suppressed, it still made more sound than he liked when he fired and killed the infected. Sam methodically worked his way down the row of infected, taking his time and placing each shot right where he wanted it. Every time he pulled the trigger a male fell dead to the steel lattice of the bridge deck. When the last one dropped, he kept his rifle aimed at the railing for several moments before telling Gonzales to get them moving.

The boat surged forward, the SEAL at the controls giving it more throttle than he had so far. He wanted to get them under the bridge as quickly as possible before more infected arrived. Sam stayed frozen in place; rifle trained and ready to fire in the event another male showed itself. He detected movement, raising his weapon to a steep angle to keep the muzzle aligned with the target area.

Another male appeared and Sam fired instantly, raising up more and shifting left as two more heads popped up. He fired, killing the first one, and was shifting to the second when there was a flash of motion several yards to the side of the pair. A sprinting female screamed as she hurdled the rail.

Sam turned and snapped off two shots, but couldn't tell if they hit home or not. The Master Chief cut the wheel, his quick reaction all that saved them from the falling body. As the boat turned, carving into the water, the female missed, except for her head. It struck the railing only inches from where Sam lay.

Stainless steel bent and fiberglass splintered from the impact, her skull exploding like an overripe melon and splashing hot blood and brains into Sam's face. Gonzales whipped the boat back into a straight line, cutting their speed as soon as they cleared the bridge. Sam pulled his night vision goggles off, spitting and cursing.

"You OK, LT?

"Got the bitch's blood in my mouth," Sam spat over the rail. "Keep going; I'm fine."

The Master Chief gave his boss a look before turning his attention back to driving the boat. The channel widened some and ran straight for a short distance before curving to their left and narrowing to less than a hundred

feet. Another bridge spanned the perfectly
straight canal. Beyond, the water opened out
into Lake Washington, but he cut their speed to
idle when he saw movement on the bridge.

"What's up?" Sam asked, still rinsing
blood off his night vision goggles so he could see.

"Another bridge and there's movement
along the rail," Gonzales said.

"Full throttle," Sam ordered. "You know
how hard it is to hit a fast moving boat. We'll be
through before they can even come over the rail."

The Master Chief shook his head, grinning,
and slammed the throttles to the firewall. With a
bellow of power, the engines spun the propellers
up to full speed, and the boat leapt forward. The
other SEALs had to grab on to anything within
reach to keep from being thrown out of the craft
by the sudden surge of acceleration.

They roared safely beneath the bridge,
Gonzales cutting power as they came out on the
far side. Sam donned his freshly cleaned goggles
and looked behind them. There were several
large splashes as infected fell into the water in
their attempts to reach the boat. He exchanged
glances with the Master Chief then nodded,
telling him to get them moving again.

Speed had been their friend to safely pass
beneath the bridge, but with speed came noise.

Anvil

As they continued to transit the narrow canal, both SEALs, who were watching their flanks reported female infected on the shoreline, following them.

"Engage targets," Sam ordered, knowing the excitement of the females would draw more to the area.

The two men started firing, aiming as carefully and accurately as their Lieutenant had when he cleared the bridge railing. By the time they reached the area where the lake opened out, both were reporting that all targets were down.

The boat made a sharp left, heading north and hugging the shoreline of a small island. Gonzales cut the speed to just above an idle when a second, slightly larger island appeared to port.

It only took a few minutes to reach the north end of the island and a small channel that cut between it and a broad peninsula that stuck out into the lake like a fat thumb. Shutting down the motors, he hand signed to the rest of the team that they were switching to silent. Sam remained prone on the side of the bow deck as Gonzales grabbed a long handled paddle and moved to the point of the bow so he could reach water on both sides of the boat.

Sam and the other SEALs kept a constant scan going, looking for any threats as the Master Chief carefully stroked with the paddle and brought them into the small channel. It was so narrow that branches from trees growing on the adjacent shorelines occasionally brushed the widest parts of the boat's hull. Ahead, the water ended in an indistinct line that was characterized by a dense growth of tall reeds.

He kept them going, letting the momentum of the boat push into the reeds until resistance brought it to a stop. Reaching out, he grasped a handful of the tough plants, holding them in place. Sam raised to his knees to see over the foliage, slowly scanning back and forth. Nothing moved and after a moment, he gave the all clear signal. Tying the boat to the reeds, Gonzales raised his rifle and slid over the edge of the bow.

The cold water reached his chest before his boots came down in thick mud. Sam joined him, and they pushed a few feet into the forest of reeds before stopping and waiting for the rest of the team. Single file, the Master Chief led the way forward. The lake bottom sloped up sharply and in less than five yards he reached the end of the concealment of the thickly growing plants.

Pausing, he scanned, saw nothing moving and continued across a narrow strip of mud and onto an overgrown green lawn. The SEALs behind him quickly moved into the open, again stepping into a diamond formation. Each had an area of responsibility as they moved.

On Lieutenant Sam's order, they moved together, climbing a gentle slope. Reaching the crest, the land flattened in front of them. A large parking lot with a scattering of abandoned vehicles was directly to their front. Beyond the lot was a large sports field.

Careful but fast movement brought them across the parking area, then each of them scaled a low fence that defined the edge of the field. Back in formation, they cut diagonally across the artificial turf, reaching the far edge and climbing over another fence. Ahead was a massive parking lot that extended farther than their night vision could see.

They set off across the asphalt, occasionally adjusting direction to give an abandoned vehicle a wide berth. Following the pavement north, it was almost ten minutes before they came to the exit they were looking for. Stepping through and beyond a row of trees, Sam looked at the hill to their front where the physics laboratory was located.

He could just make out the low, stone building at the limit of his goggle's range. Looking slightly to the left, he made note of two large, multi-story structures. Dorms. Within a stone's throw of the lab. And according to thermal satellite imaging, they were full of infected. He just hoped they were the men's dorms.

28

The SEALs moved silently across the road and into the near total darkness of a heavily forested area at the base of the hill. Two of them fired in near unison, taking down a duo of infected males that were standing next to a large maple tree. They continued moving, nearing the edge of the trees when the point man halted them with a raised fist.

He was known to have the best hearing of all of them, by far, and it was nearly ten seconds later before the rest heard the sound of approaching rotors. Four Russian Havocs and they were coming fast. Without the constant hum and roar of an urban environment to mute them, the noise of the helicopters bounced off the surrounding buildings, growing louder until the machines screamed overhead. They were heading east and were in one hell of a hurry.

Resuming their forward movement, they came out from under the trees and onto a rain-slicked, sloping lawn. Fifty yards up the slope was the edge of the parking lot for the nuclear physics lab. The building wasn't visible from their location, and remaining in their diamond movement pattern, they carefully climbed the hill.

Dirk Patton

Rain was falling steadily, masking any inadvertent sounds they might have made. But it also covered the swift footfalls of the small group of female infected that charged out of the trees when the men came into view. The SEAL responsible for their right flank security spotted them immediately, calling a warning as he began firing his rifle.

The females were close, inside twenty yards when they came into the open, and they were sprinting. The man got off three fast shots, killing two of the females before the remaining five slammed into the group. The other SEALs had turned at the warning, but the attack was so fast that none of them were able to get a shot off before the infected were at hand to hand combat range.

Sam killed a young woman with his knife as Gonzales snapped another's neck with his thick hands. The SEAL on the right flank had been unfortunate enough to have two females tackle him to the ground, and one had succeeded in locking her teeth on his throat and tearing it open. He lay on the ground, legs twitching as blood fountained out of his damaged artery.

The SEAL on the rear rolled down the slope and disappeared into the trees, a female at least as large as he was embracing him as if they were lovers. Sam killed another infected with a quick knife thrust to her heart, turned and raced

248

down the hill as Master Chief Gonzales battled with the final attacker. She was small, no more than five feet tall, and Gonzales met her with an extended arm and open hand.

He grasped her neck as she charged in, lifting her off her feet. Twisting his hips, he gripped one of her flailing legs and raised her over his head. Turning, he drove the female into the ground, head first, her neck snapping like a twig from the brutal impact. Glancing in the direction his two surviving team mates had gone, he took a moment to scan the area for other threats.

The sound of a suppressed rifle came from the trees and a moment later Lieutenant Sam emerged. Meeting Gonzales' eyes, he shook his head. The Master Chief cursed silently as he turned and continued scanning their surroundings. Their first encounter with a small group of females and they lost half the team.

"We'll get them on the way back," Sam mumbled.

He was referring to the bodies of their two fallen brothers. Gonzales didn't like leaving them laying on the ground even to complete their mission, but losing teammates was nothing new, and they didn't have any other choice. With a nod, he turned and began climbing the slope again. Sam stayed five yards behind him and kept a close eye on the trees at the bottom of the hill.

They reached the parking lot without further attacks. Pausing at the edge of the pavement, both men dropped to a knee to perform a careful scan of their target. The stretch of asphalt wasn't large, no more than fifty yards across. At the far edge squatted a sprawling, two story building constructed of brick. There were no windows visible on the front, only a pair of glass doors protecting the entrance.

Sam already knew they were ballistic glass and only opened into a small vestibule. Inside, a small security desk took up nearly half the space. It was set up for staff and visitors. They would check in before being buzzed through a heavy steel door.

There was only one other entrance or exit from the building, a large rolling door at the loading dock on the back wall. All other doors had been sealed, the Department of Homeland Security citing national security reasons to ignore the fire codes that required emergency exits.

Of the two entrances, they had decided access through the front would require less time and explosives. The glass doors were controlled by powerful electro-magnets. The hope was the electricity had been off to the building long enough for the backup generator that came on automatically in the event of a power failure to have run out of fuel. There were battery banks to bridge the gap between loss of power and restoration from the generator, but they lasted for fifteen minutes at best.

The two SEALs dashed across the parking lot, heads swiveling as they watched for infected. Reaching the glass doors, they paused as the Master Chief tried to see through them with his night vision goggles while Sam turned and watched their backs. He couldn't see through the glass and would have to clear the vestibule the hard way. Grasping the steel handle, Gonzales gently tugged, testing the lock.

The door moved easily, and he pulled it fully open. Bracing it with his shoulder he looked into the small space, rifle tracking in sync with his eyes. Nothing moved, but the stench of a rotting body made him grimace and breathe through his mouth.

The corpse of a security guard was half behind the armored desk. It had been there a while, the torso having swollen from the gasses of decomposition, eventually rupturing and spilling putrid fluids across the floor.

"Clear," Gonzales mumbled, moving into the vestibule.

He ignored the corpse and stepped up to the steel doors guarding the interior of the building as Sam came in behind him and silently pulled the glass door shut. Using a thick, nylon flexi-cuff, he secured the doors by looping it through the handles and pulling it tight. Nothing would get in, and to get out all they'd have to do is quickly swipe a sharp knife across the cuff, and it would part and release the doors.

"Too quick, LT," Gonzales said when he saw what Sam had done. "Gotta blast and we don't want to be in here when the C-4 goes boom."

"Shit," Sam muttered, drawing his knife.

Cutting the nylon, he pushed the door open and stepped through, keeping watch while the Master Chief worked. He had prepped his breaching charges before they left the institute and it was only a matter of a few moments of work to locate where he wanted to attach them, then insert the detonators.

"Ready," he said when he pushed back out into the rain with Sam.

The two men moved to either side of the glass doors and placed their backs against the brick wall. Gonzales activated the remote trigger, lifted the protective gate that covered the "fire" button and pressed it with his thick thumb.

Anvil

There was a low crump of sound, and the two glass doors pushed open a foot from the pressure wave.

Gonzales grabbed one of them before it could swing shut and slipped back into the vestibule. It only took a moment to verify the locking mechanism had been blown out of the steel doors. He called the all clear to Sam and stood waiting by the breached entrance as the Lieutenant put a fresh flexi-cuff on the glass doors.

When the outer doors were secure, the two SEALs stacked up and carefully pushed the large steel door on the right open a few feet. Nothing leapt at them, and Gonzales kept pushing until it swung fully open. At a tap from Sam, he moved, the Lieutenant tight against his back until they were through the opening. Separating, each man scanned a large lobby, seeing nothing alive.

Satisfied the immediate area was clear of threats, the Master Chief led the way to the closest door. He had no idea where they were going, but they had to start somewhere. Reaching the door, which was made of a thick slab of laminated wood, he noted the dark keypad that restricted access.

"Nuclear physics lab, right?" He mumbled to Sam.

"Yeah, why?"

"Just wondering if they had any experiments going when the shit hit the fan. You know, uranium or plutonium or some nasty shit that's going to zap us as soon as we walk in."

"Afraid of a little radiation, Master Chief?"

Sam noticed the sweat beading the man's brow. Then realized he was sweating too. He knew enough about radiation exposure to scare him. All things considered, he'd rather go back outside and fight a whole herd of infected.

"Just thinking about the cojones, sir," Gonzales said, reaching out and pulling the door open.

A long hallway stretched out ahead of them. Several doors were spaced along it at uneven intervals. Not seeing any threats, they moved into the hall, and Sam kept a hand on the door, so it closed softly.

There were no decaying bodies in the area, and both men breathed deeply even though the smell of rot had clung to their clothing and come into the untainted air with them. Hugging opposite walls, they moved deeper into the building, the soles of their boots nearly silent on the polished tile.

Anvil

For a moment, Sam had forgotten they were in a university, not a government building. He was pleasantly reminded when they came to the first door and after clicking on a small flashlight he was able to read a plaque that clearly labeled the room's purpose. Government and military buildings typically only assign a number to a room, and if you don't know what you're looking for and don't have a directory, you're screwed.

There's good reason for this. It helps with keeping the facility more secure. But it's a bitch if you don't know your way around. A university, on the other hand, has a new batch of students showing up every year, and those students need to be able to find their way around. So buildings, rooms, and offices are normally well labeled. And that was the case here.

The first door was a private office for the lab director. No need to even open the door. Moving on, they cleared three restrooms, one for men, one for women and one for families.

They passed another office, a lecture hall and two storage rooms. Forcing the doors to the storage, they made a quick scan of the contents but quickly moved on when all they found were office and classroom supplies. The hall ended at a blank wall, and they went back to the lobby, carefully entering in case anything had shown up while they were out of the area.

Three more doors opened off the space, two of them leading to identical looking hallways, the third to a staircase that accessed the second floor of the building. They checked the other two halls, only finding more offices and several large lecture rooms. No labs.

"Upper floor," Sam mumbled as they moved back into the lobby.

Gonzales nodded, and they moved into the stairwell. Climbing slowly, they moved sideways, rifles up and trained on the second-floor landing. Passing through the door at the top of the stairs, they entered a large vestibule with two doors opening from either side.

"We're in the right spot," Sam pointed at both doors.

He used his light to read the plaques bolted to the wooden surfaces. The signs read "*Fission Research Labs*". Beneath it was a prominent radiation hazard symbol and another sign that stated: "*TLD BADGES REQUIRED BEYOND THIS POINT*".

Gonzales nodded. He was familiar with dosimeter badges worn by people who work in proximity to radiation, such as an X-Ray tech in a hospital or anyone working near the nuclear reactor on an aircraft carrier. The badges were used to monitor a person's cumulative exposure to radiation over a period of time.

"Good lock," he mumbled, dropping to a knee in front of the left-hand door and reaching into his pack for a breaching charge.

Sam checked the other door while Gonzales worked. The right side door was also secured with an additional label that read "*Materials Storage*". When he reached out and tried the handle, there was an immediate thump from the far side of the door, followed by loud pounding.

He jumped back, his rifle snapping up as he moved far enough away to fight if something came through into the vestibule. Gonzales had stopped what he was doing, spinning and raising his rifle in response to the sounds. When it became apparent the door wasn't going to open; Sam told him to continue with his work.

"Ready," the Master Chief said a moment later.

Sam turned to take shelter from the blast in the stairwell, pausing when he heard more than thumping coming from the far side of the door. He took a step closer, turning his head to align his ear and hear better.

"Hear that?" He said softly.

Gonzales moved to stand next to him, also turning his head to find the best angle to try and hear what the Lieutenant was talking about. Both men listened carefully for several moments before the Master Chief shook his head.

"All I hear is pounding, LT."

"Thought I heard a voice," Sam said, finally shaking his head and following Gonzales into the stairwell.

The breaching charge cleanly blasted the lock free of the door. The two SEALs quickly came out of the stairs and stepped up to the opening. Sam noted the door was very thick, mounted on six heavy hinges and two additional pivot support arms. A half-inch layer of lead was sandwiched between two layers of solid wood.

Beyond was a broad hall with half a dozen doors. Each was a lab, labeled A through F. A and B had thick, leaded glass windows adjacent to their door which allowed observation from the hall. As they moved through the opening, Gonzales glanced to his right and held up a hand to stop.

Two large, open front cabinets held a variety of equipment. From a rod mounted to the wall, a dozen full body radiation suits were on hangars. Sam thumbed the switch for his light, quickly scanning all of the gear. He stopped the light moving, shining it on a two-inch diameter, bright red button set into a stainless steel plate and sticking out from the wall.

"It's an emergency response station," he said.

Shifting position, he peered at the screen on a piece of equipment attached to the wall beneath the alarm button. It was dark, coming to life when he touched it. The display showed several different values, another string of number scrolling across the bottom. Looking closer, Sam recognized it was a sophisticated Geiger Counter, used to measure the radiation levels in the lab.

"How bad?" Gonzales asked, recognizing the device.

"Not bad. Inside," Sam said, gesturing at the lead lined door. "And we've got everything we need right here."

He opened an empty duffel brought just for this purpose. Folding the radiation suits, he stuffed them inside while Gonzales kept watch. A large bottle of potassium iodide pills went in as well as a smaller Geiger Counter.

"Think we should put these on before we go back outside?" Gonzales asked.

Dirk Patton

Sam paused, considering the idea. He didn't like the thought of wandering around in a radioactive environment with no protection, but the suits would restrict their movement and interfere with their hearing and vision. And they wouldn't protect them from all the nasty Alpha, Beta and Gamma rays that could be bouncing around. All they would do is prevent radioactive dust, debris, and rain from coming in contact with their skin, or being inhaled as they breathed.

"Let's see what the levels are when we go out," he said, jamming more equipment into the bag before closing it up.

Gonzales helped him lift and position it on his back. Once it was in place, Sam tightened the straps, bounced it a couple of times to get a more comfortable fit and tightened again. With what they came for, the two SEALs moved back into the vestibule and headed for the stairwell.

The pounding from the far side of the other door had stopped, and it took Sam a moment to realize the significance of the absence of the noise. Pausing, he signed for Gonzales to stay quiet before walking over to the far side of the room. Carefully, he leaned in and pressed his ear against the smooth, cool surface. He didn't hear anything, but if this door also had a thick, lead core he didn't think he would.

260

Anvil

He reached for the heavy lever that controlled the lock, Gonzales giving him a look that said he thought the LT was crazy. Sam hadn't fought a lot of infected, but he'd been around them enough to learn that they didn't give up. If there was an infected inside, why had it stopped pounding on the door?

Grasping the handle, he jiggled it to make noise that would be clearly audible on the other side. A few moments passed in near perfect silence; then the steel lever moved slightly as it was pushed from the inside. Sam jerked his hand away like he'd received an electric shock, but kept his ear pressed against the wood. Very faintly he could hear a female voice crying out for help.

29

Jessica breathed a sigh of relief when the third layer of encryption fell. She had been working non-stop for several hours in her effort to break in to the Thor System and now had only a final security measure to defeat. But it would be the most difficult as she had already determined it contained a rolling algorithm that would re-encrypt itself with a new key every six hours.

Opening a new window on her terminal, she typed in a command. Leaning forward to view the lines of text that scrolled across the screen, she nodded when it told her what she already suspected. A new key would be generated in seventy-three minutes.

There wasn't enough time to crack the system before the security refreshed itself and she would have to start over from the beginning. Even a six-hour window was tight, and she wasn't at all sure she would be able to complete her work in that timeframe. But it was a much greater possibility than only seventy-three minutes.

Looking around, she noted the Marine guard assigned to watch her. He was standing ramrod straight next to the exit; hands clasped behind his back as he kept his eyes focused on her. The man hadn't moved in hours. Hadn't shifted his feet, rolled his shoulder or even scratched his nose. She knew because she had been keeping half an eye on his reflection in one of her monitors that wasn't in use.

Jessica wanted a cigarette and a change of scenery. She was reaching for her keyboard to lock her terminal when her cell phone beeped. The cellular networks in Hawaii were still up and running, to some degree. There wasn't a civilian internet or email any longer, and Facebook, Instagram, and Twitter were things of the past.

But local calls that could be routed by the switching equipment located on the islands would still go through. So would text messages. Picking up her phone, Jessica was surprised to see it was a message from Mark asking if she could take a break.

A wave of heat flushed through her when she saw the words on the small screen. Why wasn't he in custody? He should be sitting in an interrogation room with the Commander from NIS and a criminal investigator from NCIS. They should be grilling him about passing secrets to the Russians. But he was obviously running around, free as a bird, without a care in the world.

She almost dropped the phone when it beeped again. This time, it was a photo with no message, but she understood his intent. It was a pic he had snapped of the two of them engaged in sex. Jessica was on top as he lay on his back and captured the expression of ecstasy on her face while they coupled.

Anger surged through her belly, spreading into her limbs until they quivered. The son-of-a-bitch! The motherfucker had used her and was still trying. Thought all he had to do was throw a few good fucks into her, and she'd come running whenever he called. Tell him secrets.

With a profound sense of despair, Jessica acknowledged that was exactly what had happened. She had avoided romantic entanglements for a long time, focusing on her budding career with the Navy. She'd had plans to put in her twenty years, building a skill set and reputation that would land her a high-paying job in the private sector when she retired in her late 30s.

But Mark and his Russian masters had smashed that dream. There were no civilian jobs any longer. No civilian world she cared to be a part of. For that matter, if they survived, there wasn't even retirement to look forward to. Just more of the struggle to live that was now the new normal.

Anger returned, and with it came cold calculation. She knew that she was on borrowed time. The only reason she had any freedom was there was no one else with the skills to complete the job she was doing. What would happen when she finished? Interrogation? Jail, or worse? Did they really think she was a traitor? And in this new world, did anyone have the time or resources to keep someone branded a traitor alive?

Jessica was angry, but she was also a patriot. The Navy was a means to an end, but she had enlisted because she genuinely felt a calling to serve her country. Maybe she wasn't one of the warriors out there shooting a rifle or flying a combat mission, but her job was just as vital to the security of the United States, perhaps even more so.

She might be going down for having let her carnal desires cloud her judgment, but she wasn't going down alone. If the Navy wasn't going to do anything about Mark, she was. Securing her station, she stood and walked to Lieutenant Hunt's console.

"Yes, Petty Officer?"

He didn't bother to look up. Jessica did her best to ignore the cold demeanor of the normally warm and open man.

"Sir, the system is going to regenerate keys in seventy minutes. There's no point in me starting until then, so I'd like to take a break. Get some chow and a shower."

Hunt looked up, staring at her for several uncomfortable moments. Finally, he looked across the room and motioned the Marine guard over to where he sat.

"Sir?"

"Corporal, escort the Petty Officer to her personal quarters so she can shower, then the mess hall. After that, straight back here," Hunt ordered.

"Yes, sir," the Marine snapped.

He remained at attention for a moment, then stepped back and gestured for Jessica to lead the way. With a sigh, she grabbed her purse and phone as she walked by her station, the Marine close on her heels. As they rode up in the elevator, she texted a reply to Mark, telling him to meet her in the mess hall in half an hour.

Walking into the fresh air outside the building, Jessica almost faltered in her steps when she realized they hadn't taken her phone. That didn't make sense. One of the first things they should have done was to cut off her communications with anyone. But she still had it and had even used it in full view of her guard, who had not so much as blinked to see it in her hands.

Anvil

Was it an oversight? No, the Navy was many things, but they weren't incompetent. Were they hoping she'd use it to contact someone and give herself away? What was the term? Stalking horse. Was that it?

Not seeing how she could use it to her advantage, Jessica walked quickly across the base towards the large building where she shared a room with another female Petty Officer. She smoked a cigarette as she walked, thinking about what she was going to do.

Jessica showered quickly, her long hair tucked under a shower cap. Body clean, she dressed in a fresh uniform and checked her look in the mirror. Satisfied that she was squared away, she grabbed her purse and opened the door to find the Marine Corporal waiting patiently.

"How do you do that?" She asked as they began the walk to the mess hall.

"Do what?"

"Just stand there, not moving. Not talking. Waiting patiently. I couldn't do that."

"I'm a Marine," he said, feeling that was all the explanation necessary.

Jessica shook her head, not understanding and not in the mood to try. It was a long walk to

267

the mess hall, and she moved slowly. Stopping, she lit a cigarette, suppressing a smile when the Marine moved upwind away from the smoke.

"Can I ask a favor?"

She had started walking again. The Corporal just looked at her, not speaking.

"When we get to the mess hall, would you please wait outside for me? I don't want my boyfriend to find out what's going on. Not yet, anyway."

Jessica looked up at the much taller man as she made her plea.

"I can't do that," he said. "My orders are to keep you in sight at all times."

"Did you watch me shower?"

Jessica put a little something in her voice when she asked the question. The Marine blushed slightly but didn't waiver.

"No, but I was right outside the door, and there wasn't anywhere for you to go," he said. "The mess hall has more than one door."

"You think I'm going to run? Afraid I'll outrun you?" She teased.

"You won't outrun me," he said, unamused.

Anvil

Jessica sighed, recognizing that making the man uncomfortable had been the wrong approach. She slowed slightly, puffing on her cigarette.

"OK, how about this. We go in together, but not like we're together. Like two people that don't know each other and just happened to arrive at the same location at the same time. You keep an eye on me from somewhere else in the room, but like you don't know me. Can you do that? Please?"

Jessica came to a stop and looked up into his eyes as she said the last. He looked back at her for several moments, finally sighing and looking away.

"I guess that doesn't violate my orders," he said. "But if you try to get away, I'll drag you back in cuffs. Understand me?"

"Thank you," Jessica smiled, resisting the urge to rise up on her toes and kiss his cheek. "I'll behave. I just don't want my boyfriend to know until I'm ready to tell him."

The Marine nodded, and Jessica picked up the pace for the rest of the walk to the mess hall. They entered together, the guard holding the door for her and peeling off to a mostly empty section of the large, open space. Jessica looked around, spotting Mark seated by himself at a large table on the far side of the room.

He was sitting with his back to the wall and had already seen her. She walked over to him, smiling despite the revulsion and anger that were threatening to overwhelm her. Taking the seat next to him, she allowed him to briefly take her hand underneath the table.

"Why here," he complained. "I can't even kiss you here."

"There're other things we can do here," Jessica said coyly.

Turning in her seat to face him, she placed her hand on his leg and slid it up into his crotch. Mark jumped slightly, not expecting the intimate touch in a public location.

"What are you doing?" He gasped as she squeezed his quickly stiffening penis.

"Having fun," Jessica said.

She squeezed him again, hard, then found his zipper and pulled it down. Reaching in the opening, she worked her hand through his underwear and grasped his now fully erect cock. Roughly, she pulled it through his fly, continuing to stroke it.

"Jess..." he said, trying to maintain his composure.

"Shhhh. Hold still," she whispered, leaning down as if she were going to take him in her mouth.

Jessica's right hand slipped inside her purse as she continued to stroke Mark's cock. She had positioned her head so that when she withdrew a small dagger she had retrieved from her quarters he was unable to see the danger. Her first strike was lightning quick, to the inside of his thigh. She severed his femoral artery, but the knife was so sharp the pain didn't register in his brain.

Then, grasping the end of his penis, she slashed with the razor sharp blade. There was little resistance as the appendage came free from his body. Hot blood spurted across her face, dripping from her hand and chin as she held the severed penis up for him to see.

"Dos Vedanya, bitch," she hissed in his face.

30

"Is it time?" I asked when Colonel Blanchard appeared out of the darkness.

I was sitting on a scrounged poncho in the snow, leaned against a large rock. Rachel was snuggled against me, my arm around her shoulders. Irina sat a few feet away, but none of us had been talking. We were just sitting, staring into the flames of a small campfire. We'd been that way for several hours.

I was exhausted and hungry but was too tired to sleep and had too much on my mind to worry about food. Rachel and Irina had tried to share an MRE, but neither had much of an appetite. Rachel and I had argued, at length, but she hadn't changed my mind.

"No," he said, and I thought I detected something in his voice. "Come with me."

I gently pried myself free of Rachel and got to my feet. Blanchard led the way to one of the tents. When I followed him inside, I recognized the wiring embedded in the fabric. This was a portable SCIF or Sensitive Compartmented Information Facility. The wiring was part of a system that blocked electronic eavesdropping. On the modern battlefield, this was about the only way commanders could have a conversation that was guaranteed to be private.

"What's going on?" I asked.

"I just got off the phone with Admiral Packard," he began, dropping into a folding chair and waving me to take a seat. "It sounds like they have a regular Lifetime Movie going on at Pearl. Petty Officer Simmons is under suspicion of espionage, and now she's being charged with murder. But she's still working."

"What?" Was all I could manage to say.

"Long story short. She came forward and confessed to telling her boyfriend, a Chief Petty Officer, about the help she was giving you. Apparently she told him enough for him to pass it on to the Russians. That's how they kept showing up whenever you changed locations. She claims it was innocent, but Naval Intelligence isn't sold."

"For what it's worth, I believe her," I said, deciding it was time to come clean. "Actually, I'm the one that gave her a heads up there was a problem."

Blanchard stared at me for a long pause before shaking his head.

"Colonel Crawford was right. You are a pain in the ass," he said.

"By the way, where is the Colonel?"

"You don't know," Blanchard said, sadness passing across his face.

"What happened?"

"He made it to Seattle after the Russians captured the ladies. Linked up with the SEALs securing the research facility, but decided to stick his thumb in the Russians' eye. The SEALs helped him make a pair of limpet mines, and he went to the waterfront and sank their flagship and a destroyer. He didn't come out of the water."

I sat there speechless, knowing the look on my face mirrored the one of loss on Blanchard's. Colonel Crawford had been one of those leaders, and there are damn few of them, that you would follow to hell and back. He was just one of that rare breed that inspired that level of loyalty in the men under his command.

"What about Igor and Dog," I asked when I was able to speak.

"Igor called it a war. Stayed back and took up residence in a house in the mountains overlooking Seattle. Dog is with him. They're safe, for the moment."

"For the moment?"

Anvil

"The Russian flagship the Colonel sank was Peter the Great. Nuclear powered. The reactor core was breached and is sitting right next to downtown Seattle. That and the Navy engaged the Russians off the Pacific coast. It went nuclear. Fallout is spreading towards the region. We don't know how bad, but the SEALs are getting some gear to keep tabs on it."

"We need to go get them," I said, already trying to work out how I was going to get to Seattle and pull Igor and Dog out to safety.

"For the moment, they're OK," Blanchard said. "If the SEALs have to move I'll make sure Igor gets evac'd. There's more. There's a chance to turn this around."

I shook my head, not understanding what he was talking about.

"The Petty Officer. The murder she's being charged with is the boyfriend. She cut his dick off."

"She did what?" I asked, stunned.

"Cut it off. Sat in the mess hall giving him a hand job under the table. Got him nice and hard, then leaned over and sliced it off. Also got his femoral artery. He bled out before they got him into surgery."

"Holy shit," I breathed. "But wait a minute. You said she's still working."

"She is. Admiral Packard is beside himself, but apparently she's the only person who can get through the security into some mystery system. Before the attacks, there were supposedly about a dozen people in the world that could have pulled off the hack. Now, as far as we know, she's all that's left. The Admiral doesn't have a choice. And, she got in half an hour ago."

"What is it?"

"Don't know. The Admiral won't tell me, and frankly I don't want to know. Not sitting here, with the Russians just a few miles away. What he did tell me is that if we can get it operating, we can counter Barinov's threat. That means you don't go to the Russians and Hawaii doesn't get nuked."

Blanchard sounded hopeful, but I'm a little older and little more jaded.

"What do you mean "if we can get it working"? I thought Jessica had gotten in."

"She did. But the system was still under control of the contractor that built it. Hadn't been signed off yet. So, while she's in, she can't control it. Not without the software. To do that, we have to get into the contractor's servers and transfer the operating system. And it's offline," Blanchard said.

Besides being a little more jaded when you get older, you also learn to recognize when someone is leading up to something they want you to do.

"Where's the contractor?" I asked.

"Salt Lake City," Blanchard said.

"Are you fucking kidding me?" I blurted. "That's where the goddamn Russians sent all the infected they pulled out of the west coast cities."

"I'm not kidding," Blanchard said, shaking his head. "And you're right. There's over five million infected, all within a ten-mile radius of the center of the city. We don't know if this is just a coincidence, or if the Russians know what's there and are trying to make sure we can't get to it."

"A small nuke would take care of that," I said.

"For some reason we don't understand, Barinov wants North America. Wants it as unspoiled as possible. Maybe it really is just a coincidence."

I shook my head. No way was this a coincidence. Whatever this was, this weapon or

Dirk Patton

weapons system, I was willing to bet the
Russians knew all about it. The mystery a few
days ago had been why were they drawing huge
herds of infected into Salt Lake City. Now the
mystery was solved. Or maybe I was giving them
too much credit. If they knew enough to send the
infected, why do that and not just go in and
capture or destroy it? They certainly had the
troops available and in close proximity.

"OK, doesn't matter if they knew about it
or not. What's it going to take to activate it? And
how do we keep them from figuring out what I'm
doing and dropping a bomb on my head?"

"What you're doing?"

"You're not telling me all this just to keep
me entertained," I said sarcastically.

Blanchard leaned back and grinned. He
looked at me for a moment before standing and
moving to the tent door. Pulling the flap open he
stuck his head out and said something. Stepping
back in, an Air Force Captain followed with an
open laptop. Pulling a portable table in front of
me he placed the computer on it and began
briefing me on the facility in Utah.

31

Thirteen hours. That's how much time I had left to pull this off. I was in a Black Hawk helicopter, sitting on the deck with the back of my head resting against a vibrating bulkhead. We were screaming along a few thousand feet in the air, having just left Mountain Home Air Force Base after a quick refueling. We were heading for Salt Lake City, about 250 air miles to the southeast.

Several helicopters had made the flight to the base, one of them peeling off and heading into town to try and convince Titus to leave his bunker and be available for the virologists. I would have liked to go with them to talk to him. Convince him to help. I also wanted to know how he'd taken out the sniper that had me pinned down in the park, letting me escape from the Russians.

But the clock was ticking, and I had a job to do. If I didn't get it completed in time, well… to put it in no uncertain terms, I was fucked. Just under thirteen hours from now I'd be in Russian hands. To make matters worse, if Barinov wasn't already holding a grudge, I'd royally pissed them off over the past few days.

Rachel and Irina had been with me for the short hop to the air base. They were catching a ride on a C-130 that was transporting wounded back to the Bahamas. Once there, they would lay over for a couple of days, waiting to see what happened. If I did my job, and whatever the Thor System was actually worked and prevented the Russians from bombing us, they'd fly to Hawaii and eventually on to Australia.

We had all climbed out of the helicopter while it was being fueled. Irina had embraced me tightly, kissed each cheek as she liked to do, and walked away without saying a word. I appreciated her goodbye. I'm not one for drawn-out, emotional parting scenes. But I didn't get off easy with Rachel.

When Irina headed for the plane, Rachel fell against me, wrapping her arms around my waist and burying her face in my chest. She was crying and didn't want to let go. I wished there was something I could say that would comfort her, and me but nothing came to mind. All I could do was hold her tight and try to control my own emotions at the sense of loss.

When the Black Hawk crew chief shouted that the aircraft was ready to go, I had to gently pry Rachel's arms from around me. I took half a step back, maintaining my grip on her upper arms, so she didn't try to wrap me up again.

Anvil

"I hope you find Katie and she can be saved," Rachel said, sniffing back tears. "I'll be waiting for you. Or both of you. Just be safe."

I looked into her red-rimmed eyes, fighting to maintain my composure. Leaning forward, I kissed her on the lips, softly, letting it linger for a moment.

"Thank you for everything," I said when I broke the kiss.

Rachel looked at me for a beat, fresh tears flowing, then turned and began walking towards the C-130. After only a few steps she broke into a run. I would have stood there watching until she was on board, but the crew chief shouted again. Taking a deep, shuddering breath, I jogged to the helicopter and jumped aboard.

Finding some open space on the floor, I sat down and stared at my boots as the pilot lifted off. Distressed. Heartbroken. Emotionally wrung out. Those were all the things I was at the moment, and that wasn't good. I needed my head in the game, or the already slim odds of pulling this off would drop to about zero.

I was making this trip on a wing and a prayer. No one outside of Pearl Harbor knew anything about whatever type of weapon or defensive system this was. Not that I blamed them. Too much information had already been slipped to the Russians. There was no point in widening the circle of people that knew the secret. I didn't need to know anything more than what I already knew to complete my job.

My body was tired, wanting sleep, but my mind was racing with concern for Katie and angst over sending Rachel away. How the hell had I managed to fall in love with two women? Before Katie, there had been plenty, but they hadn't been anything more than a momentary distraction. For not the first time, I reminded myself of how much alike they were, trying to salve my guilt for having feelings for a woman other than my wife.

"You OK, Major?"

It was Dutch, sitting a few feet away and staring at me with a concerned look on his face. I met his eyes, forcing down my feelings, and nodded.

"Just fucking great," I growled.

I was in no mood to discuss my situation and didn't like the fact that I'd let the façade crack open far enough for someone else to see my pain. But he was right to ask. His ass was on the line, just like the rest of the men coming with me. If one of us was distracted, it could mean failure which would mean death.

Anvil

Looking around, I mentally ticked off each man that was in the helicopter with me. I'd had about half an hour with them before leaving the front. All but one were Rangers, so I knew they'd had the training and experience to do the job we were going to do. But I didn't know the men. Each would have unique strengths and weaknesses, and what makes a team truly effective is when the leader knows the capabilities of the men under his command.

To achieve that requires lots of time spent together. Training. Fighting. Bonding. We hadn't had that, and I was as unknown to them as they were to me. But it was what it was. Not only do you fight with what you have, *you fight with whom you have*, I reminded myself.

In addition to Dutch, there were three more Rangers sitting on the deck of the helicopter, two Sergeants, and a Staff Sergeant. Farthest from me was the Staff Sergeant. He was a huge, blocky blonde guy from Minnesota named Brooks. He reminded me of a young Dolph Lundgren. I guess I wasn't the first to think that as everyone called him Drago, after the Russian fighter played by Lundgren in one of the Rocky movies.

To his right, Sergeant Rodriguez from Miami. Chico. A first generation American and the only son of Cuban refugees. Short, big shoulders and hands that looked like they could crush anything they grasped into pulp. His arms were covered in tattoos that almost disappeared against his bronze skin. He was already asleep, head back as he snored loud enough to be heard over the Black Hawk in flight.

Finally, there was Tayvon James. TJ. He was a tall, almost painfully thin black man from Houston. He had played college basketball for Rice University and had been drafted by the Miami Heat. He turned them down and joined the Army instead.

His story bothered me at first. Turning down a multi-million-dollar contract with an NBA team to earn a few hundred dollars a month wasn't something you heard about every day. The last thing I wanted was to have someone along who was looking to prove themselves. I needed confident, motivated warriors.

Dutch had allayed my concerns when he explained that TJ's father had been killed in the opening days of the first Iraq war. His mother found out she was pregnant with him the same day his father died.

One man was along for the ride that wasn't a Ranger. He was a young Air Force Lieutenant named Edwards. Short, thin and soft looking, he was our nerd and would handle the computers and comm gear once we got inside the building. He sat a little to the side, by himself, eyes closed. Nervous sweat stained his shirt.

He was about as far from his comfort zone as he could be. He lived in big, dark, air-conditioned rooms full of computers, staring at monitors. I doubted he saw the light of day often unless it was time for him to pass his physical testing or certify on the firing range. We'd let him have a pistol, without a round in the chamber, and Drago was assigned to stick with him and ensure his safety. And make sure he kept up.

Then there was Dutch. A First Sergeant. The same in rank as a Master Sergeant, but a step up in responsibility and authority. He was from a large family of Polish immigrants and had grown up in Chicago. He had been in and out of the Middle East almost his entire career and had a total of seven tours between Afghanistan and Iraq. The way the world was headed before the attacks, he'd probably have gotten to visit Iran and Syria before he reached retirement.

Satisfied I had a good team going in with me, I changed mental gears and began replaying the briefing I had received before leaving the front. The Department of Defense contractor was called RWA Systems. I'd never heard of them, but then I'd had other things to worry about in life than staying current on DOD contractors and what they did. They were

285

located near Interstate 15, a few miles north of downtown Salt Lake City in a very large, very secure facility surrounded by acres of asphalt parking lots.

"Here's what I've been able to find out," the Captain who prepped me had said, clicking a button on the laptop to display a series of satellite photos. "Two story building. Total of just over forty thousand square feet. Entrances here, here and here. Interior stairwells here, here, here and here."

With each "here", he pointed at a spot on the overhead shot of the facility. I leaned in for a better view, memorizing each location and going back over it a couple of times before nodding for him to continue.

"First order of business is to restore power," he said, clicking to a new photo. "There are two large, diesel generators here on the north side of the building. They appear undamaged and are likely only out of fuel. Once they are running and supplying power, the computer systems have to be restarted, and comms restored."

He brought up another overhead photo, zoomed onto a section of the roof. Several thousand square feet of space was devoted to an array of satellite dishes, microwave radomes, and UHF antennas.

Anvil

"You know I have no fucking clue how to do any of that," I said.

"Yes, sir. The Colonel informed me you might be technically deficient. I am sending Lieutenant Edwards with you. He works for me and is an IT specialist. You just have to get the power on and get him into the server room. He'll take it from there."

"Do we know where in that monster the server room is?" I asked, looking back at the image on the laptop screen.

"No, sir. You'll have to locate it once you're inside."

"OK," I grumbled, not really surprised at the answer. "Sit tight. I'm going to grab the rest of the team and have you start over from the beginning."

Once I had Dutch and the others gathered, the briefing lasted for another forty minutes. There really wasn't that much the Captain was able to tell us. We were limited to exterior photos of the building. Pre-attack he would have been able to access floor plans and a few thousand other details online, but... Well, that just wasn't an option now.

I spent the rest of the flight thinking about anything other than Katie or Rachel or what would happen when the Russians got their hands on me. Instead, I focused on the loss of Crawford, Martinez, and Scott. Their deaths had hit me hard, Martinez more so. Crawford was my CO and to a degree my friend. Scott was a fellow warrior that I would have done anything to save. But Martinez was family.

"Would you look at that shit!"

I looked up when TJ spoke. He was leaned sideways, peering at the ground below us through night vision goggles. The rest of the men crowded around him, quiet curses being mumbled as they saw what was below us. I stayed where I was. I didn't need to look. I'd seen more herds of infected than I cared to think about.

32

The pilot came in low and fast. We streaked over the heads of a sea of infected, our speed making the writhing bodies blur together in our night vision. A second Black Hawk carrying a fuel bladder of diesel for the generators was two miles behind us. Our pilot would flare into a hover a couple of feet over the rooftop helipad at the RWA building, and we'd all pile out, and he'd be back in motion instantly.

We would have just enough time to make sure the roof was clear of threats and form a perimeter before the second helicopter arrived. This one would actually land, the crew unloading the fuel, some hoses and other equipment while my team provided security. Assuming everything went according to plan, we'd be pulling lines and getting the generators operating within minutes of setting foot on the roof.

Unless we had a problem, like the generators had sucked their tanks dry and wouldn't start because there was air in the lines. Or if they were damaged. Or any of a dozen other things that could go wrong. I was hoping Mr. Murphy of Murphy's Law fame wasn't along for the ride, but the sadistic fucker was probably already planning how to screw with my night.

Dirk Patton

"One minute," the pilot called over the intercom.

Dutch and I were wearing headsets, and he looked around the noisy cabin and shouted the message to the team, holding his index finger straight up in the air. Both side doors were open, cold air flowing in and swirling through the aircraft. I was glad for the layers of fabric protecting me, surprised that Chico was only wearing a sleeveless shirt and battle vest on his upper body.

I checked on Lieutenant Edwards. He looked like he was about to throw up. But I had to give him credit. He was stacked tight against Drago, ready to go out the door the moment he was told. For a cyber-dwelling nerd, he was showing some intestinal fortitude.

"Thirty seconds," the pilot called another warning.

Pulling my headset off, I hung it on a hook, high on the bulkhead. Dutch's joined mine a moment later. I moved to the door on the right side of the helo as Dutch moved to the left. Chico, Drago, and Edwards would follow me out, Dutch and TJ going the other way.

Looking down, I marveled at the sheer number of infected covering the ground. Well, I had to assume there was ground beneath their feet. There were so many of them, pressed so tightly together, I couldn't see anything other than raging faces looking up at the noise of our passage.

A fence flashed beneath us, and I was surprised and encouraged to note it was still standing. We were over one of RWA's massive parking lots, and for the moment at least it was empty of infected. They hadn't had a reason to push against the fence and knock it down, yet, I realized as the helicopter suddenly flared to bleed off speed.

With the Black Hawk's nose up and tail down, the pilot brought us over the edge of the roof and transitioned to a hover. The helipad, painted white with a large, blue "H" in the middle, was right beneath us.

I jumped, dashing ten feet forward as soon as my boots touched the roof. My rifle was up as I dropped to a knee and began scanning for threats.

"Dog one, down and clear," I called over the radio.

"Two, down and clear," Dutch answered a moment later.

The other two team members quickly responded with an all clear, the rotor wash from the helicopter threatening to blast me across the roof like a piece of trash in a storm as the pilot gained altitude and sped away.

"Make room for the gas station," I said, standing and moving forward.

I was on the western edge of the roof, overlooking the large parking lot we'd just flown across. On the far edge, the infected were piling up against the tall, chain-link fence, drawn by the noise of our ride. It wouldn't be long before it collapsed under their constant pressure.

I took a moment to check in with each of the team members over the radio, ensuring the roof was still clear. As I did this, Edwards ran to each of the corners of the helipad and placed IR strobes to help guide the second helicopter. Not that the pilot wasn't capable of landing without them, but every little visual reference helps when you're operating at night.

"Dog one, Sam two-seven," I heard in my earpiece.

"Go for Dog one," I answered the inbound Black Hawk with the fuel on board.

"One minute from LZ. Call status."

"LZ is green. Repeat, LZ is green," I answered, watching in dismay as the western perimeter fence began to bow inwards under the pressure of thousands of bodies.

Anvil

"Sam two-seven copies LZ is green," the pilot answered.

By now the fence was bent inwards at least thirty degrees and only moments from collapsing completely. If the infected rushed in before we got to ground level and started the generators, we had a problem.

"Sam one-niner, Dog one," I called.

"Go ahead, Dog."

"Got any hellfires you can spare?" I asked, watching two females climb over a throng of males, up the angled fence and get tangled in the coils of razor wire lining the top edge.

"Maybe. You wanting to throw a party?"

Everyone's a fucking comedian, and I've always found helicopter pilots are the worst.

"Trying to, but there's a whole bunch of party crashers at the fence. If you could find something about a klick west of the LZ to spark up it might distract them long enough for me to kick the party into gear."

"Copy that, Dog one. Sparking up just for you."

As the pilot answered, he modified his voice and did a pretty good imitation of Cheech Marin taking a hit off a joint. I couldn't help but smile and shake my head, as the fuel carrying Black Hawk came into a hover and set down in the middle of the helipad. The crew was out the door in a flash, struggling to get the heavy bladder onto the roof.

More females were scrambling over the heads of the males, most getting caught in the wire, but a couple dropped to the pavement and began sprinting towards the building. I fired two shots, both of them tumbling to the ground and beginning to crawl in their quest to reach the noise of the idling helicopter.

I hadn't tried head shots as they were still a good distance out, rather had put a bullet into each of their pelves'. This slowed them, and I took my time aiming, drilling first one then the other through the head. In the time it took me to do this, four more topped the fence and charged.

Five quick shots, yes I missed once, put them on the ground. I was opening my mouth to update the team over the radio when there were two sequential flashes of light to the west. Two hellfire missiles being fired. A moment later there was a brilliant flash that lit the night sky and briefly blanked out my night vision.

It took about three seconds for the sound of the explosion to reach my location, and it was brutally loud. Loud enough to have a physical presence, vibrating the organs in my chest and the fillings in my teeth. A massive fireball was forming, boiling into the dark sky and it was hard to tear my eyes off it and check on the infected at the fence. They weren't all leaving, many still with their heads raised and zeroed in on the noisy Black Hawk, but more were turning to head west than were staying.

"Sam one-niner, what the hell did you just shoot?" I asked.

"Truck stop along the Interstate," the pilot chuckled in my ear. "Couple of tanker trucks were just sitting there begging for it."

"It's working," I said, appreciating the man's sense of humor and trying not to think about how much I wished it was Martinez at the controls. "Think you can repeat about a klick north?"

"Thought you'd never ask, Dog. Stand by."

I fired several more shots, putting females down permanently, then glanced over my shoulder to check on the fuel delivery. The large bladder, looking like a fat amoeba, sat on the roof and two crewmen were unloading the last of several reels of hose. Tossing their burden onto the pile of equipment they'd already deposited, they scrambled aboard the aircraft, and a moment later it was airborne.

Checking with the rest of the team over the radio, I was surprised and pleased to find there weren't any other spots where the fence was failing. And many of the infected were moving away now that the helicopters were gone, and there was a very loud and visible distraction in the opposite direction.

It wasn't long before there was another flash of light to my right. I was busily engaged in shooting females who were charging across the parking lot, pausing and looking up. I had time to look back, target and drop another female before the sound reached me. This one, as impressive as it was, wasn't on par with the first.

"You're slipping, Sam one-niner," I grinned into the radio as I pulled the trigger on another runner.

"Propane tank at an RV dealership," he said. "Want me to find something bigger?"

I could tell by his voice that he was enjoying blowing shit up. Hell, who wouldn't? But we didn't need to continue expending missiles, and there was a mission to complete.

"Negative, but thanks for the assist. Stay in the neighborhood in case the natives get restless," I said, shooting another female.

"Copy. Sam one-niner standing by."

Anvil

I swear, when I told him to not shoot anything else, he almost sounded like a kid who just had his favorite toy taken away. For a moment I had a mental image of a little boy standing in the dirt, looking down as he pouted and dug the toe of his shoe into the ground.

"Dog team, let's get busy," I called on the radio. "Three, come to my position and take over."

Dog three was TJ. Dutch had assured me the younger man was the best shot he'd ever seen, and I wanted him keeping the females knocked down as the rest of us worked on getting the generators up and running.

Seconds later the Ranger knelt down next to me, rifle up and a round going downrange before he had even stopped moving. A female climbing over the top of the fence flipped backwards and landed in the slowly thinning throng.

"Showoff," I said.

He grinned without looking up and began squeezing off fast shots. Not hanging around to see the results, I ran to where the team had already gathered around the fuel bladder.

"Edwards, kill the strobes," I ordered as I grabbed a reel of hose and headed for the north end of the roof.

Dirk Patton

I didn't want the strobes left on in case any Russian patrols happened to swing by to check out the two brightly burning fires. It was possible they'd pass them off as something caused by the massive herd of infected. But if they saw IR strobes flashing away on the roof of a building, they wouldn't have to be the smartest of Ivans to figure out Americans were on the ground.

33

The reel of hose was heavy, and I was puffing with exertion by the time I reached the northern edge of the roof. Leaning out and looking down, I spotted two giant generators fifty yards to my right. Trotting to a spot directly over them, I set my burden down and stuck my head over the low parapet. Dutch ran up behind me and dropped a coil of fifty feet of fuel line before grabbing the end of the hose on my reel and dragging it back along the path to the bladder.

With Chico and Drago helping, he would get the hoses laid out and connected. It just so happened I was the most mechanically inclined of the group and had responsibility for getting down to ground level to start the generators. That wasn't necessarily a good thing. I knew about enough to be dangerous.

As Blanchard and I were throwing this whole thing together in record time, I'd had the thought that it would be good to have a diesel mechanic along for the ride. There's plenty of them in the Army, trained to maintain all sorts of heavy engines, but none had made the trip from the Bahamas. Combat troops and aircraft mechanics only.

Dirk Patton

Shrugging out of my pack, I looked around
and spotted a large air conditioning unit a few
yards away. It was really big and probably
weighed well over a ton. Running to it, I secured
a climbing rope to one of the steel struts that
anchored it to the roof, tugging hard to make
sure it was secure. Returning to the edge, I
tossed the coil over and watched it play out and
slap against the ground.

Next, I connected an end of the coiled fuel
line Dutch had delivered to a port in the center of
the reel. Slapping the connector until I was
satisfied it was seated properly, I stood and
looked across the roof. I could see the three
Rangers, along with Edwards, finishing hooking
up the hoses.

"Dog three, one. Status?" I said into the
radio as I waited.

"They're still coming over," TJ answered,
and I heard two suppressed shots over the radio
as he spoke. "Males have mostly pulled away to
the diversions, but females are still pressing in."

"Copy," I said. "Break. Dog two, stay with
three. Everyone else on me."

Dutch acknowledged the order and a
moment later I saw him run to TJ's position as
the others began running across the roof to
where I waited. When they arrived, I told Chico

and Drago to watch the area as I pulled on my pack, picked up the rope and backed up to the parapet.

"What can I do?" Edwards asked, continuing to impress me.

"Feed the fuel line to me when I tell you. And stay glued to him and be safe," I said, nodding in Drago's direction as I stepped over the edge and put my boots against the exterior wall.

The rope was tightly gripped in my hands, and I began walking backwards down the vertical surface. Halfway to the ground, I paused and looked over my shoulder when suppressed rifle fire sounded from the parapet above. One of the Rangers, I couldn't tell which one, had taken out two females who were charging the wall. Glad they were keeping an eye out, I kept moving and stepped onto the smooth concrete at ground level a few seconds later.

I was in a large area that stuck out from the exterior of the building probably thirty feet and was at least as wide. An eight-foot chain link fence surrounded it, protecting the equipment. And me too, I thought as three females slammed against the wire trying to reach me. They were quickly put down by my teammates, and I forced myself to ignore them and focus on the task at hand.

Dirk Patton

The two generators were actually giant diesel engines bolted to the thick slab they rested on. Both were bright yellow, emblazoned with "Caterpillar" across the smooth sheet metal that covered them. Each was taller than me and ten feet long.

Before I bothered to spend time fueling the tanks, I needed to make sure the motors would start. That meant finding an override panel on each to verify their batteries hadn't been drained. The units were wired into the buildings electrical supply from the local utility, equipped to detect a loss of power, or a drop in voltage below a predetermined threshold, from the grid. If that happened, they would automatically start and supply power until whatever had caused the problem was resolved, and electricity was flowing again.

There were likely very large tanks buried beneath my feet that had kept them running for some extended period of time. Certainly long enough to bridge the gap between loss and restoration of power. But the grid hadn't come back on line. That requires human intervention to make sure the few thousand different things that go into supplying power to a city were all in working order. Without the power coming on, the generators had run until they consumed all available fuel.

Anvil

My hope was that these were the more sophisticated units that also monitored the level of diesel in the tank and shut the engine down before it completely ran dry and air was sucked in by the fuel pumps. If that happened, this wasn't going to be easy. A diesel engine that has been run dry to that point can be a bitch to restart. It's not like the gasoline engine in your car that all you have to do is dump in some more and turn the key.

Moving around the exterior of the closest generator, I forced myself to not get distracted by the steady rate of fire from over my head. I didn't think the fence had been breached, so where the hell were the infected coming from? I'd worry about that later. First things first.

I finally located the service panel on the opposite side. It was secured with a simple key lock, and I forced it open with my Ka-Bar, slapping the door out of my way. Raising the night vision goggles off my face, I clicked on a small light and peered at the panel. It was a simple, touchscreen interface with a red and green button beneath, and I couldn't figure out how to get it to come on.

Touching the screen didn't bring it to life. Pushing the buttons yielded the same results. Nothing. I didn't know if it was me doing something wrong or a dead battery. Running to the other generator, I forced the panel open and had identical results. Shit. OK, at least we'd had the foresight to bring a battery with us.

"Dog four, Dog one. I need power," I said to Chico over the radio.

While he ran back to where the helicopter had dropped our equipment, I began checking to see if there was air in the line. Finding the big fuel filter, I cracked open the bleed valve, cursing when nothing happened. Fuel should have come out.

Digging some tools out of my pack, I removed the fuel filter while I called Edwards on the radio and told him to feed the line down to me. Before I hooked up the batteries and tried to start the engines, I needed to prime the system by filling the filters. Hopefully, that would displace enough air for the engines to start. Placing the filter on the ground, I headed for the other generator.

Taking a moment, I lowered my night vision goggles and looked out across the parking lot. There were a large number of dead females scattered around the area, taken down by the Rangers watching over me. Unfortunately, there was an even larger number coming in my direction. Shit on a stick, where were they coming from?

Anvil

I didn't have time to worry about it. Had
to trust the rifles above, and fence around the
area, to keep me safe. Quickly I removed the
other fuel filter and snatched the line off the
ground. Cracking open the valve on the end, I
had to wait for diesel to flow from the bladder on
the far side of the roof. It took a while, the
volume of infected increasing as I fought my
impatience.

Females were slamming against the fence,
and their numbers continued to grow. Drago
was forced to stop engaging them as they
approached, spending all his time just knocking
down the ones that were trying to scale the
barrier that was keeping me alive.

"Battery coming down."

I looked up when I heard Chico's voice in
my earpiece. A large battery taken from a
damaged Hummer was being lowered at the end
of a rope. Turning my attention back to the task
at hand, I was relieved when thick fuel began
running out of the line and into the open end of
the filter. It filled quickly, and I closed the valve
and reinstalled it. Running to the other unit I
repeated the process.

I spent several precious minutes looking
for the fuel tank, not spotting it. Where the hell
would they have put it? Then a bad thought hit
me. They probably wouldn't want to have to

open up the secure area where the generators were located every time they received a fuel delivery. Raising the goggles, I turned the flashlight back on and began searching for the filling point.

When I spotted it, I muttered a string of curses. A long pipe, secured to the wall, stuck up out of the ground ten feet outside the fence. Fuck me. There were about fifty females in the immediate area, and I didn't think they would let me just stroll out and stick the fuel line in the filler tube.

Lucas Martin stood waiting for the first of two security doors to open. It was heavy steel with a small window set at head height. As a loud buzzer sounded, it slid open, and he stepped through, another identical door impeding his progress. Buzzer still assaulting his ears, the door behind him closed with a hard thump.

To Lucas' right was a large, wire reinforced window. On the other side, a man wearing an Australian RAAF uniform watched him, hands resting on the controls for the sally port. He nodded at Lucas and a uniquely different sounding buzzer went off as the second door went into motion.

Foul air immediately flowed through the opening and made Lucas crinkle his nose. Sour sweat, fear, anger, despair and the sharp tang of human urine all mixed together to create the nauseating odor of a prison. Ignoring it, he walked through into a long, well-lit hallway. Behind him, the second door closed with an ominous thud.

Lucas was entering a prison that didn't have a name and didn't officially exist. Known only as "the cottage", it was located deep in the Western Australia desert and was built completely underground. There were no roads and nothing above the surface other than what appeared to be a dilapidated house on an abandoned sheep station.

Numerous air and ground defensive weapons were well concealed in the surrounding terrain. They would engage any vehicle or aircraft that came too close to the entrance unless it had been pre-authorized. Lucas had arrived in an RAAF helicopter that carried the correct transponder codes to allow it to approach and land. It was painted to match a popular helicopter tour company that operated out of Perth and was just part of the landscape to the locals.

After getting off the phone with John, Lucas had started making calls. His CO was the first, and his request had gone up the food chain from there. Only his badgering, by seeking the help of fellow NCOs who could put a bug in their CO's ears, had gotten him permission. And he had received it in record time. He owed his life to his American friend and wasn't going to fail when that man asked for his help.

Walking down the hall, he passed a number of high-security doors that lined each side. They were offset from each other, so when one was open, the occupant could only see a blank wall on the opposite side of the corridor. These were maximum security cells that housed

some of the most dangerous people Australia had
encountered.

None of the doors were labeled other than
by a simple, two-digit number painted in black
on the smooth, battleship grey surface.
Somewhere in the prison were a couple of men
Lucas had been involved in capturing, but he
didn't care about them and wasn't here to renew
old acquaintances. He was here to see the
turncoat American CIA officer, Steve Johnson.

At the far end of the hall, another man in
an RAAF uniform waited for him. Lucas walked
up and held out his ID badge. The man held it
over a tablet computer, waiting as the RFID chip
in the badge was interrogated. A beep sounded
from the tablet, and the man peered at it briefly
before handing Lucas his ID and tapping a series
of commands on the screen. A door to his rear
buzzed and began trundling open. The man
stepped aside and gestured for Lucas to enter.

The room was small, cramped, and very
stark. The floor, walls, and ceiling were painted
bright white. Harsh light from an overhead bank
of recessed fluorescent tubes reflected off every
surface, making Lucas squint when he stepped
through the door. A surveillance camera was
mounted in each corner of the room at ceiling
height, recording everything that was said and
done from four different angles.

The heavy door closed behind Lucas with a solid boom, and he took one step forward and sat in an un-upholstered metal chair. The seat and back were hard and cold, but he didn't notice. Opposite him, across a small metal table that was bolted to the floor, sat Steve.

He was dressed in a fluorescent orange jumpsuit and wore shackles at his wrists and ankles which were connected to a length of chain that encircled his waist. The short length of chain that connected his wrists was locked to a stout metal ring bolted to the seat of his chair.

Steve looked like hell. His face was slack. Black circles darkened the skin around his eyes, which were dull. Defeated. Lifeless. His hair was buzzed close to his scalp, and he was clean shaven and bathed, but Lucas knew that was only due to the strict hygiene rules enforced by the guards.

"Who are you?" Steve asked after several minutes of silence during which he studied Lucas' face.

"I'm no one," Lucas said.

He had worn a mask during the raid when Steve was captured, his face hidden. He didn't continue speaking, letting the uncomfortable silence draw out.

Anvil

"What do you want?" Steve asked, clearly nervous.

"I need you to help me work something out," Lucas said, noting the instant dilation of Steve's pupils.

"What?"

Lucas made a show of opening a file folder and reading its contents. He hadn't brought a file on Steve, didn't need one. The folder had been borrowed from one of the guards that had checked him in to the prison and was full of blank paper Lucas had grabbed out of a printer. He spoke as he turned pages, appearing to read from documents.

"You are Stephen Ridley Johnson. Born in Utica, New York in the United States. And you are an officer of the Central Intelligence Agency. Correct so far?"

Lucas looked up, miming the head position of someone peering over the top of a pair of reading glasses. Steve nodded, audibly swallowing, and Lucas continued.

"You betrayed your country. Made a deal with the Russians. Murdered another CIA officer. Still correct?"

Steve stared at him, the hope that had appeared in his eyes fading as he listened to

Lucas. He didn't acknowledge or deny the accusations.

"The only law you've broken in Australia is committing murder. There's even some doubt about that. The argument is being made that the outpost was technically US soil. Kind of like an embassy. Perhaps you haven't committed any crimes over which Australia has jurisdiction."

Lucas closed the file and placed it on the table in front of him, watching the impact of his words on Steve. Hope flared anew, and he tried to sit straight, coming up against his restraints with a jingle of chains pulling taut against the metal ring.

"What do you want?" Steve asked, his voice sounding strong for the first time.

"Are you familiar with the CIA system that allows activation of beacons embedded in the person of specific officers?"

Steve paused a beat before nodding.

"Can you access the database that holds the codes for each person?"

"Why do you need that?" Steve asked.

"You don't want to be asking questions," Lucas said. "You want to be answering them."

"Why? What do I get out of it?" Steve asked.

"Now that's a good question. But the better question is what do you get if you don't cooperate. The Americans want you back. With what's going on over there, I suspect they don't have the resources to keep you in a nice, safe prison cell. Besides, don't you Americans execute traitors?"

Steve stared at Lucas, Adam's apple bobbing up and down.

"Yes, I can get in," he said after a moment. "But you can't send me back! You're right. They'll execute me. And you said it yourself. I haven't committed any crime in or against Australia. Let me go and I'll help. I'll even leave Australia if you want!"

Steve's voice rose, and he spoke in a rush, grasping for a lifeline he had thought he'd never see.

"First, I need to know you can really do this," Lucas said. "Then we'll discuss what's going to happen with you. Tell me how you would access the database."

"If I tell you how you don't need me any longer," Steve whined, panic spreading through him.

313

"The method," Lucas said patiently. "How would you do it?"

Steve stared back for nearly a minute, trying to evaluate Lucas. Hoping to be able to figure out if this was a genuine opportunity for him to regain his freedom. Unable to read the big man, he sighed and began speaking.

"It's a multi-tier system," he said quietly. "First level is just standard user ID and password authentication. Second level is a supervisory password. The third and final level is biometric."

"And you have all the passwords? And biometric access? Why would someone at your level have access into such a sensitive area?"

"You came to me," Steve snapped. "Do you want me to help, or not?"

"Answer my question," Lucas said softly. "Or I can leave and come back next month. Doesn't much matter to me, mate."

"Who are you trying to find?" Steve suddenly asked, suspicion clear on his face.

"That's not your concern," Lucas said, wanting to steer the conversation away from the "who" question.

Anvil

"If you want my help, you tell me. Or you can go try to hack in," Steve said, his mouth set in a defiant line.

"How about I take you outside, shoot you in the leg and leave you for the dingos?" Lucas smiled for the first time, but it wasn't a warm and friendly smile. "Ever seen a man taken by dingos? They're nasty little buggers. See, they don't kill you right off. The pack will tear out your Achilles tendons so you can't run. Then they rip open your arms so you can't fight. And when you're laying there helpless, they move in and start feasting. Tear open your stomach and feed on your organs. They like 'em nice and fresh. And the whole time, you're just laying there. Wide awake. Feeling everything until they bite into something that'll kill you quick."

"You can't do that!" Steve exclaimed. "That kind of thing doesn't happen here!"

"Where the bloody hell do you think you are, mate? This place doesn't even have a name. No one besides me even knows who you are, and there sure as bollocks isn't anyone that cares about what I do to you."

Lucas was playing free with the truth. Not that he wasn't willing and capable of carrying out his threat, but he would never be allowed to harm a prisoner. He was counting on Steve having knowledge of the rules in American black

315

site prisons and not realizing that Australia wasn't willing to go quite that far. With prisoners. But, once he had him outside…

"So, mate. What will it be?" Lucas asked, giving Steve time to fully develop the mental image he'd painted.

"I have my supervisor's password," he finally said. "That's the man I killed at the listening station. My biometrics are still active from when I was at Langley. I checked a couple of weeks ago and still have all of my old access. I guess they forgot to disable it. I get you in. Then I go free. Immediately. Wherever I want."

Lucas stared at him, thinking. He had no idea if Steve was making shit up about how the database was accessed or not. The whole purpose was to see if the man seemed like he did know, and was willing to cooperate. At this point, Lucas believed him, but also didn't trust him as far as he could throw him with one arm. But it was a start.

"Agreed," Lucas said. "You do this, and the government of Australia will no longer have an interest in you."

35

Sam and Gonzales sheltered behind the stairwell door. Hearing the voice from the other side had energized the Lieutenant. He had ordered the Master Chief to get the door open, keeping watch as the shorter man attached the breaching charge. In the safety of the stairs, Gonzales held the trigger up, thumb hovering over the actuator button, and looked at Sam.

"Sure this is a good idea, LT? I mean, how the hell is someone still alive in there after all this time?"

Gonzales hadn't heard the voice and was hesitant to open the door and release whatever was on the other side.

"I'm sure," Sam answered. "I know what I heard."

"OK, sir. Hope you're right," Gonzales mumbled, pressing the button.

There was a loud thump as the C-4 detonated and Sam led the way back into the second level vestibule. The charge had done the trick, neatly cutting the door around the lock and freeing it. As they approached, rifles up and trained, the door swung open. A slight figure stepped into view, one hand pushing the heavy slab open.

"Who are you?" A female voice asked.

"US Navy, ma'am," Sam answered.

Gonzales hung back, slipping to the side to keep his firing lane open as the Lieutenant slowly approached the woman.

"Is it over?" She asked, taking a timid step into the vestibule.

"Is there anyone else with you?" Sam asked, ignoring her question.

"Just me," she said. "I've been alone for a long time. Tell me it's over. Please."

"No ma'am, it's not," Sam said, stopping fifteen feet from where the woman stood. "It's worse, if anything."

Lowering his rifle, Sam clicked on a small flashlight and pointed it at her. As soon as he saw her face without night vision, he dropped the light and snapped the rifle back to his shoulder. There was a frightened gasp from the woman, and she took a step away from the weapon.

"Don't move," Sam warned.

Anvil

"What's wrong? What did I do?" The woman asked.

"You see it Master Chief?" Sam asked without taking his attention off the woman.

"Yes, sir. I did."

"Saw what? What are you talking about?" The woman raised her voice.

"What's your name?" Sam asked after a moment.

"Nicole," she answered, the fear obvious in her voice. "What's wrong? Tell me?"

"What are you doing here? How have you survived?" Sam asked, rifle not wavering.

"You're really scaring me," Nicole said. "Tell me what's wrong and quit waving that gun in my face."

"It's a rifle, not a gun," Sam responded automatically. "Answer my questions first."

"I work here. Or I worked here. I teach applied nuclear physics. There's a security system that locks down the building, and I got trapped inside a long time ago."

"How have you survived? Food and water?" Gonzales asked.

319

He moved again so he could keep an eye on the first door they had breached. They hadn't taken the time to clear all the labs and rooms in that area of the building, and he didn't want someone or something coming out of it and surprising them.

"The staff kitchen is back there," she gestured behind her. "There wasn't a lot of food, but enough to keep me alive. And a water cooler with a couple of spare jugs. I ran out of food two days ago and am almost out of water. Now, what's wrong?"

Sam and Gonzales exchanged glances.

"Thoughts, Master Chief?" He asked.

"What the fuck are you talking about?" Nicole shouted, stepping forward but stopping when Sam adjusted his rifle, and she found herself staring down the barrel.

"Ma'am, if you don't keep your voice down I'm going to restrain and gag you," Sam said.

"What?" Nicole whispered, eyes wide with fear. "What did I do?"

"Beats the hell out of me, sir," Gonzales answered, ignoring Nicole and answering Sam's question.

Sam thought for a moment, coming to a decision. Stepping backwards, he moved away from the woman.

"Take a seat. There," he indicated a small grouping of chairs pushed against the far wall. "Don't speak or go anywhere else."

Nicole stared at him, her mouth open in shock.

"Now," Sam hissed.

Wrapping her arms protectively across her chest, she slowly walked to the closest chair and lowered herself into it. Her eyes never left the weapon in Sam's hands.

"Check it out, Master Chief," Sam said.

As Gonzales came forward, approaching the door, Sam repositioned so he could see all of the entrances into the vestibule as well as Nicole. The Master Chief disappeared through the damaged door.

"Please tell me what's wrong," Nicole said, earning a stern look and a shush from Sam.

Gonzales was gone for most of ten minutes, checking in with Sam over the radio twice in that time. When he emerged from the hall, after calling that he was coming out, he

walked to the Lieutenant and leaned close to
speak with him in a low mumble.

"Checks out, LT. Big kitchen and lots of
empty food wrappers. Two empty water jugs
and one that's got maybe a quart left in it. Found
where she's been sleeping. No one else back
there and no bodies, either."

"See. I was telling the truth," Nicole said
from the far side of the room.

Sam and Gonzales both turned to look at
her in surprise.

"What?"

"You heard that?" Sam asked. He'd had to
concentrate to hear the Master Chief's low
mutters as he spoke only inches from his ear.

"Of course, I did. I'm not deaf," she said.
"Now that you know I'm telling the truth, what
the hell is wrong?"

"Any mirrors back there, Master Chief?"
Sam asked, not bothering to keep his voice down.

"Not that I found. No, sir. Small
bathroom, but no mirror in it."

"Look. I know I'm not a supermodel or
anything and haven't had a shower in a long
time, but seriously. What the hell is wrong with
you guys?"

Anvil

Nicole stood and faced them, hands on her hips. Her fear had turned to frustration and was well on its way to becoming anger.

With a sigh, Sam reached into a pocket and pulled out a battered iPhone. He hadn't had a signal for a long time, but every photo he had of his wife was on the device. He'd been able to keep it charged at the research facility, opening the pics and looking at her face every time he had a chance.

Letting his rifle hang from its sling, he stepped closer to Nicole, held the phone up and snapped a picture. Tapping a button, the freshly captured image filled the screen. Reversing it in his hand, he held it for her to see. She gasped, stepping forward for a better look.

"Oh. Oh my God," she breathed.

Looking up at Sam, she held his gaze with her blood red eyes.

36

Nicole began to freak out. She tried to snatch the phone out of Sam's hand, but he held it high in the air like he was playing keep-away with a child. Shock, fear, and revulsion were all reflected in her face as tears flowed and the beginning of a scream welled up from her throat.

Sam saw what was coming and lashed out with his fist, striking her in the solar plexus before she made enough noise to alert every infected in the area. The blow temporarily paralyzed her diaphragm, and she was unable to push the air out of her lungs and scream. Stumbling backwards from the impact, she glared at the two SEALs.

Panic momentarily replaced her other emotions as her body was unable to draw a breath. But as quickly as it had been stunned, her diaphragm relaxed, and she blew out stale air and took a shuddering breath.

"You have to stay quiet," Sam said, moving to loom over her. "There are infected outside, maybe inside, that will be drawn to your voice. You need to get it together so we can get out of here."

"You hit me, you son-of-a-bitch," Nicole spat at him.

"Did you hear what I just said?" Sam asked, frustration creeping into his tone.

"Of course, I did. But why did you hit me?"

Nicole stood up straight, and Sam took a couple of steps back. He had no clue what the hell was going on. She looked infected, but she acted normal. Was this a new manifestation of the virus? Or was this something entirely new?

Then he remembered her hearing. She'd clearly heard and understood a mumble from across the room. A mumble that had required his concentration to understand and it had been right next to his ear. That, more than the red eyes, convinced him she was infected.

"Master Chief, you read every brief that comes in. Any mention of something like this?"

"No, sir. There's lots of talk about smart ones working together and even a few of them using basic tools, but nothing like this."

"What about someone turning slowly? Eyes going red first, then they turn sometime later?" Sam was grasping at straws.

"No, sir," Gonzales shook his head without taking his eyes off of Nicole. "But we should take her back with us."

"What? Take me where?" Nicole's voice sounded on the verge of hysteria.

"There's a team of virologists nearby in a secure facility. That's the only reason we're anywhere near the city. They are definitely going to want to meet you," Sam answered.

"Can they help me? They have to help me! I don't want to turn into one of those things," Nicole wailed.

"Nicole, I don't know if they can help you or not, but if you don't be quiet, we're not going to make it back. If you can't control yourself I'm going to leave you here," Sam said, hoping the threat would help the woman calm herself.

"No!" She shouted. "Don't leave me! I've been alone for so long. I'll be quiet. I'm sorry."

Sam stared at her and after a few moments, she realized she'd been yelling.

"I'm sorry," she mumbled, making an effort to keep her voice down. "I'll be quiet, and I'll keep up. Just please, take me with you."

Sam glanced at Gonzales, but the Master Chief just shrugged his shoulders and went back to scanning the doors. Sighing, the Lieutenant stepped up to Nicole and spent nearly a minute giving her instructions. To her credit, despite the desperate fear coursing through her body, she listened closely and didn't make a sound.

They put her between them, Sam reminding her to stay absolutely quiet no matter what happened or what she saw. The Master Chief took point, leading the way into the stairwell. He had to pause half way down to remind Nicole not to follow him so closely. She had bumped into his back when he slowed to scan the lower half of the stairs.

When they reached the lower level, Sam called a halt by tapping his index finger lightly on his rifle's receiver. The sound was subtle, but Gonzales was listening for it and immediately placed his back against a wall, prepared to fight. But there wasn't anything wrong. Sam had just had an idea and moved to stand on the same stair as Nicole.

"Nuclear physics professor, right?" He muttered.

She nodded her head.

"So you know how to use a Geiger Counter."

It was a statement, not a question, and Nicole nodded again. Sam shrugged out of his pack and removed the device, holding it up for her to see.

"This is what we came for. This and radiation suits."

He held it out, and she looked at him questioningly as she took it in her hands.

"Time for questions later. Right now, can you use that to test the environment outside without making any noise?"

For the third time, Nicole nodded. Looking down at the Geiger Counter, she turned it on and silenced it. Her fingers flew across the controls as she set it up to not only measure the exposure levels but to also record them for later review. Watching her work the piece of equipment, Sam was glad he'd thought to ask.

Meeting Gonzales' eyes, he nodded, and the Master Chief got them moving again. They exited into the first-floor lobby, the two SEALs tightening up to protect Nicole as they moved towards the vestibule. Sam walked backwards, rifle on a constant swivel in sync with his head as he protected their rear.

The small vestibule was clear. Nicole quietly gagged and shied away from the decomposing body. Gonzales paused at the exterior glass doors and peered out into the night, motioning Sam forward after watching for a few seconds. There were nearly twenty males bumping around in the parking lot. But they weren't what was concerning the Master Chief.

Beyond the males at the far edge of the parking lot was a group of nine females. Some were turned, staring down the slope that led to the small forested area, but three of them appeared to be watching the building.

"Do we wait and see if they move on?" Gonzales asked as quietly as he could.

Sam shook his head as Nicole raised up on her toes to see over the two larger men. She gasped when she saw what they were discussing, earning a look of warning from both of them.

"Sorry," she mouthed, silently.

"You've read the same intel I have," Sam mumbled. "They don't move on unless something distracts them. You've got right; I'll take the left."

"Do you hear that?" Nicole asked softly.

Both men froze, listening for several seconds before turning to look at her.

"Hear what?" Sam asked.

"That sound. I started hearing it when we were coming down the stairs, and it got louder the closer we came to the door."

Nicole cocked her head, trying to identify what she was hearing. Sam and Gonzales faced the glass again, adjusting the positions of their heads in an attempt to hear what she was talking about.

After almost half a minute, Sam glanced at the Master Chief, but he shook his head. He would have dismissed it as nothing, but after the demonstration of Nicole's enhanced hearing, he was hesitant to discount her warning.

"What does it sound like?" He asked, moving her closer to the interior doors.

"It's like a hum or a buzz. It's not loud, but I can hear it and kind of feel it in my teeth if that makes sense," Nicole whispered.

"The Russian signal, LT. Remember?" Gonzales reminded Sam of the report they'd read about how the Russians were attracting and directing the infected.

"No shit," he breathed.

"What's he talking about?" Nicole asked, looking at Gonzales' broad back.

"Later. The good news is, you're not crazy. There really is a sound, but we can't hear it. Now, stay close and stay quiet. We've got to move, and we're going to have to fight. Better give me that back."

Anvil

Sam took the Geiger Counter from her hands and slipped it into his pack before turning and joining Gonzales at the doors, cutting the nylon flexi-cuff that was securing them. Nicole moved to stand right behind them, nearly frightened out of her mind. What did they mean, "fight"?

"Stay tight," Sam said to her, turning and meeting her eyes.

She nodded and followed the two SEALs through the double doors into the night.

37

"Gotta go outside the fence," I said into the radio. "Dog four and five, maintain cover fire. Edwards, move the fuel line ten feet east of the fenced area. Keep it high until I'm at the fill port."

Everyone acknowledged my order, the rate of fire from the roof picking up. Females were dropping, but they were barely being held back. I didn't see any way I was going to do this unless I was fighting with one hand and refueling the tank with the other. Shit. I'm good, but I'm not that good.

"Dog one, two. Fence is down, and we've got a whole gaggle flooding in," Dutch called on the radio.

"Gaggle?" I heard Drago's voice in my ear.

"Knock the shit off!" I barked. "Break... Sam one-niner, Dog one. Copy?"

"Go ahead, Dog," the pilot of the Black Hawk answered almost immediately.

"Need you on station with the minigun. I've got to take a walk with the natives," I said.

"That's a big ten-four, good buddy. Can you mark your location?"

Anvil

If I survived this, I had to have a beer with this guy.

"Affirmative. Break... Edwards, toss me a strobe."

I moved to the base of the wall, looking up. A few moments later, Edwards stuck his head over the parapet and looked down. Spotting me, he held the strobe straight out, paused a beat to let me lock in with my eyes, then dropped it. I caught it cleanly, almost dropping it from the sharp pain when it impacted my broken fingers. Cursing and shaking my hand, I activated it and snapped the hard plastic base off to expose a nylon belt with Velcro at each end.

Nearly dropping the damn thing again, I got the strap wrapped around my upper arm and secured tightly. I performed a quick check of my weapons, made sure the safety on my rifle and pistol were set to fire, and stepped to a wide gate. There was time to shoot four females and a male before the Black Hawk roared into a hover a couple of hundred feet above the parking lot.

"Dog one, ID one strobe at ground level. Confirm."

"Confirmed," I said. "That's me. I'm going to exit a gate and move ten feet east along the wall. I'll be static and need you to keep the infected off my ass."

"Copy. Watch your ass out there. Can't swing the death dealer too close to your position."

"No shit, Sherlock," I mumbled to myself.

Shooting three more females, I called on the radio that I was moving and opened the gate as the minigun cut loose. Two females were between me and the tank. I shot them and moved five feet, pausing when another screamed and charged from my left. Turning to engage, I was happy to see her head snap back an instant before she tumbled lifelessly to the pavement. Two more that were running in fell dead a moment later.

The Rangers on the roof were keeping the immediate area around me safe. The minigun was keeping the larger mass of infected farther out in the parking lot beaten back. Trusting that everyone would keep doing their job, I dashed to the pipe and grasped the greasy cap that covered the opening.

Unable to turn it with my damaged hand, I had to waste valuable time pulling a pair of channel lock pliers out of my pack. Focusing on the task while infected were charging my position was one of the hardest things I've ever had to do. If Chico or Drago missed a shot on a female, the bitch would slam into me when I was completely vulnerable. All I could do was trust the two men I didn't know to protect me.

The big pliers did the trick, loosening the cap enough for me to spin it off and let it fall to dangle from the end of a short chain. Edwards was on the ball, and when I looked up, the fuel line was hanging right in front of my face. I was reaching for it when a body struck my back.

The bitch hit me with a flying body tackle, and I was slammed against the exterior wall of the building. Fuck, that hurt! And even worse, I was a little stunned as my forehead had bounced off the stone façade. I was pulled to the ground, and I could smell the fetid breath of my attacker.

Punching with my right, I tried to get a grip with my left but couldn't hold on with two of the fingers out of commission. She batted my arm aside and grabbed my hand, twisting. I roared with pain, lightning bolts shooting up my arm and into the base of my skull. Rolling with her, I made room to really get my right arm wound up and hit her hard in the side of the head.

The infected went limp, knocked out by the blow, and I shoved her off of me and scrambled to my feet. Whipping my pistol out, I aimed at her head, pausing when I saw the damage my punch had done. I hadn't just knocked her out; I'd broken her neck. I'd like to take credit for being a brutishly strong fighter, but the truth of the matter is she wasn't very big. Probably no more than thirteen or fourteen years old.

Taking a quick glance around I saw a lot of females charging in, a few males mixed in. But they were falling dead to the asphalt at a steady pace. Drago and Chico were keeping them knocked down, but the ring that had formed around me was steadily compressing.

Forcing my attention away from the danger, I grabbed the line and pulled it down to reach the filler pipe. Opening the valve on the end, diesel gushed out on my pants and boots before I could shove the hose into the opening. Fuel flowing, I turned to head for the gate and safety behind the fence, but the closest ranks of infected had cut off my retreat.

"Moving to the gate," I called over the radio.

Leaving my rifle slung, I pulled the Kukri and Ka-Bar and moved to engage the closest infected. The Rangers did exactly what I had hoped they would as I began slashing and stabbing. Instead of trying to pick off targets that were directly in front of me, they concentrated on protecting my flanks.

Anvil

That left it up to me to battle my way to the gate. And battle I did. All of the pain, anger and frustration lent fury to my attack and before I realized it the gate was in front of me. A male was bumping against it, a female leaping for me with a bone-chilling scream.

The Kukri made quick work of her and a fast stab to the head with the knife dropped the male in his tracks. Stepping over him, I released the catch on the gate and pushed it open. As I moved to safety, a female lunged and grasped my left arm. Pulling her through with me, I kicked the gate shut, the latch automatically catching and securing the opening.

The female screamed as she spun, still holding on to my arm and trying to slash my eyes with her free hand. Leaning away from the strike, I brought the Kukri around and buried most of the blade in her skull. It stuck, pulling free from my hand as she collapsed to the ground, dead. Stepping on her face, I wrenched it free and turned to make sure the gate was solidly closed.

It was, and I wiped my blades clean on the dead female before sheathing them and dashing to the closest generator. As I worked to open the housing that protected the battery, Chico and Drago kept up their rate of fire, shooting females that were banging on the chain link as they tried to scale the fence.

337

"Dog one, Sam one-niner. There's too many coming through the breach to hold back. You'd better get your ass back on the roof."

"Save your ammo," I responded. "Almost done."

As I said the last word, the final screw came free, and I ripped the housing out of the way and tossed it to the side. Flashlight on, I peered inside and let loose with another string of curses. The goddamn generator had a 24-volt battery. Not the 12-volt vehicle battery I'd brought along. There was no way to jump start the engine.

38

Lucas Martin stood in the shade of the weathered structure that disguised the entrance to the prison. He was waiting for the guards to finish processing Steve, get the man dressed in something other than an orange jumpsuit and bring him to the surface. Their transportation, the same helicopter that had delivered him, was ten minutes away.

Once they boarded, it would fly them about a hundred kilometers to a small air strip where they would transfer to a plane that would deliver them to Geraldton. From there it was a short drive to the CIA station in Moonyoonka. Lucas had confirmed there would be a vehicle waiting for him at the Geraldton airport.

"When do you think you can come home?"

Lucas was speaking to his wife on a satellite phone. For the first time since she'd found out he was back in the service, he thought he could detect a note of warmth in her voice. He knew her anger was really fear for his safety and had been careful to not respond harshly to many of the vindictive things she'd said.

"I don't know," he answered. "Maybe in a day or two I can come see you. And the kids. How are the little buggers?"

"They're fine," she said. "They miss you."

"What about you?" Lucas couldn't help himself.

"You're a big, stupid arse. You know that? Of course, I miss you. I want you home, not off playing soldier."

Behind him, Lucas heard the whine of hydraulics as the lift that transported people to and from the surface went into motion.

"I have to go," he said. "I love you, and I'll be home as soon as I can."

He paused for a beat, hoping to hear that she loved him too. After a moment of silence, she told him to be safe and that she loved him. Smiling, he broke the connection and slipped the phone into his pocket. As he turned, a pair of doors slid open revealing Steve flanked by two guards.

They saw Lucas, nodded, and one of them placed his hand flat on Steve's back and pushed him forward. As soon as Steve was clear, the other one reached out and pressed a button. The doors slid shut, and there was another whine as the car descended beneath the Australian desert.

"Where are we?" Steve asked, blinking in the harsh light as he looked around at the desolate landscape.

Anvil

After being captured, he had been drugged, and a blackout sack pulled over his head. He had snatches of memory of being transported in an aircraft, but only knew that by the sounds and motion. He hadn't been able to see anything as he'd been brought to the prison.

"Middle of bloody nowhere," Lucas said.

"Are we supposed to walk?" Steve asked petulantly.

"Helicopter coming," Lucas grunted. "So keep your mouth shut and behave and it will all be over soon."

"You're letting me go. Right?" Steve edged away from the much larger man.

"I already told you. You do what we discussed, and as far as Australia is concerned, you don't exist. We never heard of you and never want to hear of you."

Steve peered closely at Lucas before nodding and moving a little farther away to lean against a rough wall. Lucas turned and looked to the west when he faintly heard the sound of the approaching aircraft. It was early. Good.

The sooner they were in the air, the sooner this whole thing would be over, and he could make a quick trip home to see his family. And if he was really lucky, maybe get some time alone with his wife to see if they could add another kid to the mix.

The helicopter came into view, the bright red paint serving to make it blend in with one of the more popular tour companies that operated out of Perth. It even flew out of the same airport on occasion. Only the employees of that company would recognize it as a fake. Each of them was retired from the RAAF and knew to look the other way and keep their mouths shut. They boarded and before Lucas fastened his seatbelt he handed a black, fabric bag to Steve.

"Put it on," he said.

"What? Why?"

"Secret prisons don't stay secret if every bloody wanker that comes in or out can see where they are," Lucas said, giving him a hard glare.

Steve nodded, understanding the reasoning, and pulled the bag over his head. He felt Lucas check his harness, then heard the click as he secured his own. A moment later the seat under him shifted as the pilot lifted off.

The flight to the airstrip was quick, Lucas enjoying the scenery and chatting with the pilot to pass the time. Steve sat hunched in his seat, ignoring the two men and staring at the inside of the bag. It was hot and slightly claustrophobic, but he didn't complain. It beat the hell out of a prison cell.

The plane was ready to go and less than two minutes after being dropped by the helo, they were on board, and it was turning into the wind for takeoff. It was a much longer flight to Geraldton and Lucas took advantage of the opportunity to get some sleep. Steve sat there, listening to the buzz saw snores emanating from his traveling companion.

He was frightened and excited. Fearful that something would happen at the last moment and cuffs would be slapped back on, and he would be returned to his small cell. Excited at his impending freedom.

They were half an hour away from Geraldton when Lucas stretched and sat up. He looked over at Steve, nodded and asked the pilot where they were. The man answered with a location that Steve didn't understand, but by the way he grunted it seemed to make sense to Lucas.

Several minutes later the bag was pulled off of Steve's head. He squinted in the sudden light and tried to look outside the aircraft. It was nearly a minute before his eyes adjusted, just in time for him to see rolling green hills fading away to suburban sprawl. The landing gear thumped onto the runway, and he was pressed forward against the belt as the pilot braked hard and turned onto a taxiway.

They passed several hangars before turning into one that was vacant except for a shiny black Chevrolet Suburban. An older man with brush cut hair, wearing a black suit, leaned on the front fender. A cigarette dangled from his lips.

"Who's that?" Steve asked nervously.

"Our ride," Lucas said dismissively.

The pilot shut the engine down, the propeller quickly coming to a stop. Releasing his belt, Lucas popped the door and climbed out. He waited for Steve to exit the aircraft, escorting him to the waiting vehicle and getting in the back seat without speaking to the driver.

No one spoke as they drove out of the airport and onto the 123 highway. The drive to Moonyoonka was short, even more so as the driver pushed their speed well above the posted limit. Traffic was light, the big American vehicle blasting past the locals like they were standing still.

When they turned onto the access road for the listening post, he slowed until they were moving barely above an idle. Red dust boiled up from the unpaved road. Ahead, a Toyota SUV blocked the entrance, two men armed with

Anvil

automatic weapons standing at either end of the
vehicle. The driver flashed his lights and one of
them jumped behind the wheel and pulled it to
the side to allow them to pass.

Steve turned and watched out the rear
window as the entrance was once again blocked
after they drove through the gate onto the paved
lot. All of the stations defenses had been
disabled or destroyed by the SAS raid that had
captured Steve, so getting in was as simple as
walking through the front door. The power was
on, the air-conditioned interior cool and
comfortable after the furnace-like heat radiating
from the black asphalt.

The driver remained with the Suburban,
Lucas following Steve through the doors and
down a hall to a large room full of servers and
communications equipment. A young man with
an obvious military haircut waited for them at
the closest workstation.

"Who's this?" Steve asked, pausing in
surprise.

"This is my technician," Lucas said,
pushing Steve forward. "He'll tell me if you're
trying to pull anything, or not doing what you
agreed to do. And once you get access, he'll take
over and retrieve the records we need."

345

Dirk Patton

Steve swallowed audibly, took a breath and moved forward. The technician had already powered up the station and loaded the first login screen for the database. Glancing at the two men, Steve sat down in front of the terminal and reached for the keyboard. Lucas stopped him with a heavy hand on his shoulder.

"Let me just be clear," he said. "You do anything to erase or corrupt the data; you're not going back to prison. There're lots of dingos in the area, and the sun will be setting soon. That's when they like to hunt and feed. Do you understand what I'm saying?"

"I understand," Steve said, sweat beading his brow and upper lip. "No tricks. I'll get you in then you do whatever you want to do. I don't even want to know who you're looking for."

He had met Lucas' steely gaze, finally turning back to the workstation and typing when Lucas nodded and removed his hand. Steve got past the first screen quickly, pausing when a new window popped open and asked for a supervisory password. He thought for a moment, then carefully typed in a long string of letters mixed with characters and numbers.

Hitting enter, the window vanished, and the screen remained blank. Lucas was reaching out to grab his shoulder when a new window appeared. In large, red letters it said "*Biometric scan required for access*".

Steve reached out and pulled a small device towards him that looked like a web camera. It was connected to the workstation by a long cable. He raised the device to a point nearly touching his right eye and stared directly into the lens, pressing a button on the side of the retina scanner. It briefly glowed green before beeping twice. The word "*confirmed*" flashed in the window, then disappeared as the screen refreshed to display a directory of data tables.

The younger man touched Lucas' arm and nodded. Steve returned the scanner to its place and pushed away from the keyboard. He stood and faced Lucas as the other man slipped into the seat and began working.

"I've done what you asked," Steve said. "I'm free now. Right?"

Lucas held up a finger, telling Steve to wait. He watched as the man quickly found the record he was looking for. Picking up a pen, he wrote the information down on a piece of paper and double checked it against the screen before standing and handing it to Lucas.

"Yes. As agreed. As an official representative of the Australian government, you are no longer wanted for any crimes. Australia officially disavows any knowledge of you or your whereabouts."

Lucas had folded the paper neatly in half and placed it in his wallet as he spoke. The younger man had already left the room, and Lucas stepped aside to let Steve pass.

Smiling, Steve went into the hall and strode for the front door. Lucas followed him, stepping out into the heat of the late afternoon. The Suburban sat waiting for them, the driver once again leaning on the fender and smoking another cigarette. Steve started to turn towards where his personal vehicle sat, the car not having been moved after he was arrested. He paused when Lucas called out to him.

"One more thing," Lucas said, nodding at the Suburban driver who tossed his cigarette to the ground and stood up straight. "I'd like to introduce you to Jim Branch."

Steve looked at the man, noticing something that hadn't been there before. On the lapel of his jacket was a small pin that glowed in the harsh sunlight. Steve had seen that same pin plenty of times before, but not since he had been demoted and reassigned to Australia. It was the American flag.

"He is actually Marine Master Gunnery Sergeant James Branch, assigned to the American embassy in Sydney. He pulled out all the stops to get a flight all the way across Australia in time to drive us out here."

"The embassy?" Steve asked, fear threatening to turn his bowels to water.

"The *American* embassy, you fucking traitor," the man said, drawing a pistol from beneath his jacket and pointing it at Steve's face.

"Well, since one of you has diplomatic immunity, and the other doesn't officially exist in the eyes of the Australian government, I'll be on my way," Lucas said with a broad smile.

He walked behind the Marine and across the blistering parking lot. Behind him, Steve screamed his name. Begging. Pleading. Offering to break into other American systems if he would just come back and help.

Lucas ignored him, opening the back door and climbing into the air conditioned interior of the Toyota SUV. The two guards were already in the front seats, waiting for him. The computer tech occupied the other rear seat. The driver stepped on the gas as soon as Lucas closed his door.

He touched the button for the power window, lowering it a few inches as they slowly drove towards the highway on the dirt access road. Before they reached the pavement, Lucas heard a single pistol shot from behind.

Closing the window, he retrieved the piece of paper with Katie's beacon codes. Carefully, double checking his work, he punched them into a text message addressed to Lieutenant Hunt in Hawaii.

39

Sam and Gonzales began firing as they emerged through the glass doors. They ignored the much slower males, even though they were closer. The females, with their frightening speed, were their targets. Two of them fell before they were even aware of the presence of the pair of SEALs. The rest began to scatter, each man dropping running targets, then there weren't any in sight.

Shifting focus, they methodically shot the males as they moved across the parking lot. Nicole, nearly frightened out of her mind, stayed close to Sam's back. When he paused to steady his aim she bumped into him, knocking his rifle off target.

"Sorry," she muttered.

Ignoring her, he grunted, reacquired his target and drilled the hissing male through the forehead. In a matter of seconds, all of the infected were down, and the Master Chief moved into the lead. Sam pushed Nicole between them, telling her to stay ten feet behind Gonzales. He fell in five yards behind her, scanning through the area to their rear.

Two females charged around the far corner of the building, and he shot one, the other escaping when she dove behind the shelter of a parked car.

"Fuck me," Gonzales said over the radio.

"Sit-rep," Sam said, not taking his attention off the open ground behind them.

"Goddamn things are eating Chucky," came the answer a moment before more suppressed fire began sounding from the Master Chief's rifle.

Sam glanced over his shoulder, seeing Gonzales standing at the edge of the pavement, looking down the slope where they'd left the body of one of the SEALs, who had been killed on their way to the lab. He wanted to go look, but more infected were moving into the area, drawn by the muted sound of their weapons.

"We've got to haul ass," Sam said into his radio, firing on two different groups of females who were zeroing in on them.

"Copy that," Gonzales answered, a moment later disappearing over the edge of the slope.

Sam fired five more shots, checked to make sure Nicole was on her way and followed when he didn't see her. They moved down the slope quickly, pausing for a moment by the eviscerated corpse of the dead SEAL. The plan had been to recover the man's body and take it back to the research institute with them, but Sam realized that wasn't going to work.

The torso had been torn open as the infected fed. Blood and bodily fluids stained a large area, the clothing soaking in them. A long string of entrails extended from the open abdomen still clutched in the hand of a dead male that Gonzales had shot.

"What do we do, LT?" Gonzales asked as both men fired on infected approaching from multiple directions.

"No choice," Sam said between trigger pulls. "We have to leave him."

"We can't…" Gonzales started to say, but Sam cut him off.

"Get your ass in gear, Master Chief. Now!"

With a grunt, Gonzales complied, heading for the tree line. His rifle was up and firing as he walked, an infected falling with every shot. Nicole, fighting the urge to stop and throw up, was tight against his back. The fear of the whole situation had overcome the instructions to keep some space open between her and the two SEALs.

There were less infected under the trees, but still enough to require a nearly constant rate of fire. Behind, Sam could hear the noises of males stumbling through the undergrowth and too many rapid footfalls of females on the leaf-littered forest floor.

"Faster," he hissed at Gonzales, not wanting to have to face a large group in the limited sightlines of the trees.

They passed through, emerging from the edge of the greenbelt only moments ahead of four charging females. Sam managed to kill one and slow another with a shot to her leg; then they were on him. He fell to the ground with one of them on top, her scream loud in the night as she began trying to rip into his throat.

Twisting, he pulled the much smaller woman to the side and slammed her head against the pavement of the road. The body went limp, but before he could regain his feet, the one with the injured leg reached out and grabbed his foot. Kicking free, he fumbled his rifle around and shot her in the face as she opened her mouth to scream.

Leaping to his feet, he froze when he saw a female standing only feet away. Gonzales was behind and to the side of Nicole, his rifle aimed at the infected's head, but he wasn't pulling the trigger. The female was in a partial crouch, arms swinging slightly in front of her body as she stared at Nicole, who was frozen in fear.

354

Anvil

The small tableau remained that way for a few heartbeats, then the female suddenly turned and raced away. Gonzales fired as she ran and she fell dead to the ground, her body rolling in a loose-limbed tumble. Sam grabbed Nicole's arm and shouted at the Master Chief to move.

They dashed down the road a short distance, then into the massive parking lot. Now they ran, a few males following and females sprinting in at angles, trying to intercept. They were losing the race but reached the end of the pavement slightly ahead of the infected. Before scaling the fence to cross the athletic fields, they turned and dropped the females that were almost on them.

Sam had begun the run with Nicole's upper arm firmly grasped in his left hand, frequently checking over his shoulder for pursuit. By the time they reached the athletic fields, he realized Nicole wasn't only keeping up; she would have outpaced him if he wasn't holding her arm.

This confirmed for him her status as an infected. She'd been locked in a confined area for an extended period of time, and frankly didn't look like an athlete. Yet she was running with easy strides and not even breathing hard despite the fast pace Gonzales was setting.

Scaling the final fence, they dashed around a small equipment shed, and the Master Chief ran directly into the arms of two males. Within an instant he was wrapped up and taken to the ground, one of them locking his jaws onto Gonzales. The SEAL screamed as a large chunk of flesh and part of his nose was ripped away by the infected's teeth.

Releasing Nicole, Sam dashed in and grabbed the male's shoulders, lifting and throwing him to the side. As the infected fell away, he yanked the knife off his vest and buried the blade in its head. Spinning back, he paused in surprise as Nicole tore the other infected off the stricken Master Chief with apparently little effort. She lifted the much larger man into the air, her arms wrapped around his neck.

Turning her hips, she levered the attacker away, not releasing her grip as the entire body twisted in the air. With a loud crack, the male's neck snapped, and she tossed the corpse several feet where it rolled to a stop against the wall of the shed. When she realized what had just happened, she froze, staring at her hands before turning to look at the dead infected.

Sam was also frozen, but a groan from Gonzales spurred him to action. He reached into a pouch on his vest and pulled out a small first aid kit as he dropped to his knees next to the injured man. The Master Chief was trying to sit up, Sam glancing around to make sure they had a moment before pushing him back onto the wet grass.

The bite had torn most of the flesh off the left side of Gonzales' face, exposing the cheek bone and upper gum line. At least a third of his nose was gone. The remaining flesh was ragged, and blood poured from the wound.

"Hold still, Master Chief. This is gonna hurt like a motherfucker," Sam said, tearing open a packet of blood clotter with his teeth.

Gonzales bucked like electricity was coursing through his body when Sam poured the powder into the exposed flesh. Sam emptied the packet and pressed a thick gauze pad onto the area, meeting the other man's eyes and seeing only pain reflected. Despite the clotting agent, blood quickly soaked through the gauze, spreading across the white surface.

"Can you run?" Sam asked, quickly wrapping a couple of turns of tape around the Master Chief's head to keep the bandage in place.

"Yes, sir. I'm good," Gonzales hissed, sitting up and accepting Sam's offered hand to help him to his feet.

They made it to the boat without any further incident, Sam breathing easier when all three of them were aboard. He sprawled on the

Dirk Patton

deck at the front of the boat, aiming his rifle in the direction they had just come from as Gonzales used the paddle to move them to deeper water. Once they were clear of the small islands and floating several hundred feet offshore, he started the engines and dropped into the driver's seat.

"You good to drive?" Sam asked, making his way to a seat.

"Good to go, sir," Gonzales answered, blood dripping from his bandage when he tried to grin.

"You OK?" Sam asked, turning to Nicole.

"I killed him," she said in a small voice. "How did I kill him? I was just trying to stop him."

Gonzales turned to look at her, his hand resting on the throttles.

"You saved my ass," he said, wincing in pain as his face moved. "Thank you."

She didn't seem to hear, or if she did wasn't able to respond. She looked like she was in shock.

"Look," Sam began as the Master Chief fed in some gas and got them moving. "The infected are very strong, especially the females. It's a good thing you were able to do that, or the Master Chief might not be here with us. We're heading for the institute, and I'm sure the scientists there can tell you what's going on. But hold your head up. You did a good thing."

Nicole raised her face and looked at him, red eyes glistening with tears.

40

"Got a problem," I said over the radio, shouting to be heard above the screams of the females that were pushing in against the fence. "Fucking generator needs a twenty-four volt battery to start. We brought a twelve. Anyone have any bright ideas?"

There was silence on the comm channel for several long moments, the rate of fire from the parapet above my head increasing as Dutch and TJ came over to help provide fire support.

"Two twelves in series will do it," Chico said, the sound of his rifle clear over the circuit.

He was right. I could wire two car batteries in series, effectively doubling the voltage, and maybe the generator would turn over. But there was only one problem with that idea. I didn't have a second battery.

Looking up as the Black Hawk buzzed by in its orbit of the area, I called the smart-ass pilot on the radio.

"Sam one-niner, you see any vehicles close by that are intact?"

"Stand by, Dog. I'll see if I can spot you a chariot."

Anvil

While he checked the area, I stepped around the generator that was screening me from the fence, and the throng of females, intending to add my rifle to the suppressive fire. When I got a look at the sheer number of infected surrounding my small sanctuary I paused. There were too many of them and not enough rifles.

The Rangers overhead were doing a good job of keeping them knocked down, but as the bodies piled up, the new arrivals were climbing on them and getting closer to the top of the fence. The only good news here was that this place had taken security seriously, and the generators were well protected. The fence was tall and sturdy.

The bad news, there were more infected than I could hope to count and they would eventually be able to force their way in or over. Once that happened, if the generators weren't already running, we wouldn't be able to clear them out and come back down to start them.

Before I began firing, I stepped to my right, peering through the mass of writhing, screaming bodies. I was concerned that one of them had gotten tangled in the fueling line and pulled it out of the filler neck, and the precious supply of diesel was just flooding out onto the asphalt. A sigh of relief escaped me when I spotted the hose, still in place.

"Dog one, Sam one-niner."

Dirk Patton

"Go for Dog," I immediately replied, hoping he was calling with good news.

"Got you a big Dodge pickup. One of the diesels. It'll have two, high amp batteries in it."

"Where is it?" I asked, moving back between the generators to block some of the noise from the infected.

"About a mile from you. What do you want to do?"

"Can I get to the truck or is it mobbed?"

"It's at some kind of construction site. There's a fence around the area and at the moment it's clear. But that fence looks like one of those temporary ones. Don't think it'll hold up to all those fuckers for more than a minute."

Shit. Well, I guess I'd have to work fast.

"You got an extraction line on board?" I asked.

"Affirmative," he answered. "On my way."

I glanced at the IR strobe on my upper arm, making sure it was still flashing away so the pilot could find me. Satisfied it was working, I grabbed the end of the rope I'd climbed down and cut several feet off. Coiling it, I stuffed it in a cargo pocket along with a couple of tools from my pack, which wouldn't be making the trip with me.

"Dog two, Dog one. I'm taking a ride. Keep everyone back from the edge while I'm gone. Maybe the infected will try to follow and move away from the area," I said to Dutch over the radio.

"Copy," was his simple reply.

It wasn't long before the Black Hawk came into a hover directly over my head, just above the level of the roof. The voices of the females rose to a fever pitch as the helicopter hung in the air as if it were teasing them.

"Line down," a previously unheard voice spoke over my earpiece.

A moment later, the weight on the end of a FRIES – Fast Rope Insertion Extraction System – line banged off the top edge of one of the generators before falling to the ground between them with a dull thud. Slinging my rifle behind my back, I dashed forward and stuck a foot in a loop, got a firm grip on the rope and twirled my free hand in the air.

The pilot went straight up, ascending quickly until I was a hundred feet above the roof of the building. Looking down, I noted the Rangers pulling back from the parapet. When I looked across the large parking lot, I wasn't happy to see the volume of infected that were pouring in through what were now multiple breaches in the perimeter fence.

With enough altitude to clear any obstacles in the area, he started us moving forward. I appreciated that he was careful to not go too fast with me dangling beneath him. Normally, two people will be on the line together, and each can extend an arm to the side. This acts like wings, stabilizing the two bodies and preventing them from spinning around like a top.

But I was by myself and didn't have a lot of options. Hold on with two hands and spin, or extend one arm and spin faster. I chose to hold on with both. Mercifully, the pilot didn't try to break any speed records, so the spin was tolerable. Not pleasant, by any means, but it could have been worse.

Beneath my feet was a sea of enraged faces staring up at me. So far I couldn't detect any attempt to follow the noisy helicopter and the handsome, delicious snack dangling beneath it. But there were so many infected, and they were packed so tightly; it would take some time for the momentum to build. I hoped there was enough of a distraction for the ones near the generators to back off. Otherwise, there was a good chance that fence would be down by the time I returned.

Anvil

After a couple of minutes, I spotted the construction site we were headed for. It looked like a new industrial park was being built with numerous buildings in various stages of completion. Some were nothing more than wooden forms waiting for concrete that would never be poured. Others had already been framed, appearing appropriately skeletal in the new post-apocalyptic world.

"Going to drop you and make an orbit to check the area," the pilot said as we came over the unfinished roof of a large building that was probably going to be a warehouse.

Directly ahead was an open stretch of raw mud with several large pools of water filling the low spots. A couple of small, trailer mounted generators were sitting next to a battered Dodge pickup. It may have been battered on the outside, but I didn't question the pilot's assessment that it was a good choice. Contractors have to take care of their vehicles and equipment. Even though the sheet metal had seen better days, I was willing to bet the engine had been well maintained.

He came in slow, losing altitude as we approached the truck. I had time to scan the area for infected and was very happy to not see any. But, I reminded myself, it's always the ones you don't see that can ruin your day. In hindsight, I should have had one of the Rangers tag along to keep an eye on my back while I pulled a battery out of the truck.

The line came down as we lost altitude and I stepped into nearly ankle deep mud with my free boot. Making sure my other foot was clear of the loop, I took a step away before calling the all clear. It quickly disappeared above my head, and I ran to the truck as fast as I could through the soupy earth.

The Dodge was locked up tight, so I smashed out the driver's window with the stock of my rifle after looking into the cab to make sure there wasn't an infected waiting to grab me. Reaching through the opening, I popped the door open, and a goddamn alarm began wailing. Are you fucking kidding me? Someone put an alarm on a beat up piece of shit like this? Well, at least I knew the batteries had some juice in them.

I fumbled around the driver's side foot well until I located the hood release, pulling it and feeling the click through the body of the truck when the catch opened. Moving through the muck, I pushed the night vision goggles off my face and turned on my light to see better. It only took a moment to spot the fucking alarm siren and rip the wires out of it. The absence of the noise was almost a physical relief.

"Dog one, don't know what you did, but you got company coming. Females at the fence about three hundred yards north of your location," the pilot's voice was loud in my earpiece as I began working on the nuts securing the vehicle's electrical cables to the battery terminals.

"Copy," I answered, not pausing or looking up from my work.

Sweat broke out all across my head as I forced myself to concentrate on what I was doing. My splinted fingers slowed the work, pain shooting all the way to my shoulder, but I didn't take my attention off the battery. If I looked up or worried about the infected breaching the fence, it would just slow me down.

"Fence is down. You've got a whole bunch of runners heading your way," the pilot called.

"Copy," I breathed as the nut for the positive terminal loosened enough to allow me to yank the cable free.

It took about the same amount of time to remove the negative terminal; then I had to figure out how the bracket that held the battery in place operated. Several precious moments were wasted as I peered at it from several angles and ran my hand over it looking for a release. I couldn't find it.

The Black Hawk came into a hover directly over me as I worked, opening up with its minigun. Short, controlled bursts. I knew they were low on ammo for the weapon and hoped they didn't run out before I was back in the air.

With a curse, I gave up on figuring out how to release the bracket. Pulling my Kukri, I jammed it between the heavy plastic arm and the top of the battery and twisted as I pulled up. The bracket bent, but whatever the fucking stuff was that Dodge had used to make it was tough as hell. It didn't break and didn't pop free.

"More runners coming from the north, and south fence is breached. You've got about twenty seconds."

The Black Hawk wasn't firing the minigun any longer, rather a couple of unsuppressed rifles began shooting. Were they out of ammo? I didn't have time to worry about it. This goddamn battery had to come out, and I was out of time.

"Fuuuuck," I grunted as I used two hands to lever the Kukri up.

There was a loud snap as the bracket parted. Sheathing the Kukri, I reached in and grabbed the heavy block that was the battery. With a grunt I lifted it free and set it on the ground, whipping the piece of rope out of my pocket.

"Ten seconds." I heard.

Anvil

Frantically, I wrapped a couple of loops around the battery, pulled them tight and spun the free end of the rope around my left wrist and hand. The same hand with the broken fingers. Looking up for the first time, I saw an entire phalanx of females almost upon me. When they saw me, screams erupted from hundreds of throats.

Lunging, I grasped the extraction line which was dangling five feet from the front bumper of the truck. I jammed my foot in the loop and stepped up, my left arm jerking hard against the weight of the battery.

"Go!" I screamed as three of the leading females leapt.

The pilot fed in power, and I was yanked skyward so fast the leg that was standing in the loop nearly buckled. The heavy battery came with me, my shoulder feeling like it momentarily pulled out of its socket. Then, two of the three females slammed into me.

41

If my foot wasn't tangled in the loop, the impact from the females would have torn it free of the rope. As it was, I nearly lost my grip with my free hand, which would have left me hanging upside down, swinging by one leg. Spinning and swaying like a pendulum, I began kicking with my free foot. I could tell I was striking flesh with the heavy boot but had no idea if it was doing any good.

But giving up wasn't an option, so I kept at it. Strong hands grasped the single leg that was all that was supporting the weight of three bodies and a heavy ass battery. Those hands were reaching up, trying to grasp my belt, and I got lucky with one of my kicks. As the female was reaching for a better grip, my foot knocked her other hand free, and she fell away, disappearing into what had quickly become a seething mass of infected.

There was still one holding on, and the bitch was wrapped around my leg like a python with one of her arms. With the other, she was reaching, flailing for a higher purchase on my body. She was positioned on the outside of my leg, and I couldn't kick her. Trying to think of a way to reach a blade or my pistol, I was reminded I had a fifty-pound block dangling from my left wrist.

Shifting the angle of my body, I began trying to swing the battery. I hoped to be able to gain enough momentum to smash it into the female and knock her off. As I struggled with the ungainly weight on the end of the rope, she managed to get a fingertip grip on my belt. Shifting her weight, she inched up my leg and began biting. Only the tough fabric saved me from being torn open, the pain from the bite pressure dumping, even more, adrenaline into my bloodstream.

I finally got the battery swinging, its weight causing me and the female to twist on the end of the extraction line. She was snarling and tearing at my leg, and I panicked when I felt and heard fabric tearing. She was getting through and about to sink her teeth into bare flesh!

Twisting harder, I swung with the momentum of the battery as it came around us. In slow motion, I watched it slam into the female's ribs, the impact substantial enough that I felt it in my leg. She was knocked free from her grasp on my leg, beginning to fall. Her arms reached out, and I watched as she began to drop away, crying out in pain when she succeeded in wrapping an arm around the battery.

Her entire weight suddenly came on the rope secured to my wrist, and I felt my shoulder come completely out of its socket. She screamed as she dangled beneath my feet, looking up at me with rage burning in her red eyes. I screamed back, the pain radiating from my shoulder intense enough that I would have dropped the battery if I could. But the rope was thoroughly wrapped up, and there was no way I could let go until the weight came off and gave me some slack.

I had time to remember that this was the same shoulder that had been dislocated twice when I was a much younger Soldier. Did that make it more susceptible to popping out of the socket? It sure made it ache when the weather was damp and cold, and right now all I could hope for was that the joint wasn't being permanently damaged.

Quickly, but not quickly enough, we were over the roof, and I looked down to see the Rangers waiting for me. The pilot came down fast, then paused about twenty feet above the surface.

"Shoot this fucking bitch!" I roared in pain.

TJ raised his rifle and fired a single shot. A moment later her weight dropped off, only the

battery swinging from the rope still dragging on
my arm.

"Put me down!" I shouted.

The pilot did just that, lowering the Black
Hawk quickly. The battery hit the roof first,
giving me a fraction of a second's warning that I
was next. My boots thumped onto the surface,
and I stumbled, saved from going down when
Drago wrapped me up in his big arms. Hands
fumbled with the extraction line, freeing my foot,
then the helicopter moved away.

Drago held me until I had my balance,
then removed his hands but stayed close behind.
Chico was already working on the rope that
connected my hand to the battery, gently
unwinding it from my bleeding wrist. When it
came free, he grabbed the battery and moved it a
few feet away.

"Ready for this?" Dutch asked, standing in
front of me and looking into my eyes. He already
had his hands in place, and I felt Drago grab me
from behind.

"Oh, fuck me not..." I started to say, but
Dutch didn't hesitate.

With the right pressure and a sharp, hard
pull, he popped my injured shoulder back into
place. I might have said a few choice words
about his lineage and his sexual proclivities

towards animals, but when the joint snapped he took a quick step back and smiled. Drago released me, also stepping away.

My shoulder throbbed, but at least it no longer felt like a molten knife was being inserted and twisted. Cautiously, I moved my arm to assure myself I still had use of it. It hurt like hell, but now it was a six on the pain scale, not a ten.

"Thanks," I mumbled, looking up at Dutch.

He nodded and seemed like he had something to say, but apparently thought better of it. Glancing around, I saw that Chico already had the battery at the parapet and was pulling up the rope so it could be lowered down to ground level. Looking at Drago, I nodded my thanks for his help and walked over to where Chico was busily working.

Stepping to the edge, I glanced over. A small sea of infected was pressed up against the fence around the generators, and in several places, it was beginning to bow inwards. I quickly stepped back, so they didn't try to push in harder to get to me.

"Ready?" I asked Chico when he pulled the knot tight.

"Hold on, sir." I turned to look at Dutch, who was shrugging out of his pack. "I'm going this time."

Anvil

"The fuck you are," I said.

"Sir, your arm was just out of its socket. I don't care how tough you are; it's weak. You aren't going to be able to climb down that rope and move a heavy battery around."

"Like hell I'm not," I said, rolling my shoulder and nearly gasping in pain.

"See?" Dutch said. "Mission first, sir."

I stared at him for a long moment, seething. Not because he had called me on being injured, but because he was right.

"Do you know what you're doing?" I asked, acknowledging to myself that I needed to sit this one out.

"Chico educated me while you were out swinging with the local ladies," he smiled and held up two lengths of heavy wire. "Stripped these out of that AC unit over there. Should do the trick."

I nodded, still not happy, but feeling pride that these guys hadn't just sat on their ass waiting for me. They'd thought about what needed to be done and come up with what was needed to make it happen.

Dutch smiled, adjusted the rifle slung on his back and walked to the parapet where Chico had just finished lowering the battery.

"Watch your ass, Top," Drago mumbled as Dutch grabbed the climbing rope and turned to begin his descent.

I took up position with the three Rangers, and we began picking off more females as Dutch scampered down the outside of the building. The infected became frenetic when they saw him, the fence groaning under the weight of their constant push.

"Sam one-niner, Dog one. Any pellets left in your minigun?"

I shot two females off the fence as I made the call.

"Negative, Dog. Used them all up protecting you from the skanks."

Shit!

"OK. Got anything else that's close and will make a big boom?"

If I couldn't get direct fire support for Dutch, maybe another distraction would buy him some breathing room. I wanted to look down and check on his progress, but there were just too many females trying to scale the fence. I couldn't let my attention waver, or one of them would make it over.

"Stand by, Dog," I heard in my earpiece, then a moment later another voice that it took me a moment to realize was Edwards.

The Lieutenant didn't have a rifle, so he was at the edge of the roof watching Dutch work. He must have realized none of us could spare a glance, so he was reporting on the progress.

"He's got the two batteries connected to each other and is running the jumper cables to the generator."

The infected were surging again, hands reaching for the top of the fence around the entire perimeter. I had stopped going for kill shots, settling for anything that would slow their advance. Arms and shoulders were weak points that didn't require the precision of head shots. Less precision meant I could send more lead into the bodies below.

I heard the Black Hawk fire, surprised the pilot had found a target so close. An instant later there was a brilliant flash as the missile detonated, then a fiery explosion a few hundred yards out in the parking lot rocked the night. There was a momentary pause in the assault on the fence by the infected as hundreds of males turned and began shambling towards the new noise.

But this didn't have the effect I had hoped for. The females could see Dutch and weren't about to be pulled away by a loud light show. They had him cornered and were determined to reach him. As the males pushed through the tightly packed bodies, more females surged forward and filled the gaps they left behind.

"Everything's connected," Edwards said, excitement making him sound like a junior high school kid.

A couple of beats later I heard the whine of a large, heavy duty starter. The big diesel engine coughed, sputtered and went quiet. The starter whined again, for a long time. The engine finally began sputtering, this time continuing on in a very rough idle. It kept stuttering as the air in the lines was pulled to the cylinders.

"Don't let it die," I repeated in my head several times as I shot three more females.

If the engine stalled, it would probably be necessary to pull the fuel filter and prime it again, and there was no time for that. Also, the fuel line was outside the fenced area in no man's land. Holding my breath as I kept shooting, I heard it cough a couple of more times; then the idle slowly smoothed out. When the controller software detected the engine was ready, it revved the motor to a higher speed, holding it there to spin the big generator. Lights on the exterior wall of the building came to life.

Females were screaming and charging in at a fever pitch. Just a few minutes ago we'd been able to knock them down as they reached the fence and began climbing. Now, with their renewed push, we were shooting them off the fence. Some of them were getting hands on the top rail, and I killed a couple that made it all the way up and thrust their heads above the barrier.

"Dog two, fall back. You don't have time to start the second one," I shouted without slowing my rate of fire.

"We don't know if we have power to the servers," he shouted back.

I spared a glance in his direction, noting he was frantically yanking cables free as he prepared to move to the next generator.

"That's an order, First Sergeant," I bellowed.

"Sorry, sir. Your transmission is garbled," Dutch replied.

I shut up and kept firing. He was doing pretty much the same thing I would have done. We all knew this was critical, even though we

didn't know what it would accomplish. That's
life in the military. You don't always know why
something is important; you just know that it is.

Three more females went down under my
fire, one of them so far up that when she
collapsed her body came to rest draped across
the top rail. There was another groan from the
fence, but I didn't have time to look for the spot it
was coming from.

"He's got the batteries moved and is
connecting them," Edwards shouted.

As soon as the Lieutenant finished
speaking, there was the loudest groan yet from
the fence. This time, it wasn't just a complaint, it
was a full-on protest from the overstressed metal
posts. It grew louder as two thick poles and the
chain link stretched between them began
bending inwards.

TJ and Chico both switched to full auto
and began hosing down the bodies that were
frantically climbing the sloping path into the
generator area. They were no longer trying to
kill individual targets, rather hoping to damage
the attacking bodies enough to buy a few more
precious seconds for Dutch. Drago was still
pouring fire onto the left side and I the right, but
there were just too many infected.

"Dutch, the fence is failing. Get out now!"

Anvil

Part of me knew it was pointless to shout the warning. He wasn't going to budge until that second generator was up and running. But time ran out. With a horrific screech, the already compromised section of fence collapsed. Infected immediately began pouring in, reminding me of how water sluices over a barrier that has failed.

As the first infected made it inside the fence, a starter whined. It kept whining as all four of us poured as much fire into the breach as possible. Females were killed, maimed and shredded, but we barely slowed the tide. The engine coughed once, twice, sputtered, then kept limping along, barely running.

"He's running for the rope!" Edwards screamed.

But so were the females. They had Dutch spotted, and even though he was only a few feet away, he had to grab on and start climbing. He got both hands wrapped around the rope. Despite withering cover fire, multiple females slammed into him and pulled him to the ground before he was high enough to escape.

More rushed in and in an instant I lost sight of him beneath the mob. Everyone stopped firing, staring in horror at the pile of bodies. Females were screeching their delight, but we all clearly heard the screams escaping from Dutch's throat as they tore into his flesh. I kept my rifle aimed at the pile, waiting for a shot.

Moments later the crush of infected shifted slightly, and I caught sight of Dutch's face. He was still alive, his mouth open in a scream of unimaginable horror as he was torn open and eaten alive. Blood spurted from a severed artery, painting his face in a macabre death mask. Drawing a shuddering breath, I pulled the trigger, putting a round through his forehead and ending his pain.

"Motherfucker!" I screamed over the edge of the roof at the thousands of infected below.

Emotion fed my exhaustion, and I dropped back onto my ass after a long moment of wishing for a minigun and an endless supply of ammunition. My rage quickly turned to fatigue as I sat there with my head between my knees, panting and muttering curses. After most of a minute, a pair of boots appeared in front of me.

I took my time looking up to see who it was, meeting Chico's eyes when I did. Drago and TJ stood on either side of him, a few feet to his rear. All three of them had looks of shock on their faces, tears flowing from Chico's eyes. They'd been through hell with Dutch in Iraq, Afghanistan and now the United States. They were a small band of brothers that had just watched their big brother die.

"Thank you," Chico said, extending a thick hand to help me to my feet.

I sat there for a long time, just staring dumbly ahead. Finally, the raging screams of the infected pulled me back to reality, and I accepted his assistance.

Dirk Patton

"Don't thank me," I said, popping a fresh magazine into my rifle. "I hope any of you would do the same for me."

Each of them nodded and with a sigh, I looked over the edge. Both generators were running, their engines sounding smooth. At least Dutch hadn't died for nothing. The infected knew we were on the roof and were beginning to pile up against the base of the wall. The clock was ticking. Time to put the nerd to work.

I looked around, spying Edwards lying on his side against the low parapet. He was curled into the fetal position, gently rocking with his arms wrapped tightly around his body. Just fucking great. I didn't blame him, I wanted to do the same thing, but we had a job to do.

"Lieutenant," I shouted as I strode over to him. "On your feet. Time to earn your paycheck."

He didn't respond, and I motioned Drago over. The big Ranger bent and grabbed Edwards' shoulders, bodily lifting him to a standing position. I prefer to do my own manhandling, but my shoulder didn't feel like it could take the stress. The last thing I needed was to injure it further.

"Lieutenant Edwards. Can you hear me?"

Anvil

I stuck my face an inch from his and spoke loudly. His eyes were unfocused at first, finally finding mine and sharpening.

"You shot him!" He cried. "You didn't even try to save him!"

I took a step back as if I'd been physically attacked, struggling to control my own emotions. Before I could respond, Drago spun the smaller man around. Pressing his forehead against Edwards', he began speaking in a low, rapid voice. Too low for me to hear. Sensing the Ranger had this in hand, I stepped away and gave him space.

After a minute, Drago released him and took a couple of steps back. Edwards sniffed, wiping his nose on his sleeve. He didn't look in my direction, but Drago caught my eye and nodded. Motioning to him, I took rear guard as we moved into a diamond formation with Edwards in the middle.

We crossed the roof to the helipad, pausing long enough for the Lieutenant to collect a large backpack. He had brought along a couple of laptops and a bird's nest of different cables that would be used for him to connect to the servers and complete his job.

Adjacent to the helipad was a bulkhead with a heavy door. Inside would be a flight of stairs to the interior of the building. I just hoped there would be signs to guide us, and we didn't have to search the whole place for the server room. It was a huge structure, and I didn't think we had a whole lot of time before the infected piled up enough to reach the roof. If that happened, we were stuck inside with no way out.

Drago was on point, and he stepped to the door and tried the handle. It was locked. Slinging his rifle, he pulled a four-foot pry bar out of a sheath on his back. He had brought it specifically for this purpose. We had expected to find a lot of locked doors.

Jamming the tapered end into the seam between the door and jamb, he gripped it with both hands and pushed with all of his considerable body weight. There was a moment of resistance; then the jamb deformed, and the door popped open. Chico guarded Edwards, TJ and me at the ready, rifles seeking targets when it opened, but the brightly lit stairwell was empty.

Drago sheathed the iron bar and raised his rifle, leading the way in and down. TJ followed, then Edwards, Chico and me. As I passed through I pulled the door closed, mildly surprised to hear the lock click into place. At least our backs were protected. For the moment.

Anvil

The stairs descended to a small landing, turning and continuing down to end at another steel door. We stopped, spread out on the lower section of steps as Drago placed his ear against the surface of the door. There was no window, and he was trying to hear any threats that might be waiting before popping it open.

After a long pause, he turned and looked at the rest of us, shaking his head. That didn't mean the area on the other side was clear; it only meant he couldn't hear anything. This door wasn't locked, the handle turning smoothly and quietly in his big hand. He inched it open, peering through cautiously. TJ was in position to help slam it shut if there was an attack, hands raised and hovering inches from the middle of the door.

Apparently it was clear as a few moments later Drago pulled the door the rest of the way open and stepped through, breaking to his right. TJ followed on his heels going left, Chico holding Edwards back with a firm hand on his shoulder. When two ticks sounded over the radio, Chico lifted his hand and tapped the Lieutenant twice to let him know to proceed. I followed, softly closing the door behind me.

We were in a plush hallway. This was executive country, which made sense given the proximity of the helipad. The lights were on, and while I wouldn't call them bright, they lit every inch of space and left no shadows for an infected to be lurking in. None of us had any clue of the interior layout, so I just shrugged my shoulders when Drago looked at me. His guess was as good as mine.

Searching a large building is a pain. Searching a large building that might be housing infected is a downright bitch. It's really no different than clearing a structure the enemy has taken refuge in, but the psychological stress of worrying about a female charging out of a doorway and trying to eat you makes it seem much worse. I guess in a way it is. At least when you're hunting another man, you know he's scared too.

We moved down the hall, our feet silent on the deep pile carpeting. Drago shot a male wearing a security guard's uniform, then a moment later another dressed in a five-thousand-dollar suit. Then we came to a dead end that had to be the CEO's suite. Reversing directions, I was now on point and led the small team back past the rooftop access.

There were conference rooms. Storage rooms. Large offices belonging to Directors of this and Directors of that. Then the hall opened into a huge reception area with a tiled floor. A large, imposing desk guarded the corridor we were in, tall glass doors dominating the far side of the space.

Anvil

These were exterior doors, and I paused and stopped the team when I saw the solid wall of infected pressed up against them. They hadn't seen us, so for the moment weren't trying to batter their way in. I looked around for a way to cross to another hall that led deeper into the building without the unwanted guests spotting us.

The glass would be thick and heavy, but I didn't want to trust that it could withstand a concerted attack. If the infected broke through, well, in a word, we would be fucked. There were thousands, if not tens of thousands, of them in the immediate area. They would flood into the building, and there would be no stopping the surge until we were all dead.

But, the problem was there was no way to transition to the other hall without strolling across thirty yards of well-lit floor. And we'd be in full view of the doors the whole time. An idea occurred to me, and if there weren't several clocks ticking in my head at the same time, I would probably have never tried it. Pulling back from the corner, I waved the team into a tight knot to explain what I had in mind.

"That's going to work?" Chico asked when I finished.

"Got no clue. If you've got a better idea, speak up now."

Dirk Patton

I looked at him, watching the wheels turn behind his eyes, but he eventually shook his head. Glancing around, no one spoke up with an alternative suggestion.

"OK. Just me first. If it works, follow me one at a time and do exactly what I do."

Everyone nodded, and I stood, taking a deep breath. Turning back to face the reception area, I let my rifle hang on its sling, adjusted my posture to emulate an infected male, and shambled into sight of the doors.

I'd had the opportunity to observe a lot of males over the past few months, and if I do say so myself, I did a pretty good imitation of the way one moves. I knew this wouldn't work on other males, as they're blind as bats and couldn't see me. They'd know my status simply by smell, which the glass blocked. But most of the faces pressed against the glass were female.

Even though their sense of smell was enhanced, it seemed as if they still relied primarily on their vision to detect and identify potential prey. If they thought I was just another stupid male stumbling my way through the apocalypse, then maybe, just maybe, they wouldn't be interested in smashing their way inside.

43

Lieutenant Hunt sat back in frustration, resisting the impulse to bang the keyboard in front of him. A few hours ago he had received the codes for the Major's wife's locator beacon but hadn't been able to do anything with them. The satellites that would have normally broadcast the "wake up" signal were no longer in operation. And, even if he had enabled the tracker, the GPS satellites that would have been used to pinpoint her location were also dead.

He had been trying to find a way to utilize the NSA birds, which did have sophisticated locating capabilities, but kept coming up against a brick wall. In the system that would broadcast the coded signal, he received an error every time he issued the transmit command. For about the hundredth time he glanced over at Jessica.

She was in the secure conference room, reading a book while she waited for the mission to restore power to the RWA System's servers. Admiral Packard had ordered that she was not to be allowed to do anything other than complete her current assignment. There were just too many unanswered questions about her motivations.

Two Marines stood guard outside the door, making sure she didn't go anywhere and no one came near her. He had always liked the young woman, his heart going out to her despite his anger and disappointment over her actions. But just like she was needed to complete the activation and deployment of the THOR system, he acknowledged he needed her help.

She was one of those rare people that could look at code and actually see what it did. She understood security like no one he'd ever known. There was little doubt she could activate the signal and locate the woman they were trying to find.

With a sigh, he reached out and lifted the handset off his phone. Dialing an extension, he informed the Admiral's aide that he was on his way and needed to speak with Packard immediately. The aide, aware of the critical efforts underway in Hunt's group, assured him he would get him in front of the Admiral as soon as possible.

Securing his station, he stood and strode across the room to the exit. As he walked, he felt Jessica's stare, turning and meeting her eyes. She smiled at him, and he couldn't help but smile in return. He really did like her, and down deep didn't believe she was guilty of anything other than bad judgment.

Well, that and murder. He mentally cringed as he pushed through the high-security door, thinking about how she'd killed the Chief Petty Officer. Several people had rushed to pass judgment on her after the man died. Their theory was that the two of them were Russian agents, and she had killed him to protect herself. Eliminate the only person who could testify against her.

But Hunt didn't buy it. If that was the case, she never would have given him up when she first came forward. No, this had all the appearances of a young woman who had been used by a slightly older and much more cunning man.

He even understood, to a degree, why she had killed him the way she had. Her actions weren't those of a spy. They were those of a vengeful woman seeking retribution before she was locked away.

These thoughts swirled through his head as he crossed the base. It was dark, which always surprised him when he emerged from the subterranean room he worked in. A warm trade wind was blowing, ruffling his uniform pants about his ankles as he walked. It was a beautiful night, and he tried to enjoy the fresh, sea air while he had the opportunity.

Entering the building that housed the Admiral's office, he had to show his ID to a Marine guard and wait while the man verified he was cleared to enter. Passed through the first checkpoint, he was stopped three more times by additional Marines. The final checkpoint was at the entrance to the suite of offices occupied by Packard and his staff.

The Admiral was walking from the small galley to his office, a cup of steaming coffee in his hand. Noticing the Lieutenant, he called out to the Marine to let him through. Tucking his ID away, Hunt entered the large space and followed Packard when he was waved into the large office.

"What can I do for you, Lieutenant?" Packard lowered himself into a padded leather chair behind a desk that seemed as massive as the deck of an aircraft carrier.

"Sir, as you know I'm working on locating Major Chase's wife. Attempting to activate the CIA locator to track her."

"Yes, I'm aware," Packard said, noisily slurping coffee.

"Sir, I'm unable to operate the NSA satellite and issue the signal to her beacon. I need Petty Officer Simmons' assistance."

Hunt hadn't been offered a seat, so he stood ramrod straight in front of the desk as he spoke. Packard took another sip from a chipped mug emblazoned with the name and number for the USS Enterprise. His last command before being promoted to Admiral.

"Relax and take a chair, Lieutenant," Packard said after staring at the young officer for most of a minute.

"What do you think of all this?" The Admiral asked.

"Sorry, sir. All of what?"

Hunt thought he knew what was being asked, but wasn't about to start voicing an opinion only to find out he was talking about something other than what he was being asked.

"The Petty Officer. The Russians. Was she just a dupe as she claims, or was she actively involved in passing information?"

Packard took another loud sip, watching Hunt under his bushy, grey eyebrows. The Lieutenant paused for a moment to gather his thoughts and think about what he wanted to say, feeling the weight of the Admiral's gaze.

"Sir, if I had to place a bet, I'd say that she was duped. She came forward as soon as she realized what had happened. She didn't have to do that, and frankly I respect the strength of character it demonstrated. Petty Officer Simmons has been under my command for four years, and I have never seen anything other than a complete devotion to duty from her."

Packard picked his cup off the desk and swiveled his chair until he was facing the large window behind him. The view was stunning in the daytime, looking across acres of manicured, tropical landscaping and onto the blue waters of Pearl Harbor. Now, all that could be seen was the anchor lights of several ships in port for repairs.

"Have you ever heard of Chief Warrant Officer William Peele? He was an intelligence analyst."

"Yes sir, I know the name," Hunt replied to the back of the Admiral's chair.

"One of the highest security clearances in the Navy. Dealt with intelligence on Chinese naval capabilities, keeping tabs on their buildup. Did some really outstanding work. Or we thought he did. Until we found out, he was working for the Chinese and feeding us disinformation that was fabricated in Beijing. He was married to a young, beautiful Chinese girl that happened to be his handler.

"This was quite a few years ago, and I was at the Pentagon at the time. Headed up the investigation into Peele and the work to identify all of the false intel that had affected how we prepared for a confrontation with China. One of the things that stands out in my mind is a conversation I had with the Commander, who was Peele's CO. Any idea what he told me?"

Packard swiveled back around to face Hunt, taking a sip before placing the coffee mug on his desk. He watched the Lieutenant, patiently waiting for a response.

"I have no idea, sir."

"He said that he believed Peele had been duped. Used. That he had a good character and wouldn't intentionally do anything to harm the US."

Hunt stared back at the Admiral, thinking about what he'd just been told.

"What happened to his wife, sir?" Hunt asked.

Packard looked at him for a few moments, a smile finally appearing on his face.

"He defended her to the end. Wouldn't tell us where she was. Wouldn't cooperate in her capture even though we offered him incentives to do so. She got away. Back to China. A few years later she was spotted at an event in Beijing that was attended by our Ambassador and some of his staff. She was on the arm of one of their senior Admirals."

Hunt sat perfectly straight in the chair, hoping he'd made his point with the Admiral. He had recognized Peele's name as soon as Packard mentioned it. The Navy had kept the whole incident very quiet, and the press had never gotten a whiff.

A week after graduating from the Naval Academy in Annapolis, Hunt had been assigned to a Naval Intelligence unit in Little Creek, Virginia. The same unit Peele had worked for. He'd heard the story from the inside.

"Very well," Packard said after staring at him for an uncomfortable stretch of time. "She can help."

"Thank you, sir!"

Hunt stood, coming to attention. He had gotten what he came for and was ready to get the hell out of the Admiral's office.

"I like her, too," Packard said. "But don't let your personal feelings cloud your judgment, Lieutenant. Dismissed."

Hunt thanked him again, turned and fought the urge to run as he headed for the door.

It seemed like it took forever, but I finally made it across the large lobby and into the cover of the new hallway. The females had reacted when I'd stepped out, several of them screaming as they pressed in tighter against the glass to peer at me. Thumps sounded from all across the front, but I forced myself to ignore them and continue on my weaving, wobbling, shambling path.

The infected settled down quickly when I didn't react. They were buying it. Playing my role to the hilt, I deliberately walked into the wall on the far side of the lobby. I wasn't thinking, and my damaged shoulder protested loudly with a bolt of lightning when I bumped it against the hard surface.

I stumbled back a step, not entirely faking it. Biting my lip, I adjusted directions and disappeared around the corner. As soon as I was out of the view of the infected at the front doors, I raised my rifle and made a thorough scan of the hall I had just entered.

Rather than plush carpet, it was shiny tile, and I felt a little glimmer of hope that we were getting closer. This looked like an area where work was actually performed. Several corridors branched off, and there were a lot of doors.

Dirk Patton

Some of them were closed tightly, but many were open. I glanced over my shoulder when more thumps sounded, seeing Chico stumbling along like a drunk as he made his way across the lobby.

Forcing myself to ignore him and trust he would make it without exciting the females, I moved several feet deeper into the hall before dropping to a knee with my rifle covering the unknown territory. Chico finally finished crossing the open space and as soon as he was behind cover, joined me in providing security for the rest of the team.

Edwards came next, and soon after he stepped into view, there were the loudest thumps and screams so far.

"Slow down!"

Drago's hiss over the radio made me cringe. If Edwards lost his nerve, I had no doubt the females would see through our ruse. We were already on borrowed time, but that would drastically speed up the clock. With Chico next to me, I took the opportunity to turn and check on the Lieutenant's progress.

He was walking slow, but moving normally, about half way across. He had definitely caught the attention of the infected, the pounding increasing in volume.

Anvil

"If you don't walk like an infected I'm going to shoot you in the leg. Sir."

This was from TJ over the radio and caused Edwards to come to a stop. Even from a distance I could see the fear on his face. The sweat soaking through his shirt and beaded on his forehead. The wide eyes. He was close to breaking.

"Edwards," I said softly into the radio. "You're doing fine. Just take a slow step. Walk like you're drunk. That's all you've got to do. Just walk. Nice and slow."

He looked at me from across the room, and I didn't like what I saw in his eyes. Fear was turning to panic as the infected continued to bang on the glass. The volume was increasing as they began to realize things weren't exactly what they seemed. More and more screams were sounding, muted by the heavy doors, but still clearly audible. I was afraid Edwards was about to lose it.

"Hang in there, LT. I'm coming to get you."

Drago stepped into sight and the pounding on the doors re-doubled. He was moving slow with one shoulder dipped below the other, arms swinging loosely just like an infected male. I checked on Edwards, not happy to see him trembling as he stood frozen in the bright lights of the lobby.

"It's OK, Edwards," I said. "Drago's on his way to you. He'll help you get under cover. Just close your eyes and take some deep breaths."

I was glad to see the young man take my advice. Maybe it would help, maybe not, but I had to try something before he bolted in panic. Not that I could blame him. I might have done the same thing if I hadn't been fighting the infected for as long as I had. It still didn't sound like they were seriously trying to get through the doors, but that could change in an instant.

Drago finally reached him after what seemed like hours. I had no doubt it seemed even longer to Edwards. Coming up behind him, Drago bumped into his back, pausing as he turned his head away from the glass. I could see his lips moving, but he wasn't speaking loud enough to activate his radio so I couldn't hear what he was saying.

With another jerking motion, he bumped Edwards again, and the two of them began moving forward. One excruciatingly slow step at a time. The females were calming. Not much, but there was a slight reduction in the noise coming from the entrance. Maybe we were going to make it.

Anvil

Edwards and Drago were less than ten feet from rounding the corner into the hall when there was a scream from the far side of the lobby. The scream of an attacking female. I stood to see TJ roll into full view of the doors with a small, blonde woman dressed in a business skirt tearing at him.

The reaction from the infected outside was immediate. As one, they screamed. The sound was nearly deafening; then fists were drumming on the glass so hard it sounded like thunder on a hot summer evening. Drago shoved Edwards towards me before sprinting to TJ's aide. I grabbed the Lieutenant's arm and yanked him past into the hall, stepping forward far enough to peek around the corner.

The assault on the doors and surrounding wall, which was made of the same heavy glass, was so violent I could see the surface flexing. Drago made it to TJ in time to haul a corpse off of him. TJ had killed her with his knife and blood dripped off the tip as Drago grabbed a fistful of his vest and lifted him to his feet.

"Run," I shouted, checking on the integrity of the glass again.

It was still vibrating as the females threw themselves against it and pounded with fists and forearms. We didn't have long. Sooner, rather than later, stress fractures would appear. Then the glass would fail altogether. When that happened...

The Rangers pounded around the corner as Chico fired several shots. I spun, seeing a female and two males drop dead to the floor. The males had stumbled out of an open door, the female charging in from one of the halls that opened off the one we were in.

"Edwards, what are we looking for?"

He had sunk to the floor, and I grabbed his collar, jerking him to his feet. Without thinking, I'd used my injured arm, and the pain reminded me to pay attention to what I was doing.

"It will be a secure door. Look for an IT area. It will probably be somewhere near there."

"You heard the man," I said. "Let's move!"

We set out in a box formation. The hall wasn't wide, so we settled for two of us in front of Edwards and two behind. Chico and I took point, moving shoulder to shoulder. We ignored closed doors and gave the rooms with open ones a quick scan before pulling them shut. Despite the increasing intelligence of the females, I still hadn't seen one operate a door knob.

When we reached the first intersection, I called a halt with a raised fist. The hall continued on ahead of us, looking the same. Just more doors. To our right it ran for forty yards, ending at what appeared to be a heavy steel door. A security keypad was set in the wall to the right of the handle.

"What do you think?" I mumbled to Edwards.

"Maybe," he said. "Right kind of set up, but no way to know."

Behind us, the booming sounds of the females trying to smash their way in still sounded. Frankly, I was surprised they hadn't already gotten in. But then, from what I'd seen so far, this company hadn't skimped on security and building materials. The glass was tougher than it looked.

Moving us to the right, I motioned for Chico and Drago to trade places. By the time we covered the distance to the end of the corridor, Drago had the pry bar in hand and was ready to force our way through. He tried the handle first, but it was secure. Repeating the process, he had followed on the roof, it was only a matter of seconds before the door popped free.

He was stepping away, partially off balance from leaning his weight onto the iron bar when the door was violently slammed open. The big Ranger was knocked back, losing his footing and falling. The heavy tool slipped out of his hand and rang loudly when it bounced on the hard floor.

Several females rushed us, screaming as they attacked. I was too close to use my rifle for anything other than a club. Pounding one of them to the floor, I was hit and sent spinning backwards by a flying tackle. Landing on my bad shoulder, I nearly passed out from the pain as the female lunged for my throat.

I got my good hand around her neck at the last moment, spittle from her scream spraying across my face. Pressing her away from my body, I managed to open enough space to get a knee between us and kick her clear. She turned in the air, landed on her feet and without pausing launched herself like a missile, aiming for my head.

Ducking and slipping to the side, I captured her head in the bend of my good arm as she flew in. Tightening my muscles, I savagely jerked to the side and snapped her neck as another female took my legs out from under me. I came down on top of her, hands grabbing my vest as she tried to pull her snapping jaws to my throat.

All around I could hear the sounds of the other men fighting with the females. Screams from the infected. Grunts of pain and exertion from the Rangers. I had no time to check but hoped we were holding our own. The female beneath me wasn't screaming as she struggled to reach my flesh. And she was strong, especially when I couldn't bring my damaged arm into the fight.

I battled for a few moments, shifting to keep my body weight on top of her, pinning her to the floor. Throwing two, hard and fast punches, I hoped to either stun the bitch or maybe even knock her out. She absorbed the blows without any apparent ill effects.

Flailing to keep her mouth away from my body, my hand slipped to the top of her head and into a thick mane of hair. Grasping a fistful, I started slamming the back of her head onto the hard floor. On the fourth impact, she stopped struggling, and her eyes rolled up in their sockets. I'd felt the back of her skull crack open and figured she was done, but lifted then bashed her head a final time. Bright red blood began spreading out beneath her limp form, and I rolled to my feet and pulled my Kukri.

The battle was over. Drago and Chico were both bleeding from bites to their hands and arms, but were on their feet, rifles up and scanning for more threats. A total of seven females were lying dead in the hall, and so was Edwards. TJ was kneeling over him; hand extended towards his ravaged throat as if he wanted to check his pulse.

Dirk Patton

"What the fuck do we do now?" TJ asked as he stood up and looked at me.

"We find the server room and call someone who can tell us what to do."

It was the right answer. The only answer I could give. We hadn't come this far and lost two men to give up now. TJ nodded, bending and retrieving Edwards' pack. Now all we had to do was find the server room.

From the lobby, there was a loud crash, the sound of screaming females suddenly increasing dramatically. They'd broken through the glass. We were out of time. I gestured at the open door, and Chico stepped through, Drago tight on his back. TJ and I followed, pulling the door closed behind us.

The door let into a massive space that was used for manufacturing. Lining the far wall were a series of clean rooms where sensitive electronics could be assembled without worry of contaminating particles. Closer suspended from chains attached to large steel girders, were two large somethings. Scaffolding surrounded them, providing access for the workers. I had no clue what they were.

Each was round and over forty feet long and at least half that wide. On the tapered ends facing us were thirty-six holes, each about a foot in diameter, making the device look like a massive Gatling gun. I only had a minute to look around before the door behind me shook as females slammed against it and began trying to batter their way through.

This one didn't concern me. Much. It was steel, set into a steel frame. And it opened out, towards them. I didn't see how they could get through. Still, I wasn't happy to have them this close.

"There," Chico said, pointing at the far wall.

I followed his finger, seeing another door that looked identical to the one we'd just come in. Scanning the perimeter of the cavernous space, I didn't see any other exits with the exception of a huge roll-up door that was large enough to accommodate the equipment dangling over our heads.

"Let's go," I said, heading for the door at a trot.

The Rangers fell in behind me, all of us running with our rifles up and ready. I didn't really expect to encounter any more females in this area. If there were any that could attack, they would have shown themselves.

"Maybe," I thought, reminding myself of the smart ones that would lay in wait and spring an ambush.

Keeping the thought in mind, I didn't slow as we made our way through a labyrinth of equipment. Behind, the pounding on the door continued, and I was worried we wouldn't be able to find the server room before the infected completely flooded the interior of the building. And if we did, I didn't see how we weren't going to be trapped.

We reached the far door, quickly stacking up and preparing to go through. We'd made a couple of critical errors so far. First, we hadn't thoroughly cleared the executive area, and the female's attack on TJ had alerted the infected at the entrance to our presence. Second, we hadn't been ready for an attack when Drago forced the last door open. That sloppiness had cost Edwards his life, and might very well doom our mission to failure.

A quick check to make sure everyone was ready and I tapped Chico. He turned the handle and pushed the door open, the rest of us with our rifles up and pointing into the new hall. It was empty, for the moment. We rushed into it, and TJ gently closed the door behind us.

More offices and a large area filled with a whole bunch of cubicles. I paused when Drago pointed at a discreet nameplate affixed to a door.

Tim Shamburg – IT Manager

Well, at least we were in the right area. I took a moment to look around, spying a set of double doors protected by an electronic keypad on the far side of the cubicles. Just like what Edwards had described.

We moved through the open space, rifles ready as it was a rabbit warren of waist-high walls that could conceal any number of infected. Many of the desks held pieces of computer equipment in various states of assembly. Several of them had small libraries of well-worn paperback books with titles like *The Linux Bible* and *The Existential Coder*.

What the hell was existential about coding? Guess that was for bigger minds than mine. At least it confirmed we were in the IT area. Maybe if I survived this, I'd write a book about fighting the infected and call it The Existential Shitstorm.

These doors were solid wood; not steel like the others we'd encountered. I had no idea if that meant anything, but it presented a problem. The steel doors Drago had pried open had enough flexibility in them to partially spring back into place and allow the lock to re-engage once we passed through. Where steel flexed, wood would break.

And, these were hinged on the sides and locked in the middle where they met. If we forced them, we wouldn't be able to secure them behind us. With a whole tide of females rushing into the building, that was problem.

We were very lucky we hadn't been found already, and eventually, there wouldn't be an inch of floor space that wasn't occupied by infected. Unless it was behind a locked door too stout for them to break through.

I quickly explained the dilemma to the team after stopping Drago from using the pry bar. Glances were exchanged, but no one had any good ideas. Turning, I winced when I heard screams from another area of the building. The females were coming, and they were way too close. Ignoring the swiftly approaching danger, I stepped to the doors and looked them over.

They were smooth and featureless with only handles set on the inside edges for pulling them open once the keypad released the lock. The lock would most likely be a powerful electromagnet that held tight to a metal plate attached to the top of each door. Punch in the proper code on the keypad and the magnet would be turned off long enough for the door to be pulled open. By the time the door swung shut it would be back on.

Grasping the handle on the right-hand door, I pulled. Hard. The door flexed slightly, the bottom edge moving an inch, but the top didn't budge. This didn't really do anything other than confirm my theory. Which didn't help. We were still locked out, weren't positive this was the server room, and the screams were getting closer.

"Anyone know how to defeat a keypad?"

I didn't bother to turn around. If one of them had that particular skill, I would have been surprised.

"Electromagnetic lock. Right?"

I turned to see TJ staring at a spot above the doors.

Dirk Patton

"Yeah. You got an idea?"

"Magnet needs power. Power needs wires. This isn't an outside door. Wires should just be routed behind the drywall."

He pointed with his knife at the spot he'd been looking at. Realization of the simplicity of his suggestion to open the door hit me, and I grabbed a rolling office chair and wheeled it into place. With Drago and I holding it steady, TJ climbed up to stand on the seat as Chico kept an eye on the area to our rear.

First, powdery white dust, then chunks of drywall fell as he broke through. It didn't take him long to find the wires, sticking his knife through the opening.

"Don't cut them," I said quickly, TJ's blade freezing an instant before he began slicing. "Try to disconnect them so we can reconnect from inside and keep the infected out."

He grunted, sheathed his knife and stuck his arm into the wall, feeling around. While he worked, Chico began firing as the first females appeared at the far edge of the cubicles. Telling Drago to stay put, I moved next to Chico and added my fire to support him. It was a trickle of females at first, quickly becoming a flood. In only a few seconds we went from targeting lone runners to shooting into a seething mass of infected.

"Out of time!" I shouted to TJ as the infected flowed through the cubicles like water around rocks.

Chico and I had already switched to leg and pelvis shots, hoping to slow the advance. It worked to a degree, but the push was unstoppable with just rifles.

"TJ!" I screamed to be heard over the infected.

"Got it," he shouted back.

Chico and I began moving backwards as the throng of females surged. With only feet of open space remaining between us and them, Drago grabbed the backs of our vests and yanked us through the open door. TJ was ready, pulling it shut the instant we were clear.

Drago released us and leapt forward, jamming the iron pry bar through the interior handles and gripping it tightly in both hands as he leaned his body weight back to hold the door shut. Chico jumped in, adding his hands and weight as both doors shook under the assault of the females.

TJ had shoved the office chair through ahead of him, and I held it steady as he climbed

Dirk Patton

up and broke open the wall above the door. Once
he was through it only took him seconds to reach
in, find the wires and reconnect them. When the
second one went into place, there was a loud
click from the top of the door as the
electromagnetic lock reengaged.

With a sigh, Drago and Chico carefully
released the pry bar which went back into the
sheath on Drago's back. The doors shook,
bouncing in their frame, but were held tight by
the big magnet.

"How long until they get through?" Chico
asked, fingering his rifle.

"They'll last until the generators run out
of fuel."

I was remembering the locks failing in Los
Alamos when the power went out. I didn't
bother telling them the story. It was a long one,
and if the same thing happened here, there
wouldn't be a happy ending.

Remembering why we were here in the
first place, I turned to see if we'd gotten lucky. I
was happy to see row after row of ceiling-high
metal racks, stuffed full of servers. Then I
realized I didn't have a clue what the hell to do
with them.

We spent a few minutes clearing the room, making sure we were alone. The pounding on the doors was incessant; the screams thankfully muted somewhat by the heavy wood. It was still nerve racking to have so many infected this close.

"Don't suppose anyone knows what the hell to do," I said, glancing around at the small team.

"TJ's kind of a geek," Chico spoke up.

All of us turned to look at him.

"I'm a gamer," he explained, shrugging. "I've set up a few tournaments and had to network everything together and set up servers and routers."

I shook my head, understanding little of what he'd just said. I knew the terms but didn't know what they meant.

"OK, you're the guy. Do we need to get you on the phone with someone, or do you know what to do?"

"I don't have the first idea where to start," he said, shaking his head.

Dirk Patton

We had planned for Edwards to need to talk to Pearl Harbor as he brought stuff online. On the roof, a battery powered, encrypted satellite communications unit was already synced up and connected to an orbiting bird. In the dead Lieutenant's pack was a small headset that would wirelessly connect to the comm unit.

I dug it out, turned it on and slipped it over my head, initiating a call to the only preset. Lieutenant Hunt answered immediately, and I identified myself.

"We're in the server room, but we lost our tech specialist," I told him. "One of the Rangers has some familiarity with computer equipment, but you're going to have to talk him through it."

"That's not good. This isn't like calling the help desk because your email isn't working."

"No other option, Lieutenant," I growled, irritated with his response.

I knew it wasn't optimal. But it was all we had.

"Sorry, sir. Was thinking out loud as much as anything. Let me transfer you to Petty Officer Simmons. She's leading the effort on our end and is the best person to guide you through the process."

There was silence for a moment, then a series of clicks as he rerouted the call.

"Sir?"

I immediately recognized the voice.

"Jessica. What the hell did you do?"

There wasn't really time for this, but the words just came out when I heard her voice. She was quiet for a long pause, then took a deep breath and let it out as a sigh.

"Sorry, sir. I fucked up. It was my fault the Russians kept finding you. I let things slip to my boyfriend and... and..." her voice broke as she tried to control her emotions.

"Jessica, we can't undo what's been done. All we can do is move forward. You made a mistake, and fortunately, that mistake didn't cost anyone their life. You have saved me more times than I can count, and in my book that far outweighs your error in judgment. I trust you, and I need you focused. OK?"

"Yes, sir," she sniffed. "Sorry, sir. Put me on with your tech and we'll get started."

"Well, we've got a small problem on our end. Our tech was killed by infected. You're going to be working with one of my Rangers."

"Oh shit," she breathed. "Does he know what he's doing?"

"He knows what he's doing, and he *will* make this work," I said firmly, meeting TJ's eyes and nodding.

TJ looked like he'd rather be anywhere else. I didn't blame him.

"OK, sir. Oh, before you go, I have something for you. Your friend in Australia came through. I've got the codes for your wife's beacon. I was just starting to work on locating her when you called."

Lucas had done it! I wasn't surprised, but at the same time, it was a relief.

"Thank you, Jessica. As soon as you find her, be sure to pass the data to Colonel Blanchard in Idaho. He's waiting for your call."

"Not you, sir?" She sounded surprised.

"No, probably not me," I said. "It's a long story we don't have time for. Hold on; I'm passing you to TJ."

I pulled the headset off and handed it over. TJ slipped it on, adjusted it to fit his smaller head and said, "Hello?"

Watching and listening for a few moments, I heard him give Jessica a brief rundown of what he knew. It didn't take long. Soon he wandered off down one of the aisles of equipment, looking for something. I left him to it and turned to where Drago and Chico were standing, keeping a close eye on the door.

"Think he can do it?" I asked, tilting my head in TJ's direction.

"He's got the best shot of any of us," Chico said. "You should see some of the shit he's set up. Had the whole fucking barracks looking like a mad scientist's lab. How that relates to what he's got to do here, I can't say, but at least there's a chance."

I nodded, watching as TJ pressed a button on one of the pieces of equipment. A keyboard folded down and locked in place in front of him, revealing a monitor. I shook my head, glad someone else was doing this.

"What about getting out of here when he's done? Any bright ideas?" I asked.

"I think we're about to be FUBAR, sir."

Drago answered me, meaning Fucked Up Beyond All Recognition. Chico looked at him for a moment then nodded in agreement. I didn't disagree but wasn't ready to give up yet. I knew they weren't either. They were just being realistic and not trying to sugar coat things.

"Well, we'd better come up with something," I said. "Don't know about you, but I'm not ready to be the main course for all those needy bitches out there."

I nodded at the door which was shaking in its frame from the constant assault of the infected females. If it opened in or wasn't braced by the steel frame, they would probably have already smashed their way through.

"Maybe they don't like Cuban," Chico grinned.

"You're safe. Those Cuban sausages are too small. They'll run right past you for a Viking-sized meal," Drago said with a perfectly straight face.

I snorted a laugh as Chico flipped him off, moving away to begin a methodical survey of the large room. We had cleared it already, making sure there weren't any infected in residence. Now I wanted a closer look in hopes of finding something that would get us out when the time came.

The room was large and well lit. And cold. Computer equipment puts off a lot of heat and server rooms are normally kept well air conditioned. This was the case here as well. The first thing I saw as I began looking around was a large thermostat, secured behind a heavy plastic cover. It was on the wall, just to the right of the doors. Peering at it, I could see it was set to keep the room at a constant sixty-five degrees.

Continuing on, moving in a clockwise direction, I didn't find much. Two large touchscreen panels were built into the wall. Beyond them, a couple of desks with computers, cables snaking behind to jacks located on the wall. A bulletin board with the usual notices that are required by federal law. A white board with a series of schematics that were Greek to me. And a vintage poster from my all-time favorite TV series, the X-Files.

It was the one that hung in FBI Agent Fox Mulder's office. A grainy photo of a flying saucer, the words "I WANT TO BELIEVE" printed across the bottom. I paused for a moment, staring at the poster and remembering a better time. After a bit, I shook my head and kept circling.

The wall at the end of the room was blank, and I quickly walked to the rear. Space was tight here as the server racks came to within two feet of the wall. Looking down its length, I could see there was nothing but more smooth drywall. I reversed course, not wanting to squeeze through and risk bumping into something and causing a problem.

Back by the doors I looked for TJ, finally spotting him two-thirds of the way down one of the aisles. He was sitting on the floor, another keyboard folded out in front of him. He was typing away at a furious pace, repeating the commands he was entering back to Jessica. He didn't need my help and sure as hell didn't need me interrupting.

Returning to my survey, I noted Chico and Drago doing the same thing. There were also several ceiling tiles out of place where one of them had climbed up for a look.

"What's above us?" I asked them.

"Two feet of space that's full of cabling, then a solid ceiling," Drago answered. "We might get out that way with a breaching charge, but I don't know what's up there. Besides, we blow a hole in the ceiling and all that debris is going to crash down on the computers."

I nodded and slowly started moving counter-clockwise from the doors. Even though they had already checked, I wanted to look for myself. To the left of the doors, I stopped to inspect the wall. A large, metal plate painted bright red and emblazoned with the word "FIRE" covered most of the surface. An emergency button the size of my fist stuck out from the middle of the plate, a large cardboard tag hanging from it.

I glanced at the tag, noting it was a maintenance log for the fire suppression system. Next to the button was a sign with bold lettering that read "USE BREATHING EQUIPMENT AND VACATE WHEN ALARM SOUNDS. HALON 1301 BEING RELEASED". Beneath this was a glass fronted door to a compartment built into the wall that held six emergency breathing systems with full face masks.

Pulling the door open I picked up one of the breathers and looked it over. A small aluminum cylinder was attached to the side, a short hose leading from it to a port on the clear plastic face mask. Oxygen supply, and judging from the size of the cylinder, about five minutes' worth. Enough to get clear of the area in the event the halon system was activated.

"Got an idea?"

I looked around to see Chico, standing slightly behind and watching me. Shrugging, I returned the mask to the cabinet and closed the door.

"Wish I did," I said, walking away to check the rest of the room.

I didn't find anything else other than blank walls. No secret doors. No Sci-Fi weapons we could use to kill all the infected who were trapping us. Nothing. Returning to the front of the room, I paused to check on TJ, moving on to take a seat at one of the desks when it was obvious he was hard at work.

"How long you think this will take?" Drago asked.

He had walked up and hooked the leg of the other chair with his foot, pulling it out and dropping his bulk into it.

"Edwards said it would take him half an hour if he didn't run into any problems. Now? Who knows. The woman that TJ is talking to is sharp, and he seems more than capable of carrying out her instructions, so..."

I held my hands out, palms up. Drago nodded and leaned back in his seat, stretching his long legs out. I wasn't in the mood to talk, wanting to let my mind work on the problem of how to escape. Fortunately, he picked up on that and remained quiet. A few moments later I heard him start snoring.

Sitting there, I kept running different scenarios through my head. We couldn't fight our way out. The moment we opened those doors an unstoppable flood of females would rush into the room and tear us to ribbons. Probably just as well. We were all dangerously low on ammo.

Neither was anyone going to be able to fight their way in and rescue us. There were way too many infected in and around the building for that. Would they grow bored and leave? I snorted a sardonic laugh when I had that thought. The infected didn't get bored or tired or give up. They might get distracted, but once they were zeroed in on prey, they didn't stop.

I looked up at the ceiling, remembering Drago's comment about a breaching charge. Chico had some in his pack in case we'd needed to blast to get through doors. But, the big Ranger had nailed the problem with that idea. If we blew a hole in the ceiling, the debris had to go somewhere, and gravity would pull it down on the cabling and server racks.

One of the side walls? What was behind the drywall? Standing, I kicked Drago's foot, waking him from his nap. Chico was sitting close by, his ass on the hard floor and back leaned against the wall.

"The walls," I said, greeted by blank looks. "What's on the other side? We can't blast through the ceiling and risk damaging the equipment, but what about through a wall into an adjacent room?"

"You don't think they'll all be full of infected?" Chico asked, not terribly enthusiastic about my idea.

"Don't know, but let's see what's behind the drywall."

I headed for the wall beyond the X-Files poster, drawing my Kukri as I approached. Several swings with the heavy blade cut an opening that I could then reach through and begin pulling chunks of the drywall out of my way. Drago was attacking the other end wall, and Chico was busily opening up the rear.

When I had a two-foot diameter space cleared, I clicked on a flashlight and played the beam around the void. Metal studs, which are commonly used for interior walls in commercial buildings, gleamed in the light. Beyond that was a smooth concrete surface. Maybe we could blast through, maybe not. I had no idea how thick it was.

Sheathing the Kukri, I went to check on the other two. Drago was also looking at a concrete wall. But Chico had found a layer of sound insulation, then the back side of more drywall. The walls Drago and I had checked were either interior load bearing or exterior.

Chico's wall would open to another interior space.

"Only one problem with going that way, sir," Chico said softly as he moved the sound barrier back in place. "I can hear infected on the other side."

Shit! Oh well. At least we now knew that going through a wall wasn't an option. And that was the last idea I could come up with. We were trapped, and there wasn't any way out.

48

"I'm in!"

Jessica smiled as the screen in front of her refreshed to display a command prompt. She was now logged into the system's server in the building in Utah, the signal from her terminal being uplinked to a satellite and bounced back down to a large dish on the roof above the server room.

"You're in? You've got control?"

TJ's voice over her headset was every bit as excited as hers.

"Yes. Don't touch a thing. Hold on."

Jessica's fingers flew across the keyboard. She quickly moved through the system, identifying the settings she would need to change and the files that needed to be copied. Behind her, Lieutenant Hunt stared intently at her screen. As he watched, he was reminded just how talented the young woman was. How she somehow intuitively knew how to make the system do what she wanted.

"How long?" He asked when she paused to watch a file load.

Anvil

Jessica jumped and glanced over her shoulder. She had been so engrossed in what she was doing that she hadn't realized he was standing behind her. Turning back to her station, she opened a new window that showed the progress of multiple, simultaneous file transfers.

"Probably seven or eight hours," she answered. "These are damn big files. And once I've got them I have to decrypt, unzip, then load them onto our servers. Then mount the virtual discs and install them. Likely seven hours if there's no hiccups and everything works like it's supposed to. Say nine to be safe."

Jessica had continued working as she spoke, her fingers typing one thing while her mouth communicated in a totally different language.

"Are you through with the tech on that end?"

"Yes, sir," Jessica said in a distracted voice.

"OK, I'm going to take control of the comms. I need to speak with Major Chase."

Jessica nodded and continued working without pause. The smallest of the files had completed transferring to Hawaii, and she had already made a copy of it and stored it on a backup server.

Hunt returned to his station and donned a headset. He rerouted the comm circuit and a few moments later could hear the background noise in the server room in Utah. There was the normal low roar of all the cooling fans maintaining the individual servers' internal temperatures. He could also clearly hear pounding of fists on a door and a near constant cacophony of screams from the infected.

Identifying himself, he asked that the headset be passed to Major Chase. Footsteps, a brief, muffled conversation followed by the scrape of the microphone against fabric and the Major's voice spoke in his ear.

"Major, Lieutenant Hunt. We're in the system, but it's going to take about nine hours before we have full control. Are you going to be able to keep the servers up and running that long?"

"Yes," he answered. "We brought enough fuel for the generators. Shouldn't be a problem, but nine hours is cutting it close. I'm supposed to be in Russian hands in less than ten. Besides, we're trapped. Infected in the building. We're not going anywhere."

Hunt sat back, blinking. He didn't have any idea what the Major was talking about. In the Russian's hands?

Anvil

"Major, I think I'd better try and get the Admiral on the line. Stand by."

"Copy. I got nothing else to do but stand by."

Lieutenant Hunt quickly placed a call to Admiral Packard's office, his aide immediately connecting the call. Hunt briefly described the situation before joining the two calls.

"Major?"

"Admiral. Greetings from Utah," John said.

"I understand you've completed your mission but can't get out of the building."

"Correct, sir. The infected breached, and we're trapped in the server room. We've been looking for a way out, but there's not one."

"Colonel Blanchard is only an hour away by air. I'll have him send some Marines your way to extract you," Packard said, sounding like he was ready to hang up and start issuing orders.

"Negative, sir. Won't work. There are several thousand infected in the building and tens of thousands in the parking lot surrounding us. There's no way anyone is fighting their way in. Or out."

The circuit was quiet for a long moment as the Admiral digested what he'd just been told.

"Sir," Major Chase spoke into the silence. "What does this do to the agreement with the Russians about turning me over? We're cutting it close if the weapon, or whatever it is, won't be ready for another nine hours."

"It's going to have to be," Packard growled. "Lieutenant, how realistic is that estimate?"

"Direct from Petty Officer Simmons, sir. She's usually spot on. She doesn't pad or underestimate the amount of time she needs. But I am concerned that if there's an unforeseen problem the timeline could get extended."

"That's not an option, Lieutenant. Less than ten hours from now, either we're online and operational, or Major Chase needs to be in Russian hands. If neither of those things happen, the bombs start dropping.

"You make sure that whatever the Petty Officer needs, she gets. Immediately. I'm sending my aide over. He will ensure you get instant cooperation."

Packard's voice sounded tired as he spoke. He was betting the last remnants of America on a young woman who hadn't exactly shown that she had the best judgment. But, his back was against the wall, and the only other option was unconditional surrender.

"Yes, sir," Hunt said.

"Admiral, one more thing if I may?" Major Chase interjected before the call could end.

"Don't know why not, Major. There's not a damn thing for me to do for the next ten hours except wear a hole in my carpet and smoke too much."

"Sir, I wanted to ask about Jessica. Petty Officer Simmons."

"What about her?" The Admiral asked, cautiously.

"What's going to happen to her, sir?"

"I'm not sure that's your concern, Major," Packard said, the warning in his voice clear.

"Sir, begging your pardon, but I'm making it my concern. She has saved my life more times than I can count. And, since she's still at work, she's apparently a very valuable asset to the Navy and the United States."

"I'm well aware of her value, Major. Thank you for bringing the obvious to my attention. Is that all?" Heavy sarcasm was in the Admiral's voice.

"No, sir. It's not. You've asked a lot of me. Turning myself over. And you've already agreed to do a couple of things for me, for which I'm grateful. Now, I'm either going to die in this building, or someone will come up with some way to get me out so I can be executed in Moscow. I want one more thing from you, sir.

"Don't put the Petty Officer on trial for what she's done. She's a patriot, just like the rest of us. Her only crime is that she's young and made a mistake. If you can't forgive and trust her to continue there in Hawaii, put her on a plane to Australia. There's enough dead Americans, sir."

Major Chase finished speaking and went quiet. He had put it all out there, and Lieutenant Hunt found himself agreeing. Jessica didn't deserve to be tried, convicted and possibly executed for what she'd done. Yes, it was bad, but these were desperate times. The only problem was the little matter of her boyfriend. No evidence that he was a spy had been found, yet, and murder was still murder.

"I will take it under consideration, Major."

There was a click and Packard was gone. Hunt took a deep breath, blowing it out through his mouth.

"Think he'll let her go?" Major Chase was still on the circuit.

"I don't know, Major. I just don't know."

"Jessica told me she was starting to work on activating my wife's beacon. Is there anyone else that can take over while she's involved with this?"

"No, I'm sorry. I was trying to get the satellite to issue the command, and couldn't make it work. Had to turn it over to the Petty Officer."

Major Chase was quiet for a moment. A low sigh was audible over the circuit.

"Very well, thank you, Lieutenant."

"You're welcome, sir. I'm here if you need anything."

There was a click, and the Major was gone. Hunt pulled his headset off and got up to check on Jessica's progress. He looked around when the door opened, and Admiral Packard's aide walked in. Taking up positions behind the Petty Officer's station, the two men watched as she furiously worked on her keyboard.

49

Nicole looked up when Lieutenant Sam tapped on the window. She was seated on a narrow bunk in an isolation room inside the research institute. She'd been poked, prodded, stuck with needles, X-rayed, MRI'd, CT'd and ultrasounded to death. She didn't think there was another test known to man that could be run on her.

The boat ride from the University had been uneventful compared to the trek from the nuclear physics lab to the edge of the lake. The wounded Master Chief had piloted them, putting on speed as they passed underneath three bridges. She had been terrified to hear splashes in the water as they cleared each roadway.

Upon arrival at the institute, she was quickly ushered inside. Two SEALs were assigned to watch over her as Sam hustled the Master Chief off to receive medical attention. She was handed over to two research scientists.

One of them, an arrogant prick named Dr. Kanger, rubbed her the wrong way as soon as he opened his mouth and began talking about her as if she were something he was looking at under a microscope. The other, a younger man who introduced himself as Joe, had the saddest eyes she'd ever seen.

Anvil

Neither of them had offered any theories on her condition, and they had finally placed her in the sealed room. She was told it was for her safety, but she knew it was because they were scared of her. Not that she could blame them, but she knew she was OK. She didn't have the urge to hurt, let alone eat, any of them.

Well, maybe Kanger could use a good ass kicking, but she recognized the type. Working in the sciences, she had encountered many a Doctor of this or Professor of that who thought they were the smartest person in the room, and everyone else was beneath them. She didn't have a problem with that first part.

"You said you'd tell me your story," Sam said, smiling at her through the glass.

"It's pretty boring," she smiled back, happy to have someone to talk to that was interested in more than examining her.

"That's OK. I've got time. One of the guys is outside taking measurements from several different locations. Thanks for that suggestion, by the way. He's going to print it out and bring it to us when he gets back. So, we can either talk about the weather, or you can tell me how you wound up locked in."

Dirk Patton

Sam looked around when Joe Revard walked up. He nodded at the SEAL and smiled at Nicole.

"I was just coming for the same reason," he said. "Might be helpful. Do you mind?"

Nicole looked at him for a moment, shook her head, took a breath and stood up. She found it easier to talk if she was standing. Too many years in academia, she mused. Taking a breath, she began.

Nicole wasn't just smart; she was an actual certified genius. With an IQ higher than 99.99% of the people on the planet, odds were in her favor that she was the smartest person in the room. With dual doctorates from MIT, she had begun her career at Lawrence Livermore labs in California, working with the team that was trying to develop cold fusion.

They'd had several significant breakthroughs and were within a decade of rolling out a power source that would solve one of the world's biggest problems and do it with limitless, clean energy. After a significant advancement in the technology, the entire team was given a week's vacation. When they returned to the lab, they were astounded to find that all of their work had been removed.

Anvil

Loud protests were met with a visit from a truly frightening man who refused to say which government agency he worked for. They were reminded of the secrecy agreements by which they were bound, and thinly veiled threats of life in a Super Max prison were made if they discussed their work with anyone. The team broke up after that, many of them choosing to retire as they had spent a lifetime on their quest.

But Nicole was too young to retire. Barely thirty, she looked around for something to do, jumping at an opportunity to teach nuclear physics at the University of Washington. It wasn't MIT or Cal Tech, but the school had a good reputation and would have the equipment to allow her to continue her work. Only she would have to do it quietly. On her own.

That's what she had been doing on the night of the attacks. Alone in the lab, she was insulated from the outside world. She had no idea anything had happened until the following morning when, bleary-eyed, she opened the door to go home and shower before her first class.

It was odd that there had been no one in the upper-level lobby when she walked out, but she was too tired to give it any thought. Trudging down the stairs she'd come out into the lower level, again seeing no activity. Heading for the door that opened into the security vestibule, she idly wondered if she'd mixed up her days, again, and it was the weekend.

Opening the door, she froze in horror. Gus, the affable man that worked the evening security shift, turned at the sound. His eyes were solid red orbs and black blood dripped from his nose and ears. With a hiss and snarl, he reached for her, taking a shambling step in her direction.

As his hand closed on her arm, Nicole snapped back to reality and screamed. She pulled back, tearing away from Gus's hand and slamming the steel door with all her strength. The door bounced back, having impacted his head, and she threw her body against it and pushed until she heard the lock catch.

Dashing back up the stairs, she noticed the long, bloody furrow in her forearm where one of his nails had torn her skin. Ignoring it, she dashed past her lab and into a large kitchen, fumbling her cell phone out of her purse. There was no signal for her carrier. It was still connected to the building's Wi-Fi, but there was apparently no internet connection.

She tried a hard-wired phone on the wall, but when she got an outside line, there was no dial tone. The TV on the wall only displayed a banner telling her that the Emergency Broadcast System had been activated. In a near panic, she hit the alarm button when the muted pops of gunfire from outside the building reached her ears.

The alarm would alert the University Police, the Seattle Police, the Washington State Police and Homeland Security. It also locked down the facility, securing all doors until the authorities arrived with the proper reset codes. But they never arrived. Nicole was locked in.

The day had passed with agonizing slowness. Frequent gunfire could be heard, sounding distant because of the building's thick, shielded walls. She knew it had to actually be just outside. On campus.

As evening approached, hunger drove her to inventory what was in the kitchen. Knowing many of her co-workers also kept food in their offices and work areas, she had begun a search. Half way through, she had come across a small ham radio receiver in one of the assistant professor's desks. It was about the size of a brick with a long, rubber antenna.

Turning it on, she could only hear static. Her excitement over finding it was tempered when she remembered the lead shielding that surrounded her. But it wouldn't be here if it was useless inside the building. She had kept looking until she found a small antenna mounted high on an exterior wall in one of the least often used labs. A cable from its base disappeared into the wall.

She realized it was a passive relay for the radio signal. Taking a seat directly beneath it, she turned the handset back on. For twenty-four hours she listened to descriptions of the horror that had been unleashed on the United States. Then the battery died, and before she was able to locate a charging cable the building's power went out.

Generators kicked in, but they were only wired to the security system and a limited number of emergency lights. Even if she'd found the charger, there was no way to power it. She was cut off from the outside world.

A few days later she had gotten sick. The flu, she'd thought. At least until now. She had been sicker than she could ever remember being. Body aches that caused her to pull into a ball and stay there for more than a day. A burning fever and associated delirium.

Now, she wasn't so sure it was delirium. Some of the nightmares she'd had were so rage filled and dark they had frightened her. As the fever burned through her, she tried to sleep, waking several times so frightened of the horrible images in her head that she cried out in terror.

But the flu had passed. She had been keeping track of the passing days on a whiteboard, but the illness had been so severe she'd lost count. There was no way to know how long she'd been laid up. Recovery had been quick; then it had been countless hours of tedium until she heard the noise the SEALs made as they broke into the facility.

"I was out of food and almost out of water," she said. "If you guys hadn't found me…"

"Just how smart are you?" Joe interrupted.

"Is that really important?"

Nicole didn't like talking about it. In fact, she went to great lengths to disguise her intellect. She was one of the rare people with extremely high IQs, who wasn't socially awkward. And she didn't like the reaction she got from people when they found out. Yes, she was smarter than them. Despite what they might think, this didn't make her look down on them.

"It might be," Joe said. "We've been observing female infected for some time. As the virus has mutated, less and less of their cognitive abilities are being impacted. At least that's what we think. Perhaps it's not that the virus is having a lesser impact, maybe it's the baseline intelligence of the subject to begin with."

"The subject?" Nicole asked eyebrows arched sharply.

"Sorry," Joe said.

"I'm just yanking your chain," she smiled, even though she actually had taken mild offense to the term. "I tested at 189 when I was a child. At MIT, I went through a battery of three separate tests. The mean result was 194."

"Oh, my God," Joe breathed.

"Is that high?" Sam asked.

"One hundred is average," Joe said, trying to contain his excitement. "You seem reasonably intelligent, so I'd guess you're around 115 to 120. I tested at 123. Einstein was 160."

Sam's mouth dropped open, and he turned to stare at Nicole. She looked back at him and shrugged her shoulders.

"This is amazing," Joe said excitedly. "The first thing we have to do is test you again. See what you score now. Determine if the infection has impacted your cognitive reasoning ability."

"That's going to have to wait," a new voice spoke up from behind them.

Joe and Sam turned to see Echo, the SEAL, who had been outside sampling the radiation levels. He held several pieces of paper in his

446

hand, extending them to his Lieutenant. Sam scanned them quickly, grimacing, then placed them in an open drawer and pushed a lever which slid the mechanism into Nicole's room.

"Are those numbers as bad as I think they are?" He asked as she snatched them up and moved under a light.

"Yes," she said a moment later, looking up from the papers. "You need to run the same tests inside the building. We need to know how well it's protecting us, but I'm pretty sure we need to leave."

Sam turned to issue the order, but Nicole stopped him.

"Wait. Do you know how to check the calibration on the unit?"

The two SEALs exchanged glances before looking at her and shaking their heads.

"Let me out of here," she said. "We have to be sure we're getting accurate results."

Sam stared at her for a long moment, turning and looking at Joe, who just shrugged his shoulders.

"For Christ's sake, I'm not going to hurt anyone!" Nicole shouted, red eyes flashing.

Dirk Patton

After a long pause, Sam stepped forward and released the lock on the door to the isolation room. Pulling it open, he stepped aside as Nicole swept through the opening and told the SEAL to take her to the equipment.

50

With nothing to do other than wait, the Rangers and I sat in silence. TJ had finished his job, modestly accepting our praise for stepping up. We had briefly talked about what life had been like after the attacks, then had drifted off into our own private thoughts.

We'd been sitting like that for a couple of hours when Drago spoke up. I'd thought he was asleep, his big frame relaxed in a chair with his long legs stretched out in front of him.

"What was that nonsense I overheard about you turning yourself over to the Russians?"

"It's a long story," I said.

"Seems like we've got nothing else to do," Drago said. "Besides, these other two are boring. Chico there can't talk about anything other than his kids, and TJ… well, TJ talks about video games like they were important or something."

"Who was the first one of us that knew to shoot them in the head?" TJ said without opening his eyes. "Didn't get that shit from watching documentaries about Vikings. And are you sure there's really such a thing? Always thought they were just a crappy football team from Minnesota."

"Nah, they're not crappy," Chico chimed in. "Crappy is the Cowboys. The Vikings are lousy."

"Suppose you're a Dolphin's fan." I couldn't resist when football was being discussed.

"Oh, hell no! Forty Niners! All the way!"

"Chico, I may have to shoot you," I said with a grin.

"Don't tell me," he moaned. "Cardinals?"

"Nope. Seahawks."

That was met with groans from all three men.

"Thank God there's not a Patriots fan in the room," Drago said, eliciting chuckles and agreement from all of us.

"If there was, we could feed him to the infected," I grinned.

We bantered back and forth for a bit, talking football and remembering our favorite players and some of the games that stood out in our memories. Chico killed the mood when he said he had scored tickets for the upcoming Superbowl, his face falling when reality came crashing back in.

Anvil

"So. 'Bout those Russians?" Drago prompted after several quiet minutes.

With a sigh, I shifted in my chair and started talking. I told them everything. Not just why the Russians wanted me so bad, but everything I'd experienced since the attacks. By the time I was finished, all three were sitting up and hanging on every word.

"Fuck me running, Major, but what the hell? Do you really think if you turn yourself in the goddamn Russkies aren't still going to make Hawaii glow in the dark?"

Chico shook his head as he talked. TJ and Drago nodded in agreement with him. I just shrugged my shoulders.

"And what about your wife?" TJ asked. "I know you said the Colonel promised to take her to Seattle but fuck. How can you walk away from her?"

He wasn't judging me. He was just voicing one of many thoughts I'd already struggled with.

"If I don't, it's a certainty that they'll bomb Hawaii and Nassau. If that happens, well... Anyway. If I do, there's a chance. I can't pass on that chance."

"But what about this?" TJ asked, waving at the racks of servers. "Isn't this supposed to give us some super weapon to stop them?"

"I honestly don't know what this is supposed to do," I said, shaking my head. "Don't know if it's offensive or defensive. Don't even know if it's going to work in time. But I guess it doesn't matter. We aren't getting out of here."

Everyone fell silent, slowly withdrawing into their own thoughts. Once again, Drago surprised me when he spoke.

"What's halon?"

"Fire suppressant," I answered, somewhat familiar with it from working for a tech company in the civilian world. "Why?"

"What does it do?"

"Puts out fires," I said, not trying to be a smartass. "It's used in places where a traditional sprinkler system would cause just as much damage as the fire. Like in here, around sensitive electronics."

"OK, but how does it work?" Drago persisted.

"I'm not an expert, but it displaces or disrupts the oxygen. Something like that. When

452

the system activates it floods the space, and the fire can't burn, so it goes out."

"Is it toxic?" He asked.

"Not sure," I said. "About all I know is you're not supposed to be in a room when the system goes off, and if you are, you should grab a breather and get the hell out. Got an idea?"

"See that cabinet with the breathers in it?" He asked, pointing.

"Yeah..." I said, turning to look despite knowing exactly what he was talking about.

"Saw several of those scattered throughout the building. Think they've got a big ass halon system instead of sprinklers?"

I turned back to look at the breathers, my eyes traveling up to the warning sign.

"I have no idea," I said.

"Assuming that's the case, what happens to all those females out there if the building gets flooded with halon? If it kills fires, well, just maybe..."

Drago looked at me and lifted his eyebrow questioningly. I thought about what he was saying for a moment, feeling a small glimmer of hope.

"I have no idea, but I'll bet someone in Hawaii can tell us," I said. "But, before we make that call, let's think about this. Assuming the whole building is covered with halon instead of sprinklers, and assuming it would actually do something to the infected, how do we trigger its release anywhere other than in here? Any fire system is going to be zoned."

"Automation," TJ said. All of us turned to look at him. "Building like this, it's going to be computer controlled. And were sitting inside the brain."

TJ looked around, standing and moving to twin touchscreens embedded in the wall. I'd noted them earlier when I was searching the room but hadn't paid any attention. Reaching out, he tapped on first one, then the other, the screens flaring to life. He looked at them for a moment before facing us and grinning.

I moved to stand next to him. Each screen displayed unique halves of the layout of the building with hundreds of red dots scattered throughout the schematic. Controls ran down the right edge and across the top, each was labeled as "*Master Fire Control*".

"Right fucking here!" TJ said excitedly, pointing at the two displays. "We can control all of it from right fucking here!"

"Is it all halon?" I asked, trying not to get my hopes up.

"Yep," he answered. "Look right there."

I leaned and saw what he was pointing at. It was a legend. Red dots were gas. Blue was water. It must have been a default legend as there wasn't a single blue dot on the display, and I assumed *gas* meant halon.

"OK, that's great," Chico said. "But don't get ahead of yourselves. Even if the halon will knock down the infected, and we don't know it will, what do we do? There's still about a million of them outside. Won't they come charging in if the ones in here fall over dead?"

"Probably," I said. "But there will still be halon filling the building. It takes a while to disperse. We should have enough time to make the roof."

"Definitely," TJ said. "There's another stairwell. Closer to us. We don't have to go back through the lobby."

I looked where he pointed at the layout as Chico and Drago stepped close to see. Sure enough, the diagram showed a flight of stairs going to the roof only about a hundred yards from the server room. We should be able to cover that distance, climb the stairs and reach fresh air well before the breathers ran out of oxygen.

"That only leaves the biggest question," Drago said. "What happens to the infected?"

"Let's make that call and find out," I said, picking up the headset that would connect me to Lieutenant Hunt. "While I'm doing that, someone call up our ride and make sure he's still in the area."

Drago nodded and stepped away, pressing his earpiece back into his ear as he started calling the Black Hawk that hopefully had refueled and was orbiting the area.

"It's not halon," the man on the comm circuit said.

I had called Lieutenant Hunt and within minutes, he had found a Navy engineer that maintained all of the data centers at Pearl Harbor. He was an expert, and he was telling me our idea wouldn't work.

"Halon was banned in the early nineties," he continued. "Bad for the environment."

"But the warning sign says halon 1301," I protested, looking to make sure I was remembering the placard correctly.

"Yep, it's probably old, and they didn't bother to take it down. What you've got is an inert gas suppression system."

"Say again," I said, not liking the sound of that. Inert didn't seem like a term for something that could kill thousands of females.

"You're actually better off than if it was halon," he said. "Halon isn't good for you, but they could survive it. This is inert gas. Most likely it's a mix of argon and nitrogen. When the system is activated, it will flood the building and drop the oxygen content to nearly zero. Fire can't burn without oxygen."

"They'll suffocate?" I asked, starting to get the picture.

"Exactly. And fast, too. It's called Inert Gas Asphyxiation. The body breathes in as normal, but there's no oxygen coming in. Two, maybe three breaths and a person is unconscious. After that, death comes pretty quick. You want to be sure you either have the breathers already on when you activate the system or hold your breath until you put one on.

"You can survive several minutes on the oxygen in your lungs as long as you don't exhale and breathe in the inert gas. We train and drill on this all the time. Anyone who works in an area with an inert gas suppression system will know how to react when the alarm sounds."

"OK, so what else should I know?" I asked, feeling real hope that we'd get out of here.

"Nothing I haven't told you. DO NOT breathe in room air once the system is activated. And if your breather runs out and you have to put on a new one, hold your breath while changing. If someone does breathe in and goes down, get a mask on them as fast as you can."

I thanked the man and turned to fill in the team on what I'd just heard. They were as excited as I was, smiles breaking out all around when they heard how fast the females would go down. Drago, not surprisingly, was a little skeptical.

"We're sure the infected can't survive this?"

"They're still human," I said. "They still have to breathe air. I've seen them drown, so they need oxygen just like us."

He nodded, his smile a little bigger when I finished speaking.

"Is Sam one-niner on station?" I asked, stepping to the breather cabinet and gathering up all the masks.

"He's orbiting the area. Waiting," Drago said.

I slipped my night vision goggles on and looked down at the IR strobe that was still attached to my arm. It was flashing away. Passing the breathers around, I handed one spare to Drago and the other to Chico. TJ and I would grab extras when we exited the server room.

Only one thing left to do. Pressing a button on the headset, I waited for Lieutenant Hunt to answer.

"We're ready to bug out," I said when he picked up. "The power's on, and the servers are running. Does Jessica need anything else from our end before we leave? Once we're out, we aren't getting back in."

"Stand by," he said, putting me on mute.

I looked around as the team moved into position, ready to go. TJ stood by the fire control panels, waiting for the order to activate the system and flood the building with gas. Chico was waiting to hit the button that would release the door's electromagnetic lock, so we could exit.

"She says you're good to go, and we wish you luck," Hunt said a few seconds later.

I thanked him and broke the connection. Removing the headset, I stuffed it in my pack. Pulling my night vision goggles off, I put them in as well, then took a deep breath and pulled the breathing mask on. It covered my face from hairline, if I had a hairline, to below my chin. A rubber gasket sealed against my skin as I tugged the straps tight around the back of my head.

Glancing around, I looked at each of the other men, making sure their masks were in place and snug. Other than the black rubber gasket, the masks were made of clear, flexible plastic which slightly distorted my vision. But only slightly.

"Oh-two on," I called out, twisting the valve on my mask's oxygen cylinder.

Anvil

I could immediately smell and taste the slightly metallic air as it began flowing. Satisfied everyone was ready, I met TJ's eyes and nodded. He pressed several different spots on the touch screen panels, then stepped back and looked expectantly at the controls.

After a beat, he looked over his shoulder at me and shrugged his shoulders. The clock in my head was ticking, and I was about to tell him to try it again when a strident alarm began blaring so loud we all jumped. Two white strobes mounted high on the walls began flashing and a pleasant female voice came from speakers mounted in the ceiling.

"Fire suppression system has been activated. Do not breathe in. Put on oxygen masks immediately and evacuate to your designated rally point. Do not breathe room air."

The prerecorded message continued playing, looping, loud enough to be understood over the raucous fire alarm. TJ dashed over to form up with us, and I checked my watch. We had five minutes of breathable air, and only had to cover a hundred yards then climb a flight of stairs. More than enough time, so I held us back, waiting a full minute. I wanted to make damn sure the females were down and out before we opened that door.

When the time had passed, I slapped Chico on the shoulder with the "go" signal. He pressed the green, exit button and the magnets holding the doors closed released with loud thunks. Chico and Drago pushed, but they didn't budge. What the hell?

Chico pressed the button again, but they were already unlocked. With a feeling of dread, I shouted for everyone to push as I rushed forward. TJ came with me and working together, the four of us were able to move the doors until a two-foot gap appeared between them.

Looking through I could see a chest deep mass of dead females. They had been packed in so tightly that when they died their bodies had only been able to slump. And all that mass was blocking the doors.

"Holy shit," Drago breathed when he got a look.

"Move," I shouted, grabbing TJ and shoving him at the opening.

He was by far the thinnest of the four of us, slipping through easily after shrugging out of his pack. Scrambling up as he cleared the gap, he climbed on top of the carpet of corpses, grabbing one of the doors and trying to force it open a few more inches.

Anvil

Chico was next. Tossing his pack through first, he wedged himself into the gap and with the three of us helping, squeezed through with a minimal amount of cursing.

Drago and I looked at each other for a beat. As thick as my chest was and as broad as my shoulders were, he was bigger.

"I'll push while they pull," I said, shoving him forward.

His pack went through first, and he ripped his vest off over his head and tossed it through before turning sideways and jamming his huge frame into the void. Chico had his arms, pulling as I pushed with everything I had. TJ pulled on the door, struggling to get solid footing on the shifting bodies beneath him.

With screams of effort, we finally got Drago through. He might have left some skin behind, but he wasn't complaining. I glanced at my watch as I took my pack and vest off. Three and half minutes gone. And we were using up oxygen fast with all the exertion.

"TJ. Find more breathers. We're going to run out," I shouted over the radio.

As I stuck my head through the gap between the doors, I noticed the air I was breathing was getting stale. Pushing with my legs, I shoved my shoulders through, but that's as far as I got before the sharp door edges dug into the top of my chest and my shoulder blades. I pushed, legs churning, but couldn't get good traction on the slick tile floor in the server room.

The air was getting worse, the humidity inside the mask shooting up and creating a damp fog on the inside of the plastic. I was gasping now, my body struggling to extract every last molecule of oxygen from the foul air. Chico and Drago each grabbed under my shoulders, linking their hands together in my armpits. They started to pull, but a voice shouted at them to wait.

"Hold your breath!"

I couldn't see who was speaking through the fogged lens, but recognized TJ's voice. Fingers were loosening the straps that held the mask tight to my face then it was gone. Cool air flowed across my skin, and it took all my effort to not let myself draw a deep, refreshing breath.

Without the mask I was able to see, watching as TJ slapped a new breather in place and wincing when he yanked the straps tight. He twisted the valve on the fresh O2 cylinder and leaned in, his mask inches from mine.

"You good?" He shouted.

I exhaled, then gulped in fresh oxygen. Immediately my head cleared, and I nodded. Drago and Chico were changing their masks, and a moment later they grabbed me again and began pulling. My damaged shoulder screamed a constant complaint but was the least of my concerns.

They pulled, grunting with the effort and I began moving. The doors pinched, hard, and I wasn't sure I didn't leave both nipples behind when I passed through. A few seconds later my chest was clear, and they pulled me free with no resistance. Getting to my feet, I pulled on my vest and pack and nearly fell over when the bodies beneath me shifted.

Difficult doesn't begin to describe what it was like walking on corpses that are upright and jammed in like cordwood. I quickly learned that if you stepped on a head, it would shift right out from under your foot as soon as your weight came down.

Shoulders were the ticket. Pick your footing, and make sure you stepped on shoulders only. It still wasn't easy as the body would shift until the ones around it kept it from moving. There were all different heights of females. So every step had to be planned before it was taken. It was slow going, and it was creepy as hell.

I have a good imagination, often to my own detriment. As we picked our way across the tops of the corpses, I kept picturing all of them suddenly reanimating. Hands would reach up, grabbing legs, and pull me down until I disappeared beneath the sea of death I was walking on.

Caught up in the waking nightmare, I missed a step, and my foot sank into a void between two bodies. I went down to my hip, cursing and twisting my body just in time to prevent my other leg from being injured. Drago bent and grabbed the back of my vest, helping me to climb back up.

As I took my next step, a low whine started from over my head. Looking up, I saw steel louvers in the ceiling open as the whine quickly spun up to a loud roar. I felt a strong current of air blow across my body and cursed again when realization dawned on me.

"What the fuck is that?" Chico asked, looking around with his rifle up.

"Ventilation fans," I shouted. "Clearing out the inert gas so people can come back in. We've got to move!"

I wasn't positive that was what was happening, but it made sense. The fire suppression system was automated. It flooded the interior atmosphere with inert gas to extinguish the flames. There was probably a timer that would turn on fans to suck in fresh, outside air to clear out the gas once enough time had passed.

I spared a glance at my watch. Eight minutes. More than enough time to ensure the fire was out. Now, the system was restoring breathable air, so it was safe to come back into the building.

We moved as fast as we could on the treacherous footing. TJ was on point, leading us out of the IT cubicle farm and down a long hallway. Far ahead was a steel door with a large blue sign attached to its face. I couldn't make out what it said, but it was in the right place to be the stairwell entrance I'd seen on the building schematic.

Far ahead was a relative term. It was probably no more than fifty yards to the exit, but we were moving so slow that it barely felt as if we were making progress. Another glance at my watch as the air in my mask began to be difficult to breathe. Ten and a half minutes since TJ had activated the system. Two and a half since the fans came on.

I wanted to rip the mask off and breathe fresh air, but the ventilation system was still roaring over my head, and a strong flow of air was rushing past me. With no idea how long it took to clear out the inert gas, I wasn't willing to take the chance. Struggling and cursing, I kept

moving, returning the favor when Drago mis-
stepped and went down.

As I pulled him up, the pre-recorded voice
stopped in mid-sentence, and the alarm went
silent. We shouldn't have, but all of us paused. A
moment later a new recording began playing as
the fans started to spool down.

*"Atmosphere is clear and safe to breathe.
No fire detected."*

The fans spun down, the metal louvers
closing with loud clicks. The automated
announcement was on a loop, loud in the
suddenly quiet building. Reaching up, I loosened
a strap and cracked the mask an inch away from
my chin. Taking a cautious breath, I gagged and
nearly threw up inside the mask.

Thousands, perhaps tens of thousands, of
infected had died inside the building. Death is
not the clean, sterile passing often portrayed on
TV and in movies. When the body ceases to
function, muscles relax. And it's muscles that
control bladders and sphincters. The
overwhelming stench of human waste was
indescribable.

Slapping my mask back in place, I looked
to TJ, who had extras dangling from a strap on
his pack. I gave the team a quick warning over
the radio, and fresh breathers were passed

around and put on. Everyone held their breath as they changed, even though the air was technically safe to breathe.

As I was tugging the straps for my new mask tight against my head, I began hearing infected screams. There weren't close, yet, but the females in the parking lot were coming into the building. I had no idea if they'd be able to find us easily. Certainly doubted they'd be able to track us by smell, but didn't really care. It was time to get the hell out of here.

52

We reached the door at the end of the hall after what seemed an interminable amount of time. The screams behind us steadily drew closer as we moved, motivating us like nothing else could. Getting caught in the open wouldn't be good. With the tricky footing, it would be damn difficult to fight off an attack *and* make our escape.

Once at the door, it took way too long to clear out dead females so it could be opened. The hallway was packed tight, and we had to pull bodies up and stack them out of the way. This was more difficult than it sounds. As soon as a corpse would come free, those around it would flop into the freshly vacated space.

Soon we were all cursing, sweating heavily as we worked. Breathers had to be changed again, and I got a snoot full of the horrid, cloying sewer smell when I was swapping mine out. Even with a new mask and fresh oxygen flowing, the stink stayed with me, trapped in my sinuses.

Handling corpses absolutely sucks. It drives home the term *"dead weight"*. A 140-pound dead body is more difficult to move than a live one. Every joint is loose, flopping and shifting as you lift. It reminded me of a summer

job I had in high school, working in the oil fields
near Odessa, Texas.

At the time, the massive drill bits were
kept from overheating by injecting mud into the
hole. That mud was packaged up at another
location, put into large burlap bags and stacked
on a flatbed truck. My job was to unload those
hundred pound sacks of mud, one at a time,
when the trucks arrived.

Picking up one of those wasn't unlike
trying to pick up a corpse. As soon as you think
you have a good grip, the mass shifts. You react
to the change and the fucking thing shifts again.
Finally, you get pissed off and just throw it,
hoping it lands where you want it. Sometimes it
does, and sometimes you have to move it again.

And doing this with a bad shoulder wasn't
helping my disposition. By the time we had
cleared enough bodies for Chico and me to stand
on the floor, I was in the mood to face the
infected with nothing but my bare hands. The
rest of the team wasn't in any better frame of
mind, but we kept our frustration to ourselves
and worked without pause as the screams drew
closer.

Chico and I were using our backs and
arms to support the edge of the mass of corpses;
feet braced against our exit door. Still on top,
Drago was pulling out one female at a time,

471

passing the body on to TJ, who had taken to rolling them like logs. He had built a stack a few feet back down the hall. I could hear the females hunting, screaming to each other, and not being able to see the direction they would come from had ratcheted up my tension.

"That's enough," I grunted in the exertion of holding back the wall of dead.

Drago dropped into the small open space a moment later. He helped hold as Chico, and I shifted to make room for him to pry the door open. It was a slow process to shift around and not let an avalanche of bodies bury the area we'd worked so hard to clear.

"Contact!"

I heard TJ's voice on the radio an instant before his suppressed rifle began firing.

"Hurry," I hissed to Drago, throwing myself against the wall of ever-shifting bodies.

TJ was firing single shots, well-spaced, so I didn't think there were a lot of females approaching. Yet. But they were screaming, and others would be flooding into the hall in response to their calls.

I turned to get a better angle and make room for Drago to work. My face was pressed against the chest of a dead female as I leaned into the constant pressure, and I was thankful for the plastic mask that covered my skin. Behind me I heard the sharp bang of Drago forcing the pry bar into place, then his grunt of exertion.

"Let's go!" He shouted as I felt the bottom edge of the now open door bang against my foot.

No one moved. I was waiting for Chico, who was waiting for me. TJ was continuing to fire, the rate picking up significantly. For fucks sake, we must have looked like the Keystone Cops.

"Chico, go," I shouted.

When he moved, the whole wall shifted, threatening to inundate me. With a scream of effort, I pushed. My hands began slipping, then disappeared in amongst the bodies. An arm fell free, flopping against my head and coming to rest on my shoulder. I could feel the mass of corpses beginning to shift without the second point of resistance Chico had provided.

"TJ! Move your ass!"

I screamed at the young Ranger as another arm came free and the corpse directly in front of me slipped a few inches. My face was no longer pressed against her chest. I was now face to face with the bitch, only a thin layer of plastic between us.

TJ fired several long bursts; then I could feel the vibration from him moving across the top of the pile. He bounced off me as he jumped into the open space. The screams sounded like there were females right over my head, but I was hesitating. I was afraid to release my hold. Worried the mass would collapse towards me so fast that I'd be trapped under its weight.

Drago solved the problem for me. Reaching out, he grabbed onto each edge of my vest at the arm holes. Chico had his arms wrapped around Drago's waist, and TJ was locked onto Chico's belt. The three of them pulled in unison, and I was yanked backwards through the open door.

I wound up on top of a pile, Drago and Chico beneath me. TJ had sidestepped our falling bodies and was reaching to close the door as the wall of corpses began to tumble towards us. As TJ's hand wrapped around the door handle, a live female appeared and launched herself forward with a scream.

She impacted TJ squarely on the chest. The back of his legs came up hard against my hip, and he fell backwards over me, the infected riding him to the floor. More females were screaming, and I saw movement in the hall as I tried to extricate myself from Drago and Chico. Two more females were leaping, but the door was closing.

Anvil

TJ's hand had pulled it slightly as the female struck him, starting it swinging on its hinges. As the females were preparing to leap, the wall of dead infected that was no longer being supported suddenly broke free and tumbled against the door, slamming it closed with a resounding boom.

There was no time to celebrate as the female that had come through and attacked TJ screamed right behind me. Finally getting my feet under me, I turned just in time to take her charge. I was slammed against the door, which thankfully didn't budge.

The female was tearing at me, her face lunging forward as she sought a mouthful of my flesh. I had a forearm up and against her throat, levering her away as my free hand fumbled for my knife. Before I could find it, her head was violently snapped to the side as Drago hit her with the iron pry bar.

Her skull broke open with an audible crack, her limp body flopping to the side. Drago looked at me a moment, breathing hard, then ripped the mask off his face. Wiping sweat out of his eyes, he took a deep breath, held it a moment, then grinned.

"Thanks," I said, removing my breather.

"Hey! TJ!"

Drago turned, and I moved past him.
Chico was kneeling over TJ, who was on his back
and not moving. I dropped to the ground on the
other side and looked over the Ranger's body,
not seeing any injuries.

"What's wrong with him?" Drago asked,
bent over my shoulder.

Chico had two fingers on TJ's neck, feeling
for a pulse. After a long wait, he withdrew his
hand and looked up at us, shaking his head.
Fuck! Reaching out, I did the same. Not that I
didn't believe Chico, but I needed to feel for
myself.

There was no pulse, and when I lifted his
eyelids, I could see that his pupils were fixed and
dilated. Chico grunted, looking at the floor right
next to TJ's head. Blood was slowly pooling,
soaking his tightly cropped hair. He looked a few
inches above the dead Ranger's head and pointed
at a smear of hair and blood on the front edge of
the first step leading to the roof.

I slipped my hand under TJ's neck and
gently worked it up the back of his skull. There
was a large depression, and his scalp was split
open. That's where the blood was coming from.
Removing my hand, I sat back on my haunches
and cursed long and loud. When the female had
hit him, he'd tripped and fallen back, his head

cracking open on the steel covered edge of the step.

If we hadn't needed to wear the breathers, he would have had a Kevlar helmet with his night vision goggles on his head. It would have protected him. He would still be alive. Goddamn it, I was tired of this shit!

53

Chico carried TJ's body up the stairs, gently laying him on the roof next to the helipad as we waited for the Black Hawk to pick us up. It wasn't a long wait, and the constant screams from the ocean of females packed into the parking lot faded into the background as I thought about what was to come.

Glancing at my watch, I did the math and realized that after the nearly ninety-minute flight it would be close to time for me to surrender to the Russians. Time for me to remind Colonel Blanchard of his promise to find Katie and get her to Seattle. Unfortunately, I'd probably never know what happened to her. I didn't expect to survive long once I was in Moscow.

Watching the Black Hawk approach, my thoughts turned to Rachel. I missed her. She had become a part of me, and if things had been slightly different... I shut down that line of thought, standing and helping Chico hoist TJ onto his shoulder.

We rushed forward as soon as the landing gear touched the roof. TJ went in first, the door gunner reaching out and helping so the fallen Ranger's body was placed gently on the deck. Drago and Chico followed, then I climbed up and flopped down on a web sling. We were airborne an instant later.

The flight was long, and no one was in the mood to talk. I was lost in thought. Chico sat on the deck, cradling TJ in his arms. Drago sat next to him, his big hand on Chico's shoulder. They stayed that way for the entire time it took us to reach our destination.

I had expected to be taken back to the front, surprised when I saw we were landing at what looked like a small, civilian airfield. Stepping out, I waited as Chico and Drago lifted TJ's body clear of the helicopter. There wasn't an ambulance or morgue detail waiting for us. That didn't happen anymore.

"Take him to that hangar," I said softly, pointing across the tarmac. "We'll figure out how to honor him properly."

The two Rangers nodded, Drago reaching out and placing a hand on my shoulder. We locked eyes for a moment; then I looked over at Chico. He stood there, holding TJ in his thick arms like a child. After a moment he turned and began slowly heading for the hangar, I had pointed out. Drago dropped his hand and followed.

I watched as they walked away, turning when a Hummer pulled to a stop behind me.

Dirk Patton

Colonel Blanchard stepped out and walked forward to greet me. I shook his hand, then realized I should have come to attention. Oh well. If he wasn't going to make a big deal out of it, neither was I.

"Congratulations, Major," he said.

"Thank you, sir. But we lost three good men making it happen."

I knew Blanchard didn't need me to remind him. He was just like Colonel Crawford. Every Soldier in his command mattered to him. To him, they weren't expendable pieces for the chess board, even though in reality we all knew that's exactly what we were.

"What's the word from Pearl?" I asked.

"Not good," he said, shaking his head. "Admiral Packard wants to speak to you."

I nodded, not looking forward to the conversation.

"Remember your promise to me," I said, facing him squarely and looking into his eyes. "Find my wife and get her help."

"I haven't forgotten," Blanchard said. "I've already got patrols out searching her last known location. No luck so far, but as soon as her beacon gets activated we should be able to zero in on her."

I nodded, waiting patiently as he pulled out a sat phone and hit a speed dial key. He identified himself when the call was answered and a moment later held the handset out to me.

"Major Chase," I said when I lifted it to my ear.

"Major, Admiral Packard. Job well done in Utah."

"Thank you, sir."

"We've had a small problem, Major. The software that was copied over from the servers in Salt Lake City corrupted when it was loaded. A critical, hidden encryption file was missed. It's been downloaded and the system is being rebuilt, but we aren't going to be ready before the deadline for your surrender."

Fuck me. Of course, we weren't. Nothing ever went the way it was supposed to.

"Sir, how firm do you think the Russians are on that deadline?"

"Admiral Chirkov just called to remind me that we have thirty minutes. We're monitoring Russian C2 traffic and the order to prepare to launch has been issued. Unfortunately, they're very serious." C2 stands for Command and Control.

"How long until the software is ready?" I asked.

"Four hours. Minimum."

"Well, sir. I guess that doesn't leave me with a whole lot of options, does it?"

"No, Major. It does not. But let me be clear. I am *not* ordering you to do this. I will understand and fully support your decision if you decide not to surrender."

"Sir, I appreciate that, but you know as well as I do that there's no other way to stop the Russians from wiping Hawaii off the map. Just tell me one thing. Will the deaths of the men I lost in Utah and my surrender be worth it?"

There was silence on the line, and it only took me a moment to realize the Admiral wasn't going to answer. He'd probably already said too much on the phone, even if the signal was encrypted, and wasn't going to say any more.

"Understood, sir," I sighed. "Have you given any thought to my request about Petty Officer Simmons?"

"Investigators found evidence that the man she killed was a Russian agent. They also discovered three others working here in Pearl that he had recruited. I have a hard time charging someone with the murder of a man that I would have stood up against the wall and shot in the head. As far as the rest of it, I agree with you that she made a mistake. One which I'm hoping she has learned from.

"She will not be facing any charges, but will have her security clearance revoked, demoted in rank and placed on restricted duty until further notice. But, I have a feeling she'll be back on top of the heap in no time. She really is a remarkable young lady."

"Thank you, sir."

I was genuinely surprised. Packard had everything he needed, evidence wise, to charge and convict Jessica. The fact that he was willing to take circumstances into account spoke volumes about the man in the uniform.

"One final thing, sir. My wife. Colonel Blanchard has assured me he will find and help her. I would like your word that you personally will make sure everything that can be done for her will be."

"You have my word, Major," he answered quickly. "And thank you for what you're doing."

"Don't thank me, sir. Just help my wife."

Dirk Patton

"Godspeed, Major," Packard said, a moment later cutting the connection.

I handed the phone back to Blanchard, looking around the area, not really knowing what to do next. Out of old habit, my hand strayed to my breast pocket, looking for a pack of cigarettes that I knew wasn't there. Blanchard smiled, reaching into a cargo pocket and pulling out a crumpled pack and battered Zippo, handing them to me.

"Got in the habit of carrying them for Colonel Crawford," he explained when I gave him a questioning look.

"So how do we do this?" I asked, lighting a smoke and inhaling deeply.

"I've already been contacted by the Russians. They have a helicopter standing by, waiting for my call."

I nodded, puffing away on the cigarette. Glancing at my watch, I saw there was twenty-three minutes left to the deadline.

"Call them," I said. "Tell them to be here in twenty-three minutes. Can I borrow your phone? I've got something to take care of first."

Blanchard nodded and waived his aide over. The Captain ran up and handed over a radio handset.

Anvil

I walked a few yards away and made the call. Lieutenant Húnt quickly connected me to the Australian phone exchange, and I listened to half a dozen rings before a breathless Lucas answered. Soft music was playing in the background. Not the kind of music I knew he would choose to listen to.

"I didn't catch you with your pants down, did I?" I asked.

"Bloody hell you damn wanker! You have the worst timing," he laughed, and I couldn't help but laugh with my friend.

"Sorry," I said, even though I really wasn't. "I don't have much time, so listen close. OK?"

I talked for five minutes. Told him everything I could. Told him that Rachel and Irina would be arriving sometime in the near future. Then told him where I was going.

"Are you fucking daft?" He exploded when I explained about the surrender. "You know what they'll do to you?"

"Yes," I said, tired of explaining my decision to people.

We talked for another minute, Lucas promising to take in the two women when they arrived. He made a couple of other promises I hoped he could keep; then we said our goodbyes and I hung up.

Returning Blanchard's phone, I lit another cigarette and checked my watch. Seven minutes. Walking over to the Colonel's Hummer, I began taking off my weapons and placing them on the back seat. After most of a minute, I was unarmed. Taking my vest off, I placed it on top of the pile of knives, firearms and spare magazines.

Turning back to Colonel Blanchard, I pried the gold wedding band off my left hand and held it out towards him.

"When she's better, give her this," I said.

He nodded, taking the ring and slipping it onto the chain around his neck that held his dog tags. After that, we stood there in silence, waiting for the Russians to arrive. I smoked the rest of the cigarette, lighting another from the butt of the first.

The Captain was monitoring the radio with a headset and from the corner of my eye I saw him step forward and speak softly in Blanchard's ear. The Colonel nodded but didn't say anything to me. Moments later, right on time, I heard the sound of multiple rotors approaching.

Looking up, I saw a large Hind Mi-24 approaching, escorted by four Apaches. It came in low and slow, touching down on the tarmac a hundred yards away from where we stood. The troop compartment door opened, and two men stepped out of the aircraft.

"Sir, it's been an honor serving with you," I said, turning to Colonel Blanchard and extending my hand.

"The honor is mine," he responded, snapping to attention and raising his right hand in a salute.

After a moment, I too came to attention and returned his gesture of respect. Taking a deep breath, I walked across the tarmac and up to the two Russians. Both were Spetsnaz, one an officer, the other a senior Sergeant.

"I am Major John Chase, United States Army."

Igor lay on his stomach, mostly concealed behind the thick trunk of a fallen cedar tree. Only his rifle, head, and part of an arm were visible in the dappled, early morning light. Next to him, Dog lay with his eyes and ears above the cover. Both of them intently watched a spot in the brush on the far side of a broad meadow.

They had tracked a large buck, picking up its trail before dawn. Now, it was busily scraping its antlers against the bark of a Hemlock tree. Igor had a shot, but it was a low percentage one because of the brush that mostly concealed the deer. He was waiting, hoping it would move into the open, and he didn't have to continue tracking it.

The terrain and foliage on the western slopes of Washington State's Cascade Mountains reminded him of central Russia's Ural Mountains. He had hunted there with his grandfather many times, learning the skills and patience that would serve him well in the Spetsnaz. But he was tired of tracking this damn beast. They were miles from home and had a long walk back ahead of them.

A gentle breeze was blowing in their faces, Dog's nose twitching as he picked up the scent of their prey. Both were hungry, having quickly consumed the meager rations Igor had with him. There had been a few cans of food left in the pantry of the house they had claimed as their own. Igor had scavenged in several neighboring homes, finding nothing, and they needed the meat the deer would provide.

Igor had considered walking into town to look for food supplies but had opted to go hunting instead. He preferred fresh to what would be available in cans. As Dog healed, high protein, red meat was what his body needed as much as anything.

The buck finally stopped scraping its antlers, pausing to look around and test the air. Unable to scent the man and dog that were downwind, it slowly moved towards the open meadow. From the corner of his eye, Igor saw Dog tense as the large animal came into full view. He muttered a calming word in Russian, then repeated it in English. Dog went still and silent.

Finally, the big animal was in full view and Igor marveled at its size. There was enough meat there to feed both of them for weeks. The weather was cold, snow on the ground. He'd be able to butcher the animal and hang much of it high in a tree where it would freeze and be preserved until they were ready to eat it.

Carefully sighting in with his suppressed AKMS rifle, Igor pulled the trigger. His shot was true, the buck's spine severed along its powerful neck by the heavy bullet. The deer's legs buckled and it dropped in its tracks.

"Let's go," Igor said to Dog in English.

Dog sprang over the fallen tree, turning and waiting for the slower human. Smiling, Igor stood and stepped into the meadow. Together, they crossed the open area, stopping and looking down at the animal. It was still alive, paralyzed from the neck down. Igor quickly set about tying a long rope to its back legs so he could hoist it into a tree and drain the blood.

"Say "thank you"," Igor said to Dog as he worked. "Because of him, we eat and live."

Igor spoke haltingly. During his short time with Colonel Crawford, he'd begun to learn English. Once he and Dog had settled in to the home, he'd found a small solar charger and used it to juice up an iPad that had been laying on the kitchen floor.

Once it was powered, he'd looked through and found a small collection of movies. He watched these over and over, working hard to understand the dialogue and improve his rudimentary command of the language. His favorite movie was a western starring John Wayne. It was a story about an estranged husband and father who returned home when his grandson was kidnapped and held for ransom. The kidnappers had gotten what they deserved. Igor thought John Wayne would have made a fine Russian.

With the deer hanging head down from a thick tree branch, Igor slit open the major arteries in its neck and sat down to wait for the animal's heart to pump out most of its blood. Gravity would drain what was left after it expired. He would have to butcher the animal here as it weighed several hundred pounds and he was on foot.

As the hot blood ran, steaming when it came in contact with the snow-covered ground, he set about collecting wood for a fire. A freshly cut deer steak would go on a spit over the fire for him. Dog would take his raw, but would have to wait until Igor's meal was ready.

"Leave that," he said when he noticed Dog nosing towards the growing stain where the blood was soaking into the ground.

Dog looked at him, snorted and grudgingly walked away. He came to sit next to Igor as the Russian gently blew on the fire he had just lit. As the flames grew, he straightened up and ruffled Dog's ears, telling him he was a good boy, first in Russian, then in English. Dog's tail swished in the snow briefly before his head snapped around and he emitted a low growl.

Igor snatched up his rifle and aimed in the direction Dog was looking. At first, he saw nothing, then the brush on the far side of the meadow shook, and two infected males appeared. Both were walking with their heads tilted back, following the scent of fresh blood.

Lowering his rifle, Igor cursed in Russian and climbed to his feet. Telling Dog to stay, he strode to meet them with a large knife gripped tightly in his right hand. It only took him a moment to dispatch both males. Returning to where Dog waited, he rinsed the blade with water from his canteen before thrusting it into the fire to sterilize it.

Not leaving it in long enough for the steel to be damaged by the heat, he stood and carved two large pieces of meat off the deer's flank. Skewering one with a thin, green branch, he placed it over the flames. The second one went onto the snow in front of Dog.

Igor didn't have to tell him to leave it alone, but Dog's attention never wavered from the cut of fresh steak. As he sat watching it, a long rope of drool appeared from each corner of his mouth, stretching to the ground between his paws. Soon Igor's steak was sizzling, the flames popping as fat dripped into them. Turning it several times, Igor finally lifted the spit and sat back to enjoy his meal. Before he took his first bite, he looked at Dog.

Anvil

"Eat," he said.

Dog lunged, grabbing the food in his mouth and stretching out to hold it with his paws as he tore off chunks of raw flesh. Igor smiled and began devouring his.

Several hours later they were ready to start the long trek home. The deer had been butchered, close to a hundred pounds of meat neatly secured in plastic bags in Igor's pack. The rest of the animal had been lifted high into the tree with the rope, hopefully out of reach of any scavengers. The carcass had cooled, and he knew it would be frozen solid by the next morning.

They stopped once to share some more meat that Igor had cooked before extinguishing the fire. Dog sat close, gently taking bite sized chunks from Igor's hand. They didn't encounter any more infected and arrived at the perimeter of their home's property just as the sun was brushing the western horizon.

Igor paused inside the heavy trees, slowly performing a visual inspection of the trip wires he had rigged to guard the area. None of them appeared to have been disturbed, and Dog remained quiet. After satisfying himself that there were no infected, or worse, laying in wait, Igor emerged into the open with Dog at his side.

He carefully entered their adopted house, rifle at the ready and paying close attention to Dog. Even though he didn't growl or act like there was any danger inside, Igor still took the time to carefully clear every square foot. Dog followed, giving him a look when he didn't find anything. A look that said Igor was stupid for not trusting him.

Relaxing, Igor shed his pack in the large kitchen. He glanced at a large window set in the wall over the kitchen sink. On its sill was a satellite phone Colonel Crawford had convinced the SEALs to leave with him when they parted ways. He didn't understand why, as there was no one for him to call and no one who would want to call him. But, he'd accepted it and kept it powered with the same solar charger he used for the iPad.

For some reason he'd left it turned on, even finding a place for it in the house where it could pick up a signal from an orbiting satellite. He hadn't touched it, other than to charge it, since he'd placed it in the south facing window. Now, he slowly stepped over and tentatively picked up the handset. A small red light on the top edge was flashing.

When he turned on the screen, it told him he had a new text message. He had to read the words several times to understand the English, then struggled to find out how to view the text.

Anvil

Figuring it out, he frowned when it was nothing more than a phone number. Looking at the screen until it shut off from inactivity, he grunted and placed the phone back in the window.

As Igor worked to secure the butchered meat high in a tree in the expansive backyard, he thought about the text. Was it really for him? Who knew he had this phone? Maybe it was Colonel Crawford? There wasn't anyone other than the Colonel or the two SEALs that knew he had the device, and no one other than the Colonel would want to speak with him.

Still trying to decide if he wanted to call the number, Igor finished his work. Satisfied the food would be safe, he spent several minutes throwing a ball for Dog before it was too dark. Going inside, he cleaned up, washing the deer's blood from his body. Clean and wearing fresh clothing, he picked up the phone and took a seat in the luxurious living room.

Dog lay down next to the overstuffed leather chair Igor settled in, sighing his contentment with a full belly and time spent playing. Igor activated the phone, stared at it a moment longer then pressed a button to dial the displayed number. It only rang twice before it was answered.

"Hello?" A male voice spoke in oddly accented English.

Dirk Patton

Igor didn't respond. He didn't know any men who spoke English with an accent he was unfamiliar with. He was about to disconnect when the voice spoke again.

"Is this Igor? I'm sorry, I don't know your last name. Don't hang up. My name is Lucas Martin. I'm a friend of Major Chase."

"Da. I am Igor," he grumbled into the phone after hearing the Major's name.

Lucas talked for several minutes. He relayed what had happened to the Major and the rest of the group after Igor had parted ways with them. Sadness descended over Igor when he learned of the death of Colonel Crawford. Then anger replaced it as he was told the rest of the story.

He asked a few questions in his broken English, not liking the answers he received. After several more minutes, he ended the call without bothering to say goodbye.

He sat in the chair, staring straight ahead for a long time. Arriving at a decision, he looked down. Dog was watching him, sitting up and putting his chin in Igor's lap when they made eye contact.

"John is in trouble. We go to Mother Russia," he said to Dog, gently rubbing his ears.

The mood in the Navy's cyber warfare center was somber. Admiral Packard had addressed the staff after Major Chase surrendered to the Russians. Shocked and horrified looks quickly spread across the room as he explained the turn of events.

Jessica, tears rolling down her face, lunged at her terminal and brought up a satellite image of the airfield in Idaho. The Russian helicopter carrying the Major had already departed, but she was able to locate it quickly. It was still being escorted by Apaches, the American attack helicopters peeling away when they reached fifty miles from the exchange point.

The system automatically tracked the Hind, maintaining visual surveillance as it flew west. When it landed at the airport in Bend, Oregon, she zoomed, and they watched as the Major, in shackles, was escorted to a long range Antonov jet. Within minutes of the door closing behind him, the large aircraft took off and turned north, following a flight path across the pole that would terminate in Moscow.

The jet had taken off three hours ago on its eleven-hour journey to the other side of the world. Fighting her emotions, Jessica had kept working furiously. The initial error that had caused the delay in bringing the Thor System online was her fault, which meant the Major surrendering to the Russians was her fault.

Guilt gnawed at her, despite that fact that there was no way she could have known about the hidden file. It was a security measure, intentionally housed on a different server with a name so generic as to be invisible. Without it, the software automatically corrupted itself during the installation process. It was clever, and she was still kicking herself for not having thought to check first.

At least she'd had the foresight to make copies of every file, and when she realized her mistake was able to erase the bad data and start fresh. If only... She stopped herself. All that mattered now was getting the system operational. She was not going to allow the Major's sacrifice to be in vain.

The software install was finally complete. Jessica checked several things, nodding in satisfaction when they appeared functional. Now, all that was left was to set up the communications protocols so the software could talk through the satellite relays in Hawaii. That took another fifteen minutes as her fingers flew across the keys, then five minutes to double check her work.

Anvil

When everything showed green, Jessica typed a command that would initiate the system. With a muttered prayer, she pressed the "enter" key. The screen remained black, nothing other than a blinking cursor showing for several long seconds. Then it refreshed.

THOR SYSTEM ONLINE

"Yes!"

Jessica jumped up from her seat, looking around. She was momentarily surprised to see half a dozen people, including Lieutenant Hunt and Admiral Packard, standing behind her chair. They were all smiling at her.

"Sorry, sir," she said, unable to stop smiling.

"No apology necessary, Petty Officer," Packard said. "How soon can you be ready to launch?"

Jessica spun back to her station and dropped into the chair. Her fingers were flying again as she navigated deeper into the system. In less than a minute, she was in the targeting system, a cursor waiting for her to enter coordinates. Admiral Packard handed her a piece of paper with three sets of coordinates printed on it.

"Lock them in, but do not engage," he said.

"Yes, sir," Jessica answered, already entering the second set.

"Time to targets?" Packard asked when she finished with the third set.

"Twenty-seven minutes, sir," Jessica reported after double checking the data displayed by the system.

"Initiate launch," the Admiral ordered.

Jessica took a deep breath, typed in a command and hit enter.

Far above the earth, a small constellation of large satellites were in orbit. Twenty-four in all. They were simple devices, linked to a ground controller through the top-secret NSA satellites. They didn't contain targeting or tracking computers. They were nothing more than launch platforms.

What each did contain was thirty-six, nine-ton rods made of tungsten. Each rod was twenty feet long and a foot in diameter, with a sharply tapered nose and aerodynamic trailing edge. When Jessica's command was accepted by the satellite, nine circular doors on the tapered end pointed at the Earth slid open.

As soon as the holes in the bottom of the satellite were fully exposed, hydraulic rams in the tubes gave each rod a gentle push. As they emerged and dropped free, small canisters of compressed carbon dioxide mounted to the tail section activated and small control surfaces deployed. The small push from the jet of escaping gas accelerated the rods into their fall towards the Earth's atmosphere.

"Successful deployment, sir," Jessica said when she received a confirmation that the rods were clear of the launch platform.

Packard looked at his watch and noted the time. He nodded at his aide who handed Jessica another piece of paper with two long columns of coordinates.

"These are follow on targets," he said. "Get them entered into the targeting system and ready to go. On my order only."

"Yes, sir."

The rods quickly built speed as gravity pulled them down. Several minutes later they began encountering the outermost layer of the atmosphere. They were traveling in excess of forty kilometers per second. As the rods continued to fall, the air grew denser, and they slowed due to atmospheric friction.

The control surfaces, useless in space, made minute adjustments, guiding the weapons as they continued their plunge towards the Earth's surface. A final course correction was made, three groups of three rods each forming up and spreading apart as they raced for their targets.

Admiral Packard checked his watch and turned to his aide, telling him to get Russian Fleet Admiral Chirkov on the phone. Three minutes later a handset was handed to the Admiral, and he lifted it to his ear. His eyes were glued to the computer generated track of the inbound weapons.

"Admiral Packard, so good to hear from you," Chirkov crowed over the phone. "I'm so glad you decided to hand over Major Chase. I have always wanted to visit Hawaii and would have hated to have to destroy it."

"Where are you right now, Admiral?" Packard asked, not rising to the bait thrown out by the Russian.

"You know where I am. I'm on a plane on my way to accept your surrender and take control of your fleet."

"Sorry, I must have forgotten that was today," Packard said sarcastically. "Do you have access to satellite imagery?"

"What are you doing, Admiral?" Chirkov asked, the threatening note in his voice unmistakable.

Anvil

"I suggest you find a screen that can give you a real-time view of the Kremlin. And your naval base on the Kamchatka Peninsula. Oh, and let's not forget your nuclear power station in Smolensk. You'd better hurry."

"Admiral, what are you doing? Do you not believe we will destroy you?" Chirkov screamed over the phone. Packard held it away from his ear for a moment.

"Chirkov. Time's almost up," Packard said, his voice perfectly flat.

"I am watching," the Russian growled a few moments later. "And I am not amused. Whatever you are doing, it will be met with swift and devastating retribution."

Packard ignored the man, shifting his gaze from the computer generated tracks to real-time views of the three targets he had listed. The sprawling naval base was the first to be struck. There were three distinct flashes as each rod impacted the surface of the Earth.

At terminal velocity, the tungsten rods were traveling at six kilometers per second. As each 18,000-pound projectile struck, it released all of the kinetic energy created by its fall from high earth orbit. Explosions equivalent to five tons of TNT were generated by each, effectively destroying the majority of the base and heavily damaging most of the ships in port.

There was strangled gasp over the phone, but Chirkov was apparently unable to speak.

The next target reached was the huge nuclear power plant in Smolensk. All three reactors were in operation when the rods impacted. Each containment vessel was shattered in the resulting explosions, exposing the cores to the atmosphere and creating a disaster far worse than the meltdown of Chernobyl.

Finally, the Kremlin. The sprawling complex located in Moscow itself. The most well-protected national seat of power in the world. All three rods came down within its thick walls. Every living thing within the Kremlin, as well as a half a mile radius around it, was killed instantly. Admiral Packard watched the monitor in satisfaction as the symbol of Russian might was laid to waste.

"Admiral Chirkov. Are you there?"

Packard had waited for nearly a minute after the destruction of the Kremlin. He wanted to be sure the impact of what had just happened had time to sink in.

Anvil

"What have you done?" Chirkov bellowed. "I will rain nuclear fire until there are no Americans left alive on the planet!"

"You will do no such thing, Admiral. I am currently targeting 147 locations within Russia with the same weapon your defensive systems didn't even detect. I only have to push a button, and all of these targets will be destroyed. Russia as you know it will cease to exist. You'll have no power. No communications. No military. Not even food. And winter is coming, Admiral."

There was a long silence. The only thing Packard could hear was the ragged breathing of the Russian. He remained quiet, leaving the next move up to Chirkov.

"What do you want?"

Packard smiled a tight smile when he heard the question.

"All Russians off US soil immediately. Full withdrawal of your military to within your borders and a cessation of all hostilities. If I so much as think I hear a submarine coming shallow to launch a missile, I'll rain fire on you until there's not a fucking thing left. And turn that goddamn plane around that's carrying Major Chase. I want him back on US soil. Now!"

Made in the USA
San Bernardino, CA
12 August 2016